Snowfall

Snowfall

K. M. PEYTON

Houghton Mifflin Company
Boston 1998

First published in 1994 by Scholastic Children's Books,
Scholastic Publications Ltd., 7–9 Pratt Street,
London NW1 0AE, United Kingdom

The text of this book is set in 11.75-point Old Style 7.

Library of Congress Cataloging-in-Publication Data
Peyton, K. M.
Snowfall / K. M. Peyton
p. cm.
Summary: Desperate to see the world beyond her
grandfather's vicarage, sixteen-year-old Charlotte convinces
her older brother to take her along on a mountain-climbing
trip to Switzerland, where her life becomes intertwined with an
assortment of people in Victorian society.
ISBN 0-395-89598-7
[1. Orphans — Fiction.   2. Interpersonal relations — Fiction.
3. England — Fiction.]   I. Title.   PZ7.P4483Sn   1998
[Fic] — dc21   98-12213   CIP   AC

Printed in the United States of America
BP 10 9 8 7 6 5 4 3 2 1
MV 10 9 8 7 6 5 4 3 2 1

For David

Part One

1

In the seconds it took to fall, the snow sliding from under her feet, her early life flashed through her mind with startling clarity, just as the books always said. One wasn't to know, until it was happening. In a flash, she saw the buttercups in the field below the vicarage, spread yellow and wide in the sunshine, knee-deep to the pinafored children passing. She saw the meadows and woods beyond filmed in the milky blue haze of spring, and smelled — yes, smelled — the blossom pungent where it swagged the hedgerow. All in the seconds it took to fall. And then the darkness as the snow overtook her and bowled her body down as if in a joyous mountain game. The buttercups and the hawthorn went with her, held tightly before the ultimate darkness, spurring her last not unhappy thought: it has been good, God, it has been good! And her body crashed against him and caught him, and they fell together, still holding.

◆   ◆   ◆

Oh, how the view bored her! Charlotte, parting the limp net curtains, saw the flat fields below the vicarage unchanged as ever. There was a stream and the drive from the vicarage following it. Past a few cottages, over a bridge and the drive joined a lane that joined a road that went to London. Charlotte had never been to London. Nor even to Oxford, thirty miles the other way. She looked out often, dreaming, and never so often as now when her brother, Ben, was expected home.

"Ben, hurry, come quickly! I can't bear it!"

Charlotte was sixteen. Her grandfather was arranging for her to marry a man who repelled her. Ben did not know yet. Ben would save her.

"You can't make me."

"Charlotte, my dear, it's for your own good. I've only a few more years left to me and I must make good provision for you. If you marry Mr. Carstairs you can go on living here. You will have a position and security. It's very important in this life."

"I don't love him."

"He loves you. He's a kind man, and patient. You will learn to love him."

But Charlotte wanted to marry for passionate, overwhelming, instant love. She wanted a husband who was tall, clever, handsome, witty, athletic, courageous, and fun. She had not yet met such a man, but she thought — logically — he must be in existence, somewhere. Hubert Carstairs was repulsively unattractive to her. Her grandfather's curate, he was a boneless, colourless, speechless young man of twenty-one. When he saw her he flared up red as a beetroot — which improved him somewhat, for his natural pallor was not attractive, along with scanty, fair hair and pale rheumy eyes. He had a thin stooping figure and long white hands like clumsy spiders. He had never managed to declare with his own tongue that he loved Charlotte — the tribute came via his vicar. But his excessive stupefaction in Charlotte's presence seemed to confirm the fact.

Although her life was cloistered, boring, and lonely, Charlotte had accepted her lot until this frightful prospect had been thrown in her path. She did not ask for much, God knew — her wishes were only dreams, after all, and dependent girls without money or status, such as herself, would be lucky to get any sort of a husband. The parish abounded with spinsters of all ages — one only had to run a fête or a bazaar to see how they crowded in to help, to gossip over the rummage stalls, admire each other's hats and criticize the jam exhibits . . . there were droves of them. There was nothing for them to do apart from looking after their parents. Any man of spirit — like her brother, Ben — had long departed from this dull countryside, to London or Oxford, or even Manchester, but it wasn't given to girls to go away. Only to become governesses which, as anyone knew, was a fate worse than death. Neither servant nor mistress, a governess hovered in limbo in the outposts of the nursery, meeting no one save her charges. Charlotte, being clever, had considered the idea. Ben had rejected it for her.

"You're worth more than that, Charlie. Hang on, we'll think of something sooner or later."

It must be sooner now that Grandfather had

hatched this plan. Charlotte could see how good it appeared to him, all the loose ends nicely tied up before he died: his two orphan grandchildren settled and his living passed on to the blameless Mr. Carstairs. Ben, now in his second year at Oxford, was well on his way to being an educated man of the world (fit for what was still a question, as he was rather wild, but Grandfather had not noticed this) and Charlotte had learned all her tutor had to teach her and now had nothing to do but get married.

"But I can't! Not Hubert!"

Charlotte's knowledge of sex was limited but her instincts were strong. It had not gone unnoticed by the vicar that at sixteen his granddaughter was suddenly a mature and very attractive young woman. The idea of her getting tangled up in the biology of life terrified him. He was only too familiar with the desperate appeals of young servant girls "in trouble" and the tearful outpourings of quite respectable matrons whose daughters, he advised, should be sent away to stay with distant relations for a few months. He could see only too plainly that Charlotte was not a backward girl. Her straight, strong figure was already firmly corseted and her hair no longer in a thick plait but skewed adventurously on the top of her head. He could see the way Hubert Carstairs looked at her — not in a godly way, unfortunately. He made up his mind.

Charlotte wept. Elsie the housekeeper — and surrogate nurse, companion, and mother — comforted her, but with a sparing sympathy.

"Count yourself lucky you've got a roof over your head, my girl, and haven't got to go out cleaning like my sister's girl, Queenie. Near killed with work she

4

is — four o'clock in the morning till nine at night and blows and curses all day long. He's a kind lad after all, Mr. Carstairs."

"I don't love him!"

"Don't be so silly! Love's a bonus in this life. It's nearly always the wrong person, even then. I've seen a bit, I can tell you. Marrying for love is very dangerous. Look at your own dear mother — a disaster. She died of love, if the truth were told, and all for what! For a scoundrel. Is that what you want — this love you talk about?"

"Don't be so horrid!" Charlotte whispered.

"It's for your own good, my girl."

Elsie was a rock in Charlotte's life, but a rock in more ways than one — not a soft bosom to weep on, but a sharp, spiky breast of resolution and bracing sense. She had been at the vicarage for nearly forty years, from a girl, and knew more about the family than either Ben or Charlotte. When their mother, the vicar's daughter, had died from pneumonia at the age of twenty-four Elsie had brought the children up virtu ally single-handed. They had scarcely ever left the vicarage, and Charlotte's quiet — her stultifying — childhood had been almost entirely bounded by the high hawthorn hedges of the fields below the vicarage. The track to the village post office, carved through the buttercups, was the only highway familiar to her. If James the gardener took her in the trap to the "town" five miles away — in reality only another village, but with real shops — it was the great excitement of the week. Grandfather, a recluse, a bookworm, and old, led no social life.

For Ben, the boy, it had been quite different, of

course. Ben had gone to boarding school, then to university. He knew everything. He had been to London, and Scotland once, and had been to parties and other people's houses to stay. He had once met the Prince of Wales — well, nearly . . . the Prince was leaving somewhere just as Ben was arriving, and Ben had had to get out of the way. Ben would understand how she felt, Charlotte thought. If anyone could save her from Hubert, Ben could.

It was June, the buttercups fading, the hawthorn flowers already flushing softly into their afterlife, the autumn crop of berries. The woods beyond were heavy with summer, full of nightingales, which sang heartlessly with what sounded like joy. The beauty was lost on Charlotte. She craved far horizons and chattering people, movement, life. And love.

The vicarage was full of chiming clocks, hastening life away. At noon it seemed like an orchestra played, upstairs and down. But apart from the clocks the silence was profound. Charlotte could hear the spiders weaving webs and the ants running across the scullery floor. Dead bluebottles lay trapped in the yellowing curtain nets and dust lay on the shiny leaves of the aspidistra. Grandfather was going to die and wanted it all to carry on in the same way with Hubert in charge, dreariness to deadliness, life without end, amen.

And Charlotte felt herself burgeoning like the chestnut shoot thrusting out of the shining conker, strong and eager. She needed deep soil to grow in, and air and sunshine and storm. She did not want to be a vicar's wife. Boys looked at her now, she had noticed, and reddened, and she had become adept with a swift glance at summing up desirability, the glint of an eye, the fine lift of a handsome jaw. She was a romantic, living on fantasy. Elsie secretly lent her novels, which she borrowed from the cook at the Hall, and Charlotte fed her fantasy on tales of Indian princes carrying off swooning white English ladies and housemaids becoming heiresses and spurning young dukes in favour of the honest son of the soil. Charlotte was a great reader. She had brains and had learned everything the lame tutors hired by her grandfather had been able to teach her, but girls did not go to university. Ben was not as bright, but Oxford had always been his goal, his right. He had had a fine education. Charlotte envied him but knew that life was so. Girls were expected to marry, not be clever.

"But I won't marry Hubert," she said out loud. "Never."

◆　◆　◆

"So, what's different, James? Anything happened?"

Ben, having loaded his copious suitcases into the back of the dogcart, got up beside his grandfather's do-it-all man on the driving seat. "Don't get down, I can manage," he had been going to say, but James hadn't offered. James too was getting old, like his employer. Likewise the horse, a grey mare called Daisy. Used to the fast pace of university life, Ben felt an involuntary sinking of the heart as they set off for home. God, he'd forgotten just how backward it was out here.

"Charlotte well, I hope?"

Daisy couldn't be much fun for her to ride any longer, judging by her stiff trot. What did the girl do all day?

"That tutor fellow still teach her?"

7

"He's stopped coming. I think she knows it all now, sir."

"All!" That was rich. Ben laughed.

He had always found school holidays a terrible drag, the vicar's social life revolving around the old ladies' tea parties and fêtes in aid of the church spire. The old boy had never cared for hunting or travelling or even shooting the odd pigeon. He was always closeted with his books or — for outdoor exercise — pruning his roses. Thank God, Ben breathed, he wouldn't be spending much of the vacation at home. Just long enough to renew acquaintance with his sister.

"She's grown into a real young lady this last year. Spitting image of her poor mother," James said.

James, having worked at the vicarage for thirty years, like Elsie, knew more of the family history than Ben. Ben couldn't remember his mother. She was said to have been a saint, as beautiful as she was good. Charlotte, said to be very like her in looks, had never been considered a saint. Ben could remember painful fights with Charlotte, when she made up for her disadvantage in years with pure ferocity. Elsie used to beat her with a slipper.

The old vicarage of his childhood was very beautiful, Ben had to admit, as they approached it across the common meadow where the villagers put out their cows and horses. It stood up on a slight hill, superior in all respects, with trees and shrubberies behind and lawns and rosebeds in front, framed by black iron railings. Its front was Georgian, perfectly symmetrical, of rose-red bricks. There were no other buildings near it; even its church was on the village side of the meadow,

8

as if in opposition. The old mare slowed as she came to the incline. Ben's luggage was heavy.

"I'll get down," he said.

He was very quick and athletic. Sport was more his thing at Oxford than books, and he wasn't troubled by too keen a conscience where work was concerned. He swung up the hill ahead of his transport. Charlotte had seen the trap and came flying out of the front door.

"Ben! Ben!"

She flung herself into his arms and hugged him. "Oh, thank goodness you've come! I do need you so, Ben. You've got to help me — everything is so dreadful! Oh, Ben!"

Her greeting was that of an eager child, but Ben quickly discovered that his sister had blossomed since he had last seen her. One could scarcely call her a child now, with her gorgeous figure and arresting looks. The hair she had once worn in a plait was now piled in a luxurious mass at the back of her head, with odd ringlets trailing in splendid disarray around her ears. It was a dark chestnut brown, thick and curling, and was obviously difficult to confine. Charlotte, impatient, shed hairpins like the hawthorn its dead blossom. She had a translucent indoor skin, porcelain pale, and large grey-blue eyes that fixed him purposefully — Charlotte, he remembered, was a willful girl. But how gorgeous she had become since he last saw her! A bud come into flower, the richness unfurled, the old vicar's hothouse flower blooming away with no one to see. Had he noticed?

"Grandfather says I've to marry Mr. Carstairs. Can you believe it?"

Yes, obviously he had noticed. Grandfather was not so unworldly as he thought, Ben decided.

"Lucky Mr. Carstairs! Who is he?"

"Oh, Ben, stupid, you know — Hubert — the curate! That feeble ass — you *know*!"

"Hubert — yes, of course. Oh, he's not a bad egg. Good at cricket."

"Don't be so ridiculous!" cried Charlotte, not unjustifiably. "Life's not about cricket. It's about love — about doing things together — about exciting things —"

"He might become a bishop."

"Ben! You've *seen* him. I won't marry him!"

"All right. Let me get my luggage. I can't arrange your life before I've settled in."

"Are you staying long? All the holidays?"

"A couple of weeks. Then I'm off to Switzerland to climb in the Alps. Think of it, Charlotte! A whole party of us from Oxford — we're going to hire guides and climb the Matterhorn."

"Ben!"

At his words her whole being cried out. Her heart felt as if it were torn apart with longing. To go away, to go in a crowd, young and adventurous — as soon as he said it, she realized it encapsulated exactly what she most desired in life.

"I'll come with you. Oh, please!"

Ben was lifting his cases down from the dogcart, which had now arrived outside the front door. He wasn't prepared for this crisis before he had even set foot inside the door.

"Steady on, old girl. It's only chaps going, you know. I don't see how I can take you."

"I'm your sister. It's perfectly respectable."

"What, in a crowd of chaps? You'd want a chaperone."

"Oh, I'll find one. Elsie will arrange it. I'm sure grandfather would like me to have a holiday. I've never had one, have I?"

Lord! thought Ben. This is going to be tricky.

He threw her his bag of rackets and flannels. "Carry that. Guides carry your stuff, you know, and you drink champagne on the summit."

"Oh, Ben, how marvellous!"

The tropical flower was glowing, the colour changing, the hairpins sparkling. She gathered up his things reverently. She would be his slave, hanging on every exciting word.

They staggered into the hall and grandfather came out to meet them, and Elsie came up from the kitchen. It was greetings all round and more cheer than the vicarage knew in a month.

"I'll bring some tea into the sitting room, sir," Elsie said. "And there's a nice cake, the cherry you like, Master Ben."

"Great stuff, Elsie."

Ben was a cheerful, uncomplicated boy who had taken to life in boarding school and university without crisis or misery. He thought well of everyone. He was loyal and stoical and kind and made friends easily because of his transparent goodness of heart. To Charlotte, he was her measuring stick: she wanted a sort of Ben as a husband, but perhaps more mysterious, and, of course, more handsome. Ben was tall and strong and had the easy, quick movement of the athlete.

11

He was highly prized by his college for his prowess at rowing, football, and tennis.

He went upstairs and dumped his gear in his old bedroom and changed into his ancient Norfolk jacket.

"Don't say anything to Grandfather about coming to Switzerland," he warned her. "Not yet. I might be able to wangle it, if we can work out the chaperone bit. Perhaps one of the other chaps has a sister who might want to come. Milo — the chap that's organizing it — he won't mind a few girls along. He's a great one for the girls."

"What's he like?" Charlotte's mind leapt in anticipation.

"Oh, he's marvellous. He can do anything. He's fabulously rich, which helps. It's all titles in his family, but he's the youngest — no, second youngest — son and the black sheep."

"Is he nice?"

"Yes, he's very sound at bottom. If you're in a jam, Milo will stand by. Always."

"Is he handsome?"

"Oh, Lord, yes."

"Has he got a — you know — anyone special?"

"Well . . ." Ben hesitated. He looked at the eager face of his young sister and thought of her deadly future. It was a damned shame. A few weeks with Milo in charge would cheer her up no end. And Milo was no threat for he was in love with someone else.

"Yes, he has. But she's —" He hesitated, stopped. "I don't know, he doesn't talk about it. It's no one at Oxford. But everyone knows he's — well, he's not interested in anyone else."

"Who is she?"

"I don't know."

By Ben's tone Charlotte knew he was lying.

"I must come. Please, Ben, you must make it happen!" Her earnestness frightened him, shining out of her gorgeous smoky eyes. He hardly recognized this Charlotte, this woman of sudden and intense longing. The prospect of going to Switzerland, a sudden magic door of escape whose handle Ben had unexpectedly put in her grasp, possessed her utterly.

"You will put it to Grandfather? You must, Ben, please. If you think it's all right with — with Milo."

Milo sounded rather like the sort of person who made his own rules. He also sounded deliciously interesting.

"It won't matter a jot to Milo — the more the merrier. But I don't know about Grandfather."

Typically, Charlotte had saddled him with trouble before he had scarcely arrived. Over the cherry cake Grandfather learned that Ben was going to Switzerland. He approved of foreign travel and did not demur. He went away to write a sermon. He said he had invited Mr. Carstairs to supper.

"You will see him. You will see what's in store for me. You've got to save me, Ben, please. Switzerland, please."

"If I get you to Switzerland, will you do as you're told after that?"

"Yes. If only you get me that."

Anything could happen in Switzerland, she thought. She might never come back. From deep despair she now swung with giddy optimism towards deliverance. Her longing frightened her. She had never felt such determination; it almost made her sick. Whether it was the sheer image of freedom that was so heady, or the practical escape from Hubert's hot looks, she did not know. Grandfather's plan had frightened her; her life seemed to have changed completely in the last few days.

She dressed for dinner carefully. It mattered for Ben. She wanted him to be so proud of her that he would want to show her off to the impressive Milo and his Oxford friends. She must look grown-up and calm. She had a dress of her mother's that had been sent to a dressmaker to be altered for her, and it was of the deepest green-blue, heavy silk. It set off her dark chestnut hair and eyes to perfection. Elsie had to come and lace her up as tightly as possible so that she could get into it. (Last holidays Ben had told her that girls at Oxford didn't bother with corsets, but Charlotte found this hard to imagine. She thought it would look very common. But she had seen pictures of Bohemian ladies at poetry readings in London wearing funny draperies, like curtains, and they were supposed to be fashionable.)

"Your Mr. Carstairs'll be all eyes, you in that dress," Elsie said, looking at her with a motherly satisfaction.

"No! It's for Ben, not him!"

"You've no imagination, Charlotte. If you don't want him to love you — wear your brown serge."

"Elsie!"

It was sad indeed, Elsie recognized, that the girl had no greater occasion to dress up for than her brother's coming home.

14

"Can you do my hair for me?"

"I've got the dinner to see to. You'll have to manage by yourself."

"Elsie!"

"You've plenty of time. Far more than I have."

All the time in the world, Charlotte agreed. Fashionable hair required a great deal of time, no doubt because time was available. With a heap of tortoiseshell combs and a large box of hairpins, Charlotte set about arranging her hair. This impatience of hers was new. She was generally happy to see the minutes whiling away as she tackled some useless task, but since Ben's arrival she had been infected by a powerful impatience. Ben, with his aura of worldliness and irreverence, had given her a jolt. She felt she had come out of her chrysalis and suddenly had eyes and feelings and hopes — as if she had been dead before. The prospect of marrying Hubert had started her disaffection, and Ben's talk of Switzerland had carried her unhinged mind into realms of pure fantasy.

"But I *must* — " she said to her image.

◆ ◆ ◆

The sight of Charlotte in her finery overcame Hubert Carstairs as he stood sipping sherry with the Reverend Campion before dinner. Ben, entering the room at the same time, saw the pale, slender curate fire up like a red-hot poker and the sherry shake in its glass. He knew how it felt, having loved in that tongue-tied way several times himself, and instead of scorn for Hubert he felt a considerable sympathy. He shook hands warmly and saw immediately that Hubert in no way

15

measured up to the Milos of this world. He was wan in appearance, and his pale blue eyes had an absent-minded look. If he was twenty-one, he looked no more than eighteen. His lack of confidence made him stammer and laugh nervously. Ben's heart rather went out to him, seeing Charlotte's absence of sympathy so transparent. She was too young to appreciate his difficulty and could only see the obvious ineptitude. She had no lack of confidence herself and did not appreciate its meaning in others. Oxford would bowl her over, Ben suspected — she was so uneducated in other people.

Elsie quickly announced dinner, and they went into the dining room. The heavy velour curtains were drawn across the damp June evening, and the gas lit as if it were winter. There was a fire in the grate, James having filled the coal bucket. Ben felt himself back in another world, a hundred years ago. Yes, Charlotte must see something else before she married: security wasn't everything. This was a fortress of security, like a prison. Only Elsie's rather slapdash serving animated the scene. She was familiar, having been mother and nurse as well as cook and housekeeper, and told them the state of the potatoes — "floury" — and of the mutton — "not as tender as it ought to be but blame the butcher, not me" — and spilt the gravy on the cloth — "Oh, lawks, sorry!" Elsie was a sprightly fifty-year-old of great energy, a little sparrow of a woman whose spirit had been the mainstay of the truncated family. No close relation could have bettered her devotion. She was taken utterly for granted and wanted it no other way. Thanks would have been scorned. Hard work was her expectation and her salvation, and she did not know what it was to sit down and do nothing.

"Ben is going to take a vacation in Switzerland." The vicar opened the conversation himself, directing the information towards his curate. "He is going to do a little mountaineering."

"I believe there is great sp-spiritual solace to be found in high mountains," Hubert stuttered.

"Well, yes," Ben agreed, obviously not having thought of that department. "But the sport is what we're going for. Knock off a few summits, we thought, get the great views. Quite amazing, I believe."

"The Alps rise to fifteen thousand feet, if I'm correct." Hubert spoke like a book, Charlotte thought hotly. Her heart was hammering. She needled Ben with her clear eyes. He caught her look and hesitated.

"There's a place for Charlotte if you would allow her to come."

The vicar smiled.

"It's out of the question."

Hubert said, "Mountaineering is hardly a sport for ladies."

"Women do it, you'd be surprised," Ben said. "You must have heard of Lucy Walker and Miss Brevoort. Miss Mayer. Miss Richardson. Even Queen Victoria has climbed Lochnagar."

"All the same, it's not for Charlotte."

"Oh, Grandfather, it is!"

The passion in Charlotte's voice made the vicar raise his eyebrows. Her eyes blazed at him across the table. Hubert thought she looked magnificent and felt himself trembling with passion. To be hand in hand with Charlotte, strolling in Alpine meadows . . . what bliss! She was magnificent, like a little feral cat claiming its territory. He did not correlate her fierce inclinations with his own love of peace and meditation, not understanding that she, like Ben, wanted the heights, not the flowery meadows.

"It's such an opportunity — to travel and improve my French and German." Charlotte's voice sounded strangled in her effort to put the argument less abrasively. "Ben said he would find me a chaperone."

Ben blinked.

The vicar sighed. "A few weeks in Lucerne or Montreux, perhaps. But where would you stay? And you'd need an older woman, a mentor, my dear. Next year, perhaps, something might be arranged. A year at a finishing school, perhaps."

As Charlotte opened her mouth to protest, Ben kicked her sharply on the ankle.

"One of my friends has relations in Lucerne," he said smoothly. "It might be arranged that she could travel out with us, and back as well, and spend a holiday on the lake."

"That might be a possibility," the vicar conceded. "She has led a rather cloistered life here, I'm afraid. It would broaden her outlook."

He smiled benignly. Hubert looked worried. Charlotte's pulses were racing with excitement. She dared not look at Ben.

"I'll write, if you like," Ben said, very calm.

"If the references are impeccable, I would consider it. And a companion of course. But there will hardly be time to arrange it if you are going in July."

"It could be done quite easily, I'm sure. I'll write tomorrow."

"And who will accompany her?" The vicar now looked slightly worried, not having expected his concurrence to be exploited like this.

"Leave it to me, Grandfather. Truly it's no problem. My friend Milo has the handiest relatives — they're all over the place. And sisters and aunts and things. All dying of boredom, looking forward to visitors."

"Who is this Milo? What is his family?"

"He's a Rawnsley. Milo Rawnsley. His father is Lord Fambridge."

"Fambridge? My word, Ben, you are moving in elevated circles! The young Rawnsley is up at Oxford then? You are friends with him?"

"Yes, Grandfather. We share the same rooms."

Ben had such an amiable, open face that no one would suspect they shared more trouble with the proctor than studious afternoons at college.

Hubert was looking deeply worried. No wonder, thought Ben. He must know that Charlotte needed to be snapped up now, before she was diverted by the enticements of the big, wide world. He almost laughed out loud, seeing Hubert's anxiety, and sensing Charlotte trembling over her mutton and spinach, too frightened to put in another word. Hubert knew he was no match for the Rawnsleys of this world.

"You wouldn't, of course, think of exposing Miss Campion to the dangers of mountaineering during her travels?"

"Oh, lord, not if she's with the ladies in Lucerne! Not a hope. It's all tea parties there and excursions on the lake steamers. You'd love that, eh, Charlotte?"

He kicked her again.

"I would love to go, oh, yes."

"Lucerne is a beautiful town, I believe. And the air splendid." Grandfather looked almost animated. For a dreadful moment Charlotte thought he might decide to travel too.

"I was once in Munich. That is the sum total of my foreign travel, I am sorry to say."

Charlotte could scarcely eat now for excitement. She knew Ben was making it all up, about the relatives in Lucerne, but the way was open, the plan was afoot. Ben was wonderful. When they were alone at last she embraced him so heartily he had to fend her off.

"He agreed! You've done it, Ben! I love you! I love you!"

Ben was rather more serious.

"I've got us in a sticky pickle, to put it mildly."

"You made it all up?"

"Yes, of course. I don't know anybody who knows anybody in Lucerne — of course I don't. But I'll post off to Milo tomorrow. He's bound to have an idea. You only want an invitation with the right postmark, after all. After we leave here, we're free."

Charlotte was afraid to believe it was going to happen. It was too good to be true. But Ben was tremendously resourceful.

"You can't marry Hubert, I do agree to that. I'll do my darnedest, Charlotte, but don't rely on it. I can't promise absolutely."

"No. But I'm sure you'll manage somehow."

"I'll do my best."

20

Charlotte was too excited to sleep and lay listening to the nightingales in the shrubbery. The rain had stopped and the evening was clear, the stars shining. Next door she could hear Ben snoring. Charlotte, in her prayers, earnestly asked for him to be made strong and successful, and for God and all his angels to confer their blessings upon him.

2

Ben received a telegram three days later. "Second cousin in Domodossola. Best I can do. Arranging invitation. Milo."

"There! What did I say?" Ben was triumphant. "Milo can do anything."

"I don't actually have to go there, do I? I can stay with you?"

"Yes, of course. But we want a real address, don't we? The invitation's got to be convincing."

"What about my companion? My chaperone? He'll never let me go on my own."

"Don't you think he'll let you travel with me? We can easily invent a chaperone to meet you there. Honestly, Milo knows exactly what's wanted. All this etiquette business — he knows all that backwards. I bet you he comes up with everything you need."

Milo was taking on the attributes of a magician-cum-god in Charlotte's mind. She dreamed of conquering snowy heights at Milo's side, the others trailing far below. Ben spoiled it by saying, "He's visiting people in Geneva first. We're going to meet him out there, later."

"Who's we?"

"A chap called Roland Palmer, a couple of others I don't know very well — Albert Weaver and Norky Rhodes."

Norky Rhodes did not sound as romantic as Milo Rawnsley of the Fambridge aristocracy, but Charlotte's mind whirled to accommodate him. It was all part of the magic. But her great worry was that all this was to happen in less than ten days' time. Surely Milo would never get the required invitation from Domodossola in time? Where on earth was Domodossola?

"It doesn't really matter, does it, if you're not going there? You can bone up on it later, to tell a tale when you get home. Grandfather won't know, if he's only been to Munich."

Charlotte tried to behave as if it were immaterial whether her trip took place or not, but it was hard. She packed in readiness, her toughest skirts and gardening boots, and thick woollen stockings, and hid her case under her bed. Having Ben home broke the routine of her days, which was a great relief. The two of them went for long rambling walks or drove Daisy to "town."

"I don't know how you keep sane here," Ben observed. "Why have you no friends?"

"Because Grandfather doesn't entertain. He only visits parishioners if they're dying; he hardly ever goes out. He's not a very good vicar, you know — everyone complains about him. He won't have garden parties like ordinary people and even the church fête — he leaves it all to the ladies. I help with that, but there's no one any fun — they're all old. And we've no relations, no cousins to go and stay with like most people."

"I suppose that's why he wants you to marry Carstairs. Leave you safe when he dies. It's a pretty awful prospect, old girl. I can see that. No. You've got to get away. If not this time — you must —"

"Oh, I must go with you this time! I shall die —"

Ben, not for the first time, looked worried.

"If Milo can't . . . I'm sure he will, mind you, but — if you had another girl, a maid even, you could stay at a hotel I should have thought. Come out with us. There must be someone."

"There's only a week, if I'm to travel with you."

"Don't you know anyone?"

"No!"

But the next day a letter came addressed to Grandfather with a foreign stamp. It was extremely dog-eared, but the postmark was Domodossola. The handwriting was Milo's, Ben recognized. It said, "I shall be delighted to receive your granddaughter for a month's sojourn here. She will have the company of my own daughters who are of a similar age, and perhaps there might be an exchange of lessons to improve each others' language. It would be a most convenient arrangement. She will be received into the family with great affection and enjoy every consideration and care, as if she were my own. My second cousin Evelyn who is, I believe, travelling out at the same time, will gladly chaperone her on the journey. I remain, sir, etc. etc." It was signed with a great flourish: Arabella Asquith Monte Rosa, the Countess Weisshorn.

The signature was so flagrantly false that Ben

feared the vicar's suspicions might be aroused, but he swallowed it with gratitude and awe.

"How frightfully kind! How splendid for you, Charlotte, to have this opportunity for foreign travel with such well-bred people! And Ben will be nearby to support you if you are homesick. And a chaperone too! How very fortunately things have turned out."

Charlotte found it hard to believe. "It's all right? I can go?"

"I see no objection. Ben can vouch for the sincerity of his friends. Isn't that right, Ben?"

Ben had the grace to flush. "Yes, sir. Of course."

Afterwards he told Charlotte, "Evelyn's a chap, actually. And still at Eton. He's only fifteen."

Hubert Carstairs, they could see, was outraged.

"I think a young lady in Miss Campion's situation should travel with a maid, sir," he said to the vicar. "Surely the Countess will expect her to be attended?"

"Do you think so, Carstairs? I daresay that could be managed. We must do what is correct."

Elsie, her opinion being asked, much to Charlotte's dismay, agreed with Hubert. "It will give her a standing, certainly. She will be treated better if she travels with a maid. My niece Queenie would go with her, I dare say."

Charlotte kept quiet. She knew exactly what Elsie was up to, but feared that Elsie knew what she and Ben were up to. Queenie worked on a farm five miles away as a kitchenmaid and hated it. She came and wept in the vicarage kitchen on her days off. She was a moderately attractive girl of limited intelligence and in appearance more like a dairymaid than a lady's maid.

"Yes, she's a good girl. Splendid," said the vicar.

"Seventeen and still not pregnant," Ben said later. "That's what he means by a good girl."

"Ben!"

"Oh, Charlotte, you can see why he wants you married off. So he doesn't have to worry about you. You know what I mean. Look at you — why — in Oxford you'd be a real wow, I can tell you. The boys would all be after you."

"Really?"

"Oh yes. The girls at university are pretty stuffy on the whole — you know, intelligent. Bluestockings. They look like it."

Charlotte found these dropped snippets of Oxford life fascinating. She didn't dare tell Ben no boy had even kissed her yet . . . his talk of pregnancy was shocking. Only low girls did that, surely? She hadn't even known there were any girls at Oxford.

"What do they do?"

"They study, like us. Harder, actually. They're very, very earnest. Not much fun."

There now seemed to be very few days left in which to order the journey. It had happened so quickly Charlotte still found it hard to believe. Now her worry was how hard it would be to come back — almost impossible after tasting what she was sure were the delights in store. Somewhere, somehow, she was convinced there would be a way forward for her, leading from this magic door that was opening at her touch. She was so excited she made herself ill and had to stay in bed. She kept being sick.

But the cool, quiet room was a sanctuary for once, not a morgue. It was the lull before the storm, this too-familiar room, its window brushed by the old lilac tree, the blackbird singing in its branches. She had slept here every night of her life. "But after this, never again — never, never, never," she told her white reflection in the wardrobe mirror. And because it was the last time, she took stock soberly, listening and looking, trying to cool her excited brain. She could see where she had picked at the wallpaper as a child, and the scars between the rosebuds where Elsie had glued it back; she could hear the sound of the mower blades on the front lawn where Daisy was pulling the machine up and down, her shoes covered with felt boots to stop the marks. The room smelt of starch and camphor balls, a comforting homely smell. She had been safe here, and happy in the sense of being well-fed and unafraid, and she tried to tell herself that she had taken it for granted. Elsie's niece Queenie cried from worse things than boredom and was coming away to avoid a worse fate than ever she, Charlotte, had envisaged. Elsie said Queenie got beaten and locked in her room. The world was not a kind place, necessarily. But in spite of feeling sick, Charlotte could feel the determination shoring up her spirit. "Life is what you make it," she had heard Elsie say many times, and now it seemed she must do the making. She knew quite irrevocably that, although they had tricked Grandfather, they were right. She had her own way to go, and she must take her opportunities. Elsie would look after Grandfather; she was doing no one any harm by going (only Hubert perhaps, and he was of no importance).

Grandfather lived in his own world. She too must find her own place.

Twenty-four hours of calm meditation strengthened

her spirit. Her manic excitement gave way to a state of deep tranquil optimism. She felt wiser, and several years older. Although it was still a lark to Ben, it was now a meaningful adventure to her. Ben noticed the difference.

"Are you sure you're better?" he asked her when she appeared downstairs again.

"Yes. It was only the excitement."

Ben grinned. "Aren't you excited any more then?"

She smiled, shakily. "I — I've thought myself into it. It's very big, you must see. It takes getting used to."

"That's true." Ben respected her new authority. Thank God he wasn't a girl! She had never yet spent a night away from home! If he wanted to frighten himself, he could think seriously about what he was doing to her. But Ben was not a worrier.

"You mustn't expect it to be too civilized," he warned. "Not smart hotels, or anything. Mountain huts, more like." He had been going to say hovels but stopped himself. More earnestly, because of his sister's obvious euphoria, "It might be jolly hard at times. You know that? It's not just a lark. We want to do some serious climbing. We've been doing a good deal in Wales — learning, you know — and we've been up to Wastdale a few times, climbed on Gable. Milo and Roland and I, that is. You won't be able to come with us, not all the time."

"No."

She pictured herself waiting for them, sitting in the sun outside a chalet with window-boxes full of petunias. Brawny young Swiss lads would be yodelling down from the Alpine pastures with their cream-coat-ed cattle, and young Swiss maids in embroidered blouses would be hanging out white sheets to dry. She was well versed in geography.

"Having Queenie with you — it could be useful." He could safely leave her if necessary.

Queenie came over on Sunday to find out what was expected of her. They all went to church together — for the last time, Charlotte's mind sang! She sat in the front with Ben, in the pew behind Queenie's employers, the rich farmer Aaron Sinclair and his shrewish wife, and tried in her prayers to find justification for the deception they were practicing on dear silly Grandfather, and to ask forgiveness. Prayers rarely engaged Charlotte's heart, only when she wanted something badly enough, but this time she tussled severely with her conscience. What she was doing could scarcely be passed over in the usual mumbling form of apology she used for her usual sins of bad thoughts, getting cross, or being rude to Elsie, yet every time she lifted her eyes to the ancient and glorious stained-glass window behind the altar she was raised up with an equally glorious sense of "rightness" that wanting something more, wanting actually to live, was in accordance with God's will, not the kicking of a naughty girl. She wanted to engage herself in God's creation, not die in a backwater.

Ben, singing lustily, seemed to have no doubts at all. Charlotte envied him his untroubled temperament. She loved the way he glowed with enthusiasm for the adventures of life. He was so strong, unlike poor Hubert reading the lesson, stumbling over the lines because he was aware of Charlotte's piercing attention.

Charlotte preferred to be guided by Ben. Hubert was still deeply opposed to the idea of her going away. He *disapproved*, like an old woman. Charlotte would not acknowledge — or could not understand — the intensity of his young love.

James came for Grandfather with the dogcart, but the rest of them walked back to the vicarage together, Ben with Hubert, and Charlotte with Elsie and Queenie. Charlotte was not sure how she was supposed to behave towards Queenie, never having had a maid before. If Queenie was up to the part, she could become a friend, be one of them. After all, there would be little occasion, from the sound of it, for standing on ceremony. Charlotte rather fancied herself as a free thinker, like the ladies who dressed in curtains and attended poetry readings. My maid, my friend . . .

"Are you looking forward to the journey?" she enquired of Queenie.

"No, miss. I'm terrified. "

"Oh."

It occurred to Charlotte that Queenie thought she was going to stay in an elegant house in Lucerne for several weeks, ironing dresses and heating curling tongs. Were they being fair to her? She glanced sideways and took a shrewd look at the farmer's ex-kitchenmaid. She was — thank goodness — not ravishingly pretty nor pert looking, rather a thick country girl, stocky and strong. She had an honest, rosy face, pale blue eyes, and blondish hair pinned up severely under her black velour hat. She did not know she had far more to be terrified of than the journey.

"I want to do plenty of walking in the mountains,"

Charlotte warned her. "Would you like that?"

"I dunno, miss. I always walk plenty. Dunno about mountains, never seen any."

"Not even in pictures?"

"No, miss."

Queenie didn't look in books. The farm pictures consisted only of old oil paintings of winning bulls and hunters. But Charlotte's vicarage was full of leather-bound volumes of articles and engravings of the wonders of the world from China to South Africa, and Charlotte had seen Edward Whymper's engravings of his travels in the mountains — and knew of the frightful disaster on the Matterhorn in 1865. She had strong mental visions of the appearance of Switzerland, of the Lucerne lakeside, and the interior of Basle railway station, likewise the white cliffs of Dover, the Eiffel Tower, and Brighton pier. She had never actually seen any of them. It was hard to know what went on in Queenie's head if she had never read a book or seen a picture. Charlotte could not envisage such a mental desert. She did not know what else to say.

"I do want to come, miss, however," Queenie said.

Charlotte saw, quite suddenly, that it was as desperate for Queenie as it was for her to depart from this place.

"Yes. We're going. Don't worry."

Queenie gave a sort of gulp. She was white. Elsie gave her arm a little shake.

"She'll be a good girl to you, Miss Charlotte, don't you fret. She knows her good fortune."

So do I, thought Charlotte. The last time, the last time, she kept thinking, looking at the meadows below the vicarage. She saw everything with eyes honed by

30

gladness, each flower sharply delineated, each blade of grass separate like a spear, the dust in particles, the air in clear, spinning globules of heady ether. She saw the Matterhorn hanging over the low woods and the chamois leaping from rock to rock. She kept laughing. Elsie gave her some shrewd glances and said, "You lace yourself too tightly, young woman. I've told you you'll give yourself fits."

But when she was free she was going to wear her gardening clothes to climb in and curtains in the evening like Oxford girls. Her feet were leaving the ground. Elsie would never guess what was afflicting her.

3

"You've got to get down," Ben said. "It's too steep for the horses."

Everyone was piling out of the coach on to the dusty road. Charlotte and Queenie, sitting on top facing backwards, had been only too aware of the diminishing speed. Slowly and ever more slowly the town below had receded, a handful of dollhouses clustered beside the winding Rhône, shimmering and distorted in the heat. The railway line glittered in its curve to the west like a sleeping snake.

"Oh, lawks," said Queenie. "We gotta walk!"

But they were high already. The scent of pine trees was fresh after the smells of the steaming town. They were proceeding up a side valley to a village far above, and from there were going to walk over a pass — "easy stuff" according to Ben — and meet up with Milo in Zermatt.

"You can stay in a hotel there and do easy walks," Ben had told them. "While we go high."

"I want to go high," Charlotte said.

"You'll have to do as Milo says."

"Who is this Milo?" Queenie whispered.

"God, I think," said Charlotte.

Once out of England Queenie had pulled off her hat and shaken out a mass of yellow curls. Her nature had changed. She stared at Frenchmen and when they looked back she winked at them. They offered her chocolate and drinks from little flasks. Charlotte was slightly worried. Ben had met up with Roland Palmer, an amiable blond boy, and Norky Rhodes who was hearty and boring. The two girls were thrown together, and Charlotte found it impossible to treat Queenie like a maid. She wouldn't behave like one, and Charlotte had no experience. But the confusions were small compared with the pounding excitement of being unleashed from the vicarage.

They jumped down from their seats. Charlotte wore her gardening boots. They had left their travelling trunk in a hotel in Berne, to retrieve on the way home, and now had only a leather Gladstone bag between them. Already Charlotte felt her skin prickling with the heat under her serge coat, and she was envious of the boys in their white shirts. She would have to learn to wear less when she climbed, however shocking it might be.

Charlotte found it hard to believe in her freedom

and felt permanently amazed. Queenie seemed to take the new sensations in stride. She was not aroused, as was Charlotte, by the sight of eagles drifting over the crags high above, or the thunder of a waterfall bursting out of a gorge. She was more interested in the oddities of foreign money — "Why, it's got a hole in the middle! Some stupid penny, eh?" Already, three days out, she had declared she would never go back to the farm where she worked.

"Oh, don't talk about going back. We've weeks yet," Charlotte almost shouted.

It was not to be touched on, that dreadful subject.

"It's going to get tougher now," Ben said to her as they walked. "I hope you girls are going to cope. After this place, it's going to be pretty primitive."

Charlotte soon saw what he meant. The coach ride finished in a bustling village, which was reasonably civilized; it boasted two hotels, but there the road finished. Beyond were high pastures and mountains, dotted here and there with small haybarns. The far peaks they were making for were still hidden by the meanders of the valley.

"Milo won't be in Zermatt until Thursday, so we've three days to get there — break you in gently. We have to cross two or three ranges sideways, so to speak, to get into the valley that goes up to Zermatt. By then you'll have found out how fit you are and if you like roughing it. We'll hire a man to carry the luggage, so don't fret about that. How do you think Queenie will take to it? We can leave her here if you like."

"Oh, no! She's as fit as I am."

"She hasn't got the motivation though. Wanting to

33

do it is half the battle. Does she want to?"

"Yes," said Charlotte firmly. She did not want to lose her female accessory. Ben had become more remote since he had joined up with his friends, perhaps embarrassed to show her his normal affection. Or perhaps this was a truly masculine thing she had pushed her way into, and now she was to be found out, found wanting. Charlotte was determined not to be found wanting.

"We'll stay here the night while I find a porter," Ben said. "See if we can start off first thing, as soon as it's light."

"Oh, lawks," said Queenie when she heard the news. "Up them mountains? I dunno as I can do that."

"Why not?"

"Me boots won't hold up."

Practical reasons were acceptable: Charlotte breathed a sigh of relief. She doubted whether her gardening boots would stand the toil either. They would have to find stronger ones.

The afternoon was very hot. They were shown to a primitive room in the so-called hotel: two roughly made wooden beds with straw mattresses but — thankfully — clean sheets, shoved into a narrow space under the rafters, with a bucket of mountain water set beside a table with a china wash bowl on it. This was their last night of what Ben called luxury. Charlotte set about sorting out more suitable clothes for the expedition. She threw out her serge coat and replaced it with a long woollen jacket, belted. Underneath went a peasant blouse of coarse cotton that she had bought in Berne. The high-necked blouses with their fussy frilled fronts that she had brought with her had already been discarded, along with her hats and afternoon dresses. She put her hair back into its thick, heavy plait and set out with Queenie to buy boots. Already she felt far better and more free.

There were a few shops, converted from the original ancient chalets that lined the main street. They found one selling boots and farm wear and stood hesitantly in the doorway. Charlotte would have lingered longer, but a young man with an air of quiet desperation came and stood beside them, staring, which made her feel distinctly uncomfortable. He had a strong and menacing presence and was striking in appearance because of his colouring: he had hair of flaming golden-red. Charlotte tried not to look at him but was disturbed by his presence and pushed into the shop.

The farm boots were heavy and clumsy but would clearly last out the trip so Charlotte bought a pair for them each, with woollen socks to cushion the hardness of the leather. They left them on and had their other boots wrapped so that they could take a turn round the village to try them out. But when they came out of the shop the red-haired character was still there, as if waiting for them.

Presumably prompted by seeing their boots, he said to Charlotte, "Excuse me, madam, but are you with a climbing party?"

His accent was Irish, his voice soft and cultured, belying his appearance.

"I'm with my brother, Ben Campion," Charlotte tried to sound distant and severe.

"He wouldn't know the whereabouts of Milo

35

Rawnsley by any chance?" The desperation Charlotte sensed in her first moment of setting eyes on this man was evident now in his voice.

"I think you'd better ask him that yourself," Charlotte said.

"Where can I find him?"

"He's staying in the hotel tonight — there." She pointed it out. And then, because of the boy's politeness, she added with more sympathy, "We're leaving very early tomorrow."

"Thank you. I shall endeavour to see him before he goes."

Charlotte and Queenie walked on quickly, awkward in their boots. "He was hungry, that one," Queenie said. "You could tell. He's after some money, I'll bet."

"Do you think so?"

"Up to no good."

Charlotte supposed Queenie's tart appraisal was correct, but she was curious about the red-haired boy, even attracted by the contrast of his aggressive presence and soft, beguiling voice.

"Those Irish," Queenie said, "are all rogues."

Everyone was looking for Milo, Charlotte thought. Milo could solve everyone's problems. Certainly he had solved hers. But he was so splendid now in her mind that she knew, when they met, he could only be a disappointment.

In their new boots the two girls researched the way ahead. In the late afternoon the valley was empty and somnolent, disturbed only by the faint clanging of cowbells. It was open and easy above the village, but higher they could see it narrowed and small patches of snow glittered against the sky. "You can't see the high ones from here," Ben had said. Yet Charlotte felt that their presence was palpable, a massive, brooding silence that was almost frightening when one stopped and took it in. She would have liked to have been alone, undisturbed by Queenie's squawks and clattering. Queenie was never going to see beyond her blisters, Charlotte knew. But already she could see that there was far more to this mountaineering business than the merely physical. She felt deeply excited by what lay ahead.

When they got back they saw Ben and Roland drinking beer in the hotel with the red-haired Irishman.

Queenie clucked her tongue.

Ben came over and said to Charlotte, "When you come down we'll eat together. A chap I know is joining us."

"There," said Queenie when they were changing out of their boots. "He knows a good touch when he sees it, that one. I'll bet your brother is paying for him."

"That's his business," said Charlotte.

Queenie was very impertinent for a maid, but living together in such close proximity made for familiarity. Charlotte washed and put her hair up, although she had resolved not to bother again. There was no mirror and Queenie had to help her. When she went downstairs she was aware of a disturbing quickening of the pulse, such as Mr. Carstairs had never inspired.

The three boys stood up as she came to the table, and Ben introduced her to the newcomer.

"Charlotte, this is Marchant Merchant-Fox. My sister, Charlotte."

The Irishman bowed. Charlotte held out her hand

and he clasped it. His hands were strong and beautiful. The name Fox suited him for he had a quickness about him, and an air of cunning. His skin was golden pale beneath the shouting of his brilliant hair, and the eyes golden-light, missing nothing. Charlotte sensed that he was wicked. She felt herself flushing up.

When they had all sat down he said to Ben, "I think under the circumstances I should be known in future as Marchant. Mr. Marchant. Mar to my friends. I was always called Mar at Oxford. We'll forget the other part. It's a ridiculous name, in any case."

"Yes. Whatever's best. I'll remember that." Ben turned to Charlotte. "Mar will be coming with us to Zermatt."

He did not look entirely happy about the situation. Knowing him so well, Charlotte could tell that he was worried, even shocked, by the introduction of Mar into his circle. As if in confirmation of her suspicions, he said, "Are you sure you want to make this journey with us? You could stay here if you like, and travel up to Zermatt on the railway from Visp."

"Oh, no! We've bought boots. We want to come."

"If the weather holds it should be quite pleasant. I've managed to find a man who will bring a mule for the luggage — as long as he turns up. You can never be sure with these peasants."

"They want the work surely," Roland said. "Tourists are their trade these days."

The innkeeper brought them a rough meal of soup and a sort of lamb stew. Charlotte found she was very hungry and had to make an effort not to eat like a peasant herself. Mar was even hungrier. Although he appeared to have had a wash, and his anxieties seemed to have been quietened by his meeting with Ben, he gave out a kind of jumpy electricity that affected them all. There was no mention in the conversation of what he had been doing or where he had sprung from. The chat was banal, of Switzerland in general and the latest exploits of the climbing fraternity. Charlotte learned nothing about Mar and when he departed — presumably to sleep in a barn or under the stars — neither Ben nor Roland wanted to talk about him.

"He's someone we know — not very well . . . in a spot of trouble. I said he could come with us as far as Zermatt."

"He's run out of money?"

"Yes."

"Not just that? Something worse?"

"Don't quiz me, Charlotte. I don't want to talk about it. It's just — well, it's not very fortunate — I've got to think of you too."

"My reputation!"

"Yes. And you're supposed to be in Lucerne, besides. We don't want any infernal complications. Mar's always in hot water but this time — well —"

"He's surpassed himself, to put it mildly," Roland said.

"It's better not to talk about it. The less we know the better."

Charlotte thought Ben was talking like Mr. Carstairs. His enthusiasm had been quenched temporarily by his meeting with Mar; Charlotte did not press him, but her curiosity was sharply aroused. She thought Roland would have told her all about it, but

Ben, having instigated the great adventure for Charlotte, obviously found the responsibility weighing rather heavily.

"I'm not Dresden china, Ben," she said. "If you're going to worry about me, I'll wish I hadn't come."

"No. But — all the same — it's best to steer clear of Mar."

"She's going to have a job," said Roland, "if he's coming with us."

Roland wasn't worried, Charlotte observed. Roland was a very easy person, much less of a worrier than Ben. Ben had never seemed like a worrier at home, but when the strain came he became slightly pompous, she thought. It covered up a certain lack of confidence. Perhaps when he had suggested his plan for her to come he had never thought it would actually happen.

"Ben, darling, I can look after myself, truly."

"Well, I shall feel happier when we meet up with Milo. He'll know what to do about Mar." Ben was speaking to Roland.

Roland seemed to agree.

"Milo the god," said Charlotte.

Ben looked rather put out. "You should complain! If it weren't for Milo —"

"I know. He's wonderful. Tell me more."

"He comes from a very high-powered family," said Roland. "The Rawnsleys are a naturally bossy lot. His mother and father are horrific. They came down to Oxford once to see him, stayed at the Randolph with about a thousand servants, complained about everything, demanded an interview with the Dean, offended

the proctor — Milo had dinner with them the first night
and then disappeared. They never saw him again. He's
the black sheep of the family and of course, now, he has
scandalized them all by his affair with —"

"Roland — for God's sake! She doesn't need to
know all —"

"Oh, why not?" Charlotte cried out, entranced by
Roland's tale. "I don't know anything! I'm not to know
what Mar's done — now I'm not to know who Milo —"

"I'm just trying to keep faith with Grandfather —
can't you see? I've got you your freedom — I've deliv-
ered you from that Carstairs fellow, but I've a responsibility to keep you in good company. I'm not doing
very well so far."

"I'm stainless," Roland said.

He grinned.

Charlotte thought him very amiable. He was pale
and spotty and had untidy hair the colour of dead
grass. At the moment he seemed more of an ally than
Ben.

"What are you studying?" she asked him.

"Botany. I've finished now."

"What are you going to do?"

"Ah, that's the question. I'd like, ideally, to be a gardener, but my family thinks that with a degree one
shouldn't get dirty hands. One should teach, or — or —"

"Botanize?"

"Exactly."

They both laughed. Roland didn't seem to take life
very seriously.

Ben was studying law. "What is — was — Milo
studying?"

"Classics."

"And Mar?"

"Officially, mediaeval history. Unofficially, very little. He takes a lot of time off."

"What for?"

"Hunting, racing, beagling, gambling, ballooning, rowing, fighting, whor —"

"Oh, do leave Mar out of it," Ben complained. "He's no friend of mine, but you can't leave a chap in the lurch when he's in trouble. With luck Milo will sort him out and we'll see the back of him."

Charlotte giggled.

"Milo the Magician. I can't wait to meet him!"

◆   ◆   ◆

The stars looked close enough to touch, as if one were on the mountain top. Charlotte stared, watching the shadows of the men round the fire. They were smoking, laughing, talking softly. She lay beside Queenie in her blanket-bag, protected by a tarpaulin awning that their guide had erected for them. It was tied down to stakes cut from the bushes. The night was still and clear and the makeshift shelter like a cave, holding off the dew, dark and snug. Charlotte was so tired that the hard earth was as welcome as a mattress. She lay curled, the smell of the mountain stream and the wood fire in her nostrils. They were high, camping in a small hollow in the mountainside where a stream came tumbling down between boulders. The ground was a carpet of flowers, and there was just room for the two tents. Mar might fit in with Ben and Roland, but the guide, Casimir, would sleep out with his mule.

42

Tired as she was, Charlotte could not sleep for excitement. The beauty of the mountains was equalled only by the beauty of Casimir, with whom she had fallen passionately in love. This was her dream man, the one she had always known existed when she had been listening to the drone of Mr. Carstairs' admiration. Both Roland and Mar, so recently of interest, were completely eclipsed by Casimir. He was a boy of nineteen, a native of Zermatt, tall and lean and strong as his own mule. He had black, curling hair and eyes like Mar's, golden-brown, which kept their own counsel, shyly, not meeting. He moved over the hard ground with the ease of a chamois. Even Ben, no mean walker, was envious, sweating behind him. Charlotte thought, if she were to grow faint, Casimir might take her in his shining arms, but to impress him with her courage was more seemly, and she walked like a Trojan, long after the blisters had started burning and the muscles trembling. The high mountainsides of Switzerland went on forever, the stony track twisting and turning, mounting into the colder air over steeper and harder crags.

"Short steps," Ben advised her. "Try to find a rhythm. Slow and steady is best."

She followed him, taking his path. Queenie trailed, letting out wails at intervals. "If you don't like it, you can go home," Charlotte said to her sharply. "I'll give you your return ticket." As Ben had truly remarked, it was the motivation that spurred. Once motivated, by threats, Queenie soldiered on manfully. In their tent, they compared blisters.

"If we hadn't bought those heavy socks we'd be flayed!"

43

"Two pairs tomorrow — the light ones underneath," Charlotte decided.

The bliss of stillness, rest! Ben brought them mugs of cocoa after they had retired. Casimir had cooked a wonderful stew — "Goat," said Roland — and the mule had departed to find succulent feed on the edge of the stream. They had crossed two ridges and were camping high up in the second valley, just inside the tree line. Ben loved fires and was laying on more branches. Flying sparks and stars mixed. They had bottles of red wine, and Casimir was invited to take a drink. Charlotte lay watching, elated by the strangeness of it, feeling herself a part of this bare-boned living. The physical hardship and the primitive food and drink, the fire and the cold and the smell of the earth and of the glacier water combined to make a heightened awareness of mere living. There were none of the trappings of vicarage life, but it was richer here by far. She would not have been anywhere else in the world at this moment. Although so weary, she could not sleep. Queenie snored, unimpressed.

When the men turned in she was still awake. The dowsed fire hissed and complained. Casimir, humped into a tattered blanket, lay under a rock, still as the dead. What did he dream? Of his mountain work, leading and submitting, being polite, cooking, carrying, bearing all the burdens his rich employers put upon him? Or of girls in peasant blouses with come-on eyes and newly stirred blood? Did he have a girl he kissed, rolling over the Alpine flowers? Charlotte shivered. She was having wicked thoughts, the sort she had to apologize for in her prayers. Her pulse was leaping. The smells and the stars and the boys excited her, and she could not sleep.

4

"I say, it's a bit crowded, isn't it? How are we going to find Milo in all this lot?"

Roland spoke the feelings of them all as they came down from the sweet-smelling pine slopes into the ant heap that was Zermatt. Three massive hotels and several smaller ones spilled their visitors into the narrow streets where they mingled with cowherds, old women smoking pipes, grey-garbed guides, and hordes of climbers strung about with coils of rope and bulging sacks. Invalids lay out on balconies and terraces, drinking in the sun. Fat, rich men came rolling down from the slopes mounted on donkeys, and their smart wives went past carried by three porters apiece in sedan chairs.

"Cor," said Queenie, "I could use one o' those."

"I thought this was a climbing place," Roland said.

"Since the railway — it brings all," Casimir said with a shrug. "High up, we are alone." He gestured to the strange and isolated peak of rock, which was the famous Matterhorn, towering above the upper end of the village. "Down here, all the world."

"I say, it's ghastly," said Ben. "All these tourists! I reckon we want to climb it and get out. Go somewhere peaceful."

"What, you're going to climb the Matterhorn!"
Charlotte was appalled.

"Of course. We agreed; that's why we're meeting
here."

"It looks dreadful."

"No, it's easy. Ask Casimir."

"Is it easy, Casimir?"

"Ah, one can get the lady up today. Tomorrow, perhaps, a cow."

He smiled. Charlotte glowed. Casimir was less shy
after three days and had a way of looking at her that
made her feel faint. His black hair curled in front of his
ears, needing a cropping, and his golden eyes now met
hers softly, full of questions. Or so she thought. She
read all sorts of things into his words and his looks. His
voice was deep and quiet, and his English perfectly
adequate to say all the things she wanted to hear. He
had been a porter since he was fourteen and was now
starting to guide. Charlotte had heard Ben say to Roland, "He's a reliable chap. If we want anybody we
could do worse than hire Casimir."

"But we don't need a guide, surely?"

"He might take the girls, Charlotte at least. She
seems set on getting up a mountain, but Milo won't
want her holding us up."

"Ah, yes, he might do for that."

"I'd rather that than me have to stay behind with
her."

Charlotte, swallowing the insult, hung on to this
heady idea — what bliss! Her life was now one thrilling
day after another. Their way had been hard and high
and she had survived, not once holding the party up,

46

and Queenie had been admonished to do the same —
"Or I'll see you get sent home, just think of that."
Charlotte was ruthless. The company was marvellous,
Ben having relaxed and stopped being pompous,
Roland revealing himself as kind and sweet, and Mar a
good laugh, full of infectious enthusiasm once his mysterious troubles were put on one side. Once or twice he
had shouted out in his sleep, waking them all up, and
sometimes he could be seen with a blanched-out, ago-
nized expression when they rested in the lunch break.
But he was a strong and agile walker.

Charlotte heard Ben say to him, "I suppose you'd
rather be on a horse, all the same?"

Mar had grinned. "I'm used to moving fast, agreed.
But there's something very agreeable about this mountain business. It takes the mind off —" His voice trailed
away.

"Yes, that's the way of it."

High up in the sweet-smelling pine woods, the sun
slanting down from the clear sky above the mountains,
problems — futures — were nonexistent: the mind was
completely occupied with the surrounding peace and
beauty. Or so Charlotte felt. Queenie could still be
heard, swearing about her blisters, but only if she
thought no one could hear her. Charlotte's threat had
tamed her.

"Where have you arranged to meet Milo?"

"He said he would check into the Monte Rosa hotel
on Thursday — that's tomorrow."

"The Monte Rosa? Trust Milo," said Roland. "I
can't afford to stay there. Ask Casimir if he knows of a
cheap place."

Charlotte was desperate that Casimir would be paid off and disappear. He unloaded the mule in front of a small chalet, which he said would give them rooms. The street was narrow and the chalets rose high and overhanging with rickety balconies hung with washing and ancient staircases mounting at unlikely angles. Most of the downstairs seemed to be cowstalls, empty now but odiferous with the remains of the winter dung. Casimir deposited their bags outside the front door. The mule yawned and shook itself vigorously.

"Where do you live, Casimir, in case we want you again?" Charlotte had waited for Ben to say these words, but so far he hadn't.

"I live at Winkelmatten, where the path goes up to the Riffelalp."

Charlotte repeated these awkward names. "Winkelmatten?" Ben had the maps. "I hope we shall see you again." This was very daring, and she blushed scarlet.

Casimir gave a small bow. His shy glance lifted to hers. Charlotte felt herself burning with love for him and tried desperately to read a message in those golden eyes. She stared back, and he flushed too. He turned to tie up the straps on the mule's pack harness. Ben counted out some coins and gave them to him.

"Cheerio, thanks. Much obliged."

Casimir walked away down the narrow street and the mule followed, switching its tail. They disappeared.

Charlotte followed their landlady up to the room she had chosen for them. It was furnished with a huge wooden bed covered with a vast feather eiderdown, and had doors that opened onto a balcony over the street. Tubs of red geraniums stood on the balcony, and

48

the late afternoon sunshine flooded in. The room was scrubbed and shining and wonderful after the privations of the journey. Charlotte convinced herself that Casimir was just around the corner and could appear again at any moment. She borrowed Ben's map and saw that Winkelmatten was, in fact, very close, a part of Zermatt.

Queenie was sniggering. "I reckon you're sweet on that Casimir."

"Just you watch your words. You're supposed to be a servant, remember."

"Sorry, miss." But she wasn't, Charlotte could see. She was shaking loose her hair and undoing her old black jacket. With the freedom and fresh air a new spirit had come into Queenie's bearing and for the first time Charlotte noticed that, in her coarse way, she was very attractive. Her brown skin set off her cheerful smile and curly yellow hair. Her eyes were light blue like those of a china doll and summed up male figures with a quick and hungry swoop. Once Charlotte had seen Mar pinch her bottom when they were scrambling up a rock, not something he would have dreamed of doing to her. Oh, Casimir! Charlotte could not get his lovely look out of her head and felt herself trembling. So this is what it was like to be in love, what she should have felt for Mr. Carstairs! If Casimir were to pinch her bottom . . .

Charlotte washed and changed, and Ben came and told her that today was Thursday — they had thought it was Wednesday, until the landlady had corrected them.

"That means we have to meet Milo tonight, not

tomorrow. Lucky we found out! We'll eat somewhere cheap first, then see if we can find him up there in the hotel."

Ben told Queenie to order herself a supper from the landlady. Mar seemed to have disappeared.

"Isn't he coming with us?"

"No. He doesn't want to be seen by — well, it's all English in the Monte Rosa — he's got to lie low, in case he's seen by someone who — who —"

"Who would have him arrested?"

Ben groaned and would not reply.

"I think you should tell me what he's done."

"Wait until he's seen Milo. It will all come out, no doubt, and with luck we'll shake him off and we can forget about him."

"With hair that colour, it's impossible for him to lie low."

"I know. Especially if he comes into the hotel."

Mar had worn a battered felt hat since coming near Zermatt but would have to remove it if he went indoors. The three days walking had cheered him, but he still gave the impression of carrying a fearful burden of anxiety.

Charlotte found it difficult to concentrate her mind on meeting Milo after the experiences of the last week. She was physically tired and mentally excited by her conflicting emotions and felt that twelve undisturbed hours in bed would have suited her better than an evening in the Monte Rosa hotel. Zermatt seemed suffocating after the tranquility of their mountain tracks, its narrow streets crowded with returning climbers.

"The Matterhorn is a honeypot," Ben said.

"Everyone comes here."

Charlotte had seen the Matterhorn's distinctive summit several times from the highest ridges they had crossed on their way but was unprepared for its towering proximity above the village. It hung in the sky above them, its tilted, triangular apex now catching the last of the sun so that it appeared isolated from the ground. Its rocky faces were so steep that little snow lay there, unlike the surrounding high mountains whose summits were covered in snow. Brushing the first faint stars, the sharp ridges stood out in austere profile. It seemed to dare the antlike humans to despoil its heady solitude. Charlotte shivered. The air was cold now that the sun had disappeared; she pulled her wool jacket over her shoulders. She would be afraid to climb the Matterhorn, she thought. But Casimir said ladies climbed it. With Casimir at her side, perhaps . . . she shivered again.

Ben, reading her thoughts, said, "You won't be climbing it, don't worry! As far as the hut, perhaps."

"I don't think I want to."

"It's a tough climb — long — but nothing very difficult."

"But people have died on it."

"Yes, the first ascent — that was very unlucky. They died coming down. One slipped and pulled the others off, four of them. The one who slipped was very inexperienced; he shouldn't have been there. And one or two since — people make mistakes."

"You won't make a mistake."

"No. Milo's been climbing round here since he was ten, you know. He'll lead us. He's climbed Mont Blanc, the Wetterhorn, Shreckhorn — lots. After the

Matterhorn we're going down the valley to climb the Weisshorn. We passed below that — you saw it, do you remember? Down there." He pointed back down the main valley where the railway came up.

"Yes."

The Weisshorn was covered in snow. It looked much better.

"It's difficult, much harder than the Matterhorn."

Milo, Charlotte assumed, would succeed. Ben had complete faith. Was he stupid, or was Milo as competent as Ben thought he was? Charlotte could see already that these mountains were unforgiving to those who did not know their ways. One had to learn.

So much to learn . . . She had never been in a place like the Monte Rosa, which swarmed with leisured Englishmen and smart ladies. Her unsophisticated dress was not out of place, but her ignorance of social etiquette certainly was. Ben and Roland seemed perfectly at ease.

"It's like a public school common room," Roland remarked. Roland never got worried. He accepted everything with his quiet smile.

No wonder she didn't feel at home. An orchestra played somewhere; waiters scurried about, carrying drinks. A restaurant beyond the double doors seemed to be doing a roaring trade and the foyer swarmed with young — and not so young — men in climbing gear, their boots abandoned for slippers. They were lean and brown, or else painfully sunburned, eagerly exchanging stories — of climbs, no doubt — and laughing uproariously.

"Lord, where do we find him in this lot?" Roland murmured.

"Let's find a table first," Ben said. "And order a drink."

Some people were opportunely departing and Ben moved in. He ordered two beers and a lemonade for Charlotte.

"Do you know if Mr. Milo Rawnsley is here?" he asked the waiter.

"I believe he is staying here, yes, sir."

"Can you find out if he's arrived back?"

"Yes, sir."

"Are you friends of Milo's?" A couple of men at the adjoining table turned round to speak to Ben. "He went off climbing two days ago and said he'd be back tonight."

They pulled their chairs round and started into mountain talk. Charlotte was content to sit taking in the atmosphere. Life in the vicarage now seemed very far away, and quite unreal. She had spent seventeen years of her life not knowing anything at all about what went on beyond the village green, and by sheer chance had escaped to find out what she had been missing.

Having fallen in love with Casimir, she expected meeting Milo to be something of an anticlimax, but when he arrived she saw instantly why he loomed so large in Ben's allegiance. He was the sort of person who seemed to dominate the room he came into, not by size nor by bravado, but by some intangible magnetism. He was only twenty-one but had an indisputably authoritative air, yet without arrogance or conceit. His manner was perfect, friendly yet respectful to the older climbers, in no way obsequious like the dreadful Carstairs; one could tell he had a considerable standing amongst them, whether because of his climbing skill or because of his personality Charlotte could not tell. He had some tale to tell about his day, for he stood talking for some minutes at the bar, although he had acknowledged Ben and Roland with a grin and a nod, and was obviously making his way gradually in their direction.

"Everyone wants to know Milo," Roland remarked, without envy. "What is it about him? Not just the scandal, surely?"

"What, out here?" Ben answered. "I doubt it. Climbers don't come from the drawing room crowd."

"But Milo's in with the Marlborough set. He —"

Roland stopped, and Charlotte assumed that Ben had kicked him under the table. Ignorant as she was, she knew that the Marlborough set were the fast-living, aristocratic crowd the Prince of Wales consorted with, who raced and sailed and gambled and held Saturday-to-Monday parties where they all, according to Elsie, swapped partners. The Prince was notorious for his mistresses, and Queen Victoria despaired of him. All the world knew that. In spite of it, or perhaps because of it, he was regarded with affection by the general public. He was now getting old, and Queen Victoria held imperious sway, keeping him out of a job.

Charlotte, strung-up, said angrily to Ben, "I'm not a child, you know, that you can't talk in front of me. All your friends seem to do things I mustn't know about. What did Mar do?"

"He killed someone," Roland said.

Charlotte gasped. Ben went white and looked as if he was about to throw up. At this moment Milo arrived at their table and said, "Who killed someone? Anyone I know?"

"Oh, Lord, Milo, good to see you!" Ben shoved his chair and stood up, holding out his hand. "Charlotte, this is Milo Rawnsley. My sister Charlotte, Milo."

"Charlotte who is staying in Domodossola? I'm very pleased to meet you, Charlotte."

He made a small, easy bow and gave her an enchanting smile. Milo, unavailable because he was passionately in love with someone else (the scandal lately mentioned — at least Charlotte had picked up some of the necessary information), was infinitely desirable, Charlotte could see at a glance, if one were looking. (Since Casimir, of course, she wasn't.) Of medium size, of medium colouring — brown hair, dark blue eyes, very brown skin — he nevertheless combined every feature and manner in a way that resulted in total desirability. How lucky that she was immune was Charlotte's first thought. Without any blushing or dimpling of embarrassment she was able to say, "How do you do, Milo?"

"Glad you turned up," Milo said, pulling out a chair for himself. "My aunt's place is desperately dull. And actually my aunt is an uncle and a terrible old lecher." He laughed and turned to Roland. "Who's killed someone? Anyone I know?"

"Mar. Merchant-Fox. That red-headed idiot at Balliol."

"That's a bit extreme, even for him."

"He's here in Zermatt. Looking for you. Wants you to help him."

"What, buy him a wig? He stands out in a crowd even when no one's looking for him."

"I don't think anyone's actually on his trail. But

he'll have a problem if he tries to go home. He doesn't want to stay out here forever and he's got no money, of course."

"Oh, we'll think of something." Milo was not easily shocked. "Is he climbing with us? He's a great sportsman."

"If you ask him, I'm sure he'll come."

"Who did he kill, as a matter of interest? He's always scrapping but he must have been a shade overzealous this time. Anyone I know?"

"Well —" Ben gave a dubious glance in Charlotte's impatient direction. Charlotte glared at him. "There won't be much grieving — Ambrose Payne."

Milo's shapely eyebrows lifted abruptly.

Ben said, "It happened in Paris, at the races. Ambrose was whipping a horse — lost his temper, you know him . . . Mar hit him, and he went over backwards and hit his head against the wall. As soon as he saw he was dead Mar made a run for the railway station and got on the first train departing — landed him in Geneva. He remembered you were out here somewhere and came looking. That's the story."

"Were there witnesses? I take it there were?"

"Yes. I'm afraid so. But mostly friends of Payne's. I don't think Mar likes the thought of standing trial."

"Payne is no loss. Mar's done the world a good turn, ridding it of that swine. A lot of people would thank him for it."

"That's what I told him. But he's frightened all the same. Not unreasonably, bearing in mind Payne senior and his cronies."

Roland said, "As long as he keeps away from racecourses, he won't meet them."

"What, Mar keep away from race courses!" Milo laughed. "He never will. It's his life."

"It might be his death."

"Well, it's serious, agreed. But we'll think of something. Mar's a laugh. We need him around."

"He's rather depending on your thinking of something."

"Are we going up the Matterhorn tomorrow? Tell him to come along. The weather's set fair and we're all fit."

They fell to making plans and mountain talk. They ordered more drinks, and Milo bought Charlotte something that was definitely not lemonade, in a small glass. The two men at the next table pulled their chairs closer, and some time later in the evening Milo asked Charlotte to have a dance with him. By this time everything Charlotte saw was in a mist of unreality. The dancing was in a far room, and Charlotte floated across the floor and into Milo's arms. He laughed and held her close so that his cheek rested on the nest of her piled-up hair, which by now was falling down in untidy corkscrews round her ears. And she was dancing with a member of the Marlborough set! What would Elsie say if she knew! She would faint. I am fainting, Charlotte thought, her dancing feet obeying — by no order of hers — a faultless path in tune to Milo's lead. He danced like an angel and so did she, he holding her strongly, as if she were very valuable, yet made of Dresden china. He did not say anything at all, yet he was so close she could feel his heart beating against her breast, his strong mountaineer's heart that was pledged to a scandalous lady. Like mine to Casimir's, Charlotte thought, and danced on.

When she went back to their lodgings later, Charlotte saw that Queenie was missing. She was too tired to care and fell into bed without undressing. She took only her boots off.

In the morning Queenie was snoring in the next bed. It was very late and there was a note pushed under the door from Ben.

"We have gone to climb the Matterhorn. Back tomorrow night. Enjoy yourselves."

Charlotte took the note back to bed and lay staring at the bright sunlight playing over the ceiling. Two days on her own! She would go and look for Casimir.

5

It was as if, with new impressions and new people crowding into her life, she was suddenly released like a butterfly from its chrysalis. A month ago the idea of going out alone to seek a young man would have been unthinkable. Now, she set out full of buoyant optimism. As Elsie said, "Life is what you make it." She was making it.

It was a fine, sparkling day and the mountains quivered in a pale heat-haze above the bowl of the valley. The "railway" tourists were still in bed, and on the path down to the river she met only local people and some of the climbing fraternity setting out to make their bivouacs for the high mountains, slung around with coils of rope, toting ice axes and alpenstocks. They chattered and larked; only one woman was to be seen amongst them. Charlotte, without alpenstock or even knapsack, was disregarded. I would go anywhere with Casimir to lead me, she thought, and her pulses ran faster with excitement. This is love, she acknowledged. It must be! She felt like a flower opening to the sun, warm and excited. Grandfather thought you could do without it. Doing without it himself had landed him the man he was: dried-up, book stuffed, dreary. I shall never go back to become Mrs. Carstairs, without love, she vowed. She wanted the mountain peaks of life, not the sleepy valleys.

It was as if the fiery drink that had uplifted her the night before still flowed in her bloodstream, for when she saw Casimir she went straight up to him, smiling, and asked if he would take her on a walk — "as high as I can." He was splitting wood outside a down-at-heel chalet on the roadside and put down his axe and smiled.

"The Matterhorn?"

"I don't want to meet the others — that's where they've gone. Are you free?"

"Yes, miss."

"I will engage you — pay you, I mean."

"Where do you wish to climb?"

"Wherever you think best. Up there perhaps?"

The road ahead was inviting, winding up into the pine woods that clothed the slopes. Already in the sun the soft scent of the pine resin sweetened the air. The needled path hummed with bees.

"I will come. A moment —" He went into the chalet and came out presently with a knapsack. He wore the battered, brimmed hat favoured by the guides, a grey waistcoat buttoned over a coarse cotton shirt, and a pair of patched tweed trousers. A jacket was fastened inside the strap of the knapsack.

"Come."

He led, she followed.

◆　◆　◆

Ben and Milo and their various friends stayed in Zermatt for two weeks and made forays to the surrounding peaks: Monte Rosa, Lyskamm, the Breithorn, and Alphubel. Sometimes Charlotte accompanied them as far as the bivouac, for they camped high and started for the highest slopes very early in the morning, before the sun loosened the snow and the stone-falls grew dangerous. Casimir would accompany them and take Charlotte down when they parted company. His father, a seasoned guide, continued with the others.

"I know you would rather climb with them?" she questioned him.

He smiled, not answering.

But as the days went past she knew how he would answer if she asked again.

She thought she was in paradise. In the sunshine, on the high Alps amongst the flowers, on the rocks and the snow slopes, in rain and snow, and in the sunset, wearily sliding down the forest paths, she followed Casimir. And would have died for him. He said little; he smiled; sometimes he gave her a hand over a bad place, and sometimes his eyes met hers, not smiling, but grave and dark and worried.

"He's all right, that fellow?" Ben asked. "Doesn't

give you any — I mean, he's respectable, I hope?"

"Yes, very."

"When we try the Weisshorn, he'll come with us as well. We'll need him. You'll have to stay behind with the girls."

"Yes."

They had met several climbing companions, and Charlotte had registered two girls: a sharp-nosed blue-stocking called Phyllida Stern-Marshall, who seemed to be alone, and a large Jewish girl called Clara, who was married to a small, monkeyish man called Max. Clara was not in climbing shape and seemed stoical about her beloved Max leaving her for the mountains he seemed to love more. Fortunately she did not want to go for walks with Charlotte, as suggested by her companions. She would study, she said. She was heavy, Charlotte thought. She studied music but seemed to have no instrument. Perhaps it was one that did not travel, like a harp or a piano. Phyllida climbed with the men. Charlotte was envious of her for this but would not give up her days with Casimir. Life offered too much. Besides which, Phyllida was an experienced climber, having started young with her father. One would not want to hold up a moderately experienced party. Charlotte did not feel she had a lot in common with either of the girls. She was more at home with Queenie, who seemed now to have all the young natives of Zermatt eating out of her hand. While Charlotte was happy with one, Queenie was happy with dozens. Charlotte wondered whether she should keep an eye on Queenie but decided Queenie was old enough to look after herself. She had always been more

61

at home with the male sex than Charlotte herself. What authority had she to offer advice or stop her fun? Life was standing on its head, and Charlotte was enjoying it too much to start worrying about the rules.

She had not danced with Milo again. Usually she dined with the men when the climbing was over, but she was too much in a haze of love for Casimir to take part in the parties and incipient pairings, which she would otherwise have noticed. Although Milo, being rich, was based at the Monte Rosa hotel, none of the others had much money and they usually ate in a cheap restaurant where Milo was content to join them. The floor was bare, the tables rough and without cloths, but the bread was fresh baked and the wine came in jugs, the soup in a great tin tureen. Cheese was fresh from the mountain huts, and the stews rich and full of dumplings. After a day's climbing it all tasted as fine as anything the smart hotels could offer. Nobody dressed for dinner, and the smell of sweat and socks and burning onions all added to the heady atmosphere.

Max and Clara were German but spoke some English. They had been studying in England. Milo knew Max slightly. Phyllida was awaiting her degree results — she was ribbed about being dauntingly clever, which Charlotte could well believe from the high pale forehead and serious grey eyes. She made Charlotte feel frivolous and unworthy by comparison. But the boys treated her as an equal, and none of them made passes at her: she was too cool. Ben said she was a strong climber. She was tall and angular and rather ungraceful, slightly mannish. Charlotte found her hard to talk to: she had no chatter, only considered, intelligent conversation. An Oxford bluestocking, she fitted Ben's earlier description of the female undergraduate.

At the end of the second week, a young man approached the dinner table and was introduced by Milo.

"An old friend of mine. I think Ben knows him. And you, Roland?"

Ben and Roland looked puzzled. Charlotte stared. The golden eyes challenged her. She knew them, surely! Yet the hair was black, untidily worn, and the eyebrows dark, not as she remembered.

"It *is* —" She glanced at Milo. He was laughing. "It's Mar."

"God Almighty!" Ben couldn't believe it

"My friend Mr. Marchant," Milo said quite seriously to Clara and Max. "He is going to climb with us."

"Mar! Whatever —?"

"Would you have known?" he asked anxiously.

"Never, not in passing. But now — of course . . . when you speak —"

"There, Mar, you'll have to keep your mouth shut —"

"It's a confounded wig!" Ben shouted.

He made a grab. Mar ducked and knocked over a glass of wine. They all shouted and laughed.

"Milo fitted me out. I knew he'd manage something."

"A certain gentleman, staying at the Monte Rosa . . . I approached his valet. I knew his gentleman wore a wig — I had observed. Most wig wearers keep a selection, and he was no exception, as I found out from his man. For a consideration, I was able to acquire a spare."

"Oh, Mar, you look splendid." Charlotte was amazed. Yet how sad to see that exceptional, glorious colour quenched.

"It's awfully hot," Mar complained. "But it makes me wonderfully anonymous."

"I don't think anyone would ever know you," Roland observed. "Only when you speak, and at close range, I suppose —"

"Where are you staying? Where've you been?" Ben asked.

"I've found a free hotel. It's full of hay and cow dung but suits me very well. I have the main suite and a view over the valley that beats anything from the Monte Rosa."

"I thought he should join us," Milo said. "He wants to travel home with our party — it would obviously be safer — so he might as well fill in the time climbing with us as well. We're none of us in a hurry, are we?"

It seemed not. To go home . . . Charlotte shivered.

"I've nothing to go back for." Phyllida spoke for several of them.

"Here's to the Weisshorn then." Milo raised his glass. "All the time in the world."

The Weisshorn — the Weisshorn, which was going to take Casimir away from her. Charlotte kept her glass down. But the weather grew cloudy, and the Weisshorn was shelved for easier mountains. Ben, Milo, Mar, and Roland went across the valley of the Rhône to the Bernese Oberland for ten days where the weather was said to be better, but Charlotte professed to like her lodgings in Zermatt too much to go. "I want to do some watercolours," she lied. As soon as they had gone the

64

weather improved, and she hired Casimir again. A German party had required him, but he excused himself from their plans when Charlotte called on him.

"You prefer me?"

"Yes, miss."

Charlotte was breathless with her own audacity but his answer, with a troubled smile, elated her. When they climbed she wanted his hand more often and held it for longer. He made no attempt to withdraw it. Unlike Mr. Carstairs' hand, it was strong and hard and the press of the calloused fingers made her feel she was brimming over with the anguish of love. He would not meet her eye. Holding her, he picked his steps across a patch of snow to an outcrop of rock warmed by the afternoon sun.

"Let's stop here. The view —"

The rocks, high up on the Riffelberg, faced directly on to the Matterhorn, whose granite summit was softened into a rosy haze by the heat. The snowfields below its fluted arêtes spread glittering skirts to the cloudless sky, and from the heads of the deep valleys on their fringes came the faintest echoes of the cowbells, loveliest of sounds that Charlotte knew she would equate forever with her present happiness. Sitting there, still feeling the shortness of breath from the climb, smelling the clear air already touched, perhaps, by autumn, and the odour of their own honest sweat, she felt the scene etching itself deeply into her mind. She would never forget this happiness, heightened by the awareness that it was unsustainable — the ingredients were not part of her common life and quite probably, after this summer, unrepeatable.

"I love climbing. Are there many women climbing?"

"Many up here, but not many to call a climber."

"I'm a climber." She knew she was good, with a sense of balance, no fear, lacking only experience and fitness. She loved the feel of gaining, climbing steadily, the view lengthening below, the ridge beckoning above, and the feel of the body being stretched and challenged, so that at the end of the day she was tired with a glorious physical sense of earning and deserving rest. Casimir never showed weariness. He never seemed to hurry but was always ahead, very cool.

"You're very good," he said, and smiled.

She held his look, smiling back, until he turned away.

"Do you like me?"

"I like you — too much," he said.

"I like you too much too."

He laughed. "That is good. We climb with love."

But he was brushing it off, not serious, Charlotte thought. She was serious, serious to death. Perhaps it was his defence, to turn it aside. Charlotte's instincts refused to be quenched. Following him down in the late afternoon her eyes were more for Casimir than for her rocky path, and twice she stumbled against him. When they stopped to rest by the deep pools of a falling stream just above the forest she could not pretend she was interested in the last of the battered sandwiches he pulled from his sack. The flowers in the grass smelled of honey, and the swinging bells were close at hand, celebrating the gorgeous day.

"I do love you so, Casimir," she said, and put her lips to his face. She saw the flare of astonishment in his eyes, so close, and tasted the lovely salty male press of his mouth against hers. They kissed chastely, yet lingering, and Casimir brought his arm out from underneath him and put his hand behind her head and held her for a moment. She drew her face away.

"Oh, how lovely!"

She laughed.

He lay back, resting on one elbow, looking at her cautiously, the shock fading to amusement. He had broad, high cheekbones, and in the late sunlight his dark eyes shone golden like Mar's. It was a boy's face, yet there was a man's composure. She thought suddenly that he was the same age as Ben but older by far, his life compounded of hardship. Guiding and portering was not all about lying on the Alpine meadows with a young girl. It was his strength and composure that she loved and admired. The English boys were frivolous and childish beside Casimir, even Milo.

"I would like this to go on forever. I am so happy."

"It is good." He paused, sat up, and opened the sandwich packet. "But winter always comes."

"Do you climb in the winter?"

"It is the fashion now. There is work in the winter."

She could climb forever! They plunged down through the pine-wood tracks, the path twisting and turning, and when she caught him up — he waited on the turns — Charlotte kissed him again. He kept laughing, kissing her ears and her cheeks in return, but when they passed people and came out in the open above Winkelmatten he was a taciturn guide again.

"Do not kiss me goodbye," he hissed as they came to his chalet on the road, and she did not know whether he was teasing or serious.

"I will kiss you up the next mountain — tomorrow."

"Yes, madam," he said.

She danced back to her lodgings. Zermatt was now in evening shadow but up high the peaks still blazed with the glorious light of the setting sun, rose-madder mountains against the dusking sky. They called this the Alpine glow, and at dawn the sun touched the highest tips first, in the same way. Charlotte longed to be there, in the last and the first of the sun on the highest peak — it would fit her soaring spirits — but she knew no one ever was. The peaks reserved their greatest beauty for themselves, quite rightly.

She ate alone, Queenie not returning until nearly midnight. What on earth was she getting up to? Charlotte, who should have known, did not give it any further thought but lay on her bed thinking of Casimir.

6

Mar leapt up the stairs two at a time.

"Charlotte! Are you there? I've come to tell you we're back —"

He rapped sharply on the bedroom door. The landlady had said the girls were in, but there was no sound from inside, save some rather strange snoring sounds. He wondered if he had the right room.

"Charlotte?" He knocked again and listened intently.

Someone was crying.

"Charlotte, it's Mar. Are you all right? Let me in."

The crying stopped but the snoring noise continued. He waited a few moments and the door opened a crack. Charlotte's tear-stained face looked out.

"Great heavens, what's wrong?"

"You can't come in!"

"I've only come with a message. To say we're back, and you must join us. But what's happened?"

"Oh, Mar!" Charlotte broke into fresh sobs.

"Oh, come on, let me in! I can help you. Don't be silly."

He pushed the door open. Charlotte did not resist.

"It's Queenie," she said. "I don't know what's wrong with her. She's acting so strangely. I think she's ill."

"Let me have a look."

The snoring came from Queenie who was lying on her back on the bed. She was wrapped in a bath towel and seemed to be naked otherwise. She looked like an abandoned doll, her cheeks flushed bright pink and her yellow hair clinging in wet ringlets to her cheeks and neck. She looked delectable, Mar couldn't help remarking, with one shapely ankle hanging down over the side of the bed.

Charlotte said, "She's been crying the last few days and kept saying she felt sick. Then tonight she took a bath, so hot I thought she would die, and came back in here and fell on the bed as if she was unconscious. Well, like that. I can't wake her. She seems to have a fever."

"Oh, ho," said Mar, in a knowledgeable way. Then, "Oh dear, Charlotte. Show me the bathroom."

"It's downstairs, the little shed at the back. The landlady brought in the hot water, and Queenie kept asking for more. I don't know why. She's never had a bath before."

"I'll go and have a look."

Charlotte was too worried to wonder at Mar's investigation. She sat on the bed watching Queenie, noting again that, without her fusty clothes, she was remarkably pretty. She had blossomed since coming to Switzerland and put on weight, which suited her. Her hard life at home had stifled her spirits, Charlotte surmised. The two of them had flowered in this Swiss sunshine, and Charlotte had wanted it to go on forever. Queenie was spoiling everything.

Mar came back. He had an empty bottle in his hand which he held out to Charlotte.

"Gin," he said. "She's drunk. She's emptied the bottle."

Charlotte was shocked.

"She never gets drunk."

"Listen, Charlotte. You've led a very protected life. At Oxford lots of girls take very hot baths and drink a bottle of gin. Don't you know about things like that? What the reason is?"

Charlotte stared at him. "No. What is it?"

"It means they've found out that — they're — well, they think they're going to have a baby. It's a way of getting rid of it, if they're lucky."

He saw Charlotte's jaw drop. How innocent she was! Queenie's baby could well have been his if Queenie had had her way. She had come looking for him more than once when he had been lying apart from the others during their trek to Zermatt, but he had been too aware of the favours he was getting from Ben to

70

encourage her. If he had noticed then how desirable she was undressed . . . he could not help smiling. The Merchant-Foxes had the unfortunate habit of passing on their bright colouring, which was inhibiting to a young man like himself.

"Why are you smiling?" Charlotte whispered. She had stopped crying and gone very white. "It's dreadful. What shall I say to Elsie? We can never go home, not if she's —"

"Girls like Queenie," Mar said, "have babies wherever they are. Believe me, she knows all about it. You mustn't take the blame."

"I — I —" Charlotte was going to say she had hardly set eyes on Queenie during the last week or two, then realized with a shock that she too had been behaving in a way that Ben, for one, would be appalled at. But what she had been doing with Casimir was fun and beautiful: it surely would never lead to . . . The colour crept up over her pale cheeks.

"What shall we do?" she whispered.

Mar put his arm round her gently. "It happens, Charlotte. It happens all the time." Even to clever girls at Oxford, as well he knew, not just to the ignorant Queenies of this world. How many marriages took place because the heir was already on its way? Even amongst the children of the Marlborough set, the mathematics of gestation, estimated when a child was born soon after marriage, were amazing.

"Perhaps the hot bath and the gin will do the trick. Let's tuck her in and make her comfortable and then — have you eaten tonight? I can buy you a meal. I did some guiding over on the Jungfrau — would you believe? — and I earned myself some money. Nice ladies on the glacier. Of course, the Swiss guides soon put a stop to it, but I made a few francs first."

"You won't tell the others — not Ben — about Queenie?"

"No. Of course not. Will you come?"

Charlotte was still shaken and dubious, but after they had put the blankets over Queenie and decided she was in a deep and healing torpor, it seemed pointless to sit beside her worrying all night. Charlotte hadn't eaten and was hungry. She fetched her jersey jacket and wrapped it round her.

"Just an hour or two. She might need me."

"My orders were to sign up Casimir, too. I'll walk down to his place afterwards. I hope he's not booked up. He's a good chap. I expect he's been touting German chappies around since we left him. They're two a penny here."

Mar was a different person since his disguise had proved so successful.

"I met fellows — over in Wengen — who should have known me, but they didn't. It's done my confidence a world of good." He wasn't a naturally retiring person, it was quite obvious. "But I don't put myself forward, I'm very careful."

They went into the familiar café. It was an unusually grey evening, with storm clouds blotting out the high peaks, and the restaurant was crowded. Mar found them a table squeezed into a corner and ordered Charlotte a glass of hot red wine laced with cinnamon.

"You need perking up. It's been a shock for you — that stupid girl."

Mar smiled at her across the table, and once more Charlotte regretted that his lovely colour was all stuffed away under the dark wig. The golden eyes looked even yellower by contrast. They had a way of looking at her that she found slightly unnerving. If she wasn't so deeply in love with Casimir she might have found him rather exciting, as she had initially before Casimir arrived.

"I hate your wig," she said. "I love your real colour."

"I love my wig. I never take it off, day or night, in spite of its being so beastly hot. It is my freedom, my salvation. Milo is a brilliant man — he solves all problems. Alas, not Queenie's though," he added quickly.

The hot wine warmed Charlotte's very brain.

"Perhaps Milo will solve my problem — I shall die if I have to go home after this. I can never go home."

"Like me."

"You? But now —"

"Oh, come, my old Irish mother will know me, even with my wig. The men who want me will certainly be watching my home — that's in County Cork, out of the way — but they'll have their spies out, I'll wager you. So Milo's offered me a job in his stables. He has racehorses, you know — just up my street."

"Oh, how marvellous! Does he have his own place? His own racehorses?"

"Yes, he's gloriously rich, you know. A great-aunt of his has left him a pile. She loved him, unlike his own mother, and now that he's twenty-one he can spend it. He's bought an old hunting lodge on the boundary of —" He stopped. "Perhaps I shouldn't tell you this . . ."

"Oh, goodness, these secrets! Ben was ridiculous,

keeping me in the dark. Don't you start." Charlotte was highly indignant. "Roland said it was common knowledge that Milo is passionately in love with — well, I don't know who, but it's obviously someone he shouldn't be. A scandal, he said. Tell me."

"Yes, well, it's not exactly a secret. He has a great affair going with Constance Mathers — have you heard of her? She's gone forty and got children nearly as old as Milo. She's married to one of the Prince of Wales' secretaries — of course, it's a great scandal because they're both at court and very public people. And she's mad for Milo, too. She's an amazing woman, very bold. She rides like a man across country — that's where they meet, mostly, on the hunting field, and racing. They can't be seen together in London, of course, but in the country . . . Milo's not very careful and Mathers doesn't want it out in the open, of course. But now Milo's bought this old place to live in right on the Mathers' boundary. It's an absolute ruin, I believe, but Milo doesn't care. He's moving in as soon as he gets home, and there's a place for me if I want it. It couldn't have worked out better."

No wonder her brother Ben didn't want her to know about his fast friends, Charlotte decided — what a shocking tale! Grandfather would have fifty fits if he knew what was going on.

Charlotte pondered this amazing news while the Swiss girl set down bowls of thick brown broth before them. Falling in love with Casimir, dining now with a disguised murderer, nursing a fallen domestic . . . although she had set out to deceive, she hadn't intended her course to be quite so outrageous. Yet how

74

strangely one came to accept these new ways . . . going back was not now merely distasteful: it was impossible.

"Perhaps Milo would have a job for me? I can't go home. I'd rather be a parlourmaid. Kitchenmaid even."

"Ask him." Mar grinned. "You can help me in the stables!"

"Women can't do anything! Governess — that's all — "

"Things are changing. Women do work now, if they've got sensible parents. Embroidery isn't enough, after all, if you're clever enough to get a degree."

"Men like you get a degree and never intend to use it."

"Don't be unfair. I never was a scholar — look at me! I doubt if I've passed my exams. Milo will have, I daresay, and Ben — but I only went to Oxford for a way of getting to England. Not to work. God Almighty! I've only ever wanted to be around horses . . . racing, hunting — I don't want the high life, only a bit of fun. I'm happy living in my haybarn, aren't I? If Milo wants a groom, a stable boy even, I'm happy."

"I wish I was a man."

"I'm glad you're not."

Indignant, upset, Charlotte looked gorgeous to Mar. Her emotions enhanced her bright colour: her eyes were the colour of a deep crevasse but not nearly so unfathomable — ice-grey, touched with blue and violet. They sparkled like the sun on snow crystals — how well suited she was to this mountain air! What had she been doing these last few weeks? When he had first met her he had thought her a dull English miss, but something had come awake in the vicarage child. It was not

75

Queenie's impasse that had brought about the change. When she grew up, Mar thought, she would be infinitely desirable.

"Perhaps I could go to Oxford," she mused. "No — Grandfather would never allow it! Milo might think of something. He seems to have all the answers."

"For other people. Not for himself."

"He does what he wants, surely?"

"His affair with Constance tears him apart."

Charlotte thought this a strange thing for Mar to say. He was so insouciant, carefree in his manner, yet he spoke these highly wrought words without flippancy.

"But he chooses it?"

"People don't always choose who they fall in love with." Mar noticed these words caused Charlotte to blush deeply. (Who was she in love with?) "Constance is — was — a friend of his mother's. She was at their home a good deal. He fell in love with her when he was sixteen, and she thought it very amusing — then. Now, five years on, she finds it's no longer amusing. It is very hard for them to be together, and of course an affair of that sort is difficult — exciting, forbidden — doomed . . ."

Charlotte found this story deeply romantic. A month ago it would have opened chasms beneath her feet, fed frugally as she was on village intrigue, the blushes of spinster ladies and the stammering demeanour of her admirer, Mr. Carstairs, but since falling in love with Casimir she knew exactly how tortured Milo's life must be. She had not yet come to terms with the parting that she knew she must endure before long. Perhaps this knowledge of a love doomed was what inflamed her feelings for Casimir. She and Milo had a bond.

When they met again she studied him curiously. It was true that he was lively and charming and amusing and all those things that made him such sought-after company, but there were times when he seemed to put up shutters and retreat into a private world. He could be sharp when in this mood, and his friends had obviously learned to respect it. They said he was "with his black dog," and shrugged. Even when silent he radiated an air of authority, which everyone instinctively respected. Charlotte met him again when she travelled down the valley the following afternoon to Randa to rejoin the party. They had arranged to go in the morning with Casimir, but Queenie had been too ill to start. It had taken Charlotte all morning to get her on her feet again.

"Oh, Lor'! I wish I was dead!"

The cure, apparently, hadn't worked. All Queenie had achieved was a monumental hangover. Dark shadows bruised her cheeks and she wept.

"What shall I do, Miss Charlotte?" Her cockiness gone, she was a meek, subservient creature again.

Charlotte braced herself for this new responsibility she now bore. She felt like the Mistress of the House.

"Who is the father of this baby?"

Queenie wept harder. "I dunno, miss."

"What do you mean, you don't know?"

Charlotte was genuinely unable to understand. When the explanation was stumbled out, she found it hard to believe. Queenie had had no less than six lovers, hardly any of whose names she knew. Charlotte did not know that this could happen. Elsie had told her, in a muddled way, about "love" . . . that when you married the man you loved you went to bed with him and he — he — well, he put his arms round you and held you close — very close — er — and kissed you, and . . . Elsie had never fully expounded on exactly what happened, but obviously it was momentous because "if you were lucky you got a baby." Presumably if you weren't married and the same thing happened and you got a baby, the situation was not lucky at all.

"Perhaps if I climb the Matterhorn —" Queenie started.

"Don't be ridiculous."

"Lots of girls get rid of 'em. My mum jumped off the coal shed, over and over, and it worked."

"Don't be so horrid. Suppose it was you — the baby —"

"She jumped off with me too, but it didn't work that time."

"If God means you to have a baby you will have it." Charlotte was not a vicar's granddaughter for nothing.

Queenie howled afresh.

"They'll throw me out — I can't go back to the farm, and my mum and dad'll throw me out. I shall die!"

"Not yet, stupid. Elsie won't throw you out — besides, it's ages yet. Get dressed. We've got to go down to Randa to join the others."

"You won't tell 'em, miss?"

"No, of course not."

They might guess, she thought, even if Mar hadn't told them, for it was a white, bedraggled Queenie that staggered to the station to catch the train the few miles down the valley to Randa. Mar had given Charlotte an address. Whatever was to happen to Queenie — and Charlotte feared that it might prove to be her problem — could wait. Charlotte was only impatient to see Casimir again.

Milo had found a chalet that they could have to themselves. A ladder led up from the street to the first floor above the cowshed, giving onto a rough balcony and massive door. Inside was one large room furnished barely with table and chairs and a long communal bench-bed all down one side, filled with straw. In one corner stood a stove with a cupboard beside it — the kitchen. Water came from the rain butt outside. The floor was swept, and a pile of colourful blankets had been tipped on the straw bed. It was basic in the extreme. Charlotte, if she hadn't already been monumentally shocked by Queenie's disaster, should have been appalled by the immodesty of living with several men in one room, but life seemed now to have taken on a new set of values. One's modesty was very small beer beside the magnificence of the mountains. Triviality had no part in it.

What worried her far more was being faced not by cheerful Ben and Mar and by dearest Casimir but only by the ladies of the party, Phyllida and Clara. Before their high-minded gaze she withered, dithering on the threshold. Being accompanied by a maid seemed a most frightful bodge under the circumstances.

"The men have gone off on a preliminary skirmish," Phyllida said. "They'll be back tonight. Mar told us you'd be coming."

79

"You didn't stay behind for us, I hope?" Charlotte was nervous at the thought she might have inconvenienced the austere Phyllida.

"Oh, no. I'm glad of an easy day for a change. I shall climb tomorrow."

She seemed perfectly amiable, and Charlotte felt better. Clara was patching a pair of trousers, Max's presumably. Her English was poor, and she only spoke with any fervour when she had had several glasses of wine. But she smiled, doubtfully.

Charlotte told Queenie to curl up in the blankets and go to sleep again, an offer which she gratefully accepted, and which removed her conveniently from the embarrassment of socializing.

"Why do you travel with a maid?" Phyllida asked Charlotte mildly. "Milo said something about how you are supposed to be staying with his aunt in Domodossola?"

Charlotte explained, which she noticed seemed to put her in a better light with Phyllida, for she unbent and even showed a faint admiration.

"Never been away from home? I can't believe it. Not even one night?"

"No."

"Amazing." She sat on the table with her feet on the bench, very unladylike. "I don't feel at home anywhere, I have moved about so much. Oxford, perhaps, and now that's over."

Although her words were friendly enough, Phyllida had a cold, superior manner. Charlotte felt diminished by her, in awe. Possibly it was misleading. Elsie said stuck-up people were sometimes only shy and tongue-tied, so perhaps Phyllida's coolness covered an inadequacy but, if so, Charlotte could not see it — save perhaps in her looks, which were rather severe. She had a high white forehead and cool grey eyes, a slightly hawkish nose, and unsmiling lips. Her brown hair was pulled back into a large knot at the nape of her neck, and the few tendrils that escaped were straight and spiky. She was tall and agile, without curves, like a boy. She appeared extremely capable and not likely to suffer fools. Charlotte felt a bit like a fool.

She asked her, hesitantly, "Have you climbed a lot?"

"I climbed with my father — yes, a lot. But he died two years ago."

Charlotte was unable to attempt sympathy. She longed for the boys to come back, with their noise and high spirits. The afternoon was cloudy and evening would come early. It had been snowing on the high tops at night and the Weisshorn, unlike the Matterhorn, was garbed in white. Charlotte knew it was a difficult mountain to climb and was impressed that Phyllida was going. Ben had said they knew Phyllida at Oxford, and she was fearsomely clever. Not the sort, presumably, that was driven to jumping off coal sheds.

Charlotte offered to peel potatoes, which seemed a suitably humble yet useful offer, and there was a sack of them handy. Phyllida suggested Queenie should do it, but Charlotte said Queenie was ill, without specifying. Phyllida shrugged and gave Charlotte a knife.

"It's no good expecting her to do it," she said softly, with a nod towards Clara. "She doesn't dirty her hands."

A bond was established and Charlotte felt more at home. Over the potatoes Phyllida told her she had lived abroad with her father as a child — in Germany,

Greece, Egypt and India, and now that she was finished at Oxford she did not know what to do. Charlotte told her about Mr. Carstairs. Phyllida was horrified.

"Far better to be free. Marriage can be a prison."

Thinking of Casimir, Charlotte wasn't sure about this. "Not to the right man, surely?"

"Oh, but they are rare, believe me. To live with someone else you have to compromise. The weaker compromises the most. It's always the woman. You only have to look about you."

Charlotte thought of all the acquiescent wives she knew. They all appeared quite happy. At home in the village it was thought the height of bliss to become engaged. To be spared spinsterhood was the most heartfelt prayer sent up from all the cold, lino-floored bedrooms of the land. Phyllida seemed to live on another planet. Charlotte did not argue. Certainly she didn't want to marry Carstairs, but she did want to marry someone.

"Clara seems happy with her Max," she remarked softly.

"Clara is besotted," Phyllida said shortly, as if it was to be deplored.

Clara did not look made for passion, a large and apparently lethargic girl with sallow skin and thick black greasy hair. She reminded Charlotte of a cow, with her large, calm eyes and measured movements.

"Milo met them in Visp. Max is a brilliant climber, better than Milo, I think."

When they came back, Charlotte noticed that yes, Clara was besotted with her new husband. It appeared to be mutual for, as soon as the party came in at the door, the two were entwined in each other's arms as if they had been parted for a month. Charlotte longed to be the same with Casimir but had to be content with a wink and a smile. The sight of him made her pulse race and the blushes burn in her cheeks: she was terrified the others might notice. Because she could not be alone with him, she loved him more fiercely than ever.

They went to bed, late, on the straw bench, all in a row, the girls at one end and the men at the other, save Clara and Max who lay together. Charlotte contrived to get as near to Casimir as possible, but Ben lay in between, an impassable hulk. Some time during the night, Charlotte sat up under her blanket and looked at the sleeping forms around her. The moonlight through the gable window lit Casimir's sleeping face, so close and yet unassailable, like the highest peak in the world, only to be looked at, not touched. She stared and stared until she thought his unconscious would acknowledge her and the golden eyes would open to the moonbeams and receive her gaze. But he slept, unaware, and Charlotte became cold. "I do love you so, Casimir," she whispered. But the only answer was the soft whimpering of the sleepless Queenie, to whom love had a different face altogether.

◆　◆　◆

The valley sank into dusk as the sun's fiery disc slipped away behind the ridge between the Weisshorn and the Zinal Rothorn. For a few minutes the upper snow slopes were bathed in the unearthly glow of sunset. The sky flared, faded; the crimson snow dissolved softly into grey night. The valley smelled of cold earth and glacier water and dead bodies. Charlotte was wrenched with the pain of solitude, of loving to no avail.

"Oh, don't be stupid," Phyllida said roundly, "it's a long way down — they'll be back by midnight."

Charlotte, to cover her unaccountable despair, had declared herself worried by the party's nonappearance. She had climbed with Phyllida to the mountain hut the previous afternoon, where the climbing party slept before their attempt on the summit. Phyllida, unexpectedly, had decided not to go with them, and the two of them had come back together. Now, the following evening, they had set the obligatory stew simmering and peeled a mountain of potatoes. Charlotte, deprived suddenly of her honey-scented expeditions with Casimir and deeply worried about what had happened to Queenie, had fallen into a depression about the immediate future. Paradise on earth was fleeting, she realized all at once. What on earth was going to happen to her, let alone to Queenie?

"I'm going for a walk."

She wanted to be on her own, stirred up with her conflicting emotions. Phyllida offered no soft shoulder to cry on; her view of the world was sharp and unsympathetic. Self-pity engulfed Charlotte.

She took the worn path across the meadows that was the start of the climb up to the mountain hut. She thought when she met the descending party her cares would dissolve: magic Milo would find her a way out of her dilemma. Perhaps in daylight her troubles would vanish — that was the way of dark thoughts. She had gained more than she could possibly lose, since leaving home.

From way above on the path she thought she heard the sound of voices. She stopped to listen. A rattle of stones rewarded her, and voices again. Her heart lifted immediately. The warm company of Casimir and Ben, of lovely Mar and funny Roland would soon lift her out of her gloom. She hurried on, her face lifted up to the forest above.

Two figures dropped down out of the trees, hurrying, sending the stones avalanching.

"Ben?"

But she knew neither of them. Charlotte stopped, disappointed. The two men were middle-aged, agitated. They stopped by Charlotte and gabbled in French. She could not understand a word.

"I am English," she said. "*Anglaise. Inglese.*"

"*Anglaise? Ah, malheur! Vous attendez vos amis? Ah, mon Dieu!*"

Something was wrong. Charlotte was first puzzled, then frightened. The two men were climbers, judging by their ice axes and coils of rope. They pointed back towards the high peaks, hidden now by the forest below.

"*Il est mort! C'est affreux. Vous comprenez? Il est tombé —*"

"*Qui est tombé?*"

"*Mort*" meant dead. Even Charlotte's perfunctory knowledge of French recognized that word. "*Tombé*" was "fallen." She stood staring, petrified by the words. Who was dead? Ben? Casimir?

"Dead? One is dead?"

"One fell. We saw 'im." In the gloom Charlotte made out the man's gesture, his hand making a quick dash to indicate a slip, and then a hopeless downward sweep to suggest a long, long drop. Charlotte heard herself let out a terrible wail. She put her hand up to her lips to stop it, cutting it off. Her knees started to tremble.

"Who? Who is it?"

"Nous ne savons pas. Ma chère mademoiselle . . ."

They were now concerned about her shocked reaction. They insisted she come down to the village with them and, certainly, she felt that all the strength had dissolved from her legs. She could not stop trembling. Was it dearest Casimir, or dear, dear Ben? Oh, please God, she wept, not one of them.

She went back with them to the chalet, wanting to fetch Phyllida who was strong and not given to hysterics. Together they would climb up to meet the stricken party.

"Phyllida!"

"But who is it?" Phyllida's reaction was the same as Charlotte's. Charlotte, even in her distress, noticed that Phyllida was as heart-rent as she was for one of the party, but who it was she did not know. Clara collapsed in a sobbing heap, supposing it was her Max. Only Queenie stayed calm, her childlike eyes taking in the excitement. Perhaps she felt a human twist of reassurance in seeing that she was not the only one in trouble.

"Oh, Miss Charlotte, suppose it's Mr. Ben?"

Her eyes sparkled at the possibility of such disaster, which would not touch herself.

Charlotte was appalled to discover that it was Casimir her heart was pounding for, more than for Ben. She recovered her courage as Phyllida took charge. Phyllida insisted on getting dressed to set off to meet the party with Charlotte, in spite of the discouragement of the two Frenchmen.

"We know the path. We're not stupid. Of course we must go."

She instructed Queenie curtly to look after Clara, who was still hopelessly sobbing as they left the chalet.

"What a useless girl!" she fumed. "Wouldn't you want to come if you thought it might be your husband?"

"Yes, oh, yes."

Hurrying, stumbling, up the track, Phyllida and Charlotte were of like mind, spurred on by fear. A small part of Charlotte's mind acknowledged pleasure in finding herself so suddenly in accord with the daunting Phyllida. She found her legs now working strongly, her step matching Phyllida's practiced rhythm as the path steepened.

"We can't be sure it's our party, when you think about it," Phyllida said.

"They said an English party."

"There's nearly always three or more on the Weisshorn if the weather's fine. It just might be — "

She was clutching at straws. Charlotte could see that she was very frightened, but it was not in her nature to show it.

The way was lit now by moonlight, and a bitter breeze whined in the tops of the mountain pines. The path was well defined; they walked steadily, listening at intervals for any sound from a descending party. At last they heard what they both wanted and dreaded: distant voices. Only once, then silence. A few minutes later, a faint scraping and rattle of stones.

The girls stopped.

"Oh God!" Phyllida said softly.

Charlotte felt herself starting to tremble again.

"Who do you think —"

"I pray not —" Phyllida stopped. Then, tightly, "The least likely is the guide, the professional. The others —" Charlotte, her heart leaping with hope at the obvious sense of the remark, saw her shrug. "Roland and your brother Ben are the least experienced."

Charlotte could feel her breath almost strangling her with fear. They stood as if frozen to the ground. They heard the murmur of voices again, then the thudding of boots, and the first of the party came down through the trees.

Mar.

Charlotte noticed he was quite small beside the others. Ben followed, then Casimir. Phyllida gave a small, choking cry. Roland came down the path, then Milo last.

Charlotte swayed with relief. Max. Her mind flew to the crumpled, sobbing girl they had left in the chalet. Well might she cry! And how she loved him!

"You have heard?" Ben said. "Max has fallen."

"Two Frenchmen told us — an accident. But we didn't know —"

Charlotte felt Ben's arms round her and sensed his own need for comfort in his embrace. "It is terrible. He is killed, and we could do nothing."

"Oh, Ben, thank God it wasn't you. I was so afraid."

And even as she spoke, her eyes over Ben's shoulder sought Casimir's. He was looking at her. He was the professional, as Phyllida had reminded her, and must take the blame.

Milo said, "There is no one to blame. He slipped in quite an easy place. It can happen to anyone — but it was too steep a place to make a mistake. He fell more than a thousand feet."

"How ever shall we tell Clara?" Phyllida whispered.

Milo said grimly, "We're relying on you for that. That is what we are all dreading."

They started down again. Charlotte managed to drop back to be by Casimir who brought up the rear. In the darkness she reached for his hand and he grasped it.

"I was terrified it was you."

His hand restrained her and they fell back slightly. The path curved and the others filed down and disappeared from view. Casimir pulled Charlotte towards him and kissed her passionately on the mouth. She felt his sweat and salt on her lips and the bruising of his teeth. She was astonished. It was nothing like the fun kisses of the warm Alpine meadows, but something as elemental as her earlier fear. His arms bruised her shoulders, his body was hard against hers, like one of the ancient pines. There was nothing of Ben's tenderness and need. When he let her go she felt herself gasping for breath. She nearly fell over. Then he was walking on ahead and she stumbling after him with all her wits knocked out of her, half sobbing with shock, relief, amazement, and her insane love.

The moon went in behind the clouds and a few soft snowflakes started to fall.

7

Milo took the girls down to the Monte Rosa hotel and hired them a suite. Clara was literally prostrate with grief. Phyllida, after two days, declared her lacking in backbone and grit and lost sympathy, but Charlotte continued to nurse her. Someone had to. Clara decided she would never eat again — she wanted to die, but the most delicious of the Monte Rosa's chocolate mousse, left by her bedside, miraculously disappeared in the night.

"She's like Queen Victoria, after Albert died, ratting out," Phyllida snorted. Phyllida was quite obviously of the stiff-upper-lip school and, whoever it was she was frightened for that night — Charlotte supposed Milo — she would not have broken down like Clara. Charlotte too thought that it was bad form.

"She's a foreigner," Queenie said, as if that explained all.

"A German," Phyllida said stiffly. "There's no excuse."

Queenie seemed to have perked up since tragedy had overtaken them, as if she saw that there were, after all, fates worse than hers. Charlotte felt in limbo, shocked, but she had not been a real friend of Max's: she had known him only fleetingly. But the accident, so close to everything she now most cared about, had upset her already upset world disastrously.

"Whatever are we going to do?" she cried to Phyllida, and in the "we" she felt she contained the whole group, banded together by this dreadful accident. None of them felt inclined to continue the climbing holiday, yet none of them seemed to want to disperse. They milled around Zermatt restlessly while Max's body was searched for — unsuccessfully — and the formalities were paraded. Milo handled the police, the town authorities, the guides' enquiry, Max's effects, and Clara's breakdown with perfect equanimity and sat all one afternoon by Clara's couch patiently trying to elicit the names and addresses of any next of kin beside herself. But Clara sat upright, her long black hair streaming loose to her waist, her large bosom heaving with sobs ("Histrionics!" Phyllida muttered contemptuously) and declared herself alone in the world.

"Max — he never speak of his family — they are in Russia! He had only me. And I haf no one! My parents arc dead, I haf no brothers, no sisters, I haf no one!"

"She's lying," Phyllida said to Milo. "How was it she was at the Conservatoire studying music?"

"The Conservatoire of where?"

"Ask her. I don't know."

"Who said she was?"

"Max said. And she said."

Milo, endlessly patient, got nowhere. The Conservatoire was in Russia and she studied singing, that was all. She had been in England for a few months. Max had some money in a bank in Paris. They had planned to live there afterwards.

"But now — now — I wish to die."

Her large white face was blotched with crying. What had sparky little Max seen in the great frump? Charlotte wondered.

"I think you'd better come home with me," Milo said, "if you've nowhere else to go."

Charlotte could not believe Clara's luck. Go home with Milo! And Mar was going too . . . oh, the bliss! And of them all, she had the most cause for finding sanctuary, even more than Clara and Mar.

When Milo had departed, she said to Phyllida, almost weeping, "Milo says he will take her home with him. Oh, how lucky she is! Why can't he take me? I would do anything — scrub floors, wash up, do the fires, the cooking — oh, anything not to go home."

Queenie, listening, perked up and said, "If there's a kitchenmaid's job going, I'd apply, miss. I haven't got anywhere to go home to either, the way things are."

"Why not?" Phyllida asked.

"I'm going to have a baby, miss."

"Oh my God!" Phyllida, startled, suddenly started to laugh. "We could all apply for jobs with Milo! Me too. I've only got the prospect of teaching ahead of me, and I'm not patient enough to be a teacher. Or a governess, God forbid. He's bought a derelict house — we could all offer to go and clean it up for him."

She was laughing, thinking it a stupendous joke, but both Charlotte and Queenie were entranced with the idea.

"If only we could."

Now that the time had been advanced for going home Charlotte was terrified. She knew she could never carry off the great lie she had perpetrated before her grandfather, nor find the courage to say how her maid Queenie had gotten herself pregnant. The evil day had seemed far distant but now suddenly was almost upon her. She latched on to Phyllida's crazy idea as the only ray of hope in the dreary grey cloud of her future and sounded out Mar as to the faint possibility of Milo's needing help to put his house in order. Even if it were only a temporary refuge it would give her breathing space to try to arrange her life.

"What's it like, this house of Milo's? You know he's offered to take Clara home with him?"

"What, to Nettlepot Hall?"

"Is that what it's called, the place by his — his lady friend?"

"Yes. It's very romantic, behind a high wall, overgrown, with a lake, and branches scraping the windows. And stables full of ghosts, and gardens all run riot."

"Is it derelict — the house? Where will Clara go?"

"The house is empty. It's been empty for years. But not derelict, no. It's good inside, filthy, but not damp or falling down. It will need a lot of cleaning up."

"Do you think —" But she couldn't say it. She had this wild, improbable vision of them all scrubbing floors, sweeping down cobwebs — Clara and Phyllida and Queenie and herself, and Roland — who wanted to be a gardener — cutting back the undergrowth and Mar lording it in the stables. It would be like paradise, to go on living together.

"I wondered — oh, Mar, I wish I could have a job like you in the stables. What can I do? He is taking Clara because he is so kind, but she is useless. But I could scrub his floors and clean his windows and make him curtains and things! I want a job, you see, and somewhere to live, and how can I take Queenie home now she is going to have a baby? I thought — I just had an idea. I know it's ridiculous, but we could all go

home with him and do his house up for him, help
him — "

Help *me,* she meant.

"He'll need servants, that's for sure," Mar said.
"But how could you be a servant?"

"I know all about running a house. I do it at home
— with Elsie."

"A housekeeper? But you have to be a fat, cross-
grained old biddy with a face like a boot to be a housekeeper. As well say I could be his butler."

"You'd make a wonderful butler." Charlotte
throughout her childhood had had a great awe of butlers. Not having one of their own, to visit a house with
a butler had always been a great source of excitement.
To be waited on by such a proud man and treated like
a lady when one was only a child had been a never-fail-
ing excitement. Elsie said they were a terrible conceit-
ed tribe and thank God the vicar didn't aspire to one,
but that hadn't changed Charlotte's opinion.

"I suppose I'd as well be a butler for Milo as have
nowhere to go," Mar said. "He's a great man for helping lame chickens. He's got an answer for everything.
Save his own predicament."

There was a service in the English church for Max,
not exactly a funeral because there was no body, but a
service appropriate to the circumstances. Zermatt was
well accustomed to the format. It took place the day
before they were all due to leave, and Milo had ordered
a farewell dinner for them the same night at the Monte
Rosa.

It was a still, cloudless day. The Matterhorn was
like a dream mountain, scarcely visible in a shimmering haze of light, yet its dominance strangely undimin-

ished. What little pathetic ants they were, Charlotte was moved to feel, adrift on her own sea of grief, which had little to do with poor Max. There was a suitable smell of autumn on the crisp air, and the bell tolled with a sound not unlike the happy cowbells of the upper pastures. The guides who had no work scheduled attended to show allegiance to Casimir. He showed no emotion, standing next to Milo who had hired him. Charlotte, shaken with the pain of leaving him, could not take her eyes from his figure. The passionate embrace he had frightened her with on the night of Max's death had become monumental in her mind, second only to the terrible fear of going home. When the organ played the opening bars of the beautiful hymn "Dear Lord and Father of Mankind" the tears streamed from her eyes. Ben beside her took her hand kindly, but did not know she was thinking of Casimir's burning kisses, not of Max's untimely fall down thousands of feet of glacier. When they came out of church, Casimir was talking to Milo; then he went off with his fellow guides. He made no attempt to say goodbye to her. Charlotte wept all the way back to the hotel, and Phyllida gave her some sneering, and slightly puzzled looks.

"I don't want to go home." Charlotte tried to put her off.

"My dear child, you think you're the only one. What is to become of us, tell me that?"

Her voice was sarcastic, and Charlotte had no urge to unburden her woes of love on Phyllida. Queenie would have been a good deal more sympathetic, but Queenie had gone missing again. Now that she was pregnant, one supposed she had nothing to fear any longer in the arms of her lovers. Charlotte had more to worry about now than Queenie.

In the afternoon she slipped away and ran down to Winkelmatten, praying none of the others would see her. Casimir could well have gone off with clients, she did not know, but a blind compulsion sent her to his house. An old woman, presumably his mother, came to the door and gestured towards the sheds behind. Casimir was there, milking a goat.

Charlotte stood silently, her blood racing. She could scarcely breathe, let alone speak.

Casimir looked up, surprised. But he smiled. He went on milking the goat but the pail was nearly full.

"You go home now?"

"Yes."

"A sad end. I am sorry."

Sorry she was going home? She could not tell. He looked in no way desolate, whereas she was tear-stained and trembling and her hair was falling down. For Max, perhaps he thought.

He put the pail to one side and wiped his hands on a cloth. Charlotte went up to him, her feet taking her even while her brain looked on in amazement, and he took her in his arms and kissed her as he had kissed her on the night of Max's death. And this time she knew it was coming and cried out for it and felt his wonderful mouth on hers and his smell of sweat and goat and carbolic soap in her nostrils. He swung her backwards onto a pile of hay, and his whole body was close to hers just as Elsie had said happened when you were married. His hands held her head hard against his mouth, the strong fingers tangled in her hair. Charlotte's excitement, half alarm, half ecstasy, felt like a fire taking possession of her faculties. The taste of him was in her mouth, and she could not breathe for his kisses.

Someone was shouting and screaming. Charlotte half heard the noise of a virago, felt a kick in her side, felt Casimir's weight come away, abruptly. He shouted something, but was looking up, not at her. He rolled away and she was left like a doll flung on the hay. The old woman came into her confused vision, standing over her, arms akimbo, screaming abuse. Casimir got to his feet and shouted back at her, and then he was turning to Charlotte, laughing — laughing! He put his arms out to her and pulled her to her feet.

"My mother," he said, and shrugged. And laughed.

Charlotte faced the old woman blindly. The shrewish voice rang on the still air, haranguing her as if she were no more than the goat Casimir had been milking. Charlotte tried to say something, choked, and turned away. Casimir's mother laid a clawlike hand on Casimir's arm to restrain him, and he shrugged again, still smiling, and made no move to follow Charlotte.

"Casimir!"

Some fat tourists were coming up the path, and Charlotte suddenly saw them staring. She wanted to die with grief and horror, but could only put her head down and scurry away like a kicked cat. Great hiccupping sobs burst in her throat; she could not contain them. But more people were coming down the path, and in her despair she fled across the pasture and down to the river. Alone at last she flung herself onto the flowery grass and sobbed unrestrainedly.

Nobody came. The shadows lengthened and the grass grew cold eventually. Charlotte knew she had to go back, but could not bring herself to move. Did

Casimir love her? She had no experience and could not tell, but was haunted by his laughing acceptance of his mother's will. First, those wonderful kisses, then rejection. What was she supposed to make of it? Did clever Phyllida know about such things? Or Mar? Not that she could possibly ask them . . . but they would soon be wondering where she had got to: she had to make herself smart for the farewell dinner. She staggered to her feet and tried to tidy herself, pulling her blouse down and picking the straw out of her hair. She was cold suddenly, and very tired. This was her last night . . . she was beyond tears, thinking of the future.

Clara was refusing to go down for the farewell dinner, and Phyllida decided she was going to make her. Charlotte's own state went unnoticed. Phyllida's scolding was much the same as Casimir's mother's and had as forceful an effect, for Clara, after much lamenting, got off her couch and started to rummage in her trunk for her dinner dress. Phyllida, like Charlotte, travelled light, and her appearance for dinner was not glamorous, but Clara, when arrayed, was a different being. In black velvet, with a rope of pearls over her splendid bosom, she looked surprisingly commanding. She was a large girl, and had a statuesque quality, slow moving and imperious. Her raven black hair, greasy and straight, made an imposing bun at the back of her neck, decorated with ornate tortoiseshell combs. Her white face had a naturally distant, dreamy expression and, with her grief still heavy upon her, she made an incongruous figure amongst the crowd of restless, hearty people who thronged the downstairs rooms.

"I'd like to give her a kick in the backside," Phyllida said rudely to Charlotte.

Charlotte heard herself giggle. She was amazed. The dinner was a wake, as far as she was concerned. But she did her best to make herself smart — with Queenie's help with her hair — and was relieved to see that her crying had not made much of a mark. Even Queenie noticed nothing amiss. She was going out to dinner with Rudi, whoever he was.

"The father of your child?"

Queenie laughed. "He might be, miss."

"Mind you're back in time. The train's early tomorrow."

"Yes, miss. We're all packed. I've seen to it."

They joined the boys downstairs, and Milo led them into the dining room. The head waiter pulled out a chair for Clara, bowing deeply. The boys were rather embarrassed by her, Charlotte noticed, but Milo sat himself beside her kindly. They had been drinking and were all rather boisterous, but Clara put the dampers on them. They poured her a large glass of wine.

"You look very beautiful tonight, Clara," Milo said solemnly. "Here's to your future happiness. It will come, eventually. Drink up."

Clara looked dramatic and Charlotte was afraid she was going to make an affecting scene, but fortunately the wine tempted her, and she acknowledged the toast with a self-pitying smile and drank.

Phyllida winked at Charlotte across the table. Mar sat at the head, between them. Charlotte had a drink too and felt much better.

"I've got some good news for you," Mar said to her. "Drink up and be happy. You've nothing to worry about."

"What do you mean?"

"All in due course."

Phyllida gave them her sharp look and said, "I'd like some good news too. How about me?"

"You, Miss Stern-Marshall, are perfectly capable of looking after yourself."

"Meaning I'm not?" Charlotte asked.

"Exactly."

But after a few glasses of wine Charlotte thought she was. When they left the table she thought she would go down to Casimir's house and throw stones at his window. He did love her, she was sure.

She laughed at Mar. How sweet he looked in his wig, his eyes yellow like a tiger's. He wore a spotted cravat and looked horsy and rather raffish. Milo wore a white shirt with a stiff collar and an expensive suit. They should all have been in dinner dress, and Milo had made a compromise so as not to embarrass them. He was the kindest person, Charlotte thought.

Ben, sitting beside her, got morose instead of happy with his glasses of wine, and said, "I'm feeling guilty about you going back to Grandfather spinning a tale about staying in Domodossola. Have you done your homework on it? He's bound to ask lots of questions about what you did. It was a crazy idea of mine, to suggest it."

"Oh, don't be so stupid. It was the best thing that ever happened. I've been walking, haven't I? He doesn't have to know where, or who with. Besides," she added, "I'm not going back."

"What do you mean?"

"I can't. It's impossible."

"She's got a job," Mar said.

"*What?*"

Charlotte dropped her fork, as startled as Ben.

Mar was smiling. "Milo's offered her a job as housekeeper."

"Milo! What on earth —?"

"It's true, isn't it, Milo? You've offered Charlotte a job at Nettlepot Hall?"

"I'm offering everyone employment at Nettlepot Hall if they want it. God knows, it needs it. The first thing I do when I get back is hire people to make it habitable. If you want to get in ahead, you're very welcome. Nothing intellectual, you understand."

"For me, Milo, what can you offer me?" Phyllida looked suddenly pale. "If Charlotte is your housekeeper, can I be your cook?"

"Yes. Splendid. I assume you can cook?"

"I can cook as well as Charlotte can keep house."

"But —" Charlotte thought this was some cruel, enormous joke. She stared at Milo across the table. "Do you mean it? I can be your housekeeper?"

"Yes, dear Charlotte."

"She's only seventeen!" Ben cried out.

"A good age to start."

"You're mad, Milo."

"Not at all. She's never left home in her life. She must be domesticated — how can she be otherwise? You are domesticated, aren't you, Charlotte?"

"Terribly."

"First class degrees won't matter at Nettlepot — it's all sweeping and scrubbing and hacking and repairing. Roland, apparently, wants to be my gardener. Mar's my groom. Queenie the kitchenmaid. I only need a butler now. Ben — how about it? You'd make a splendid butler."

"Milo!"

Ben, of them all, could not see the joke. Charlotte was deliriously happy: her dream had come true. All of them living together, the wild idea she had thrown out to Mar — it was Mar who had put it to Milo, Charlotte realized.

Ben said, "Grandfather would never allow it. You're mad to think you could be a housekeeper, Charlotte."

"Oh, come, Ben old chap, don't be so stuffy," Mar said. "She can't go home and marry this old boot we've been hearing about. You got her out of that nicely — you've got to support her now."

Ben was not wild like Mar nor confident and privileged with wealth like Milo and floundered when life grew complicated. He was not the strong oak that Charlotte had always imagined. His recent heady friendship with Milo Rawnsley had spurred him to plan Charlotte's escape — it was in keeping with the wild ways of the more privileged Oxford set — but when reality set in he lost confidence. He was too steady and honest by nature to be proud of his behaviour towards his grandfather. This new situation they were all laughing over was beyond his comprehension.

"Charlotte's too young —"

"If she's too young to be a housekeeper, it follows she's too young to marry the curate," Roland said equably.

"And she can give up being a housekeeper, whenever she likes, but once she's married the curate — well, it's for life. Think of it, Ben." Mar looked very stern.

"You'll come round to it. Have another drink."

Everyone but Ben was entranced with the prospect before them, even the brilliant Phyllida with the offer of cook.

"Better than governess. Thank God, it will give me some breathing space, until I know where I'm going."

Roland said, "If I can make a decent garden at Nettlepot I can make my name. That's what I want to do, like Paxton and Repton. I don't want to teach botany. You'll give me a free hand, Milo?"

"It's yours to do as you like with, old chap. Gardens aren't my province. Just grow the food and some decent grapes — impress the folk next door — and you've a free hand as far as I'm concerned."

Charlotte sat back feeling that the crowded dining room was spinning round her head. Whatever Ben might or might not do, an escape route had opened up for her at the very last moment. In only a few hours the train would be bearing them back down the Rhône valley towards Geneva, the journey she had been dreading. But now the journey was towards friends and independence, a life of her own. If her grandfather tried to stop her she would run away . . . she would go on a hunger strike . . . her head was whirling.

When she fell into bed, even Clara's sobbing across the room did not keep her awake. Clara's love was so great a thing — although she dramatized it, Charlotte knew that it was real and that Clara's misery was real. It did not mean that she liked Clara, but she was deeply sorry for her. Suppose it had been Casimir? But Charlotte could no longer work out her relationship with Casimir. He had loved her with such passion — which had turned to laughter. Laughter! Charlotte ached for the feel of him again.

But in the morning, early, when they assembled on the station platform with their luggage, Casimir came to say goodbye. They all shook hands and promised to meet again.

Charlotte could not stop the tears coming. She had to walk away down the platform. She hid herself behind a large crowd of Germans laden with shoulder packs as large as themselves, and here Casimir came to her and took her hands and looked into her eyes and said, "I love you, Charlotte. Will you come back?"

Charlotte could not believe it. A great rush of joy made her feel dizzy, drowning out all her doubts and fears.

She flung her arms round him and pressed his hard cheek to hers.

"Oh, Casimir, I love you too. Oh, how I love you!"

And the train bore her away, afloat on a cloud of bliss and longing, to a life of she knew not what, and no longer cared.

8

Dear Grandfather,

As you can see from the address I am back in England, staying with a group of Oxford girls at the home of Milo Rawnsley, Ben's friend. My stay in

Domodossola had to be cut short as my hostess's nephew was killed in a climbing accident, and she had to leave home suddenly to see to his affairs. Mr. Rawnsley very kindly invited me to join this party, which I am enjoying very much. I have made some very pleasant friends. We are all working together to restore and decorate this house which Mr. Rawnsley has bought.

Charlotte stopped to chew the end of her pen. She wasn't used to writing novels and was unsure of this mix of fact and fiction. She gazed out of the window. The view was almost obliterated by the ivy that half covered the mullioned panes, but at least a gap in the all-encroaching woodland outside revealed a narrow but breathtaking view of Constance Mathers' establishment in the distance. A high brick wall separated Nettlepot Hall's dishevelment from the magnificent gardens of Goldstone Manor, but by a chance in the planting of the trees that surrounded it, there was a view from this one window of a small section of the back terrace of the manor and three of its bedroom windows — just enough to hint at its opulence and beauty.

"Jolly handy to send signals from," as Mar had remarked, although whether Milo was likely to use it for this nobody knew. They all knew about Constance Mathers, Charlotte noticed, and appreciated why Milo had decided to buy Nettlepot. "Pretty risky, if you ask me," Phyllida had commented once, but otherwise Charlotte had not heard the subject discussed. She was rabidly curious to meet the famous beauty and had hoped to meet her when out walking with Clara. (They had to take Clara for a walk every day, Milo's instructions. "Like a dog," sniffed Phyllida. "She is getting fat," Milo remarked. "Getting? Got," Phyllida said.) But Mar said that Constance was still in Scotland for the grouse-shooting.

Phyllida was busy cooking while Charlotte groaned over her letter, for Milo's sister Kitty was coming to stay. Nobody seemed to know about Milo's sister. They knew about his spoilt young brother Evelyn, but Kitty was a mystery. She was two years older than Milo and married, and that was all they knew. Phyllida was worried, Kitty being the first guest, but Milo had said airily, "Kitty doesn't count. We'll eat in the kitchen as usual." "Sounds hopeful," Mar said. "Wait till his mother comes, not to mention the beloved."

The dining room was being prepared for such guests. Along with the sitting room it was the most beautiful room in the house. Situated on either side of the large entrance hall, these two rooms had been rebuilt in the 1820s giving a modern front to the old house. From the approach, one saw a beautifully proportioned Regency house. But wander any further than the sitting room and dining room, and the house immediately revealed its Tudor, even mediaeval, roots, with dark flagged passages, crooked backstairs, rooms of odd shapes at strange angles, joined by curving corridors, up two stairs and down three. Unexpected windows looked out on higgledy-piggledy roofs and spiralling chimneys, even a hidden courtyard full of weeds with a tortoiseshell cat sunning itself on a well top. It took them all their first week to find their way around. The girls were offered rooms on the top floor which had once been guest rooms. Phyllida had chosen one at the front, the best one (of course), which looked out over what had once been a smart gravel drive between smooth lawns, leading away in a fine curve to cross the end of an elegant lake and so out to the road. But what it looked out over now was a dirt track winding through tangled woodland to skirt a large pond choked with bulrushes and fallen willows.

"You're going to improve my view, I hope, Roland," Phyllida remarked.

But Charlotte rather thought the view from the room she had chosen would be more likely to be improved by Roland, for she looked out over the back to the old kitchen gardens, surrounded by high walls, and the glasshouses where the vines were escaping through panes of broken glass. Her room was small and caught the early sun, which she thought would be an advantage. It was next to the "signalling" room in which she was writing her letter. The signalling room had a table and chair in it, which was why she had chosen it — there was very little furniture in the house so far.

She could not think how to expand her letter without telling any more lies or giving something away, so she ended it rather abruptly:

I am very well and happy and send you many kisses and my kindest respects.
> *Your loving granddaughter,*
> *Charlotte.*

Nettlepot Hall, being in Northamptonshire, was con-

veniently inconvenient to get to from her old home —
a cross-country rail and hired carriage journey, which
she knew her grandfather would be unable to face. He
might, of course, send Elsie, or he might order her
home. She wouldn't go. Ben had gone straight back to
Oxford and then to Durham to stay with friends. He
was putting his head in the sand about the whole holiday business, Charlotte realized, but could hardly
blame him. Milo had promised that he would send a
letter to reassure the old man but he hadn't written it
yet. Charlotte decided she must remind him.

Having finished her letter, she nearly fell asleep
across the rickety table. Since she had landed at
Nettlepot Hall she had spent twelve hours a day scrubbing floors, brushing down stairs, cleaning windows,
and getting down cobwebs. The boys had fed vast fires
to air the place, cut ivy away from the windows, and
made valiant attempts to put the plumbing and the
drains in order. Milo had worked as hard as any of
them.

He had employed some casual labour to clear the
dead trees and cut logs to feed the voracious fireplaces
but Phyllida had declared she didn't want any local
women in her kitchen "to take gossip home"; she could
manage with Queenie.

"Just imagine," she said to Charlotte, "the stories
that will be going round about us! Lucky your grandfather's sixty miles away."

"What do you mean?"

"Oh come, Charlotte, don't be so green. Heir to mil-
lions takes on derelict house next door to his declared
lover, his servants Oxford graduates. . . It's very queer,

108

you must admit. Just moved in — we're bound to be hot gossip at the moment. Give it a few weeks and the place is straight and we've learned our jobs — it won't be so bad then if we employ a few helpers. We need them, God knows. What we don't need is adverse opinion."

Charlotte had supposed that the reason she didn't want her grandfather visiting was because she sensed the whole set-up was far from respectable to outside eyes. She would not admit it, for in truth it was perfectly respectable, but small village people saw things differently. She had also gone into the situation blinded by her love for Casimir, which showed no sign of abating and which stopped her thinking seriously about anything else. If only he hadn't completely demoralized her by declaring his love for her at the moment of parting, she thought she might have stood a better chance of putting him out of her mind. If she could have remembered him laughing — laughing when his mother had kicked them apart — that would have been easier. But that last moment of tenderness had overwhelmed her. She was as lovesick as Milo himself, wrapping herself in such dreams as she had never experienced before, exploring emotions she did not know existed.

Two days ago Milo had found her weeping over her bucket of dirty water at the top of the back stairs. She had not heard him coming and was too late to mop her eyes and put on a bright face.

"It's not the work, is it? You mustn't exhaust yourself," he said.

No.

He stopped and stared at her.

"It's Casimir, isn't it?"

She could not reply. She stared back at him like a stupid sheep and saw in his expression a deep compassion.

"Yes."

He squatted down to be on a level and said, "You mustn't cry. You can go back, in the spring. Time passes."

"How can I go back?" Her voice came out like a wail.

"I will take you. We can all go climbing again."

"But — but I — I'm only a housekeeper —"

"Look, Charlotte, the servants in this house are my friends. I want it that way, it suits me. We are not bound by convention. Why shouldn't we do as we like? Life is for being happy. We obey the rules that matter, but the silly rules of convention don't matter."

Charlotte could find no answer to this.

Milo said, "Climbing is part of my life. I go every year, always. You will see Casimir again, if you wish. Don't be sad — not you."

He had then departed, leaving Charlotte amazed. She did not think anyone — save perhaps Queenie — knew about her love for Casimir, yet Milo seemed to take it for granted. He would take her back to Switzerland! She could climb with Casimir again and bring him back to Nettlepot to work! Her dreams were inspired.

As long as Grandfather didn't interfere . . . she was under age and he could order her back home if he wished.

Queenie had written home to say she had a new

post at Nettlepot Hall, and her parents were only too pleased for her. They didn't, of course, know that she was pregnant. If only it could be as easy for her, Charlotte yearned!

She put the letter in an envelope and addressed it and left it in her room. She had come upstairs to clean herself up to get ready for Kitty's arrival. She knew Phyllida was nervous, although Milo had told them Kitty was "nothing to worry about." What did that mean? There were no rooms yet fit to receive anyone. They all lived in the kitchen, even Milo. Their own bedrooms were barely furnished, having only beds and washing jugs and chamber pots, and all the guest rooms were empty.

The kitchen smelt marvellous. Phyllida and Queenie were hard at work, and even Clara had been forced to lend a hand. A whole sheep was cooking on the old-fashioned spit.

"Mar said he found it," Phyllida said dubiously. "He brought it in last night. I don't believe half of what he says."

"It smells wonderful."

"Well, Mar's in charge of that. He prepared it on the spit. I think where he comes from — you know — the bog — he knows about these things."

The back doors were open to the yard outside, and the evening sun poured in. The kitchen was enormous and bare, except for a huge scrubbed table in the middle. It had archaic cooking ranges with myriad ovens and the spit down one side, and great stone sinks and draining boards down the other. Hot water was drawn from the range. They carried it up to their own bedrooms to wash, even Milo, but if they wanted a bath they used an old scullery nearby and a tin bath which they filled themselves. (Nobody washed much.)

Charlotte went to the doors and breathed in the lovely autumn-touched air. Casimir, she thought! The air was touched with that Alpine freshness that was sharp in her memory, along with the feel of Casimir in her arms. She had been greatly comforted by Milo's kindness and thought now of Casimir not with despair but with an excited anticipation, until they should meet again. Milo had promised. Spring was only eight months away. She wondered if she dared write to him? Would that dreadful mother steal her letters? How sweet Milo was. The unattainable Milo. If only Grandfather had proposed Milo for a husband, she would gladly have agreed. She was tired. Her thoughts wandered and were disturbed rudely by the sound of rapidly approaching hooves along the back drive. They had no horses yet — it must be a visitor. Kitty?

"Someone's coming!" she shouted over her shoulder.

"Oh, not yet!" Phyllida wailed. "Find Milo!" she shouted at Clara. Clara moved like a snail towards the hall.

There was a large yard behind the kitchen which gave onto the walled kitchen gardens opposite and, further on, to the stables. A back drive led into it from the road, very useful for deliveries. But if this was Kitty . . . a real visitor should arrive at the front door by way of the front drive over the bridge.

A pair of magnificent chestnut horses was approaching at a fast trot — so fast that Charlotte was alarmed that they wouldn't negotiate the archway into the yard. They were pulling a fashionable gig, rather high and racy, and were driven by a woman without an attendant. She made the archway with military precision and pulled up sharply, immediately outside the door. Slotting her whip into its holder, she shouted down to Charlotte. "Hello! I'm Kitty! Will you hold the horses while I get down?"

Charlotte moved forward nervously and took the two bridles, not sure how to greet Milo's sister. She didn't know whether she was Milo's friend or Milo's housekeeper. It was a problem that hadn't arisen before. Kitty hooked up the reins, jumped down, and came round to relieve Charlotte.

"Are you Phyllida or Charlotte? Charlotte, I think? That nice Ben's sister?"

"Yes, I'm Charlotte."

She had to force herself not to add ma'am. For Kitty was a strikingly authoritative figure. Although small, she was a female Milo in looks, with his lovely blue-grey eyes and clear skin. But more skittish than Milo and given to laughter. She wore a tweed driving suit and a red hat with a long feather and buttoned leather boots.

"Has he got a groom yet, or shall I have to see to them myself?"

"I'll think you'll find Mar in the stables. I'll take them round if you like."

At this moment Milo appeared round the side of the house, prompted by Clara. He came up to Kitty and kissed her excitedly.

"You drove on your own? All the way? You're crazy!"

"It's just near enough — thirty-four miles! Aren't they splendid? I was longing to try them as a pair — they went like Trojans. They hunt too, you know. You are clever, Milo, buying a place just within reach."

"Oh, it's lucky to be near you! You come second to being near Constance, of course, but a pretty good second. This is Charlotte Campion — have you introduced yourself? My sister Kitty Lytton, Charlotte. My favourite sister. I have six and the other five are all dreadful, aren't they Kitty?"

"Frightful," she agreed. "And our brothers too. There's only us. Look, unload those boxes out of the back before we go to the stables. I've brought you a few things."

The "things" turned out to be plates, cutlery, glasses, saucepans, buckets, jugs, carpet beaters, brushes — all things that they fell upon with delight when the boxes were opened in the kitchen.

"Look, a real cloth!" Phyllida shook out a huge damask tablecloth, richly embroidered with the Fambridge monogram in the corners. "Oh, put it on the table, Clara! We'll be sumptuous tonight!"

There was also a case of the best claret and a tin trunk full of towels and servants' clothes — striped afternoon dresses, black dresses, and aprons of all kinds. So far they had worn their own old clothes all day.

"I suppose when the house is all set up, we'll have to act the part properly," Phyllida decided, trying a striped dress against her lanky figure. "You'll have to wear black, Charlotte, and have keys hanging from your belt."

"Only when proper people come."

They had no idea what Milo's future plans for them were. So far nobody had bothered to act their parts.

Mar hacked enormous slices off the sizzling lamb, and Phyllida served up roast potatoes and great steaming bowls of hot gravy. Kitty's bottles of claret sparkled in the candlelight. It was like their days in Zermatt, all hungry after their heavy work, with Kitty making it a special evening. She sat opposite Milo, questioning him about his plans.

"All this for Constance? Oh, Milo, you are crazy! You surely won't entertain here?"

"Only my special friends will come here. Constance, of course, and my hunting and racing friends. You, Kitty — no one else in the family."

"Mama and Papa are sure to want to call when it's all set up, even if they're not speaking to you now. Out of nosiness."

"I won't receive them. I shall be out."

"And when you entertain Constance . . . how will it work, with your friends here?"

Milo's friends, who had not understood this clearly themselves, listened with interest.

"On those occasions, they will dress and behave like proper servants, and I will treat them as such. The rest of the time, we just do our work and we are friends."

"Do you think it will work?"

"Yes. Why not? We all know how to behave as servants. We've been surrounded by them all our lives."

"So, how is it arranged? What does everyone do?"

"Phyllida is the cook, a splendid one, I might add. Queenie helps in the kitchen. Charlotte is the housekeeper. But she will have to wait at table when visitors come, and so will Clara. Clara does the linen — the sewing and the ironing. She looks after my clothes. All the girls help with the washing, and the men make the fires for it. Roland does the grounds and the kitchen garden, and Mar is in charge of the stables. He will also double as butler when visitors come."

At this last everyone roared with laughter. Mar looked rather offended.

"Why do you all think that so funny? That I can't be a butler?"

"He knows how to pour wine," Roland pointed out.

"He'll be wonderful!" Phyllida cried. "But your brother would have been better, Charlotte. Why didn't Ben join this household? He would make a perfect butler."

"He's too serious — he thought we were all mad," Charlotte said.

"I'm serious," said Mar.

"Nobody needs to be serious," Milo pointed out. "Even when you're being a servant, it's not all that serious, after all. I could be a butler standing on my head, if necessary."

"How is Mar going to receive your visitors' horses round in the stables, and be at the front door to meet the same visitors?" Kitty asked.

"I'll have hired some help by then — outside help from the village. We shall need gardeners and grooms and boys to clean — no gossiping women! I don't want a terrible hierarchy of old retainers around me, like we've got at home. For God's sake, Kitty — my own place — I don't want stuffed-shirt servants breathing down my neck! I can have all that in London. But when I'm here, in my own place, I don't want ceremony."

"Sometimes you'll want ceremony — you could be a laughingstock. Bertie comes shooting round here — suppose he were to walk in one day?"

"I'm not inviting the Prince of Wales, idiot! And yes, I agree, sometimes I will want ceremony. But how often? I've bought this place so that I can enjoy myself. Mar, Charlotte, Phyllida will be tact itself when I require them to be servants, and the rest of the time — well, we behave as it suits us. We run the house and enjoy ourselves."

"You must understand, Kitty, that we are using this place rather as a sanctuary — it suits us too," Mar put in. "Milo isn't entirely mad. In fact, he is our saviour. None of us has anywhere to go and we're only too happy to be his servants in exchange for his hospitality."

"We *like* it!" Roland said, with a happy sigh. He worked in the kitchen garden all day, from first light, cleaning out the glasshouses and clearing the rampant growth from the brick paths. He dreamed of ordered beds and shining produce and grapes hanging in lustrous clusters from the ancient vines, and Milo's garden was a gift from heaven, awaiting the transformation that he knew was in his power to effect. Of them all, he had no threats hanging over him: his respectable suburban parents did not object; he desired nothing that he did not have already. He had worked out how to clear the "lake," then enlarge it by a system of dams. His head was full of pictures of the future. He was always last to the table, smelling of carbolic, and sometimes fell asleep after supper while the others were still talking. Charlotte always envied him his total happiness. Hers was in patches, bliss and agonies falling over each other. Roland was steady and kind, while the rest of them were of all humours like herself.

"I love it; I'm not criticizing — I'm jealous! I wish I could join you!" An expression of great sadness crossed Kitty's face fleetingly.

"You can, any time, dear Kitty," Milo said softly.

Charlotte sensed that there was a great unspoken link between the brother and sister, which she envied deeply. Much as she loved Ben, she had never felt that he was close to her, or that she meant very much to him. She had a great surfeit of love to use on someone, and sometimes felt she would burst with frustration and her sense of loss. The expression she saw on Kitty's face made her feel that she was not alone. Yet there was no way of putting these confusions into words.

Kitty, tossing the emotion aside, looked sharply at Mar and said, "I've seen you somewhere before. But not with Milo. What is your name?"

He had been introduced casually as Mar. He replied, avoiding her question, "At Oxford, perhaps?"

"I've never been to Oxford. I connect you with race-meetings. On a horse. Is that right?"

Mar glanced at Milo.

Milo said, "Mar mentioned that this place was a sanctuary. More for him than the others. He doesn't really want his name known here."

"His name is on the tip of my tongue, and I fear I shall remember it very shortly," Kitty said.

"Have some dessert," Phyllida said. She nipped sharply from the table and fetched a huge apple pie from the stove. "We've no cream, I'm afraid. Milo promises a house cow shortly, but I've never learnt to milk."

"Queenie can milk," Charlotte remembered.

(Queenie, the real servant, was something of an embarrassment at mealtimes, refusing to sit down with them, although invited. She preferred to do the fetching and carrying and eat by herself afterwards. Tonight, she had retired to her room, saying she was tired, but Charlotte thought she wanted to avoid Kitty.)

"Oh, good. I thought I might have to learn."

"Marchant Merchant-Fox!" Kitty cried out suddenly.

"Oh, dammit, Kitty," Milo said crossly.

"But Fox had red hair. Orange, like a lighthouse. I thought, 'how well-named.' It is you, isn't it, and you've dyed it?"

"I wear a wig, madam."

"Oh, heavens, I know why you're hiding — everyone thinks you're in Geneva."

"Who is everyone?" Milo asked.

"Ambrose's brother — what's he called? The really awful one? Jacob. Jacob Payne. And his nasty wife, aptly called the Weasel."

"How is it you know these very undesirable people, Kitty?" Milo asked.

"It's racing gossip. At Goodwood. Merchant-Fox has disappeared — he's on the run because he murdered Ambrose rather than settle a debt."

"Is that the story?" Both Milo and Mar were outraged.

"I've always settled my debts! Find someone to say otherwise, apart from that crook."

"Ambrose had a funeral, a very ostentatious one at Newmarket, so everyone knows he's dead. Did you murder him, Mar?"

"No. We had a fight and he died. That's different. And I owe him no money, nor ever have done."

"They're after you, though. Jacob has sworn 'to bring you to justice' — his words. Rich, coming from him, the biggest crook of the lot. But it seems to be accepted that he has a point. Ambrose is dead, after all."

Milo and Mar exchanged glances, and there was a short silence. Mar's habitual bounce was extinguished, and the drawn and anguished expression Charlotte recognized from the first days of meeting him had come back to his features.

He said, "Out of touch — down here — and in Zermatt — one tends to think . . ." He shrugged. "I felt justice was on my side. It was an accident, and he deserved a thrashing. But, of course — " He shrugged. "It will be pursued. Why should I think otherwise?"

"They are dangerous enemies, Mar," Milo said. "They must never find out where you are."

"I can't hide forever!"

"Someone told me they'd hired a private detective to trace you," Kitty said.

"God's truth!"

"As long as no one discovers he was with Milo in Zermatt," Phyllida said, "how can they trace him here?"

"They know he travelled to Geneva. Someone must have seen him on the journey. That hair . . . Oh, Mar, your disguise is splendid. No one in passing will recognize you. The voice gives you away, your lovely Irish

120

voice. I never gave it a thought — who you were —
until we sat here in conversation."

"How do you know all this, Kitty?" Milo asked. "If
this is racing gossip, it's very inside gossip . . . a private
detective? Who told you?"

Kitty hesitated.

"If you want to know . . . our young brother Evelyn
is friendly with the Paynes. He told me."

"Evelyn?"

"He's a bit of a skunk, Milo — between you and me.
Mother spoils him frightfully, and he's into gambling
and bad company."

"He's still at school —"

"Not often. He skives off, comes to me because I'm
near. He gets to all the big race-meetings, believe me."

"Brat." Milo glowered at the head of the table. The
jolly evening was now taut with anxiety. Charlotte
could feel a cold creeping of fear taking hold of her,
threatening the warm intimacy of the house.

Across the table, Roland was silent, and Phyllida
frowned ferociously. None of them knew much about
this fashionable racing world of crooks, dukes, gam-
blers, and the Prince of Wales, but had gathered that
racing was the passion of Milo and Mar's lives. Milo's
racehorses were arriving shortly, his hunters were coming up from grass, and soon the house would revolve
around the winter scene of sport. They all rode, of
course, for transport, and took horses for granted —
and also hunting, which was a common country pursuit — but racing was another sphere altogether. Milo
rode his own horses when he went racing, and was
apparently a well-known and successful amateur rider.
Charlotte guessed that the thrill and the edge of danger

was very akin to the excitements of the difficult climbing around Zermatt and that Milo needed such a spur in his life to give it purpose. His love affair was equally difficult and dangerous. Milo did not choose an easy path.

"It's as well you've told us this, Kitty," he said gravely. "We've tended to put Mar's problem to one side since we came home. Lying low . . . it's all right for the present, but no one can live like that forever. We'll have to work something out."

"Getting something on Payne shouldn't be difficult," Kitty said.

"Blackmail. What fun!" Mar said, smiling.

"Make sure Evelyn doesn't come here, Kitty," Milo said.

"I'll tell him he won't be welcome. That won't be a surprise. But everyone is very curious about your hideaway, Milo. Very daring, it's considered. Are you leaving calling cards on your neighbours?"

"Only on one."

The conversation veered away from Mar, and by the time they were all ready for bed the frisson of fear had been forgotten. Kitty had been earmarked a hastily cleaned and aired room near Charlotte's, and Charlotte had given her bed to Kitty. Queenie had lit a fire in the grate, and, in the light of the oil lamp Charlotte carried to lead the way, the room looked cosy and inviting. Kitty followed Charlotte up, bearing her own small bag of luggage. When Charlotte started to depart, Kitty said, "Don't go for a moment."

Charlotte turned back. Kitty was sitting on the bed, her face softly lit by the lamp. She looked very small, even frail, yet a powerful energy emanated from her slender frame, as it did from Milo's. There was an impressive authority, and Charlotte felt at that moment as if she were indeed the servant. Perhaps it was good practice.

"Why have you nowhere to go?" Kitty asked.

Charlotte explained about Mr. Carstairs and her stultifying home life.

"Is he kind, Mr. Carstairs?"

"He's kind, probably. But he repulses me."

"You're not in love with Milo?"

"No!" Charlotte was startled by the question.

"Good. So many girls are, and it's quite useless. He loves only Constance, and it's hopeless, blighting his life."

"But she loves him?"

"Yes, I think she does. But of course she won't leave her husband, she won't upset society. We are all allowed our affairs, as long as we don't rock the boat, as long as it's discreet and no one's hurt. But Constance — she's a friend of our *mother's* — in fact, I think that's how it came about . . . she was a mother to Milo when he needed one — and our mother, to put it bluntly, is not a maternal woman. Of course, he loved her for it. He has a romantic nature, and she is very beautiful and sophisticated — perhaps, he thought, unattainable. Milo always wants the impossible in whatever he does — the most difficult: the Matterhorn, the Grand National . . . Constance is also very bold, which appeals to him enormously. She is an amazing horsewoman. They went hunting together, and they fell in love in a different way altogether. Constance too. That was when he was barely seventeen. A passing whim for Constance, but for Milo it's been like being chained. It's a terrible thing to have happened. How will it end?"

Charlotte was astonished at hearing these confidences, wondering why they were being given. Kitty had only met her three hours before. She stood awkwardly by the door, silent, listening to the fluttering of the fire in the grate, and the distant bark of a fox from away down the drive. The night was never silent here, full of rustlings and creakings, barking and hooting, and small animal shrieks. She had already grown used to its seclusion, its feeling of withdrawal inside a small world, edged by the Goldstone walls and the uncleared woods.

As if answering her unasked question, Kitty then said, "I thought — I hoped — perhaps you were here because —" She shrugged. "You met in Switzerland. You are lovely. The other girls, no, but you — oh, Charlotte, I love Milo so. And he does so need someone like you to be his partner. He isn't nearly as strong as he appears — I don't mean physically. But in his emotions — he's so vulnerable. You wait till you meet Constance! You will see what I mean . . . she eats him up. He is her amusement. She is *forty-eight,* Charlotte! And now, when she comes back from Scotland, it will start all over again."

Charlotte could think of nothing to say.

Then Kitty said, "Are you in love with someone else, that you aren't in love with Milo?"

Charlotte felt her cheeks firing up.

"Yes."

"Oh, Charlotte, what a pity. That other girl,

124

Phyllida, is in love with Milo, I could see. And even Clara, she will be when she gets her wits back. The way she looked . . . Who are you in love with? Not Mar?"

"No. The guide, in Switzerland. Casimir."

"Was he very beautiful?"

"Yes."

"Did he kiss you?"

"Yes."

"How lovely! It cannot last though. It's impossible." Kitty looked pleased. "Then perhaps you will love Milo. When he needs you."

Charlotte was disturbed by Kitty's remarks. That she should presume to love Milo! How wild Kitty was.

Spurred by such confidences, she asked boldly, "And who do you love? Your husband?"

Kitty burst out laughing. "No. I love no one. If you were to meet my husband, you would see . . ."

She did not explain, and Charlotte dared ask no more. She left Kitty the lamp and departed, much disturbed. There was still the washing up to do, and she made her way back to the kitchen where Phyllida and Clara were clearing the table. The boys had gone upstairs. Charlotte put her apron on and started to stack the dishes at the sink. Phyllida and Clara were discussing Kitty, and Charlotte listened curiously, wondering what their reaction would be if she told them what Kitty had said about them. It was true, she thought, that Phyllida loved Milo, and it was her real reason for staying as cook. But she was such a spiky girl — her love was not displayed in soft looks and words, but covered up by her brusque exterior. Clara, recovering from the shock of Max's death, had discovered that the homely routine of Nettlepot suited her essentially domestic outlook. The high drama of her grief had ebbed and, although she wore unadorned black at all times, she was beginning to take an interest in her new life.

"You were a long time," Phyllida said rather tartly to Charlotte.

Charlotte did not say why. She changed the subject.

"It's serious, those men being after Mar. Suppose they find out where he is?"

"God knows. It's bad, really bad. He was sick, when he heard that." Phyllida was setting the table for breakfast, polishing the knives on her apron. "It's hard to keep secrets. When we have boys to help, from the village, they notice things, talk."

"Milo will think of something."

"He does usually, but he's not a magician."

Charlotte hardly slept, confused by Kitty's talk, worried about Mar, and missing her bed. The floor was hard. She got up early to help Phyllida. She took hot water up to Kitty and found her still asleep, the covers thrown back, a slant of autumn sun burnishing the thick plait of her hair. She wore an exquisite silk nightdress, embroidered all over with flowers. Seeing her, Charlotte felt a stab of jealousy — Kitty with her confident questions, rich and secure, privileged and lovely. By comparison Charlotte felt like a blind woman feeling her way into life, knowing nothing, not even what she wanted. Kitty knew everything, like Milo, and had tossed away her confession of love for Casimir as "impossible." But when Kitty opened her eyes and smiled at her, Charlotte felt herself melting as if warmed by fire.

"Oh, dear Charlotte, what a lot we have to do. Milo has no idea."

It was the start of a maelstrom of activity at Nettlepot Hall. The house was at least clean and ready to receive the train of pantechnicons that shortly started to issue up the drive from the railway station five miles distant. Furniture, great rolls of carpet, and trunks of curtains were unloaded into the empty rooms.

"Where on earth did Kitty get it all from?" Phyllida asked, amazed as ten railwaymen manhandled a vast grand piano through the hall towards the sitting room. Two more men stacked enormous family portraits and hunting pictures at the foot of the stairs, and when Charlotte went to her room in the afternoon she found it furnished with a lovely brass bed, an oak wardrobe and chest of drawers, a faded Persian carpet, and a pair of rather ragged but cheerful yellow velour curtains. Dear Kitty!

"I recognize some of these things. They're all from home," Milo said. "Kitty must have ransacked the place. Mother throws things out all the time — everything must be the new fashion for her. Of course, she's in Monte Carlo just now — she'll never know they're gone. Good old Kitty. I'd never have had the brass to go home for stuff."

"Some of it's beautiful," Charlotte said, amazed at such profligacy. The vicar's household had darned and repaired voraciously; Charlotte had been brought up on thrift. She helped hang some beautiful, if faded, tapestry curtains in the sitting room, shortened by Clara on her machine to fit the new windows. The soft autumn sunlight shone in on chairs and sofas upholstered in gold brocade, and across an old silk carpet patterned in gold and red, faded to the colours of the leaves outside. The huge black piano filled an alcove, which could have been designed for it. In the dining room Queenie was polishing a long Jacobean sideboard, and Phyllida was setting chairs (not matching, but near enough) round a long oak table, grand enough for a banquet.

"Oh, we are so smart! It's a proper house now." The girls were thrilled.

Milo's horses had arrived, led down the drive two by two by men from the station, and Mar had all their stalls and boxes ready, scrubbed out and deep in new straw. As well as the hunters and the steeplechasers and Milo's darling mare Goodnight Glitters, there was a pair of smart carriage horses — "The girls can ride them. They're quiet as kittens, ridden" — and a couple of ponies for pulling a trap and carting Roland's rubbish.

"Thank goodness, we'll be able to go shopping," Phyllida said to Charlotte, tired of improvising on basic farm fare from their neighbours. "I want currants and spices and sugar and rice and fish and macaroons and angelica and —" There was no end to it. "Do you drive?" she asked Charlotte.

"Yes, of course."

"I never have," Phyllida said. "You'll have to teach me."

The next day Charlotte got an answer to her letter. It was from Elsie.

Dear Charlotte,
Your grandfather has shown me your letter and ad-

vised me to visit you to see that you are all right. If it is convenient to your hosts I shall be coming on Thursday to the nearest station. There is a train that arrives just after noon. If you do not meet me I trust there will be a carrier I can hire. Wire to confirm.

Your affectionate,
Elsie.

Charlotte read it aloud, with mounting horror. Queenie nearly fainted.

"Oh, Lor', me stomach! What'll she say? Oh, for Gawd's sake, I'll have to — oh, Miss Charlotte — what'll we do?"

Charlotte was as shocked as Queenie. Since hearing nothing from home, she had been living in a fool's paradise, pretending that all was well. Elsie on Thursday . . . in three days' time . . .

"Come on, Queenie, it doesn't show a bit," Phyllida said. "With your big apron, she'll never notice. Who is this Elsie, that you're both so horrified?"

"Queenie's aunt. Grandfather's housekeeper."

"Lucky they didn't send your Mr. Carstairs."

"We'll all be as good as gold, Charlotte, don't worry," Milo said. "We'll charm her off her perch, say we can't live without you. Leave it to me."

And he smiled at her, and Charlotte saw at once that he would win Elsie over with his sweet manners and the attention from the shadowed blue eyes beneath almost girlish lashes. He had such genuine charm, yet, according to Mar, was a daredevil out hunting and racing. "That mare of his, Goodnight Glitters —" Mar said. "She trusts him utterly, even the things he asks of

129

her — you wouldn't believe it. He is a superb horseman."

Milo was her dream husband, she realized. What a pity that they both loved someone else. The realities of life were a far cry from dreams.

9

When she saw Elsie standing on the platform with her old carpetbag, Charlotte was so excited she burst into tears. She flung her arms around her, a flood of homesickness overtaking her — *dear* Elsie! Friend of her childhood, nurse, servant, scolder, confidante . . . Elsie was more intimate than a mother, safe and approachable in the kitchen, handing out raisins, letting you scrape the cakebowl. The whole of her sheltered, kindly upbringing rushed back at Charlotte; even the smell of Elsie, so familiar — a mix of mothballs and strong soap, a dash of violet water — overwhelmed her with nostalgia.

"Dear Elsie! How lovely to see you!"

The two grey carriage horses stood in the station yard, with Mar playing professional groom in dark livery, white breeches, shining boots, and a top hat. "Treat me like a servant, remember," had been his last words as the train steamed into the station. Immediately, Charlotte could see that Elsie was impressed. This was no old swaybacked Daisy with the gardener-handyman, but a real toff's set-up.

"My, Charlotte, how smart! Whatever sort of a place are you in? I thought just a country sort of farm."

"Oh, no, we're quite smart, Elsie, you'll see."

"Oh, my word, I don't know what to think. I thought you were hiding something down here, straight I did. I said to your grandfather I'd call and see what tricks you're up to. He's very worried, you know, that you never came home after Lucerne."

"Elsie, I couldn't stand to see Mr. Carstairs again. You know that. I don't want to get married. You'll see what good friends I have here."

"You're so young, Charlotte, to have a job away from home."

"But not too young to marry."

"Oh, hush now. Let's not argue."

Elsie, unused to carriage drives, looked around, enjoying the country lane and the autumn trees arching overhead. She settled herself with a contented sniff and watched Mar's stiff back in front of her. The horses were bowling along, striding out at a good pace. Elsie gave Charlotte a nudge and whispered, "He looks a right young tartar, that driver."

"He's only the groom."

"A bonny lad."

Charlotte wanted to giggle. "How do I know she's not a private detective, your Elsie?" Mar had asked. "The Paynes might have hired her." It was characteristic of him to turn his fears into jokes.

When they came to the high golden walls and splendid gates of the Mathers' establishment, Elsie was quite excited. "Whoever lives there? What a grand place!" The lane to Nettlepot left the road just past the gates and followed the wall round, the woods encroaching. "Your neighbours, Charlotte? Who are they?"

Charlotte mumbled the name Mathers, making it sound like Matthews, and Elsie showed no sign of recognition. Charlotte was fairly sure the Establishment gossip had not reached home and, if it had, would go unremarked. Elsie was well up on the Royals' and Bertie's carryings-on — "Poor dear Alex, what a saint the princess is" — but had not cottoned on to the scandals of the lesser ranks. Grandfather had heard of the Rawnsleys, but Charlotte doubted if Elsie had. She did not read the newspapers, only paper novels.

"Our place isn't as smart as that," Charlotte said — unnecessarily as the tumbled woods closed in on them. "It's been neglected. That's the job: to get it back in order. You'll see."

Yet already she loved the romantic approach through the trees and the first glimpse round the bend of the sheet of water edged with reeds where the moorhens clucked and the grey herons stood patiently in the dawn. The pretty Palladian bridge had been cleared of debris, and the front of the house, denuded of its overgrowth, now stood invitingly in the mellow sunshine. As the carriage drew to a halt, Roland came to take the horses' heads — as instructed during the plan of campaign — and Mar handed Elsie down and took her bag to the door.

"Thank you, we can manage," Charlotte said in her housekeeper's voice. Mar backed away sycophantically, rather overdoing it, Charlotte thought. Elsie wasn't the Duchess of York, for goodness' sake! But Elsie was

132

overcome by the treatment and followed Charlotte up the stairs to her room breathlessly expressing her admiration.

"If you'd like to wash and then come down, we'll have something to eat in the kitchen and then I'll show you round."

The whole twenty-four hours of Elsie's visit was to be devoted to reassuring her about the respectability of Charlotte's job. Everyone had been briefed. Mar and Roland were to stay in the background; Milo would impress Elsie as only Milo could. Phyllida, the most impressive of friends — intelligent, well-bred, sensible — would have the leading part.

Charlotte went down to the kitchen to find her with lunch ready, the table laid for four.

"Milo and Roland have already eaten. Mar's having his after we've finished, and Elsie is out of the way. Tonight Milo has his dinner in the dining room alone, and we all eat in here with Elsie." Phyllida seemed, for her, more flustered than Charlotte was expecting.

"Is everything all right?"

"Yes. But Milo's just told me — oh, God! — lover lady is coming to dinner tomorrow night. The adored Constance."

"Tomorrow!"

"Yes. So little warning! And it's for real — no fun and games. She's to think we're proper servants. Milo's deadly serious."

Charlotte felt herself go cold all over. Tomorrow!

"Mar's got to be butler."

"No!"

Charlotte was horrified. She would have to wait at

table, hand the vegetables. Her hands would shake, she would drop the cutlery. She had no doubt that Milo would expect perfection — they couldn't let him down. Their own lives depended on it.

"And the meal will have to be perfect," Phyllida groaned. "If only we'd more warning."

"We are all dying to see her — but *tomorrow!*"

The horrors to come meant that present rigours — impressing Elsie — seemed quite simple by comparison. They were. Elsie hadn't come to criticize. It became apparent that she wanted to make a good report home.

"It's true what you said, the vicarage is a prison for a young girl." She embraced Queenie warmly and noticed nothing untoward about her figure — about which, indeed, it would have taken a very practiced eye to suspect the truth. Elsie was enjoying her little break, loved being cooked for and waited on, and was thrilled with the cosiness of her room and its views.

After lunch Charlotte took her on a tour of the grounds, through the kitchen garden, and out into the woods. She avoided the stable yard because she didn't know how to treat Mar, in front of Elsie. When they came back, Milo met them in the hall, and Elsie was introduced.

Milo was a different person. He seemed suddenly ten years older and acted exactly like a high-born landowner being introduced to his housekeeper's old nanny — pleasant, distant, and patronizing. Charlotte, impressed, kept silent, like a proper housekeeper. She could feel her heart fluttering with indecision. When he left them, going upstairs, he gave an order concerning the wine he wanted for the following evening, and

Charlotte heard herself answering, "Yes, sir, I will see to it." It came quite naturally, from the way he had treated them.

Elsie was impressed. "What a very pleasant gentleman."

They ate dinner in the kitchen, with Mar and Roland, and Elsie had a glass of wine and everyone was charming to her, on their best behaviour. Milo ate in the dining room alone and Charlotte waited on him. When she went in he was perfectly normal, not like he had been with Elsie.

"Are we impressing her?" he asked. "Is she disposed to let you stay?"

"It's too good to be true, so far. She's enjoying herself, certainly — I suppose she's hardly ever left the vicarage in her life. She thought you were a 'very pleasant gentleman.'"

"Good." He smiled.

He looked lonely in the large dining room, his place lit by a branch of candles. He had a book propped up on the vegetable tureen and had not changed out of his riding clothes.

He said suddenly, seriously, "I want you to stay, Charlotte. I'm doing my very best. I'm going cubbing in the morning, early, so I probably won't see her again. But if she seems doubtful — before you go — send me word up at the stables, and I'll see what I can do."

"You are kind, Milo."

Charlotte was overcome by the trouble he took, her great good fortune in meeting him almost overwhelming her in a sudden flood of emotion. She felt tears welling up and had to blow her nose.

"I can never go back — not now. I couldn't bear it."

She turned away with the used dishes, feeling her hands trembling.

"Charlotte."

She turned back.

"You know — tomorrow — tomorrow matters to me as this matters to you." In the candlelight Milo's face was drawn and pale, his eyes lit with the reflection of two flames. "I might not be the same person tomorrow. You will understand?"

"Yes. It was the arrangement."

"She is not like us, Charlotte. You will see. It's not a game, tomorrow. Not for any of us."

"No. I understand."

He looked as fraught, suddenly, as she felt about going home. As she left the room, Charlotte remembered Kitty's words — "she eats him up." Walking down the cold corridor back to the kitchen, she knew that it wasn't a game for any of them, not for Mar who was in danger of his life, nor Phyllida who loved Milo and must watch him loving Constance. If Elsie gave her permission to stay, her heart would be the lightest of all.

In the morning, as Elsie prepared to leave, packing her carpetbag, she said to Charlotte, "I will make up a story for your grandfather. I won't tell him the truth — nor lies either, but something that will satisfy my conscience. I was a girl myself once, although you will find it hard to believe. This house has a happy feel. I want you to be happy, Charlotte. I won't stand in your way. You can always come home, after all, if you need to. But don't disgrace your good grandfather's name — I trust you not to do that, Charlotte. You know what I mean. I rely on you to behave in the good way you have been taught."

Charlotte, thinking of Queenie, flushed scarlet.

"Elsie!" She hugged her deliriously. "I promise. Oh, I wanted it so much — for you to say yes. Dear, dear Elsie! You will be proud of me, I promise — I will never let you down."

"You are a darling girl. I want you to be happy, Charlotte." Elsie then burst into tears, and so did Charlotte, and they hugged each other, laughing and crying, till they realized the horses were waiting for them outside.

Then, in spite of the terrors of the impending evening, Charlotte was walking on air. She was safe. Going back with Mar in the carriage she was still half-laughing, half-crying with relief. Mar was pleased for her.

"We'd never have let you go, Charlotte — we need you too much."

"Oh, no. You'd miss Phyllida for her cooking, but not me."

"You're wrong. Cooking's not everything. Phyllida is like the school matron, all starch and crackle. And Clara is like a great suet pudding. But you — you're — I don't know — nice — the sort of girl a chap can get on with."

Coming from Mar, a scornful young man, this was a compliment indeed. Now that Elsie was disposed of, he put the horses into a canter, and they careered home. There was a lot to do.

"What's Constance like?" Charlotte asked him. "Have you met her?"

137

"No. I've seen her — out hunting, at the races, parties and suchlike. She's stunning looking. Tall, very clever, I believe. Not my sort at all. Frightens me to death."

Charlotte had to cling on as the horses swung into the lane. Mar handled them with consummate skill. Would he be as good as a butler?

"Aren't you frightened about tonight?"

"Oh heavens, yes!"

Phyllida was taut with nerves, making meringues. Lunch was only sandwiches; there was too much to do. Roland came in with all the flowers he could cull from the neglected garden: blowsy golden chrysanthemums and fading roses, with branches of bright-berried spindle and bronzed beech leaves. Clara was put to arranging vases in the hall and making up vases for the dining room and sitting room. Queenie was helping Phyllida, Charlotte had to polish the dining table and chairs and pick out the best of Kitty's gifts — glasses and cutlery and the table china — while Mar made up the fires and filled the log baskets. He fetched up the wine from the cellar and shook out his butler's suit, also provided by Kitty. There was no point putting it on because he had to do evening stables before he became a butler. Charlotte put on her black dress and covered it with a large white apron. Strictly speaking, she was to be parlourmaid, not housekeeper, but such strict demarcations were out of their range. Somehow she would have to tame her hair, make a severe bun and prevent locks from escaping. Clara would have to help her. Meanwhile she helped Phyllida.

"No carving — I'm being very practical, to make it

easy. Soup — Milo says put the tureen on the table, and they will serve themselves. He doesn't want to use the sideboard. I've made game soup with the pheasant Mar ran over yesterday, and there's lemon sole to follow. Milo says you needn't hand it, Charlotte, nor the vegetables. He's thought of everything to make it easier. I'll put it on the nice silver dishes Kitty sent, and the sauce in the sauceboat to serve separately. Then there's saddle of mutton, but Milo says send it in carved, on a dish, with the roast potatoes round it. There's a trifle for sweet — I've done that. It only needs the cream on top and decorating. Queenie, you can do that."

Queenie, now that they were doing things properly, was more at home than when the master ate with them in the kitchen. They found they were asking her advice about details — she was, after all, the professional. The kitchen was hot with cooking, and as the afternoon drew into evening the air of tension started to heighten, and Phyllida's temper grew edgy. They all rushed to obey her orders. Charlotte managed to do her hair, and Clara wedged the recalcitrant tendrils firmly into a large bun.

"You look like the Queen," she said, staring dreamily at Charlotte.

"Oh, thanks a lot. My chins too?"

Mar agreed. "What a martinet! I won't cross swords with you, madam."

He shook out the black tailcoat and breeches.

"But wait for my transformation. The butler is boss, remember. You take orders from me."

Roland lit the lamps and the candelabra in the dining room and put fresh logs on the fire. Outside it was becoming dusk and the night was cool, the first stars hazed by mist. Although it was too soon, Charlotte was on tenterhooks for the sound of hooves on the gravel.

"I must see her," Phyllida declared. "I'm going to spy from my bedroom window when she comes, Charlotte — will you keep an eye out for me? I can run up the back stairs." Her face was set and white. "I hate her, oh, how I hate her!"

"Phyllida!"

Charlotte could see she was overwrought but was surprised by her sudden vulnerability. Phyllida usually closed up on anything that affected her emotionally, taking refuge in the scorn and cynicism that made her such a prickly character. Charlotte, seeing her suddenly without her defences, felt an involuntary surge of sympathy. How awkward of her to love Milo, without hope, when sweet Mar and even sweeter Roland were available. If I weren't in love with Casimir, Charlotte thought, I would . . .

"Charlotte."

She jumped. Mar stood before her, unrecognizable for a moment. He wore his black tail suit, black breeches and stockings and white gloves, and had smarmed his wild wig back with oil, so that he looked smooth and rather evil.

"What do you think?"

"Oh — sinister — creepy —"

Mar looked put out. He straightened himself. "I'm not tall enough to be impressive. Fine for being a jockey, too short for butlership. I shall be good though, you wait. Milo will be proud of me."

"I thought you might use your own hair."

"What, with her? She's the last person who must know me. That crowd loves scandal."

"I scarcely know you like that. I'm sure you're safe."

They went to inspect the dining table, as Mar wanted to make sure Charlotte had put out the correct wine glasses.

"Can't expect these vicarage girls to know about such things." But it was all in order.

As they inspected it, Milo came in. He was in evening clothes, and as surprised to see their new appearance as they were to see his.

"I say, very impressive. Charlotte, you look brilliant, double your age. A bit like the Que —"

"No! That's what Clara said."

He laughed.

"We shall need the minimum of attention, don't worry. Mar, you will answer the door and take her coat. Her carriage is going back, so there will be no problem there. Charlotte, you will wait in the background, in case she needs anything. You will wait in the hall, until we decide to start eating."

He fidgeted with a flowerpiece, turning a rose outward, and Charlotte could see that he was nervous too. He hadn't seen her for three months. The setting for a renewal of his doomed courtship was as beautiful as it could possibly be, the splendid room lit and warmed by firelight and candles, silver and glass glinting. Milo had never had Constance to himself in private before. "She eats him up." Charlotte recalled the strange words again, and her heart went out to darling Milo, who was courting only unhappiness. She knew that he knew it

141

too. His expression was taut with apprehension.

He disappeared into the sitting room, and Milo and Charlotte waited in the hall, silent and on edge. At last they heard the distant scrunch of hooves on the gravel, and Charlotte darted down the long passage to the kitchen to warn Phyllida.

"She's coming!"

She fled back to her place and heard the carriage stop outside the front door. She could feel herself quivering with nerves. She glanced at Mar and saw him straighten himself, playing at butler, as the doorbell rang. He moved forward. Charlotte waited, unseen in the shadows.

Mar opened the door, and Constance came in without hesitating. Milo came out of the sitting room and crossed the hall in a flash and took Constance in his arms. There was no polite, "Shall I take your coat, madam?" from Mar, or even a preliminary greeting between the two lovers, only the ardent coming together in a passionate kiss. Charlotte was dumbstruck and felt her mouth drop open. Even Mar's impassive butler's face was hard put not to show astonishment. They stood like statues, staring, until the long embrace showed signs of coming to an end.

Constance broke away and laughed. Her laughter was genuine, very civilized, a drawing-room laugh, Charlotte thought. Patronizing. She was slightly taller than Milo, with a flawless complexion, enormous dark blue eyes, a patrician nose, and hair piled high over her forehead like Princess Alex. She wore a dress of dark blue velvet, very low in the bust and the waist so tight Charlotte wondered she could breathe. A choker of pearls and sapphires lay against her creamy neck — no wrinkles or any signs of age that Charlotte could see, only an elegant line wrought by much practice of grace and carriage. She wore long white gloves and sapphire bracelets, and a huge white fur, which she handed to Mar, almost smothering him.

"Sweet Milo, have you missed me?"

Her voice was honey-sweet. Charlotte hated her like poison, instantly. If she had been Phyllida, she thought she might have attacked her. Thank heaven Phyllida had been spared the sight of this embrace! Great wafts of scent filled the hall as she moved towards the sitting room, holding Milo's hand. The door closed behind them.

Charlotte did not move, overwhelmed by — what? She was not quite sure — only that she felt personally violated by Constance's complete takeover of *their* Milo. She did not know what she had expected: curiosity, gentleness, fun perhaps, certainly not this display of power and passion. Even Mar, extricating himself from the embrace of the magnificent fur, found it hard to make any comment. His shrug, and the expression on his face, were more eloquent than words. They were servants now, and to stop and discuss the visitor was not their prerogative. Mar went back to the kitchen, and Charlotte waited for orders, as directed.

They were a long time coming. Charlotte stood patiently. After a little while she wondered if she might sit down — it had been a hectic day. But it occurred to her that she had never seen a servant sitting down, only in the kitchen. The whole ethos of being a servant then occupied her mind as the minutes ticked by, and she realized that taking orders and being treated as a piece of furniture was very foreign to her nature. Standing waiting was what servants had to do. It had never struck her before how animal-like it was, obeying orders that were so foreign to one's own desires. It made her feel rather uncomfortable, and guilty, to think that she had never given a thought to such matters before. She had seen servants treated abominably at times, and it had never disturbed her, not as much as seeing a horse beaten by a stupid carter in the street. The general opinion, even in the vicarage, was that servants were lucky to have a job at all, and a roof over their heads. They had no cause for complaint. After nearly an hour, Charlotte began to feel quite differently.

At last Milo came to the door and told Charlotte to serve the dinner.

"Tell Mar to knock when it's ready."

Charlotte fled back to the kitchen to find Phyllida in near hysterics as her dinner overcooked in the oven.

"Why have they been so long?" she wailed.

"Kissing and cuddling," said Mar. "Why do you think?"

Charlotte thought Phyllida would stab him with the carving knife she had in her hand. In spite of the warm ovens she was pale, and perspiration ran down the sides of her nose.

"Did you see her?" Charlotte whispered.

"A glimpse. Is she beautiful?"

"Yes."

Phyllida shivered as if she were cold.

"The soup's ready, in the tureen," she said. "You can take it in."

Mar put his white gloves on, and Charlotte took the tureen into the dining room and put it on the table. Mar took the warmed dishes and put them in place.

"I'll go and announce dinner. You wait by the sideboard, until he decides it's all in order."

Charlotte waited, nervously. She had a feeling that Constance could be appalling to servants.

Mar was brilliant, as if he had been a butler all his life. He pulled out Constance's chair and opened the wine and waited stiffly until Milo had poured it. Constance was silent but gave the impression of giving off sparks, darting secret messages to Milo with her fantastic eyes. Milo too seemed to be possessed of a nervous energy that was almost palpable, although he was sitting apparently relaxed. Charlotte sensed that this was no kindly, sweet love affair, but carried on — certainly by Constance — to satisfy a longing for danger, excitement, and novelty. If Phyllida had been the serving maid, Charlotte thought she would have tipped the tureen over Constance's head.

Mar kicked Charlotte on the ankle and they retreated. Relief swept over Charlotte as they got back to the kitchen. Milo would ring for the next course; she could sit down. The evening seemed to go on forever. Every time she served a fresh course she had to report back in minute detail to the kitchen as to the humour of their master. Milo did not acknowledge her at all as she attended the table; Charlotte found it hard to be treated like a dog, and Phyllida found it worse to hear of the success of the romantic liaison over her roast lamb. When the dinner was over Mar and Charlotte were dismissed — "Don't wait up" — and Charlotte cleared away the remains on the table. Phyllida was alone in the kitchen. The others had gone to bed. The two of them tidied the last of the dishes and then sat in front of the fire with hot lamb sandwiches and cups of tea. They were both exhausted.

"We got through all right. It'll be better next time," Charlotte said.

"I would rather cook for a hundred of his friends, than just for the two of them," Phyllida said. She knew she had given herself away to Charlotte. She was white-faced and bitter.

"What is she doing to him, an old hag of forty-eight? She must have bewitched him."

"Is that why you came here, because you love him?"

"Yes. I've loved him ever since I first set eyes on him. That was three years ago. I know there is no future in it, I tell myself how stupid I am, but it makes no difference. The climbs — in Switzerland — I dream of how it was . . . he said I was good enough to go with him — I couldn't believe it! Oh, it was like being in paradise . . . he praised me . . ."

At her words, Charlotte was fired with her own memories of being with Casimir on the white snow ridge, the two of them together, and his salty kisses in the hot grass, crushing the flowers beneath their embrace.

"It's different out there," she said.

The freedom and exhilaration shared on the mountaintops gave a quite different view of ordinary life, yet one could not say it was an illusion. It had seemed at the time the most real of experiences, far more natural than the forced, etiquette-ridden regime she was used to.

"Yes," Phyllida agreed. "It's simpler. Life and death. Keeping up, not making a mistake, relying on each other . . . the peak ahead, to be taken. It's not about who your father is, whether your face fits, whether you're pretty or not." She was staring into the old embers of the fire under the spit, softly greying into the small hours of the next day, and her face was bleak. She was not pretty and knew it well; she would charm no one with her face and figure, only with her sharp intelligence, which could be cruelly used and was rarely endearing. In an age when women were expected to be soft and decorative, agreeable and acquiescent, Phyllida was sharp and bright, like a rock, argumentative and opinionated. Two tears welled out of her stone-grey eyes and trickled down her cheeks. Charlotte was horrified.

"Don't!"

"I would die for him," Phyllida said.

The house was silent; the ash falling made no sound. It was growing cold, and Charlotte suddenly felt herself shivering. Even in her distress, Phyllida was too strong to embrace and comfort. Charlotte thought she would be thrown off, like a fly, yet she longed to do, say, something to help. But she knew there was no help. Life was like that; everyone loved the wrong people, who loved somebody else, or didn't love at all.

Phyllida stood up suddenly and took her plate and mug to the sink. She yawned hugely.

"I'm going to bed."

Charlotte undressed in her own small room, looking out of the window on to the moonlit back yard and the glittering roofs of Roland's glasshouses. She wondered if Constance had gone home, or whether she was going to spend the night in Milo's bed. It was a still night, touched with frost, the sky filmed with stars which, faint, all seemed to run together to make a golden, filmy roof. As she looked out, two horses came out of the stable yard, ridden by Milo and Constance. Constance was riding sidesaddle on one of Milo's hunters, a grey, and was wrapped in her huge white fur so that she looked like a ghost on a ghost horse. Milo was on his darling mare, Goodnight Glitters, riding alongside, his hand holding hers. Charlotte heard him shout something, and the two horses broke into a canter. Constance was laughing and her hair was coming loose, but she kicked her horse on faster and went away up the drive at a flat gallop, Milo in hot pursuit. Their laughter echoed on the still cold air. Charlotte stood petrified. If Phyllida had seen them, her tears would freeze on her cheeks.

She lay in bed, wondering, and thought she could hear their distant laughter as they rode across the frosty fields.

10

With the opening of the hunting season and the return of Constance, Milo was much occupied. He went hunting (generally with Constance) three times a week and racing once or twice; sometimes he went up to London, and quite often he took his horses away racing for two or three days at a time. When he was home, mostly after dark, he was tired, hungry, and happy. He would come in at the kitchen door, spattered with mud and quite often with blood, sit down and hold his legs out to have his boots pulled off. Phyllida would have hot water and hot drinks ready, Clara his fresh clothes, Queenie a tray of his favourite biscuits straight out of the oven. A large joint of beef would be sizzling in readiness, a bottle of port uncorked. Mar would come in, having gotten the horses dry and clean and fed their buckets of bran-mash, then Roland with twigs in his hair and earth under his fingernails, and eventually they would all sit round the kitchen table to devour one of Phyllida's triumphant suppers. Afterwards they would spend the evening in the sitting room before a roaring log fire. The men would talk and the girls read or sew or play cards (except Queenie, who stayed in the kitchen).

Charlotte was now so happy she felt like a purring cat in front of the fire. Her fears were over; she enjoyed her days, enjoyed her friends, and had the certainty of seeing Casimir in the spring, when Milo promised they would all go climbing again. The times when she was required to be a servant were infrequent, but she quite quickly got used to it. Constance came fairly regularly but found nothing amiss. She treated servants like doorstops, and they all hated her. When male friends came, hunting or racing men generally, they were kind and funny and did not mind if things weren't quite as they should be. The only other female who came regularly was Kitty, and she quickly became like one of themselves.

149

Kitty was a born organizer, and they had cause to be grateful for the way she conjured up new staff, arranged to have two bathrooms built, arranged for tradesmen to call, and led them to church on a Sunday to sit in the Nettlepot pew and show a united front to the village. Charlotte, in spite of everything, had missed church with a deep and uncomfortable sense of guilt. Being forced out into the village by Kitty and taken to meet the local shopkeepers in her autocratic company gave their unconventional household some standing in the neighbourhood. Milo could not be bothered with such things, but everything operated more smoothly with local approval. Kitty was forceful, with the authority that the girls could not conjure up, and this, combined with her use of the family charm, had the shopkeepers falling over themselves to oblige. Another "lady" to serve! "They are all dreadful snobs," Kitty remarked. In her wake, Charlotte and Phyllida also found themselves eagerly served, their patronage treasured. Phyllida, Charlotte noted, loved it, although she professed to be a radical and on the side of the working man. "I am a working woman," she was fond of saying. She despised Constance for being "useless," but would have blistered anyone who might suggest the same about Milo. They took care not to be flamboyant in public but drove out soberly in their dark clothes. (Elsie had sent Charlotte a trunkful of her own belongings, which had been a great relief.)

Kitty had interviewed and hired three stableboys, two garden boys, and two daily girls to clean in the house. Phyllida had turned down more help for herself — "We don't want anybody else in our kitchen" — and

Charlotte and Clara now turned, along with Queenie, to help with the extra cooking. They did not bother with demarcation lines, in the style of the usual servant hierarchy. The worst jobs — the fires early in the morning — they took in turns, and Roland was good at carrying coal. He had gentlemanly instincts. He opened doors for them and pulled out their chairs.

"Not like you, Mar," Charlotte pointed out.

"I'm run off me feet out there," said Mar, grinning.

"You've got more boys than Roland!"

"Horses are more important than cabbages."

But Mar, of them all, was not happy. "How can I be? I'm a prisoner here. I can't go hunting, I can't go racing, I can't go to town. I'm like a sewer rat, nobody sees me."

"But they mustn't."

"All the same, it must be resolved sooner or later. I can't live like this forever."

"That's true," Milo said. "We've got to get you out of this hole. I want you riding for me, not cleaning the tack. What can we do?"

"Kill the lot of 'em."

"Tempting, but not practical. They're so dirty — everyone would be glad to see them off the racecourse. We need something we could take to the stewards. Then tell the Paynes that unless they make it clear there'll be no prosecution over Ambrose's death, we'll report them."

"There were suspicions over that chestnut colt they had that won that handicap at Ascot in the spring. Useless in its previous races. People say they've got a ringer in the stable."

"What's a ringer?" Phyllida asked.

"I thought you were an educated woman!"

"It's a double," Roland said kindly. "You run the duff one a few times, and it comes nowhere, then you enter it in another race, only this time you run its double — the good one. Its price is about fifty to one because everyone thinks it's useless, so you put a lot of money on it to win and — hey, presto — it's the brilliant horse you're running and it wins. And you make a fortune."

"If you own this brilliant horse and run it properly, wouldn't you make a lot of money anyway?"

"You might. But not as much as this other way."

"They certainly wouldn't want a trick like that uncovered," Milo decided. "We'd need to get our hands on both the horses, I think, hold them as evidence. Otherwise, proving it would be impossible."

"Steal them?" Charlotte was getting alarmed.

"Borrow them."

"Heavens, it sounds dangerous."

"Round about Ascot, in June, that would be the time," Milo said. "Kitty could get her spies out — twist Evelyn's arm — find out if there's anything in this rumour. If there is, well — it would scare them out of their wits if they thought it could be uncovered."

"Yes, it's strong enough. They'd back down before being accused of that."

"Who's going to steal the horses?" Phyllida asked.

"We are, of course. You girls might help — send you in as decoys or something."

"You're not serious?"

"Are we serious, Milo?" Mar asked. "I think I am."

"Oh yes. We're serious. There's not a lot to do in the summer, after all."

"This sounds like more than an Oxford prank," Phyllida said.

"It's what we were practicing for."

"He's a dangerous man, Jacob Payne. It certainly wouldn't be a prank." Kitty put her word in. "You couldn't afford to make any mistakes."

"No. We're depending on your spy network, Kitty, to set it up for us. Dammit, Mar's right — he can't hibernate forever in the woods here. Life is passing him by."

Charlotte was shocked and frightened by the turn the conversation had taken, yet both Milo and Mar seemed to be much cheered by it. She thought the suggestion that the girls might be involved must be a joke. But the summer was a long way away yet. Before then she would see Casimir again, and who knew what would happen then? Casimir was her dream, and if her dream was somewhat impractical — "You're not going to marry him, are you?" Phyllida asked scornfully — it made no difference to the fact that the very thought of Casimir was like a warm beacon in her life. Sometimes she wondered if she was remembering him accurately, but then in her dreams his face came so clearly: the wide, peasant cheekbones, brown and faintly freckled, the brown-gold eyes smiling, the black hair hanging over his forehead . . . and the grace of his figure climbing, moving effortlessly. She felt he had been with her in her room. What was he doing through the winter, holed up with his horrible mother and the cows and goats that he had to milk? Patrons wanted to climb when the snow and ice came. Was it dangerous? He had to be responsible, make the decisions, carry the responsibility. He was her hero, climbing through the snow, saving his party by his skill and courage.

They all had their dreams: Milo of Constance, Mar of his freedom, Roland of his gardens and glasshouses and his name being known on all the big country estates. Queenie of finding a husband who would accept her baby (she was now quite large), Phyllida of loving Milo, and Clara . . . but who could tell what Clara dreamed? She was always far away, inaccessible with her broken English and her strange, withdrawn temperament.

"I think Clara gets a very poor deal. I thought you said she was a music student," Kitty said one evening to Milo when Clara was out of the room.

"What do you mean, poor deal? She had nowhere to go and I offered her a home."

"She works hard. She owes you nothing. What about her music?"

"What about her music?" Milo looked hurt.

"Exactly, you don't know anything. She ought to carry on with it, if it was important to her. You haven't asked her! What does she play? The trumpet? The organ? You've no idea, have you?"

"No. There's a piano there, if she wants it. I haven't given it a thought."

They had had sing-songs round the piano occasionally, but Clara had never joined in. Both Milo and Mar played, more with panache than sensitivity, and Charlotte had her repertoire of Chopin and Schumann, but no one had thought of asking Clara to display her talent.

"I shall take her in hand," Kitty decided. "She ought to continue her studies. She's had time to get over her bereavement. She must look ahead."

"You like it here. There's so much scope for your talent interfering," Milo said.

"Improving," Kitty smiled. "Clara and I will have musical mornings and I will find out how good she is."

"As long as I can't hear you —"

"Don't worry. That's another thing, Milo — your staff ought to have their own sitting room. When Constance comes, or your friends, you can't expect the others to live in the kitchen all night."

"Very well. See to it."

"Good. I will."

And before the week was out Kitty had cleared out a room adjoining the kitchen which had previously been the servants' dining room, and another pantechnicon arrived from the railway with carpets and easy chairs, tables and lamps and cupboards, cushions, curtains, coal scuttles, and a set of hunting prints.

"I wonder there's any furniture left at your parents' place," Mar remarked, roped in for the heavy work. "Don't they miss it?"

"There're over a hundred rooms. I just take a bit from different places and nobody notices, only the servants and they don't mind — less to polish."

Kitty had a way with rooms, making them look casual and homely and inviting. She liked to arrange great vases of branches and berries and dried flowerheads, throw bright-coloured draperies over the backs of chairs, heap cushions on threadbare chairs. In less than a week the room looked as if it had been used for years. She tamed the feral cats in the woods so that they sat purring in front of the fire and adopted two mongrel terriers from the village to keep the rats out of the stables and yard. When Constance came they had somewhere to sit between their bouts of activity, and Mar fixed a bell to ring from both the dining room and sitting room and jangle in the kitchen and the new room.

"That's much better." No one disagreed. Kitty was a valuable link between Milo and the rest of them, seeing quickly what was needed. Milo, having conceived the whole plan and set it in motion, was now too wrapped up in his own affairs to bother about the details of execution. Original thinking was his province, but the nuts and bolts of seeing his ideas through often bored him. Now that he was seeing so much of Constance he was absent in spirit and they were all aware of it. They felt that he was by nature closer to them than to Constance, and that he was the victim of what Kitty called a "bewitching." Nobody could find a good word to say for Constance.

"Except, she is beautiful."

Cold-eyed, Phyllida watched from the yard when Constance rode in with her groom to go hunting with Milo. Sometimes the meets were a two-hour ride away, and they went together, in their finery, their grooms riding behind on their second horses. Constance rode sidesaddle, wearing a black habit, a high white stock, and a black bowler tipped well forward, her hair in a severe chignon behind. She rode her favourite horse, a black gelding called Jackdaw, who had a fearsome reputation, according to Mar. "Give her her due, she's a brilliant horsewoman. Four men tried to hunt Jackdaw before her, and none of 'em could control the brute. No

156

hedge is too big for him, no ditch too wide." Charlotte — if not Phyllida — could not but agree that they made a remarkable picture, the black horse with his bold eye and satin coat, and the elegant rider reining him in. Milo, by contrast, rode his mare Goodnight Glitters who was quite small, but whose reputation for courage was as great as Jackdaw's. She was a chestnut, lean and ribby, with a white blaze and a short red mane blowing in the breeze, and she never stopped pulling.

Once, when Charlotte and Phyllida were out shopping in the trap, they had to pull up in a narrow lane when hounds poured across their path, out of one hedge, across the road, and through the opposite hedge into the wide field. The master came through a gate behind them and jumped a gap in the hedge into the field, but Milo and Constance, side by side, jumped down into the lane ahead of them, crossed it in a bound, and jumped clean up and over a fearsome hedge out to the other side. Mud and twigs flew, and the rasping of the horses' breath hung on the still air. Charlotte had her hands full stopping Herbie, their faithful cob, following with the trap behind him, but Phyllida, who never drove — "I couldn't possibly" — was rewarded with an eagle-eyed impression of the two faces, smeared with mud, taut with an excitement she knew she could never experience. To share that . . . no wonder they loved and with the same passion . . . she could not forget the woman's blazing blue eyes as she drove her horse at the hedge and Milo's tense concentration, asking his little mare for the same commitment. It was danger and courage and high excitement, heady as love itself, binding them.

When Milo came home from hunting after a good day, he could not settle, but roved about, still on a high, until the effects of a warm fire and a couple of glasses of port quietened his nerves. Mar, seeing all the same things, grew morose with jealousy. He had hunted all his life, and the opportunity now being missed was agony to him. Phyllida too, marking the competition and knowing the hopelessness of her situation, suffered equally.

Charlotte, immune, suffered for them. She was so happy and optimistic, she did not want her own joy spoiled by their troubles, but she could not bear Phyllida's self-disgust and the quenching of Mar's spirits. She was deeply involved with her friends. It all passed Clara by, but Kitty, who understood, said gently, "Time passes, and things work out, Charlotte. For better or for worse. Don't fret."

Charlotte sometimes wondered where Kitty's happiness lay. Certainly not in her home, for she was scarcely ever there. She was always on the move, coming and going, planning new schemes. What drove her? She did not have Milo's inner reserve, which nobody (unless, perhaps, Constance) penetrated. She was restless, creative, funny, and apparently happy. Her husband, she said, was in India. Who was this husband? Kitty did not volunteer, and no one liked to ask Milo. In spite of their all being friends, Milo, because of his natural authority, was in some ways the actual master of his servants, although it would never have occurred to him that this was so.

It was Milo who decided that Charlotte ought to go home for Christmas. Charlotte had had a bad conscience about this herself. She didn't want to go and was hoping, as a servant, she would be expected to stay. But Milo said she owed it to her grandfather. Charlotte knew he was right.

"I thought you might need me."

"No. Kitty will be here. She can cope. Why don't you take Phyllida with you?"

Charlotte thought this a very good idea. There would be less chance of Mr. Carstairs cornering her if she had Phyllida at her side. Phyllida liked the idea too. Queenie was adamant she did not want to go but thought it might be a good idea if Charlotte told Elsie about the coming child.

"They'll have to know sooner or later, and if you told them, miss, it would make it easier for me."

Charlotte agreed to approach this thorny subject. Much as she would have preferred to spend her first Christmas at Nettlepot, she knew that she was doing the right thing when the carriage swung away down the drive on its way to the station. Phyllida, amazingly, was quite excited.

"It's awfully dull, I'm warning you. You'll die of boredom."

"A safe, boring childhood is something I never had. How do you know I might not like it?"

"Perhaps you'll fall for Mr. Carstairs."

"He might have found Another."

They got the giggles, like two schoolgirls. Mar kissed them both goodbye.

"It won't be the same without you."

"You'll miss us? Oh, good!"

"Your charm, your cooking —"

"Charlotte's charm and my cooking, I suppose," Phyllida said tartly.

Charlotte thought she saw Mar flush slightly, but in the dull early morning light it was hard to tell. Saying goodbye, she realized how dear he was now. The great warmth of her new friendships made her quiver with a sudden rush of happiness. How lucky she was! Compared with Clara, with Phyllida, it was good to have a home to go back to, however boring. A great wave of nostalgia swamped her. She was getting ridiculously sentimental.

After changing trains twice, they arrived at the familiar station to find old James waiting for them with an even older Daisy in the shafts. The ancient mare's progress was nothing like the eager pace of Milo's pair of greys, and Charlotte felt slowed to her old ways long before the vicarage came in sight. She felt she had been away ten years.

Milo was right, of course, and there was no doubt that coming home for Christmas was the expected, the kind and considerate course of action. Grandfather was much frailer and had a transparent air, as if a strong breeze would blow him away, although he declared he was fit and well. Elsie was all excitement and bustle, making tea, arranging cakes, lighting fires in their rooms; the vicarage smelt of cooking and polish — so familiar the smells! — and Elsie had put all the Christmas decorations up, the golden bells and toy trumpets, the white snowflakes and silver tinsel that she kept from year to year wrapped in newspapers so that they wouldn't lose their shine.

"And Ben will be home tomorrow."

"It's lovely here," Phyllida said softly. "Why did you say all those things?"

Charlotte had no answer. She was ashamed. It was lovely because there would only be five days of it.

Strangely, in the vicarage atmosphere Phyllida blossomed, and her tart and bitter ways vanished. She glowed; she was kind; she laughed. Charlotte was astonished. Even her grey eyes took on a colour, her spiky hair shone with gold lights. Her Christmas dress was a striking crimson velvet, which Charlotte had never seen before. Perhaps she had been working too hard at Nettlepot, or was it forgetting Milo, not feeling his rejection every day, forgetting Constance, not seeing Milo's infatuation for the undeserving Constance dancing before her eyes? When Ben came, the three of them were in such high spirits that even the despised Mr. Carstairs dropped his pomposity and actually laughed. He seemed to have gotten over his passion for Charlotte — Charlotte was both relieved and piqued and had difficulty in persuading Phyllida that he was the reason she had felt obliged to leave home.

"You made him sound like an ogre."

"You wouldn't want to marry him, all the same."

"I can think of worse. I thought he was about fifty, the way you talked. He's only twenty-two."

"He acted fifty. You can't imagine . . . I admit he's improved since last summer."

The only embarrassment came when Grandfather asked Charlotte questions about her stay in Domodossola. She pretended that she had met Ben and went climbing with him and his friends — "I met Phyllida that way" — and managed to avoid too much outright lying. She still felt bad about the deception. But Grandfather seemed happy for her in her new interests and said, after several glasses of port, that the vicarage was a dull place for a young girl. After two glasses of port herself, Charlotte plucked up enough courage to tell Elsie about the baby Queenie was expecting. This was in the kitchen on Christmas Day, while Elsie was basting the turkey — not a good moment, for she nearly dropped the whole sizzling bird on the floor. Charlotte had to give her some of the pudding brandy. For the rest of the day Elsie was very quiet — "I'm afraid I've got rather a headache." She excused herself early and went to bed, but the next day, and up to the time the girls went back to Nettlepot, she seemed to take on a new dimension, as if the thought of the new life was giving her a fresh source of life herself. Thinking about it, Charlotte supposed, when Grandfather died, Elsie had no future, unless she was invited to stay on in the vicarage with the new vicar (Mr. Carstairs?), and perhaps another generation of her own family gave her the comfort of a sense of continuity, a reason for looking forward to the future. She made no recriminations, but a sweet dreamy expression took over when she was in repose, quite different from her usual no-nonsense, set-lipped look.

Charlotte felt things had worked out with almost unbelievable satisfaction to all parties. But when, in anticipation, Grandfather proposed a toast to the New Year and she raised her glass, looking towards Phyllida and Ben, she had a sudden lurch of fear that coming events might prove both difficult and dangerous. For a moment the bright candles seemed to flicker and fade. But she drank, and the heady port sang in her bloodstream.

11

By sheer coincidence, when Milo's little mare Goodnight Glitters turned a rare somersault at a large ditch and rail at the end of a hard day's hunting, she was only half a mile from home.

It was a raw February day, and dusk was creeping early across the ploughed fields. Charlotte had just been out for more wood for the fire and heard the distant holloas and the cry of hounds from the woods beyond the lake. She went back to the kitchen and reported, "Milo will be early tonight," and shortly afterwards there was a hammering on the front door. It was so urgent that she ran to answer it.

Constance stood on the doorstep, her crop raised to deliver another tirade. She held her own horse Jackdaw and Goodnight Glitters by the reins, but Milo was mounted on his mare, white as a sheet and with blood running down his face.

"He's dislocated his shoulder. Help me get him down," she demanded.

Charlotte gasped.

"Wake up, girl! Come round on this side. Steady him as he slides down. All right, Milo, the mare will stand."

The two horses were a handful, and Constance had chosen the harder job of keeping them still. Milo was holding his injured arm with the other, as if it were about to fall off, and looked down at Charlotte grimly.

"I'll swing my leg forward over her neck. It's the easiest way." And he gave her the glimmer of a smile.

"Catch me." And he dropped down into her waiting arms.

"Oh, Milo!" She held him as he swayed, and he put his good arm across her shoulders to stop himself falling. His weight came onto her momentarily and she staggered.

"Stand up, girl!" Constance snapped.

The two horses curvetted across the gravel, steaming in the icy dusk.

"Take him inside. I'll put the horses away. Your men are in the yard, I hope?"

"Yes — ma'am."

She shouldn't have cried out "Milo," she knew. But she was stricken by her friend's plight and wasn't playing at servants. But a glance at Constance's imposing figure cowed her. Although splattered in mud, she made an arrogant and impressive figure, dominating the two difficult animals. She struck Jackdaw over the ears with her crop, and he stopped dancing about and followed her round the side of the house.

Charlotte helped Milo up the steps.

"I'll get Roland to go for the doctor."

"No. Constance will do it. Don't bother."

"Do what?"

"Put it back. My shoulder." He was in agony and had to sit down on the hall chest.

"I'll fetch Phyllida — to help. Oh, Milo are you all right?" She thought he might faint if she left him. "I'll shout for her."

She ran down the passage, shouting at the top of her voice. Phyllida came, nearly as pale as Milo.

"Help me upstairs."

164

One on either side they supported him up the wide staircase to his bedroom. Charlotte saw that Phyllida was trembling nearly as much as Milo. She, Charlotte, was the strong one.

"There, sit down. Lean up here." She pushed all the pillows together behind his back. "I'll take your boots off. Give me your foot."

Between them they removed his boots. How could they take his coat off? It was impossible. He was covered and wet with mud, which was now already all over the bed.

"Leave it. Constance will do it." And then, with another faint smile, "Remember, dear Charlotte, you're a servant. For my sake. And you, Phyllida. Please."

He was kind, even in his pain. They fetched hot water up and lit the lamps and the fire.

"Are you sure you shouldn't have the doctor?"

Charlotte took the little gold fox pin out of his stock and started to unwind the long white silk cravat from round his neck. His hair clung tightly to his skull, wet with the sweat of pain. They wanted him for themselves, to make better, but Constance was in charge. When she came in, they instinctively drew back.

"Good. How lucky, to be so near home. Glitters never took off — not like her. I've sometimes wondered, Milo, if her sight is all it should be. She always jumps left-handed, doesn't she? For no reason that I can see. Odd. Besides that, you ought to get a bigger horse."

"You ought to get a kinder one."

Constance laughed. She sat down on the side of the bed. "Let's get your coat off."

It seemed all in a day's work to Constance. Her hands moved deftly. She, like Milo, was covered in mud, but her elegance seemed unimpaired. Her waist was as magically small, and her hair, when she tossed aside her bowler, immaculately in place. Beneath the apron of her habit, her legs in their white breeches and boots were long and shapely.

"Darling boy," she said, with a smile.

Then she stood up, put her foot hard against Milo's ribs, took his hanging arm, and yanked it with all her force against the pressure of her straightened leg. Milo almost screamed, cutting it off by some instinct of his hard public-school upbringing, but Phyllida let out a louder cry, and Charlotte thought she was going to pass out.

"Sorry. No good," Constance said, and did it again.

At the third yank, she said, "I think that's it. What do you think, Milo?"

Milo did not answer.

"Move it," Constance said. "How does it feel?"

"My arm's all right," Milo muttered. "But I think you've broken my ribs."

Constance laughed.

"Clean him up," she ordered Charlotte. "And one of you fetch some brandy and a couple of glasses." As neither of them jumped to obey, still suffering with Milo, she swung round and looked at them closely. "What a pair of ninnies! Why do you have such babies to serve you, Milo? You want someone like my Mrs. Carruthers. Your house would be run properly then."

"My life as well. No thank you."

"You are too lax. No wonder your mother despairs of you."

Milo did not look disposed for light conversation.

166

Charlotte and Phyllida ran out of the room to fetch brandy and bowls and towels. They were both quivering with shock and hate.

"What a monster she is! I could kill her!" Phyllida was white and shaking. She needed brandy more than Milo, Charlotte thought. "She *possesses* him! She is a witch. Oh, how can he —"

She almost howled her despair, running down the stairs. When they got back, Constance was sitting on the bed, her legs crossed, smoking a cigarette out of a long holder. Charlotte set the tray down on the bedside table.

"Pour it then," Constance snapped.

After she had gone, clattering away down the drive on the revived Jackdaw, Charlotte and Phyllida went back to Milo to see what he wanted for supper. He was sitting on the side of the bed, nursing his arm, staring into the flames of the now dancing fire in the grate. Charlotte thought she had never seen a sadder expression on his face. But it wasn't physical pain. If Phyllida hadn't been there, she would have dared to comfort him, she thought. But how could she tell if that was true? Phyllida was there, her brooding, emotional presence like a suffocating blanket.

They made the bed comfortable, in silence.

Milo said, "I'm sorry she was rude to you. It's her way, I'm afraid."

And that's all.

◆　◆　◆

When the doctor called, it was to deliver Queenie's baby.

"She should count herself lucky she hasn't got

Constance for a midwife," Phyllida remarked. "A few yanks and it'd be out."

Phyllida could not hide her love for Milo. Charlotte was so happy that Casimir filled her mind, else she too, she thought, would fall for Milo. There was something so vulnerable about him in his affair with Constance that one wanted desperately to protect him. What Kitty said was true. Everyone fell in love with him. Possibly because he never noticed. He was the most unassuming of them all and had the most power.

Queenie was a long time in labour and screamed a lot, but was as fit as a fiddle immediately afterwards. The baby was a fine girl with a lot of yellow curls like Queenie and lusty lungs. They all doted on her, and she lived in the kitchen, sleeping, gurgling, or screaming according to the time of day, while Queenie got on with her chores. She was christened Lily. Elsie sent her a bundle of clothes she had sewn and knitted, and Queenie's parents sent letters, which Queenie cried over. They were unexpectedly loving, which was why she cried. They wanted her to go home, but she refused.

"I know where I'm well off."

Charlotte remembered Queenie's night with the gin bottle and the hot bath and was amazed at how nearly she had eclipsed this eager baby, which now brought such happiness.

On the day she was born, the air was mild, and a carpet of daffodils miraculously came into flower on either side of the front drive.

"This was a real garden once," Roland said wistfully, surveying the show. "There are paths and arbours all hidden in the undergrowth down by the lake, and I've found the remains of what must have been an Elizabethan garden at the side of the house. It was covered over by the drive that goes to the stables — what a tragedy. If Milo would agree to have the drive rebuilt on the other side, I could restore it."

His ambitions knew no bounds. Already the kitchen garden was in order, and in the glasshouses the vegetable seedlings were starting to come up in their rows of trays. Exotic seed catalogues were strewn on the kitchen table. The orchard beyond the kitchen garden had been cut and cleared, the trees pruned, and soon would be a sea of blossom. Roland had no plans to go climbing again in Switzerland. He looked horrified when Milo started talking about dates.

"I can't leave the garden at this time of year."

"The boys can keep it going, surely?"

But it was plain that Roland preferred to stay with his garden.

"Who's for our climbing holiday then? Constance goes to Biarritz at the end of April, and I think that would be a good time to go. Then we can get back in time for Ascot. Charlotte is coming, and Phyllida. Ben said he can make the two weeks over Easter, and Julian and Henry Somers are coming. You, Mar — I think not. Too dangerous. And Clara — I know you don't want to, which is understandable."

Mar looked gloomy, although he had always discounted the trip.

"The first thing we'll do when we get back is start sorting out the Paynes," Milo said to him. "Kitty says young Evelyn's getting into debt gambling, and she thinks he'll divulge what's going on in that stable if he's paid enough money. I'm afraid our young brother is not a nice person, but his lack of honour will suit our needs. We might meet him in Switzerland. I understand he's going to be in Zermatt over Easter, and it might pay me to stand him a drink or two."

"If we could settle the Paynes —" Mar's eyes lit up at the thought. "If not — I've been thinking about it — I'll go to America and find a job there. I've cousins in San Francisco. I'm not cut out to be a coachman, Milo — in spite of the fact I'm eternally grateful and all that."

"No, well, I can see that. But I'm not going to lose you to the new world, Mar. I want you riding Glitters in the Grand National next year. She's cherry-ripe for it — ten years old, and you can do less weight than I can. Constance forbids me to ride her in the National; she thinks I'll get killed. But it would be great sport watching you, Mar."

"Begorra! I'd give my eye teeth to ride her. It's a left-handed course, and that's the way she jumps. Right-handed and you'd be in the canal halfway round. I'll hold you to that. Let's get the squeeze on the Payne family. We'll have them squeaking for mercy by the time we're through."

Both of them seemed more fired up by the prospect of nailing the Paynes than by a discussion of the climbing holiday that had started the conversation. Charlotte did not want to think about this adventure, although she recognized its necessity. She was counting the days until the journey to Switzerland.

12

Ben was waiting for them at the Monte Rosa hotel with the two brothers, Henry and Julian Somers. They arrived in the evening, just in time to see the last flames of the setting sun alight on the top of the Matterhorn. The valley was plunged in icy shadow, with a strong smell of   "Spring, it smells of spring," Charlotte decided, sniffing deliciously.

"And all the nights we have missed, while we have been away," Milo said, looking up the valley. "Missed seeing the sun kiss the mountain goodnight." He could say such things with perfect gravity. "What a waste."

Charlotte could have hugged him with joy. He understood. To him the mountains were special, not just a spree to while away the summer. "I shall always come back, always, whatever happens," he had said on the train. Constance never came to Switzerland; she hated the snow.

The swollen streams poured down from the glaciers with the melting of the snow, and the trees were bursting with bright buds. Not all the cows were turned out yet, and the streets stank with the rich manure piled up against the sides of the chalets. The thick, warm smell of the cows' breath hung in the alleys. Charlotte felt she was back in paradise. Like Milo, she knew she would always come back.

"Ben!" They hugged each other. Introductions were made all around, drinks ordered, and dinner too. Milo insisted that the girls had a room in the Monte Rosa. "For now; enjoy comfort while you can."

"Have you hired a guide, Milo?" Ben asked.

"They're quite busy, it seems. I've been asking around."

"I thought we'd try and get the chap we had last year, the one you found —"

"Casimir? Yes. I went down to his home this afternoon, but his wife says he won't be back until tomorrow. I left a message to say we would like to see him."

"Fine."

Milo sent a cautious, stricken glance in Charlotte's direction. He saw the joy wiped from Charlotte's eager face as if she had been physically bludgeoned.

"His wife!" She could not stop the words crying out across the table. Ben did not notice her anguish, and laughed.

"Yes. Apparently he married when he was seventeen. She wasn't here last summer — she was with her parents up in the pastures, making cheese. They work damned hard, these peasants, all for a pittance. He's a good chap, I agree. I'd like to have him again."

The conversation fastened on climbing plans, but Charlotte did not join in. She excused herself early, saying she was tired, and went up to the room she was sharing with Phyllida. There she flung herself on the bed and wept bitterly. The disappointment, after her excitement at arriving and the weeks of eager anticipation, was total. Her lovely, lovely Casimir! Her memories of those sweet kisses, the first she had ever tasted and the most wonderful experience of her life, treasured so tenderly all through the long winter . . . what a pathetic child she was to have read such a momentous story into what had been just a lark on his part. She had been so happy.

172

Phyllida, of course, was not sympathetic. She was as tender as she thought Charlotte's plight merited, a good friend in need, but her scorn was not well hidden.

"Whatever did you think it would lead to? You must have been in a dream world! Did you want to marry him and become a Swiss peasant?"

But it was the dream world that Charlotte had lived for: the love-play in the flowery grass, no more. It was, as Phyllida pointed out, utterly unrealistic.

"Grow up, Charlotte. Whether he was married or not, you could only have been disappointed. Think of it. If he had kissed you and then — you know — if he had wanted to — well . . . what then? You might have landed up like Queenie. And think how you despised Queenie for her behaviour."

Charlotte had supposed — she knew, really — that she only wanted the fun, the excitement, not the commitment. She had never faced it squarely, as Phyllida so brutally pointed out. Her physical body perhaps wanted more — her feelings had both surprised and frightened her — but her poor brain was not yet ready to cope.

"It could be your salvation, finding that out so soon. It settles it, doesn't it? You must put him out of your mind and enjoy the climbing — it's what you're here for. He's a real swine, playing with you like that, and all the time with a wife."

"Oh no. It was my fault, I think."

"Well, you're so lovely, Charlotte, you will get whoever you want in this life."

Phyllida's voice was bitter, and her face twisted in spite of the graciousness of her words. Charlotte felt as if she had been drenched with a bucket of cold water. She looked up and saw Phyllida looking her worst, her mouth set tightly, turned down, eyes grim, nose sharp and hawkish. She did herself such disservice. Beneath the sharp surface, she was kind and loyal. She took great pains not to let it show.

They went to bed, but Charlotte could not sleep. What a day — such happiness, coming up the valley, meeting Ben, being in this lovely place — and then the shock. But perhaps what Phyllida said was true, that she could now see clearly.

In the morning, Milo said he would go and meet Casimir and see if they could start for a hut that afternoon. It was a fine morning, cold and sparkling, and Milo said to Charlotte, "Fetch your jacket. You can come down with me."

She felt low and knew Milo was sorry for her, knowing about Casimir. She went with him, silent. She felt such a fool.

Milo said, "It's best, to face up to it, dear Charlotte. It was only a fantasy, wasn't it?"

"Yes."

"You are lucky. You don't know how lucky."

"I think I do."

"Bound by cobwebs. Not chains." That was the word Kitty had used — "chains." "A fairy tale. Remember it for what it gave you, not what you think you've lost. I'd make a good preacher, don't you think? Like your Mr. Carstairs."

"Mr. Carstairs has changed too. He's not bothered with me any more."

"That's lucky for him then. It changes all the time,

174

Charlotte, like a silly game. Nothing stays still. I wonder, when we're seventy, how it will all have turned out for us. We ought to make a pact, to meet at the Monte Rosa when we're seventy. We'll do that, eh, before we leave? We'll make a date. Casimir too. Mar and Roland — I wish they were here. Perhaps you should fall in love with Mar, Charlotte. Or Roland. Or me."

"You're in love with Constance."

"My being in love with Constance is as hopeless as your being in love with Casimir. We've that in common, at least."

And he looked grim, like Phyllida, and Charlotte felt her spirits lift, conscious that she was, indeed, lucky. Now that she no longer had Casimir to love, would she fall in love with Milo, as Kitty had suggested? "Everybody does," Kitty said. And Charlotte knew that she was not immune. In a sense she already was, and always had been. Only the arrogant figure of Constance mocked her aspirations. No one could compete with such a woman. She took a sideways glance at the lithe person at her side, dressed in his old tweed climbing suit with a yellow hunting waistcoat under the jacket, a shapeless felt hat on his head, and thought what an unusual man he was, so free of the snobberies and conventions of his kind, his outlook simple and pure. Yet sharper characters could not outwit him, nor bullies deter, for he had this godlike authority that he himself seemed unaware of. He was always looked to for decisions, for leadership. Yet he had no wish for power. The thought comforted her, that he was her guardian, her protector.

As they approached Casimir's dwelling, she grew

very nervous. No wonder the old lady had bawled her out last summer. Hot flushes of shame burned in her cheeks. Milo knocked on the open door, and a young woman came out. She was plump and rosy and very young, with large blue eyes and blonde hair and a happy smile. Milo spoke to her in German, and she smiled and nodded, while Charlotte felt herself eaten up with jealousy, thinking of this young girl being the recipient of the kisses that had so entranced her. But Casimir had loved her, she felt sure; it had been in his eyes, and he had said so. Charlotte believed everything she was told.

Apparently a deal was arranged, and they walked back to the Monte Rosa for breakfast.

"Casimir is coming here at lunchtime. I said we would be ready to start," Milo announced.

They all sat down for breakfast, and the waiter brought the coffee and fresh bread. The talk was all of climbing, but Charlotte was shivering with nervousness and disappointment.

When Casimir came, she was waiting in her boots and her tweed suit, her hair in its thick plait, on the veranda of the Monte Rosa. She saw him coming up the street with his knapsack on his back, walking with the easy stride that she had pictured so vividly during the long months of separation. The nut-brown face and black hair, the shapeless hat shading the speckled brown eyes that she had dreamed about for ten months were now a reality, and she trembled like a poplar in the wind. She felt faint, like a drawing-room lady.

"Swine," Phyllida whispered in her ear.

He shook hands all round, girls last. Charlotte last.

176

His cheeks were as hot as hers, his eyes needling hers. He smiled. She smiled back.

"Charlotte."

"Oh, Casimir!" She heard her own wail, almost a sob.

"Dear Charlotte," he muttered, and squeezed her hand.

Did he love her?

She would never know.

◆　◆　◆

It was hard.

"Think about the mountains," Phyllida hissed at her. "They don't change. That is what you're here for."

If her prowess at climbing would impress Casimir, she would climb. She climbed like a goat and found stamina she never knew she had. She progressed from staying in the hut and going down the easy way to loll in the meadows to climbing the peak itself. The boys said she was a natural. Phyllida was a natural too, but the boys took her for granted. She was one of them-selves, and she looked it. But for pretty little Charlotte, unexpectedly brave and brilliant, it was praise and admiration all the way. She thought she could wean herself from her infatuation with Casimir, now she knew that he was married. But being with him in the mountains, where the pettiness of everyday living van-ished like icicles before the sun, her emotions were equally at the mercy of this heightened act of living, uncertain as the cloud vapours that danced and writhed about the peaks. The more she knew she could not have him, the more she loved. They were never

177

alone together, and how his mind worked she had no idea. When they came close, by chance, he was the perfect guide. He never looked her in the eye. He roped her up, his hands about her breast, but never touched her. She wondered if this was how Phyllida was tormented by Milo, and she knew it was.

One afternoon, descending from the Z'mutt glacier on their way back to Zermatt, they stopped to make tea by a small stream that leapt heedlessly across their path to plunge down into the gorge below. It was warm and still; the sky was cloudless, and the mountain tops all around them seemed to float in the ether as if detached. It was hard to believe they had ever disturbed those sublime summits with their silly chattering selves. Charlotte sat apart, smelling the soft wood smoke of the pine sticks, looking at the scene and wondering at the strange state of her mind, entranced by the mountain softness and bedevilled by Casimir. The brew made her despair. She wanted so badly to be happy. Everything was there for it, and nothing. Her tea was finished, her mug packed, and the others were moving off, but she hadn't the will to move, hypnotized by her own plight.

"Wake up, Charlotte!" they called.

The peace of the high valley, as the others departed, moved her almost to tears.

Milo, shifting his pack on his shoulder, looked back. She knew she should get up and go, but it was impossible. He came back, slowly. He dropped his pack and sat down beside her.

Such was her emotional state, she burst into tears, and he put his arms round her. She sobbed with her face buried in his tweed jacket, and he held her and stroked her hair and spoke to her in the voice he used for Goodnight Glitters when something frightened her. Charlotte had never known motherly love, after all, only Elsie's rather bony comfort, and it suddenly seemed like paradise to sob one's misery to a sympathetic embrace. She was ashamed of herself, but it was lovely.

"Milo, oh Milo, I'm sorry!"

"Never mind. I've been stupid, hiring Casimir. It's hopeless for you. I'll pay him off tonight, and tomorrow we'll go away from here. We'll go up to the Oberland, to Wengen or Grindelwald. You will be free of him."

This made her cry all the more.

"Like pulling out a tooth," he said. "It will hurt, and afterwards it will be better. Or perhaps you don't want to get better?"

"I do, but I want Casimir!"

"A contradiction, dear Charlotte. I wish I could pull Constance out like a tooth. But her roots go right down into my heels." He laughed. "But you're curable. Only lime roots, clinging on by their fingernails. In a week you will have forgotten. I shall hire an old, ugly guide, and you can go home and love Mar. He would like that."

"I do love Mar. But not like Casimir."

"You are an overwrought girl. You need a slap." But he was laughing. "We've got to stop Mar going to America. Get him out of the mess he's in. Think ahead, Charlotte, not for old things you can't have. Think of all there is to do — mountains to be climbed, lives to be saved! No time for crying."

He pulled her to her feet and wiped her eyes with his own, rather grubby, handkerchief.

"Think of a way for me to stop loving Constance. It's me that should be crying."

"She's horrible."

"I know."

"Oh, Milo, I didn't mean it! Just that she's —"

"I know what you mean. She's horrible. I'm afraid there are no rules for love."

Charlotte picked up her knapsack and shrugged herself into it. She suddenly felt a thousand times better and quite ready to face a future without Casimir.

"I'm sorry. I'm sorry."

They walked on down the track together. The others were ahead, out of sight. The Z'muttbach crashed down the gorge far below them, sending up clouds of spray speared with the gold of the afternoon sun and, as if in argument, the voice of tranquillity as against the rage of nature, the cowbells clanged and tinkled from the pastures above.

Charlotte now felt bold and strong. "How can you stop loving Constance then? How did you start? Why did you start? You didn't have to."

"It's odd but I never mention Constance to another living soul, only you. I never speak about her, even to Kitty. Not to Mar or anybody. But to you, her name always slips out. Why is that?"

"Because I'm a mess too. Like you."

"Is that it?"

"I think so. How did you start loving Constance, if she's so horrible?"

"Well, of course, it's not true that she's horrible. I

180

agreed with you because she's horrible to servants, that's quite true. And you're a servant when she's around. But to my mother she was a good friend, and to me too, before we fell in love."

"When did you fall in love? Ages ago?"

"Yes. When I was sixteen. She made me love her. She was my friend, had always been my friend. She had always been in our house, ever since I could remember, visiting — a friend of my mother's. My mother never liked me much. She prefers my older brothers, who all jump to attention and do as they're told. I never did that, nor did Kitty. I was ill a lot. I was consumptive, and my mother thought I was a weakling. She thought I was pretending all the time. Constance saved my life by getting proper doctors and seeing that I was treated properly. She got me sent out here to Switzerland to get cured. That's how I fell in love with the mountains, when I was fourteen. She made my mother send me here."

"Did she come?"

"Oh, no. She wrote me letters. And when I was sixteen I was sent home, and she made me love her. She taught me."

"That's wicked."

"I needed her so badly. I felt I knew nobody at home, except Kitty, and my mother was all wrapped up in Evelyn. He's a weakling too but, unlike me, he gets all the pampering in the world. He is spoilt to death."

"Your mother sounds rather unbalanced."

"Yes, a good word for her. She's potty. Ask Kitty. She's a real egotist. If you flatter her and do as she tells you, she thinks you're wonderful. If you stand against her, she goes off the rails. She herself was spoilt to death as a child. An only child. She was very beautiful, and her parents thought she was a sort of goddess. Not good for later life."

"Constance got on with her though?"

"Yes. Constance gets her own way too. They had quite a lot in common. Constance knows how to handle her. I never did."

"Why are you so nice, with a mother like that? Your father must be a nice man?"

Milo laughed. "I'm glad you think I'm nice. I think I'm as selfish as my mother. I do everything I want to do, exactly as she does. My father — he's all right. Lives his own life, says yes to his wife, whatever she wants, and gets on with his garden. He's like Roland. Grows things. He goes all over the world collecting plants, trees, seeds. Writes learned papers and lectures. Scarcely knows one son from another, but the most obscure plant from Borneo or Mozambique — he knows its history, its antecedents, what conditions it thrives in . . ."

Charlotte digested all this, slotting Milo into this extraordinary background. Constance played a bigger part than she had imagined. But Kitty hated her.

"Kitty — who is she married to?"

"Mr. Lytton. Mr. Lytton is seventy-five. He's a gardener like my father. They are friends. He carried her away, like a little kitten, to save her from unhappiness. He's very rich and gives her everything she wants. He wants no return, unlike Constance."

"Fancy, Kitty . . ." Dear, pretty, vivacious, lovely Kitty — married to a man of seventy-five! And whatever was she, Charlotte, crying about just now? These Rawnsleys could teach her a thing or two about disaster, yet they laughed and smiled and enjoyed themselves as if they had been brought up in a loving vicarage.

◆ ◆ ◆

Phyllida was wildly jealous and suspicious of Charlotte's coming down the mountain alone with Milo. It was useless trying to explain to her how it came about. Charlotte became impatient with her bad mood.

"If you are always so disagreeable how can you expect him to like you? It's nothing to do with what you look like, which you're always saying it is — Milo is a very friendly person. You know he likes you because he asked you home. He likes you because you are intelligent and witty and interesting, but now you are spoiling everything by being stupid. What did you think we were doing? If you want to know, I was crying, because of Casimir, and he came back to cheer me up. It's because he's kind — you know what he's like. I didn't do it on purpose."

It was the first quarrel she had ever had with Phyllida, and it ended with Phyllida crying. Charlotte couldn't believe her eyes and felt terrible. Phyllida was crying over Milo just as Charlotte had been crying over Casimir. Of course, it was impossible, after all the recriminations, not to see the funny side of their pathetic behaviour, and they finished up by laughing and crying together.

That evening Casimir was paid off and departed while Charlotte was in her bedroom. She did not see him go. She felt only relief and a strange sort of numbness, a suspension of feeling. Up to then, her feelings had overflowed almost into hysteria; now they had gone into hibernation. She felt calm and adult. Milo announced that they were going to Wengen in the morning, as his brother Evelyn was staying there and he wished to see him.

"Evelyn is said to be very handsome," Charlotte said to Phyllida.

"Said by whom?"

"Kitty said. We can fall for him."

"He's only sixteen."

"Milo was only sixteen when Constance fell for him. He said she taught him to love her."

"She seduced him. She's a witch, that woman."

"Perhaps she'll come to a bad end, and Milo will be freed from her spell."

"We could make an effigy and stick pins in it."

All the same, they were quite interested to see what Evelyn was like. They found him in the bar of the Palace, the hotel they booked into after getting off the train. He was already slightly drunk, although it was only four in the afternoon, and looked horrified to see his brother standing before him. Milo introduced them all, very civilly.

"I say, Milo, I didn't expect —"

"Kitty told me you'd be here. How are you, old chap?"

Evelyn was as handsome as all the Rawnsley tribe, perhaps more so than Milo, for he had blond colouring and bright blue eyes and a golden Swiss tan overlying the flush that was characteristic of the consumptive.

He was slender and graceful, yet with the slightly gangly movement of the adolescent boy. Charlotte had a sudden vision of Milo at the same age, with exactly that same rather endearing gaucheness, being mothered by the predatory Constance Mathers.

Ben, tactfully, steered their group to a table and called a waiter, while Milo stood talking to Evelyn. Afterwards Milo came back to them and said he had arranged to have dinner with Evelyn alone, but he wanted Charlotte and Phyllida to join them.

"There's a chance here to find out something about the Paynes — you know, Ben, we want to get Mar out of his trouble; that's my only reason for looking up Evelyn. Nothing to do with brotherly love, I'm afraid. Evelyn is friendly with the Paynes. I can't miss this opportunity." He explained the plan they were hoping to use to blackmail the Paynes into dropping their persecution of Mar. "It's a long shot, but worth exploring. He's here with our revered mother, but she is away tonight visiting friends in Lucerne, so the sooner I have my chat with Evelyn and we can depart, the better. Kitty never said anything about dear mama being with him. One lady I have no wish to meet."

When Charlotte and Phyllida went to change for dinner, they both agreed they were agog to set eyes on the matriarch Rawnsley.

"What a pity we shall miss her. So near and yet so far."

Dining with Evelyn and Milo together was a good consolation. Phyllida was now in high spirits at the prospect, her jealousy forgotten. They shook out the single dinner dresses they had brought with them.

Charlotte was, thankfully, better equipped than last year and could make herself quite respectable, although she had had no new clothes since she had left home. She missed Queenie to help her with her hair. Phyllida was hopeless with hairpins.

At dinner, Milo encouraged Evelyn to drink and led him on with banter and fair talk. Charlotte was rather shocked at his manipulation of his young brother, for the boy was obviously a charmer who was already well versed in bad ways. He spoke boastfully of his gambling but admitted, under pressure, that "if mater knew how much I owed, she would shoot me."

"Kitty tells me you skive off to go racing. Won't she find out about that?"

"I'm pretty bright about not getting caught. Ascot's so close to Eton, that's no trouble, and Windsor, Esher, even Kempton —"

"Who do you go with?"

"Arthur Payne mostly. And Sugden. Arthur gets a lot of tips, his father being a trainer. They're up to all the tricks and I can get in on it quite often — you know, when they pull a coup. It's great —"

"Oh, come on, Evelyn, don't kid yourself. How much do you owe?"

"I'm going to make it up at Ascot, and everything'll be fine then. I've got a cert for Ascot."

"What if it loses?"

"It won't lose. It can't."

"You'll be in trouble if it loses?"

"Yes, but it won't."

Evelyn, in the hot dining room, was flushed and over-confident, more childish by the minute. Charlotte felt a deep sympathy for him suddenly. The blue veins pulsed in his temples; his skin was almost translucent, his full lips a rosy-red, his manner feverish with the symptoms of his illness. As Milo must have looked when he was taken to the sanitorium. She guessed then that Evelyn was in Switzerland with his mother exploring the same avenue of cure.

"If you're in trouble, Evelyn, come to me. Don't let those sharks get their teeth into you. You know the danger you're in."

Evelyn scowled at him.

"They're not good company, the Paynes," Milo said softly, and Charlotte knew he was speaking then as a newly affectionate brother, not as a plotter. Evelyn's plight had softened him, as it had Charlotte. If he was a spoiled brat, there was something very appealing about him.

"What is this dead cert that will make your fortune?"

"I'm not fool enough to tell you that."

"I don't bet, Evelyn. You should know that. But I will be at Ascot. If I know the name of the horse, I shall know whether you will need me or not. If it loses, I'll be waiting for you."

"If it loses, so will some other people." His voice shook, even as he laughed. "It's true, Milo, I'm in far too deep, and if only I can get out of it this time, I'm going to chuck the whole thing in. I don't want the parents to hear about it. I shall be expelled. Imagine the fuss."

It seemed to Charlotte that Milo had set up the situation to his satisfaction, prompted by Kitty's knowledge, but after Evelyn had departed, shakily, to bed, he was not disposed to show much pleasure.

"Poor little devil! The sooner he gets shut up in the sanitorium the better for him — and not only for his health."

He spent the rest of the evening arranging for a guide and planning routes for further climbs with the others. They were to leave at ten in the morning for a mountain hut, to climb the Jungfrau. The guide was forty-five, Milo said, and had a squint.

In the morning they enjoyed breakfast, aware that there would be no such luxury for the next one. They put on their boots and prepared their knapsacks and came down into the hall ready to depart, coinciding with the arrival of the little mountain train in the street outside. A great bustle of coming and going filled the street, and one particular party arriving in the hotel seemed to be demanding more attention than all the others. The hotel manager ran out to greet them, and the porters hustled round to attend to the luggage. A lady seemed to be the centre of attraction, a very demanding lady.

Charlotte heard the receptionist say, "Lady Rawnsley! Is her room ready? Run! *Mein Gott!*"

She looked round for Milo, but he had disappeared.

Lady Rawnsley swept into the hotel. She was quite small and well on the way to being elderly, but she had a presence that seemed to fill the busy foyer. Bumbling mountaineers fell over each other to give her room, and all the hotel flunkies gathered for her orders. She was dressed in the height of fashion, outrageous for a small, if smart, Swiss mountain village, with a hat like a cartwheel and a veil that did little to disguise the scornful hauteur of the expression.

Charlotte, hypnotized, met the self-assured blue eyes that roved over the visitors coming and going, and saw for a moment Milo himself looking at her. She was still very beautiful but with lines of bitterness about her mouth, which was thin and downturned, not wide and sweet like Milo's.

"Is my son not here to greet me?" she demanded.

"Which one, my lady?"

"Evelyn, of course. Which other son would it be, for heaven's sake? Send word to his room that I'm here."

"At once, madam."

They met Milo outside by the station where he was waiting with the new guide who was, indeed, ugly and wizened, although with a pleasant enough smile. The others ribbed Milo about his disappearing act, but he only smiled.

"One complication we didn't need — meeting my mother."

And it occurred to Charlotte later in the day, when they stopped to eat their lunch on a heady spur over-looking the village, tiny below, that there was a side to loving Milo that Phyllida hadn't considered.

"Imagine having that for a mother-in-law."

And she remembered Casimir's mother, and they both got the giggles.

13

Phyllida was in a strange mood on the way home.

"Being at Nettlepot all that time — we've been incarcerated. I'm not used to staying in one place. I'm wasting my talent. I can't go on being a cook all my life."

"It's not a prison. I'm sure you can go whenever you like." Charlotte hoped she wouldn't, all the same. Charlotte was totally used to being in one place all the time and had exchanged one place for a much better one.

"It's all wrong, being given holidays like this. We're as bad as Milo and his mother. Parasites on society."

"Oh, come on. Milo's not a parasite. He can't help being rich. What will you do if you leave?"

"That's the trouble. I don't know. I ought to teach."

"You said you didn't want to."

"No. That's true. But one doesn't necessarily do what one wants to do."

Charlotte rather thought you did, if you had the choice. She thought Phyllida was being difficult. On the other hand, they had achieved what they had gone to Nettlepot to do: clean it up and get it running, and the future, in terms of work alone, was not demanding. Certainly for a girl with an Oxford degree, Phyllida was, as she said, wasting her talent. About herself, Charlotte had never recognized any talent that she might be wasting. Without outside influences, brought up in an old-fashioned way, she was only expecting, with luck, a satisfactory marriage and a domestic future. Who with, was as uncertain now as it had always been. She felt a little thrown by Phyllida's new aspirations, and slightly guilty that she took her now privileged life as the status quo.

However, when they travelled back to England and Mar met them at the station with the carriage, even Phyllida seemed delighted to be home. As they pounded round the curving front drive and over the bridge towards the house, they saw the lawns on either side freshly shaved and roses coming into flower in great banks beyond, all cleared out and rejuvenated by Roland's loving care. The house stood fresh and spruce, newly painted, the gravel all weeded before, and the door invitingly open to show the colourful interior. Having been away, they were struck forcibly by the contrast with their return the year before, when their first impression of the place had been one of dispiriting neglect.

"You can't go away now," Charlotte whispered to Phyllida. She felt her senses lift with a rush of affection for the place, a sense of belonging that she had never had for the vicarage. It was her home. Yet Phyllida's words now shadowed her joy. It was true that their places were tenuous, after a year.

Mar, Roland, Clara, and Queenie were all obviously glad to have the house up to strength again and had made a celebration dinner in the kitchen. It was early June, and Roland's first vegetables loaded the table: tiny new potatoes covered with butter and parsley, early peas, crisp lettuces and hothouse cucumber, all to accompany a huge joint of cold beef. Constance was not expected home for weeks, and her absence added to the abandon.

Only Mar was quiet. The sanctuary of Nettlepot

was now, to him as well, beginning to feel like a prison, but he had better reason than Phyllida to chafe.

"I can't live like a monk any longer!" Hearing the talk all of climbing and freedom, he cried out in despair. "My own old horse is running at Ascot and I can't go and watch! Did you see Evelyn in Switzerland, Milo? All this time given over to frivolity and —"

"Yes. I saw him. There was more to the visit than frivolity. We had dinner together, and then in the morning, before we left, I had a chat with him in his room — he was sober then — and told him what we had in mind. I've promised to pay all his debts in exchange for some detailed information — the layout of Payne's yard and which horses are in which boxes. It's true he's got a ringer for that good horse that won the October Handicap. What's it called? Jester, is it?"

"Joker. A chestnut with a white face."

"That's it, Joker. The idea, I gather, is to run the duff ringer at Ascot — again. It's already run twice. Then spring the real Joker at Sandown or Goodwood and make a killing. I thought we could go and lift the real Joker the day before the race. Borrow him. Afterwards give him back and tell no tales, but only under certain conditions."

"They'll agree to that. They'll be out of racing if word gets out." Mar looked much cheered. "It would solve my problem all right."

Phyllida asked what Charlotte had been thinking. "Why, if you know about this ringer, don't you just threaten to tell the authorities?"

"Because by the time the authorities investigate, the ringer will have vanished — we want the proof in our own stables."

"It's a great idea." Mar was back to his old self at the thought.

"I'm seeing Evelyn at Ascot. We'll get down to details after that. You could be riding in no time, Mar, if we're lucky."

"Pension off that wig," Roland said. "It looks as if it's got the moth in it these days."

"It's a hard life me old wig leads. I can't get to the shops to buy a new one."

Charlotte and Phyllida slipped quickly back into their old life. There were no visitors to accommodate, save Kitty, and, without Constance, their roles as servants were almost forgotten. Phyllida thought they ought to have weekly practices, like fire drills, in case they forgot how, but Charlotte thought there would be time enough when Constance came back. Clara was more cheerful these days and took a more active part in the kitchen, although she was no chatterbox. She liked helping with Queenie's baby and would sit in the sunshine in the backyard singing it to sleep in its perambulator, her voice very low, while sewing or shelling peas, or darning the men's socks.

"She's a real German hausfrau at heart. I bet she can cook better than I can," Phyllida said.

"Sausages and sauerkraut. Milo might not like that. He likes your cooking."

"The way to a man's heart — if only it were true."

Charlotte was much taken aback when Milo approached her one afternoon when she was alone in the kitchen and told her he was going to take her to Royal Ascot with him.

"I need a partner, and you'll do fine, all dressed up. Kitty will see to it. She'll get you a ticket for the royal enclosure; she knows how to arrange it. Anyone in my family can get in. You don't mind coming, do you?"

He was so casual about it that Charlotte felt an instinctive resentment. What was all in a day's work to him seemed an insurmountable social hurdle to her, not to mention the appalling consequences when Phyllida found out. Why not Phyllida?

"Why me?"

"I think you might be useful in the plan — you know, the Payne thing. There's a Payne wife. She won't be in the royal enclosure, but I'd like to meet them afterwards if I can, and if I have a — a sort of girlfriend with me, it will make it seem more innocent. It's part of the Mar plan. You're to aid and abet."

"But — I — I can't!"

"What do you mean?"

"The royal enclosure! I won't know what to say, what to do. Why can't you go with Kitty?"

"I thought you'd enjoy it. I thought you'd jump at it."

"Well, I'm not jumping."

Milo looked surprised and rather put out.

"But you're so game, Charlotte. What's wrong?"

Charlotte didn't know what to say. She felt she was being used, but how could she complain of that, after what Milo gave her? She supposed she was put out by the manner of the invitation, that he needed a sort of accessory and that she would do. This sensitivity was new to her, and her feelings quite surprised her. She shook her head. It was hopeless to explain.

"Why don't you ask Phyllida?"

Milo was sitting on the table in his usual boyish sort

194

of way, picking red currants out of a bowl Roland had brought in. He was in shirt sleeves, still deeply tanned from Switzerland, so that his eyes looking suspiciously into hers seemed intensely violet-blue, like the sky at dusk. Charlotte wondered suddenly if she was going to fall in love with him. There was no one else to compete any more. How easy it would be. She gave herself quite a fright, thinking this. It made her angry.

"What will she say?" she demanded. "When she hears you've asked me?"

"Why? I asked you because you'll do it better, be sweeter than Phyllida. People will like you. Phyllida will sneer at them. You know she doesn't approve of the idle rich."

Charlotte did not reply. He waited.

"She won't mind, surely?"

Annoyed, Charlotte was impatient with his lack of understanding.

"Oh, Milo! Don't be so stupid. She'll be furiously jealous."

"Whatever for?"

And as he spoke, he got the message, which now Charlotte was cursing herself for letting slip. Charlotte saw his colour heighten, and he turned away, stood up, shrugged.

He spoke abruptly. "You won't come then?"

Charlotte was mortified.

"Yes, if you want me. It's just the way you asked. As if —" She floundered. What a mess she was making of everything! Why ever hadn't she just said yes, like a muffin? She didn't know what she felt now.

"Yes, all right. I'll come."

"It was supposed to be a treat for you. A lovely day out. You make it sound like a duty — I've ordered my housekeeper to accompany me."

Afterwards Charlotte supposed that, in a way, it was rather like that. She was to be an accessory, rather like a useful handbag. He had not asked her with any suggestion that he might enjoy her company. But why should he, she then wondered? Her living with him was purely a business arrangement, for his convenience. She was free to go at any time, as she had pointed out to Phyllida. Her mixed-up feelings worried her, and she tried to forget the conversation had taken place.

Surprisingly, Phyllida was not jealous.

"It's not somewhere I've ever wanted to go to, fortunately. Be careful what you get into with Mar — it all sounds rather dangerous to me." She obviously thought that the invitation was nothing to do with Charlotte's charm and attraction. Charlotte was much relieved and now had nothing to think about but carrying off her part. Meeting the toffs in the royal enclosure was something that worried her. But Kitty arrived to put her right.

"Dear Charlotte, it's nothing. You mutter, look down, and curtsey. If anyone asks where you come from, you can say you're a friend of mine, staying with me. You're not there to be noticed. Just about everyone else is, so you can relax. Mind you, Milo has a lot of admirers, so you might get some sour looks."

What she was to wear was terribly important, according to Kitty.

"But don't worry; I've got it all in hand. You are

staying with me the night beforehand. I shall turn you out like a duchess."

"Thank heaven it's not me," Phyllida said stuffily. "It's a proper circus."

Charlotte pretended it was ridiculous too, but secretly she was rather excited. Especially about staying with Kitty.

They drove there the day before, very fast, and Charlotte sat in the back while Milo and Mar larked and chatted up on the box, taking it in turns to drive. Away from Constance, Milo was like a boy out of school. They sang stupid songs and did some smart overtaking, which caused Charlotte to grit her teeth. But as they approached their destination they calmed down and Milo joined Charlotte in the back. He directed Mar off the main road into some minor lanes, and they passed through miles of sunlit forest and across common land dotted with ancient cottages. Wherever did Kitty live?

"It's not far now."

Charlotte had no idea what she was expecting: something rather grand, as befitted a Rawnsley, she thought. They turned down a long drive, and Mar pulled the horses to a walk to cool them down. An avenue of limes shaded the hot sun, but no grand mansion appeared at the end, only a quite modest Elizabethan farmhouse set amongst a sprawl of barns and stables and rows of glasshouses. The land was hilly, dropping behind the house into a narrow valley and rising up beyond clothed in heavy beeches, adroop in the hot sun. In the valley several horses were grazing, and mares with foals came curiously to the gate at the sound of hooves. As Mar pulled the horses to a halt there was a perfect silence, with only the soft buzzing of bees to soften it.

"Kitty's little nest," Milo said.

He sat for a moment, taking it in, and smiled.

"He rescued her, nice Mr. Lytton, from a house nearly a quarter of a mile long, with over a hundred servants. He gave her this farm, to breed her horses on, and her complete freedom. He is a nice man."

Some children, Charlotte thought, would like to live in a house a quarter of a mile long with a hundred servants, but the Rawnsleys seemed a perverse family. Possibly, having the mother in it was what made the Rawnsley home uninhabitable.

"Oh, my mother!" Kitty exclaimed later. "Do you wonder? I had to 'come out,' have a ball, be put on show like a filly for sale. Milo understands. Our other brothers and sisters — they all loved it, but Milo and me, we ran away. Milo ran off with Constance, and I went to my great-aunt Maud."

In her bedroom, with the windows wide open looking out over the valley and the afternoon sun slanting in under thatched eaves, the Ascot clothes were laid out on the bed, a confection of pink and silver glittering in the golden light, fine as thistledown. Not so fine the corsets, which had to be laced more tightly than Charlotte had ever endured.

"I shall die!"

"If you will be fashionable — I'm sorry. Breathe in. More, better. There." Kitty heaved with all her strength. "The waist is twenty-two inches. I'm sure you can make it, Charlotte — you're only a little thing."

Kitty was gasping with the effort. "That's it. Try the dress."

Magically, it slithered down over the ghastly corset and hooked up without a wrinkle. It was of palest pink lace and tulle, with silver flounces down the front, which were caught down both sides with tiny pink roses. The fashionable high, full sleeves sprung out from her shoulders like angel's wings, then were caught in close at the elbows with more roses, and round the high lace neck a black velvet ribbon was fixed with a rhinestone at her throat. The hat was like a bird of paradise sitting on her head, with one dove-grey plume curling down onto her shoulder. The delicate colours seemed to bring out the rich colour of her hair, and her eyes looked back from the mirror with amazement, a deeper, smokier blue than she had ever imagined. She was stunned.

"Kitty!"

Charlotte had never been vain, largely because she had never had a decent mirror to look into, but realized that, in these clothes and in this light, she did look — well —

"Beautiful," Kitty said.

"The dress! It's so pretty."

"You've never dressed to show yourself off, have you? It's your vicarage upbringing. And Phyllida's influence — what a killjoy she is! I always feel she disapproves terribly."

"Oh no, she doesn't." Charlotte felt bound to leap to her friend's defence. "She's very serious-minded though, it's true. Very clever."

"I don't see why being clever means you have to be

so dowdy. I'm clever, and I'm not dowdy." Kitty laughed. "You must buy yourself some new clothes. Does Milo pay you? Have you any money?"

"He gives us the housekeeping."

"What about your wages?"

"Well, we're guests, really. He pays for everything we want. And Switzerland —"

"But no wages?"

"No."

"He is deplorable. Really! I shall speak to him."

"Oh, no, please."

"He uses you. Even this — he has a plan to meet the Paynes, isn't that correct? And he thinks being with a woman will help him meet the Weasel."

"The Weasel?"

"Jacob Payne's wife. Everyone calls her the Weasel, didn't you know? She looks like one. Behaves like one too, from what I hear."

"I don't know about this. Milo didn't say —"

"No? Well, don't worry about it. It's to help Mar, after all, and he's a sweet boy. But be careful, Charlotte — the boys are very wild when they're up to their tricks. I shall tell Milo you're going to Ascot to enjoy yourself. Not as part of a plot."

Charlotte didn't like the sound of the Weasel, but was so entranced by her new appearance that she didn't give it much thought. The dress was hung up in tissue paper on its hanger by Kitty's maid, and the corsets were let out, much to Charlotte's relief. They went outside and Kitty took Charlotte out to the stables where Milo and Mar were looking at her horses. From the stables they walked through the glasshouses. "We should have brought Roland — just his province," Milo exclaimed. A riot of exotic plants clouded the glass with their exuberant breath, filling the air with heady scents. Beyond the glasshouses a garden dropped down the valley slope, full of the plants and trees that Marcus Lytton had collected during his lifetime. Several gardeners were at work and drew back respectfully as the visitors passed by. How strange, Charlotte thought, that Kitty had all this and yet . . . she thought of her own crazy dream-love for Casimir and the bliss and the tears it had cost her. Did Kitty love her elderly husband? How could she forego so coolly all the handsome young men that crossed her path? She called lovely Mar a "dear boy" like a woman a generation older, yet she was only twenty-three, a year older than Milo.

But she was obviously happy. A wonderful dinner was served later, and afterwards the four of them sat on the terrace in the cool of the evening. Kitty lit a cigarette, and the smoke hung on the still air, mixing with the fragrance of the tobacco plants under the windows.

"So, you don't want to come tomorrow?" Milo asked her.

She shook her head. "Mama might be there."

"It will be easy to avoid her. I shall."

"You'll come back in the evening?"

"Yes."

"My coachman will take you to Ascot, and Mar can spend the day with me. I have a three-year-old I've backed, but he's being very difficult. I don't know why, because he's got a sweet temperament. Perhaps you can sort him out for me, Mar? You must try him — see if he bucks you off like he does me."

"That'll be a fine way to spend the day."

"Falling on your head?" Milo smiled. "It's used to it,

201

after all. We'll get that wig pensioned off if we're lucky."

"Oh, Mar, take it off! I've forgotten what you look like." Charlotte, intoxicated suddenly with the pleasure of the evening, made a grab for Mar's hair. Mar laughed and ducked, then snatched the wig off and tossed it up in a climbing rose that overhung his chair, where it hung like a sleeping bat. The riotous orange curls that had for so long been hidden clung damply to his head. He shook himself vigorously, like a dog after a swim, and laughed.

"You look like one of Marcus's foreign plants," Kitty said. "I think you ought to go in the glasshouse."

"I thought you'd be bald after all this time," Milo said.

"Oh no, it gets thicker. I chop it off occasionally. Oh, what a release! It's fiendish hot, the wretched thing."

Charlotte laughed, delighted to see her old Mar in his real tiger colours, the golden-green eyes glittering with excitement. She was overcome, suddenly, by her good fortune, sitting in this beautiful place with these people who were, amazingly, her friends. All because of Mr. Carstairs — who, when she had gone home last Christmas with Phyllida, had not seemed nearly so bad as she remembered. It was a miracle, how life had changed for her in only a year. It was frightening, how quickly things could alter. For the good, or for the bad. And her future . . . she was not a real housekeeper, only like a poor relation, being given a roof. If Milo, after all, was one day to marry, would she want to be his housekeeper all her life? Only if she were the wife as well.

14

It took Kitty two hours to get Charlotte to her liking the following morning, the first day of the Royal Ascot meeting. To get her hair properly under the hat, with the right curls peeping out in the right places, was a mammoth task. Charlotte was none too good at sitting still, especially laced up as she was   sitting was agony.

"It's the last time you'll sit down today, save in the carriage, so don't worry. Ascot is so wearing. Especially with Milo, who wants to be everywhere. Comfortable shoes are everything." There was a modicum of rouge and powder to apply, and lip gloss, and a parasol to be carried in the correct manner, and white gloves.

"Don't touch anything, for heaven's sake."

"Oh, Kitty, I'm terrified! Suppose the Prince of Wales —"

"He likes pretty girls. If you're introduced, you just curtsey and murmur, 'Your Royal Highness.' Nothing to it. You don't speak to him, only if he asks you something. Milo knows him a bit — he's not a bit stuffy when you get to know him. Very kind. But a stickler for correctness — you mustn't wear your Garter star upside down, like the Duke of Devonshire. That was so funny! But don't worry. Milo will look after you."

When the hat was settled to Kitty's satisfaction, Charlotte got up to look at her Ascot self in the mirror. She thought Phyllida wouldn't recognize her — would Milo? She scarcely knew herself. She was like a piece of confectionery made of spun sugar, all pink and glittery.

"God Almighty!" said Milo.

"By Jasus!" breathed Mar.

"I'm frightened to move," Charlotte said. Going downstairs had been nerve-wracking, the dress right to the ground, unlike her ordinary wear, and she was unable to touch the bannisters because of the gloves. But confronting Milo was equally a shock for her, because, although he usually dressed well, if carelessly, she had never seen him in the full fig of frock coat and top hat before. His trousers and topper were silver-grey, the coat black with a silk waistcoat beneath and a gold watch chain glittering across his slender midriff. Unlike her, he seemed perfectly at home in his smart attire.

He whispered to her, "You asked why I didn't take Phyllida. Now you know. She wouldn't have stood for it, and she would never have looked half as beautiful."

Charlotte felt a great flush of pure pleasure sweep over her at his words. She knew then that she was going to fall in love with Milo if she was not very careful.

Mar went down on one knee. "Charlotte, will you marry me?"

"Not yet," she said, and laughed.

Mar was aching to go to the races, but had to stay and break in horses. As Milo handed Charlotte into Kitty's carriage, Mar said urgently, "And remember you're not there to enjoy yourself — buttonhole Jacob — remember —"

"Yes. I'll see Evelyn first. Don't worry — we'll sort it out."

"Oh, Milo, I don't believe this!" Charlotte said as they spun away down the drive. Kitty's coachman was

driving her chestnut pair, but they went far more soberly for him than they did for her.

Milo smiled. "It's a pity we've work to do. I could
quite enjoy myself otherwise."

The last time they had been alone together was
when she had wept for Casimir. It seemed a long time
ago now. She had forgotten Casimir. (It was only a
month.) As if remembering the same, Milo said, "It's a
bit different from the climbing, all this fal-lal, isn't it?
Nice in a way, for the contrast — you appreciate the
mountains more, if all this claptrap is part of your ordinary life. Because no sooner do I come home from
Switzerland than I want to go back. I was thinking,
perhaps, of going this winter — next summer seems so
far away. You can climb in the winter, in the snow, if
the weather's fine. And there's this new business,
where you climb up and slide down on skis. It sounds
like a bit of fun. You can go really fast apparently. I'd
like to try that. The trouble is, it will interfere with
hunting."

He didn't say whether he would take his "servants"
— Mar probably, if he was let out into society by then.
Milo had been lucky for Mar.

The carriage and pair soon came out onto roads
busy with traffic, mostly going to Ascot. The towers of
Windsor Castle rose palely in the heat-haze across the
river, very exciting to the rustic Charlotte — "Does the
Queen never come racing? She is so close."

"No, she abhors racing." Milo had a very poor opinion of Queen Victoria. "She's a gorgon, wrapped up in
her German relations, and hogging the throne from
nice Bertie. She thinks he can't be king — how wrong

she is. He has the human touch and knows how to mix, how to enjoy life."

"You'd think she'd be glad to retire after sixty years."

"I don't want to grow old. I'd like to go — bang — doing something wonderful. It wasn't so bad for Max, like that —"

"It was bad for Clara."

"Yes, that's true. She's only just coming to, isn't she?"

"Mainly due to Kitty." Charlotte knew that she and Phyllida made a pair and Clara stayed outside. They hadn't meant it that way, but Clara made no approaches. Kitty spent hours with her in the sitting room at the piano, but exactly what they were up to Charlotte had never discovered.

A lot of new houses were being built in the woods. Ascot seemed a popular place. They drew up outside the gates to the course and Milo arranged where to pick up the carriage after racing; then they were through into the hallowed grounds, Milo with his hand under Charlotte's elbow. It was very crowded, and Charlotte quickly found that every other girl was dressed in much the same way as herself, and all the men in the same uniform as Milo. She felt relieved to be able to melt into this crowd and not stand out; her fears receded.

She knew very little about racing. Milo knew everything, and she knew she was in good hands. They went into the royal enclosure, their credentials scrutinized by uniformed stewards, and stood in the crowd to watch Bertie and his party arrive in their open landaus, with all their outriders and liveried postillions and footmen.

When they came into the stand all the ladies dropped curtsies, and the men bowed as they made their way towards the royal box. Charlotte got a glimpse of the portly prince as he passed by, quite close. Below, all across the grounds, the less privileged were crowding to see him and cheer. The atmosphere was extremely good-humoured; it was very hot, and Charlotte began to relax and enjoy herself, her worst fears unrealized. The Prince had not stopped dead in his tracks at the sight of her and asked to be introduced; she could breathe again.

They went down to the paddock for the first race and watched the horses being led round the hallowed grass. Owners and trainers stood in the middle chatting, and one particular pair attracted Milo's attention.

"There," he murmured to Charlotte. "Our friends the Paynes. I knew he had a horse running today. The man with a carnation in his buttonhole — nose like a billhook — that's Jacob, Mar's friend. The woman in cream is his wife, the Weasel. Their young twit of a son, Arthur, is Evelyn's friend."

Jacob had a coarse and evil face, Charlotte decided (or was it just because she knew he was evil?), high colour, and an impatient manner. He was big and looked menacing. The Weasel was well named, with a prominent nose and receding chin, and rather outsticking front teeth that gave her a rodent look. She had very sharp blue eyes and tight, thin lips. She fussed round the horse, checking its girths and breastplate, and seemed a very practical lady. She was smartly dressed, but seemed not to care for fripperies.

"She is quite a formidable customer," Milo remarked. "They say she rather than Jacob runs the yard.

She certainly knows her horses and works like a man. She might be the most difficult to handle."

"What do you mean, handle?"

Milo laughed. "Where's your spirit of adventure? To trick — we are going to trick them, Charlotte. Like they trick other people."

"I don't like tricks."

"I should have brought Phyllida."

Charlotte bit her lip. She didn't know if Milo was joking or not.

"I say, Milo!"

Evelyn moved across to them as the horses left the paddock and the crowd started to drift away. He looked very hot, if not feverish, and worried. Beads of sweat stood out on his forehead.

"Evelyn. Are you on your own?"

"I am at the moment. I'm with Mama, officially. She got me the day off school — I'm leaving, you know. I have to go back to Switzerland, to be treated for my lungs, like you, Milo. It might save my bacon, if I can get away before my creditors close in."

"Oh, rough luck, Evelyn. I wouldn't wish that on anyone. But look, they cured me — you'll win through, don't worry. I was telling Charlotte — I'd like to go back there in the winter, for a holiday. I'll come and spend some time with you. Look, can we arrange to meet — after the Prince of Wales Stakes? You know what it's about."

"If my horse comes up, I'm not —"

"No. We'll meet all the same. The top end of the paddock, eh?" His voice was very authoritative. Evelyn flinched.

"All right."

He went off towards the grandstand. Milo said, "Let's stay down on the lawn. We don't want to meet Mama, for goodness' sake. I didn't think she'd be here."

"What's this horse that Evelyn's bet his fortune on? Do you know?"

"A colt called Schoolboy. It won't win."

Milo was right. The colt came in fourth. Evelyn met them under the trees in a quiet spot away from the crowds. The sweating runners were being led back to the stables, their afternoon shadows following them across the manicured grass. Charlotte watched them, not anxious to be embroiled in Milo's "tricks." The atmosphere was so rich and sweet, she wanted to enjoy it, twirling her parasol like a real lady at lovely Milo's side. Evelyn was close to tears.

"Calm down," Milo ordered. "Whatever your bills, I shall pay them. I promised. In return for your telling me —"

"They'll kill me!"

"Not if I pay up, idiot. Tell them to contact me. Did you find out what I wanted to know?"

"Yes."

"Good. Tell me."

"Joker, the real Joker, is in one of the isolation boxes behind the main yard. There are four boxes together, with three horses in. Joker is the chestnut — he has a red ribbon threaded into his tail, because it's hard to tell him apart from his double — even Jacob has a job to tell. The double, Old Tom, is in the main yard, with a plate beside his box with the name Joker on it. At night there are guard dogs loose, and a boy sleeps with Joker, the real Joker."

"Yes, well, we're not going to work at night. It's all to be done in broad daylight, when they're off guard. Jacob will be here, for a start. He's got a horse running tomorrow, hasn't he?"

"Yes."

"I will tell you the plan, and you tell me if they're likely to fall for it. They've got a two-year-old for sale, called Mr. Herring. They want a lot of money for it."

"Yes, it's a damned good colt."

"If I show an interest — say I'd like to look at it — they'd be keen to receive me?"

"Oh, yes."

"Even if I say I can only manage tomorrow afternoon? Jacob will be at the races but Mrs. Weasel Payne might stay behind to show me the horse?"

"Yes, I imagine she would. They're very anxious to sell it."

"And the yard would be empty — the afternoon siesta — the boys will all be at home, or here, with perhaps just one to run out the horse for me . . . do you think that's how it would go?"

"Yes. The head man will be here with their runner. And Jacob too."

"You think he would entrust the selling to his wife?"

"Yes. She does all that better than he does."

"Because if there's a hitch, we can overpower the lady, but Jacob is very handy with his fists."

"She's not called the Weasel for nothing. How are you going to walk out with Joker, while she's there?"

"Charlotte here is going to cause a diversion. And while the lady is occupied, Mar and I will sneak out the horse and, if necessary, dissuade any dissenting grooms."

Charlotte came to with a jolt. "Me? How? What do you mean?"

"Faint. Have the vapours, or whatever women do, their corsets being so tight. It's common enough and definitely women's work. She'll take you indoors and give you a drink, clear the decks. There's absolutely no risk to you at all." Milo spoke almost scornfully, as if she had suggested he was putting her in danger. Charlotte felt her throat go dry.

"Tomorrow?"

"Tomorrow afternoon." Milo dismissed her and turned back to Evelyn. "There is a way out behind, I take it, without coming out through the main yard?"

"Through the fields, yes."

"Is Joker a kind horse — easy?"

"I believe so."

"Good." Milo gave a little skip. "That's great. Piece of cake."

"They'll go mad!"

"That's the whole idea. Put them where we want them. They can have their horse back if they agree to our proposition." Milo grinned, very satisfied. "That's great, Evelyn. Refer your creditors to me and I'll pay your bills, and don't worry about the Paynes. By the time you come back from Switzerland they'll be in prison for some other nefarious deed, I'm sure."

He put an arm round Evelyn's shoulder in a fatherly way. Evelyn looked about twelve, Charlotte thought, his Ascot clothes hanging forlornly on his emaciated figure, his lips trembling with incipient tears. She felt sorry for him, being bullied by Milo, with the terrible disease hanging over him. She wondered how much money he would have made, if the right horse had won.

"Now, introduce me to the Paynes, and tell them I'm interested in buying Mr. Herring."

Charlotte found herself being carried along on the wings of Milo's enthusiasm, in spite of being very afraid of what was going to happen. Jacob and his wife were talking to an owner by the saddling boxes, but turned eagerly to greet Evelyn and Milo. Charlotte saw that they liked to consort with the upper classes — probably few of their owners came into this category. She saw the Weasel's beady eyes dart over her from head to toe as she was introduced — how well named she was, for she had a curiously sharp and dangerous aura, in spite of a sycophantic smile and wheedling voice.

"Delighted to meet you, sir. In the flesh, so to speak, for of course we've heard about your riding exploits."

Her husband looked like a bone-crusher — trust Mar to take on such a dangerous family, and he half the size. Charlotte wondered if the brother Mar had killed had been anything like the apelike Jacob.

"I'm interested in the colt you're selling, Mr. Herring. It's a bloodline I particularly like, and there aren't many about. Would it be possible for me to call and see him tomorrow afternoon?" Milo spoke in his usual soft way, yet the question was more an order and hardly seemed to require a reply.

"Well, I'm sure — yes."

Jacob looked at his wife excitedly and was no doubt mentally adding another five hundred to the price.

"Of course, sir. My wife will show him to you. You understand, I shall have to be here tomorrow afternoon? We have a runner in the third race."

"Yes. I'm afraid it is a slightly inconvenient time,

212

but I can't manage either morning or evening tomorrow. I will call at three, madam."

He bowed to the Weasel and walked away, Charlotte at his side. She saw that he was sparkling with the success of his plan, his arrogant manner dispersed in smiles.

"That was smart, eh? It's beautifully set up, all as smooth as clockwork. What a very successful day, dear Charlotte. How lucky we've been."

Charlotte could not see it herself, her role not appealing. But she did not want to think about it at the moment. She had a hopeful feeling that something would happen to prevent tomorrow's venture, being always an optimist. They strolled across the grass back towards the grandstand, and after a few moments Evelyn caught them up.

"It's devilish embarrassing. They're so grateful to me for introducing you."

"They're getting no more than their just deserts. It will teach you not to mix with bad company, Evelyn."

"Milo!"

It was inevitable that Milo was going to meet friends before the day was through, and in the grandstand there appeared to be a host of old acquaintances waiting to greet him and be introduced to Charlotte. Charlotte pretended she was a friend of Kitty's but was aware of raking glances, almost as bad as the Weasel's, and expressions that were not necessarily friendly. There was a lot of gushing over Milo, she noticed. But as they turned to leave after the next race, a meeting took place that Milo hadn't planned.

Coming down the steps above them with an elderly man was the tall and unmistakable figure of Constance

Mathers. Pushed by the crowd, they coincided with Milo and Charlotte at the bottom of the steps.

If the Weasel and some others of Milo's circle had looked her up and down, Charlotte felt it was nothing compared to the rake of Constance's wide blue orbs upon her shrinking figure. The look scored her, like claws. She glanced at Milo and saw the shock on his face. Yet he kept his composure. He bowed to the man Constance was with and murmured, "Sir," and then he bowed to Constance, very formally.

Then he said, "Allow me to introduce Miss Charlotte Campion. Charlotte, Mr. and Mrs. William Mathers."

Not knowing whether to curtsey or not — they weren't Bertie, after all — Charlotte stood rooted to the ground, trying to smile. Her face felt as frozen as Constance's glare. Her husband, on the other hand, appeared quite amiable and gave her a pleasant smile.

"Had any winners, Milo? I've had deuced bad luck all afternoon."

"No, sir, I'm afraid." He hadn't put any bets on, that Charlotte had noticed.

Constance looked as stunning as usual in an outstanding turquoise blue gown and ropes of pearls. Her hat was made of white feathers; she wore white gloves, and her wrists were laden with sapphire bracelets. She looked so strong and perfect and arrogant that Charlotte felt as if she herself had melted away into invisibility, her confectionery clothes diminished to cobwebs in the sun. The crowd moved them forward, and William Mathers dropped back to speak to another gentleman. Charlotte heard Milo say to Constance, "I thought you were still abroad."

She said, viciously, "Obviously."

"I'm staying with Kitty for Ascot. Why did you come back? Is anything wrong?"

"Not until now."

"Don't be ridiculous, Constance."

But Milo was shaken, Charlotte could see, and as they parted in the crowd she could feel his mood had changed, his excitement about the coming adventure dissipated by Constance's anger.

"She had a terribly good look at me. How can I turn back into a servant when she calls again?"

"Yes, it's really unfortunate. The darnedest thing to happen. We'll have to get you a wig like Mar — a ginger one. But perhaps she won't come back."

Charlotte could not tell whether he was joking or not. She thought not. He looked suddenly rather pale and tired. Charlotte had a great urge to shout "Good! If she never comes back — good!" How many years, she wondered? Since he was sixteen . . . the woman was monstrous, holding poor Milo in her jewel-encrusted talons. But the evidence that Constance was jealous — jealous of her, Charlotte — made her want to shout with joy. And she knew, however striking and magnificent the woman's clothes and arrogant bearing, she was old, she was disintegrating; however beautiful her eyes, they were finely webbed with wrinkles; however smooth her skin, it wasn't young and transparent like her own, and her body, though strong, wasn't lithe and lissome and full of fire like hers, Charlotte's. Charlotte wanted to shout and sing. She wanted to wrap Milo in her arms and cover him with kisses.

On the way home Milo gradually came out of his mood and laughed.

"I should grow out of her, I think," he said. And then he sighed, heavily.

♦ ♦ ♦

Milo and Mar stayed up plotting all night, making a plan, and allowing for every possible variation on what might happen. Evelyn had given Milo a sketch map of the yard and marked the way out of the back, where the gates were and where the paths led to. Mar was to be hidden in the boot of the carriage and would slip out to steal Joker while the others were engaged in examining Mr. Herring. Kitty arranged that their coachman would be a young groom who would understand what was going on, not the staid, elderly man who had driven them to Ascot. They were to take the fast chestnut pair, in case they were chased.

Kitty said, "I don't know why you have to involve Charlotte in this at all."

"Because with Charlotte we can do the job with guile, while without her we can only do it by force. I'm not very keen to take on the Weasel, even if she is only a woman."

"Have you asked Charlotte whether she wants to come?"

"Do you want to come, Charlotte?"

Strangely enough, Charlotte knew she would be disappointed now if they dropped her from their plans. She was keyed up to do it and flattered by being wanted. Frightened, definitely. But fear was a stimulant, and being with Milo, being wanted by Milo, spurred her to accede to her role. It seemed like a game, a joke, the way they talked about it, yet she knew it was life itself to Mar.

"Yes. But I've never fainted. I'm not sure how to."

Kitty instructed her. "You can't go pale, but you can pretend dizziness. Don't talk. Go quiet, and rub your eyes a few times. Perhaps Milo can ask you if you feel all right. It could be the heat, you can suggest. I'm sure it's going to be another scorcher."

Charlotte went to bed and hardly slept for thinking of her day at Ascot and the day to come. Her mind was jumbled with events both real and imaginary, and when she awoke in the dawn she scarcely remembered where she was. A mist lay over the fields, and the sun was a pink, shimmering blur caught in the tops of the beech trees across the valley. She slid out of bed and went to the window. Across the lawn, leaving trails in the dew, Milo and Mar were walking down to the river. They only had drawers on, and were punching each other and roughhousing, and after they had gone out of sight Charlotte heard the splashes as they leapt into the river. The thought made her shiver. The boys had always had cold baths at school before breakfast — Ben had told her — sometimes having to break ice to make the water flow, so no doubt a summer river even in the dawn was attractive by comparison.

Kitty, being much the same size as Charlotte, amused herself by finding clothes in her wardrobe that she said Charlotte could have. By lunchtime the pile on Charlotte's bed was quite high.

"What you don't fancy you can pass on to Phyllida. She looks as if she's not been near a dress shop for years. She's taller, but most of the hems will let out."

For the visit to the Paynes, Kitty decided on a blue-striped, sailorish sort of dress, with a full skirt. "You might have to run, who knows? It's very practical."

217

There was a straw hat with blue ribbons to set it off. Once dressed and ready for action, Charlotte began to feel rather nervous. Milo and Mar, having been riding all morning, came in for lunch like two overgrown schoolboys. This was the real Milo, Charlotte suspected, the Milo of the mountains and "tricks," not Constance's Milo, not Milo of the Ascot establishment. It was the Milo, she thought, that belonged to her.

"Very respectable," he said to her, eyeing her dress. "You look like my wife."

"What a good idea!" cried Kitty.

"She's going to marry me," Mar said. "When I'm back in society."

"Really?"

"When that happens, I think you'll go," Milo said. "We haven't discussed that, have we? Am I going to lose my head groom?"

"I'll chuck up head groom and apply for racing manager. How about that? Goodnight Glitters — she's got form. We could —"

"Oh, be quiet, both of you," Kitty commanded. "Let's get this afternoon over first."

Both Kitty and Charlotte were more nervous than the men.

At two o'clock they set off behind the chestnut horses. It was, as Kitty had foretold, oppressively hot. "Good fainting weather," as Mar remarked cheerfully. He was not yet hidden in the luggage boot, which might well do for him, Charlotte thought (but did not say). A young man drove, who knew what they planned to do.

"And what do you plan to do?" Charlotte asked. "How long have I got to pretend to faint?"

218

"The longer the better, to give us more time. We shall be looking at this colt, Mr. Herring, with a groom and the Weasel. No more, I suspect — I hope — because all racing stables rest in the afternoon and the lads go home. In this case they'll all go racing if they have the chance. So we're looking at this colt in the yard, and you come over faint, and the Weasel has to escort you to the house to lie down. Make out you're quite ill, else she might just sit you down in the tack room, and that's no good. We want her well out of the way."

"Then what do you do?"

"I flash a few sovereigns at the groom, and he will put Mr. Herring back in his box, and I will lock him in. He will tell the Weasel I overpowered him. I will if I have to, but I think money will do the trick. Then Mar nips out and takes Joker, and I take Old Tom and we bustle them out into the back fields and ride away."

"Leaving me behind!"

"Yes. You are in the house, recovering. The Weasel will probably leave you there and come back to the yard. As soon as she disappears you nip out of the house where Ned here — that's our coachman — will still be waiting. You jump in and gallop away. Nothing to it."

"Hmm."

Charlotte thought there was, and as they trotted steadily on their way she became more and more nervous. She noticed that both Milo and Mar also stopped being so cocky and presently ceased talking altogether. The Paynes' place was some twenty miles away. They got lost twice — not a good omen, Charlotte decided — and only found it by asking directions from gawping yokels. Smart carriages were not found in these lanes, even during Ascot week. Eventually they came to a rutty drive with the name of the farm on the gate. The young coachman pulled up, and Mar got round the back and into the boot. Milo propped it open with a brick to give him some air, for the afternoon was without a breeze and sultry, the sun veiled with an ominous, thunderous haze. When he got back onto the box, Charlotte noticed that Milo was now taut and unsmiling. A sudden cold wash of pure fear shook her.

"Please, Milo —"

"Be quiet."

"I'm terrified."

"It's for Mar. It matters."

The joke was over, she saw.

The drive led between fields towards a huddle of low farm buildings. The fields were backed by woods, and there were fields fringed with woods beyond the farmyard. As they approached they saw that a three-sided stableyard opened onto the drive. An archway in the facing line of stables led into a smaller yard beyond — where presumably Joker was installed. The house, a nondescript brick farmhouse, lay back from the stableyard on the lefthand side, up a short drive of its own. From the house one could not see into the stableyard. Evelyn had drawn Milo a sketch-map of the layout, and this fact had helped him work out his plan. Charlotte realized she would have no idea what was going on if she was left in the house. As if sensing this thought, Milo said as they approached, "Ned will keep the carriage handy, ready for you to make your escape. Do what seems best. We'll be pretty quick getting the horses away, so don't worry about us."

They were committed, and Charlotte's fear receded as she got down, ready for action. The carriage decanted them outside the house. The Weasel came out, as expected, and greeted Milo and Charlotte. They then walked back up the short drive and into the stableyard, and the carriage followed and pulled up to wait at the entrance to the yard.

The guard dogs Evelyn had mentioned were in the railed enclosure of a large kennel in the yard, snoozing in the sun. Presumably they only worked at night. They did not even look up. The yard was somnolent, empty save for a groom who waited by the door of a box presumably occupied by Mr. Herring. He jumped to attention as they approached. He was a middle-aged man and looked like a boxer, with a battered face and a cauliflower ear. Not too good, thought Charlotte, and was surprised to feel an unexpected rush of apprehension, not for herself, but for Milo. He looked slender beside the burly groom. He was in his arrogant mode, so that the Weasel gabbled, at a disadvantage. At close quarters, again, Charlotte thought Ferret rather than Weasel, for she had a yellowish colour and slightly bloodshot eyes. Her greyish-yellowish hair was scraped back without regard for fashion, and her dress, of rather dirty grey cotton, looked like a servant's dress.

The groom opened the stable door and went in with a headcollar to secure Mr. Herring. A glance showed Charlotte a lean bay beast with a gleaming coat. The groom started to lead him out into the yard, but Milo stood in the doorway looking him over, no doubt to give Mar time to escape from the carriage, and make his way round the back of the buildings to the far yard.

221

"You'll see him better outside, sir," the Weasel said.

But Milo ran his hands down the horse's legs before he let the groom lead him out. Charlotte stayed outside, leaning against the wall, feeling herself into a sickly mood. It certainly was oppressively hot. Unbecoming smears of sweat glistened on the Weasel's nose and forehead, and she fingered her high collar as she prattled on about the horse's two-year-old form.

"Let me see him walk out," Milo said.

He made his way out towards the drive, indicating that the horse should be walked towards him, to see his action from the front, and then he got the groom to walk the animal past and away from him down the drive towards the house. This made the whole group of them come nearer to the house.

"Trot back and past me," he called to the groom.

He turned to Charlotte and said, "Do you like him?" He gave her half a wink.

"Are you all right, my dear?" His voice was full of a sudden concern. He put his arm round her and Charlotte let herself droop (rather deliciously) towards him, swaying. Her heart started to beat heavily with apprehension, and for a moment she almost thought she was going to faint. He whispered, "Don't overdo it," and she realized that if she looked as if she would fall he would have to carry her. She staggered a little and then straightened up, trying to look brave.

"It's the heat. I — I — a drink — oh, please —"

The Weasel seemed to be more interested in watching her horse than Charlotte, but when she noticed that Milo was otherwise occupied she cast her gaze unkindly at Charlotte.

"Are you ill?"

"She's a little faint with the heat. Perhaps she could sit inside till we've finished."

"Yes. Help yourself," the Weasel said to Charlotte.

The door was open, unfortunately. The Weasel was obviously not a motherly type.

"I — I need a drink. Some — cold water —"

"Would you be so good?" Milo spoke to the Weasel in his most aristocratic way, taking it for granted that she would respond. "Your man can show me the horse meanwhile."

The Weasel buckled to Milo's tone with ill-concealed annoyance, turning away towards her front door without any show of sympathy. Charlotte did her best to sway after her, but as the Weasel gave no glance behind she dropped her act and hurried to catch up to her.

They went into a wide hallway. The house smelt of dogs and was shabby and dirty. A door on the left of the hall was open and showed a sitting room with a useful sofa, which Charlotte made for rapidly.

"Oh dear, I'm so sorry! I feel dizzy —"

The Weasel came after her crossly and stood looking at her with narrowed eyes, as if she were a sick horse. Charlotte was undecided as to whether she was suspicious, or whether this was her usual lack of grace. Delaying tactics, she remembered, were required.

"You couldn't — I'm so sorry — but you couldn't unlace me? I think I'd feel much better. It must be the heat."

The Weasel had responded to Milo's high-handed tone, so Charlotte decided to use the same tactics and started to unbutton the front of the dress. The Weasel obliged, fumbling with the corset strings at the back as the bodice came loose. The way Kitty had tied them Charlotte knew they would be difficult to undo, and she heard the Weasel muttering crossly.

"And then perhaps you'd get me a drink of water? Oh dear." She put out a hand to steady herself on the sofa arm, feeling that she could get quite carried away with her act. She sank gracefully across the sofa back so that the Weasel could carry on with her task. She felt the corset relaxing and took some deep breaths.

"Oh, thank goodness! That feels better already. Thank you so much."

"I'll get you some water. Then you can stay here if you like, until Mr. Rawnsley is finished."

She went out into the kitchen, and Charlotte wondered how Milo was getting on. If he'd been quick, she reckoned he might be away by now. She risked a quick glance through the window. The drive was empty. The carriage stood waiting at the top, in the entrance to the stable yard.

The Weasel came back with a glass of water, and Charlotte felt that her task was well done: the corsets had been very time-consuming.

"I'll rest here if I may. Thank you very much."

She took the water, and the Weasel went out without another word. Charlotte leapt to the window and watched her walk quickly up the drive. It was time for her to move.

Scrabbling to button her dress as she went, she ran for the door. The Weasel was out of sight. The carriage looked miles away. Charlotte ran.

She had almost reached the carriage when a loud scream came from the yard ahead of her, and almost immediately the Weasel came belting back round the corner. Charlotte leapt for the carriage, but her undone dress slipped down, and she caught her foot in the hem. Her leap was cut short, and she fell against the step, nearly knocking herself out on the carriage lamp. Ned held out his hand with a shout, and she reached up; but the Weasel, with amazing strength, pushed in front of her, seized Ned's outstretched arm, and pulled him violently off the box. She was so quick that Ned was taken unawares and seemed to cartwheel out of the sky. The startled horses reared; the carriage lurched forward, spraying them all with gravel, and then shot off down the drive as the horses bolted. Charlotte rolled over just in time to stop the front wheels from decapitating her and scrambled to her feet. The Weasel and Ned were locked in combat beside her, and as she stood, not knowing what to do, Ned wrenched himself out of the Weasel's grasp and shouted at her, "Run for it, miss! The back way!"

Charlotte took his advice. Gathering up her sagging skirts she tore round the corner into the stableyard, expecting to see Milo and Mar, but the stable doors swung open and there was no sign of them. She ran through into the second yard and saw that one box was open and empty. Certainly they had been quick. But what about her, abandoned and horseless? Even as she hesitated, a ferocious scream followed her from the drive, and a quick glance showed her that the Weasel had shaken off Ned's restraint and was now running in her direction. Close behind her was the old groom, roaring like a bull, and behind him Ned. Charlotte had no option but to take to her heels and run, preferably faster than the Weasel.

A strong sense of self-preservation guided her.

There was a gateway into a field out of the second yard, which was obviously the get-away route. Milo and Mar could have taken no other way. Charlotte dived through the gate, tripped up again on her hem, and scrambled completely out of the dress altogether as she started to her feet again. The freedom was a godsend. At the far end of the field she could see Milo and Mar on the two chestnut horses, looking along the hedgerow for a way out. Mar seemed to have found a spot. Charlotte saw him ride his horse hard at a thin place in the hedge, and Milo swung round to follow him. Charlotte cupped her hands to her mouth and screamed, "Milo!"

On the quivering hot, still air, her voice carried like the scream of a hare. Milo reined in and glanced back. Charlotte started towards him. The Weasel was through the gate behind her and in close pursuit, shouting the most frightful epithets, and Charlotte, spurred by terror, shot across the thistly field, praying for deliverance. Milo turned his horse and came cantering back to meet her, and Charlotte ran faster still, terrified that the Weasel would treat Milo as she had treated Ned. But Milo kept well clear of her pursuer and circled neatly to come alongside. He held out a hand.

"Get a hold of its mane!" he shouted.

He grabbed her under one armpit and half lifted her off the ground, riding on to get clear. Charlotte got her other hand to the horse's neck and grabbed a handful of mane as directed and ran, half pulled, half flying through the air, towards the hedge. Somehow they crashed through. Spears of sharp hawthorn caught at her flying petticoats and she screamed out. Milo pulled up abruptly.

"The carriage horses bolted!" Charlotte sobbed out.

"Get up! Get up!" Milo held out both arms and heaved her violently up over the horse's withers. He had no saddle; there was nothing to hold onto. She lay head down as he pressed the horse on and found a handhold on Milo's breeches. After some desperate bumping and crashing during which she had no idea where she was or what was happening, the horse at last pulled up, and Charlotte slithered off in a heap onto the ground. Milo jumped off beside her.

"She's gone back — to get a horse, I daresay. Here, get up. Give me your leg. What happened to Ned?"

Charlotte tried to explain, while Milo legged her back onto the horse, the right way up this time. With an impressive bound, he then hopped up behind her.

"What's happened to your dress?" He was laughing. Laughing! Charlotte burst into tears.

"Oh, come," he said. "We've got the horses — be happy! I'm sorry if you got a fright. I only hope Kitty's chestnuts don't hurt themselves. She'll never forgive me."

He was riding the horse through the wood, twisting and turning and ducking under branches. It was cool and quiet, and Charlotte suddenly realized that he had his arms round her, and she was sitting there in her chemise. Her tears turned to laughing, and she got the hiccups.

"Where the devil is Mar? I'm supposed to be on the fast horse — he's on the dud. The idiot should have waited."

But he was only a minute ahead of them, and they soon caught him up. He was not pleased to see Charlotte.

"This is going to slow us down."

"We can always throw her off if we're chased," Milo said cheerfully.

"I thought you were fainting in the drawing room and going home in the carriage."

"The carriage bolted. I had to run for it."

"Lor'! What about Kitty's horses? Was Ned on the box?"

"No. They went without him."

"I suppose we ought to find them," Milo said. "They're valuable, and Kitty's darlings. You'd better go back, Mar, and I'll go on with Joker."

"I could be looking all night."

"True."

"I'll go on foot. If I meet the Payne woman, she won't know me on foot."

"Yes. Then Charlotte can ride Old Tom."

Mar nobly took off his jacket for Charlotte to wear. He bunked her up onto the chestnut and put the reins in her hands.

"Sit tight. Don't get hurt. Remember I'm going to marry you."

Charlotte laughed. "Only when you've got red hair."

"We've done well today. I'm on my way."

"Seriously, avoid the Paynes," Milo said. "They're not stupid, and you might be recognized, wig or no wig. They would kill you now, if they could."

"And you too, I daresay," Mar said. "I swear they'll be after their horse! You'd better ride fast, the two of you, before she's back."

He turned and went sprinting back the way they had come.

"I can't ride fast, not without a saddle." Charlotte had to admit her limitations. Nor had she ever ridden a horse so lean and raking as Old Tom before. The Weasel could ride fast, she had no doubt.

"Do your best." Milo's voice was brisk.

She should be riding in the carriage now, driven by Ned, back to home comforts. Old Tom's stride was long and smooth, but his back was slippery. Charlotte took two good handfuls of mane along with the reins and gripped her legs as hard as she could around the horse's flanks. Milo went ahead, and they shortly came out onto a road. There was common land on the other side with bushes and trees and some cows grazing. Milo turned onto the road.

"Now, if she's decided to chase us, we should see her from the top of the hill. Come on."

He went off up the road at a fast canter, and Charlotte's horse followed without any urging. The faster they went the easier it was to stay aboard, and after a few minutes Charlotte began to gain confidence, sitting up a little straighter and breathing more easily. But she could see Milo was worried. He kept glancing back, and when they came to the top of the long hill he pulled up. Charlotte supposed it was to give the horses a breather, although neither of them seemed to need it. He turned and looked back down the long valley behind them.

"Ah. Dammit. They're coming."

The jokiness had gone. His face was taut and pale. Charlotte knew it had been a laugh, just him and Mar. They could have escaped on the two good horses easily. But now she was the liability and Milo was on his own.

229

"You must go on without me," she said.

"I need both the horses," he said. "We need them both for proof and they know it."

Charlotte slipped off Old Tom instantly and gave his reins to Milo. Milo fumbled in his coat pocket and thrust her a handful of sovereigns.

"Good girl! Mar will come back this way if he finds Kitty's pair . . . with luck you —"

His voice was lost as he sped away. Bareback on Joker, leading Old Tom, it seemed to Charlotte that he travelled as fast as any lone rider with a saddle. He had not hesitated to desert her, not even made a sketch of an apology nor voiced anxiety about her welfare. Charlotte was shaken by the suddenness of these events, left abandoned now in Mar's jacket on the public highway with no idea of her whereabouts. But she had offered. In her confusion, only instinct reminded her to hide from Milo's pursuers. She plunged away into the bushes that lined the road and lay down in the hot grass under the spread of a kindly thicket of broom. The thud of hooves on the hard road grew rapidly louder. Perhaps they had seen her — surely they had — but it was the horses they wanted, not the girl. She risked lifting her head and peering through the leaves and saw the Weasel riding astride like a man, her face set with determination. Round her waist was a belt with a pistol in it and in her hand a whip with which she kept clouting the horse. Charlotte was stunned by the sight, not believing a woman capable of such aggression. The old groom was some way behind, also leathering his horse, but obviously not driven with the same bitter determination. The sight of the pistol was terrifying.

The thud of hooves receded and all was silent. The landscape shimmered in the heat-haze, the white dust settling. In both directions there was now nobody to be seen, the only signs of life two cows and a donkey grazing in the distance, some bees in the roadside flowers, and the sound of a cuckoo echoing in the woods behind. The road onwards was shaded with trees, curving over a ridge and dropping into a valley of sleepy hayfields and wooded commons. No town or village was to be seen, only an occasional cottage roof of thatch or brown tiles. Charlotte scrambled out onto the road and turned her face in the direction the horses had gone. There was nothing to do but to walk on and try to find Kitty's horses and stay her fears with positive thinking: Milo would outpace the Weasel; he was in no danger. Yet she remembered the expression on his face. He had not been without fear; there had been no jokes in his departure.

How stupid they were to meddle with such dangerous people! Yet Mar had killed a man. There was a side to the two men that she had not appreciated: their love of danger and excitement, which was only half satisfied by sport. The image of the Weasel with her pistol disturbed Charlotte, and her own predicament seemed nothing by comparison. The evil woman would use her pistol if it would gain her anything, Charlotte felt sure. It wasn't for show. And Milo did not know she carried it.

She did not know whether to walk back and look for Mar or walk on and try to find Kitty's home. Instinct drew her in Milo's direction. The afternoon was so hot that there was nobody on the road, although in the distant hayfields work was in full swing. It was a long time since she had set off on a walk of some seven or eight miles, which was the distance they had come, but there was no alternative now so, having made up her mind, she started off briskly.

And as she walked she knew, from the nervous way her thoughts dwelled on what might be happening ahead, that her blessed imperviousness to Milo's beauty was failing since her dream of Casimir was dashed. She could not keep her mind from his anxious face as he galloped away. If only she could have helped him! Constance would have ridden like a dervish at his side, not rolling and slithering on the thoroughbred's back like a kitchenmaid. He had not hesitated to abandon her — no wonder! At least she had offered, not waited to be ordered, but in her mind the comparison between herself and the glorious Constance whose face haunted her from the day before was hopeless. Milo was accustomed to sheer class. There was no way he could switch his allegiance to the stupid child she still was.

Everybody fell in love with Milo. Kitty said so. She was no different.

15

"So, what happened?"

Phyllida wanted to know. Charlotte had slept like the dead since arriving home.

"Milo said he left you on the road, miles from anywhere."

"I walked for an hour, and then Mar came along with Ned and the pair. They had caught them safely. I was never so glad to see anyone!"

"Milo was really worried about having left you. He must love you, Charlotte! Thank God it all went off safely. He said it was nearly a disaster."

"Yes. And he never knew the Weasel had a pistol in her belt. She would have used it, I'm sure, if she'd had the chance."

"No. He never mentioned that."

"Where are they now — Mar and Milo?"

"Mar's standing guard over the two horses. Milo left them at Parson's farm on the other side of the village, and Mar has instructions not to let them out of his sight until Milo gets back."

"Back from where?"

"He's gone home, to his parents! Can you believe it? He took Glitters out this morning. Apparently he's asked the Paynes to meet him there. He says going to the Rawnsley home and being met by his mother will put the wind up them before they've started. And he doesn't trust them enough to ask them here. There are eighty servants in the Rawnsley house, and he said he would make sure there were about forty of them standing around when the Paynes arrived!"

"Thank goodness! They are wicked people, the Paynes. But fancy Milo going home, after avoiding his mother all this time —"

"He said it was braver than facing Payne, meeting his mother again. Do you remember how he avoided her at Wengen?"

At last there was time to talk. Charlotte and Phyllida were alone in the kitchen. Clara had gone off with Lily in her perambulator, and Queenie was picking strawberries in the kitchen garden (flirting with the boys, Charlotte guessed). Now that Milo had left, Phyllida wanted all the details. She wanted to know about Kitty's home, what they had for supper, what Charlotte wore for Ascot, who they met there, how Milo treated her, what they talked about . . .

"How did he treat you?"

"Don't be stupid! How do you think?" In her indignation, Charlotte remembered that Constance had been jealous. That was not a figment of her imagination: it had been in Constance's reaction and in the look in her eyes. She did not tell Phyllida this, only that Constance had been there.

"Oh, that woman!" Phyllida spat out.

When she got into her jealous, despairing mood, Phyllida always talked about going away. Charlotte could not bear the thought. What had started out as a schoolkid lark, with friends, was running its natural course, and Charlotte knew that there would be change. She could not be Milo's housekeeper forever.

"Is Mar going to stay, if he's free now?" she wondered.

"You can take his supper up to the farm," Phyllida said. "He's sleeping up there until Milo comes back. You can find out what his plans are."

If they were for change, Charlotte did not want to know. She did some housekeeping (checked the clean sheets, made out a shopping list, swept out her bedroom and cleaned the windows), then took a basket of food that Phyllida prepared and went out to the stable-yard to get Herbie and the trap. Mar's "boys" (one was sixty-five) harnessed the cob for her, and she drove out down the back drive. It was still very hot, and over the wall she heard Queenie giggling amongst the strawberries. Roland was working on the far side of the garden, supporting the heavy fruit branches of the trees that grew against the wall. He was one who would not leave, Charlotte knew.

She sat watching the flickering shafts of late afternoon sunlight dancing through the archway of trees as they bowled along, thankful that the excitement of the previous afternoon was behind her. It had all turned out safely. Mar had found Kitty's horses unhurt, Ned had turned up at Kitty's late in the evening, and Mar had come home on one of Kitty's hacks. There had been no sign of the Weasel in pursuit. But until Milo returned home she would worry. He had not been looking forward to his visit to his parents' home, but the plan was sound.

Charlotte found Mar sitting outside the farm stables where the racehorses were ensconced, idly watching the haymaking that was going on in the fields opposite. His wig was hanging on the prongs of a pitchfork beside the stable door; he was the old Mar with the shouting orange hair tumbled over his forehead and the tiger-gold eyes that brightened at the sight of her.

"I'm dying of boredom here. Don't take your eyes off 'em, his Lordship said. How long will he be? Do you want the job, Charlotte?"

"No fear! Yesterday was enough excitement for me."

He had a gun propped up by the stable door, she noticed.

She put the basket down, and they explored its contents: a meat pie, some fresh bread, tomatoes, a cold custard, and two bottles of ale.

"She's a good provider, Phyllida," Mar said appreciatively, spreading it out on the cloth provided. "She'll make a good wife to someone when she mends her sharp ways. If," he added. "She frightens me."

Charlotte laughed. "A bit of stick — it's what you need. Keep you in order."

"She's like Constance Mathers. I don't like sharp, intelligent women. I like your sort, Charlotte."

Charlotte picked up a small, soft tomato and squashed it in his face. He laughed, and ate it.

"I mean friendly, not dumb."

"A good egg, I know. Phyllida's a good egg, underneath."

"She ought to let it show more."

"It's her way."

Charlotte helped herself to a few spoonfuls of the cold custard. It was pleasant, having a picnic with Mar in the hayfields, the clack of the reaper making its familiar summer noise across the meadows, mixed with the shouts of children playing while their mothers plied their pitchforks. She could have been at the vicarage, looking down across the home fields — the sounds were the same, and the women's labour, and the children's cries. Ascot seemed an age away, almost like a dream.

"What are you going to do, if you're free from your troubles now? Will you go away?"

"It depends on Milo. I'd like to train for him — the racing side is my scene. Not driving carriages. If he could disentangle himself from the wretched Constance, we could get some good winners between us —

jumpers, I mean. That mare of his would jump round Aintree like a stag. But he won't go racing in the winter because he wants to be hunting all the time. With that woman."

"Perhaps he'll get tired of her. It can't last forever." Constance was afraid, Charlotte knew. She knew by the look in her eyes at Ascot.

"I'm glad you don't want to go away," she said.

"Why?"

"I like things the way they are. I don't want it to change."

"You like 'things' . . . what an answer! Do you like me?"

Charlotte laughed. "Of course I like you. Especially without your wig."

"Could you love me, Charlotte?"

"Love you?" Charlotte was jolted by the question.

"I could love you quite easily, Charlotte. In fact I think I do."

He sprawled against the hay bales, screwing up his eyes against the evening sun, not looking terribly earnest, but amused. He wasn't dying of love, like Mr. Carstairs, was her instinctive thought — thank goodness. She couldn't do with that. But there was something in his expression that told her it wasn't exactly a joke. She wasn't sure how to handle it. She said nothing, watching the haymakers.

"If I'm free now, you see, I'm not going to live like a monk. I feel like wooing a nice girl, and the nicest girl I know is you."

Just as Milo said, nothing stood still. The patterns of their lives had become woven together, and now another thread had appeared, strong and bright. She had loved Casimir; she did not feel for Mar what she had felt for Casimir. But now she suspected that what she had felt for Casimir had been transferred to Milo. Yet Milo, she thought, was out of bounds.

She dropped her gaze and remembered Mar the first time she had set eyes on him, and the compulsive attraction that had stirred her outside the boot shop. Before Casimir. She was not fit to answer his question, so confused were her feelings.

"Oh, Mar." How sweet if they could love each other unequivocally. How simple and satisfying it would be. But in truth she could not commit herself.

"I don't know what I feel, about anybody," she muttered.

"Kiss me, Charlotte."

He stretched out a hand and touched her cheek gently. He was such a joky person, but now his face was serious. He turned her head to face him. His eyes, so close, she saw were like Casimir's, golden-brown, and the same expression was in them. Greener, she decided, but the same expression. She did not move away,

"I've always loved you, Charlotte," he whispered.

He kissed her, very gently. She put her arms round his neck and hugged him, moved by his affection, but reminded forcibly of the pleasure she had experienced when she had wept on Milo's breast in Switzerland. She had been starved all her life of simple, loving caresses. Because a man held her and comforted her, and she liked it, it did not mean she was in love with him. Did it?

"I suppose," he said, "you love Milo?"

"I don't know."

"Then perhaps I can persuade you to love me. It all

takes time. I'm not in a hurry. I'm only young." He laughed, much to Charlotte's relief. "I've told you, at least. You can think about it."

Charlotte smiled. She wanted her freedom still, and his understanding was a great bonus. If she was going to love, she wanted it to be fun. At least, with Mar, most things were fun. She did love him, truly, but perhaps not in the way he wanted.

"If I were serious," he said, "I'd go away, out from under Milo's shadow where the girls can see me. They'd all come flocking then, Charlotte, I bet, and you'd be sorry you hadn't snapped me up when you had the chance." He laughed. "Shall I do that?" His eyes were dancing, screwed up into the sunshine.

"No, don't."

"You want me?"

"I want you around. Oh, Mar, I want —" But she didn't know what. She started to scramble the empty dishes back into the basket. "I only brought your dinner. I didn't expect —"

"A declaration of love? Never mind. Take it as a bonus." And he laughed, his love lying easily. If only it were so easy for her.

Charlotte drove home in a daze, relieved as the sun slipped down behind the heavy summer woods. She could not help brooding on Mar — it was impossible not to be moved by his feelings . . . dear Mar. Yet she was thinking all the time of Milo — when would he be home? She would not rest until she knew he was safe. She rather thought that that was love, rather than joking with Mar.

Milo didn't come home that night, nor the next day. It was still very hot, and after supper Phyllida went to bed early with a headache. Clara also went up, and Charlotte was left alone in the kitchen. The door was open to let in the air, although the night was close and threatening thunder. The air smelt of fresh hay — lucky the farmers to have had such an early cut and no rain to spoil it. The last carts had trundled home, and the shaved fields now craved fresh showers to grow again.

In the distance Charlotte heard the soft scrunching of hooves on the drive. It could only be Milo. She felt an instinctive alerting of all her senses, and a sudden pounding of the bloodstream which dismayed her by its force. Surely she was not falling so blindly into the Milo trap, like Phyllida and Clara? Yet all the symptoms pointed to it. She had half a mind to run up to bed and avoid the issue, but her feet would not run, and her eyes would not be turned from the archway where he would appear.

Goodnight Glitters was tired and sweating. Milo pulled up and slipped out of the saddle. He looked as tired as the mare, his face pale and drawn.

"Shall I take her to the stables for you?"

Lie down and you can walk over me, something inside Charlotte said, and she shivered with the joy of it.

"Charlotte. No, I'll take her. Come with me. Is all well?"

"Yes. Mar is still sleeping with the horses. He has a gun. No one has come."

"No. Well, that is settled. They will come for Joker tomorrow. Old Tom will stay with us in case they are tempted to renege on the deal."

240

"And Mar —"

"It worked, Charlotte. They will clear Mar's name, and no more will be said. In return for Joker back, and no word to the Jockey Club. Of course they will hang themselves in due course, but that will be no business of ours."

"That's wonderful for Mar. At last."

"Yes. We were lucky."

The stables were in darkness. Most of the horses were turned out in the summer night to graze, and Milo took off Glitters' saddle and bridle and sponged the sweat off her and turned her out too.

"It's best for her."

He shut the gate, and they stood watching as the mare walked away down the big meadow to the stream at the bottom where it flowed out of Roland's improved lake.

"It's fifty miles from my parents' place. I'm tired, and I daresay she is too. But I couldn't stay another night there. I longed to come back."

We longed for you to come back, Charlotte thought. What shall I do? I am so stupid. And Mar loves me.

They walked back to the house. In the soft darkness Roland's flowers — the pinks and the white-faced tobacco plants — drenched the air with their scent.

"Are you hungry? Shall I fetch you something?"

"No. A glass of ale, that's all. I'm thirsty."

Milo unwound his stock and pulled it off, opening the neck of the white shirt. He sat down at the table and took off his boots, and Charlotte brought the ale from the cask in the cool-room.

"Is there anything else?"

"Are you playing at servants? Don't, Charlotte. Sit down. It's not too late, is it?"

"No. The others went up early. We thought you'd be back earlier."

"It's five hours riding. If my mother had her way . . . oh, what a monster she is! And Constance . . . Constance came there, after Ascot. I wasn't prepared for that. Not the two of them together, and me the pig in the middle. The Paynes were easy compared to those two. It was a mistake to go home, although it certainly intimidated the Paynes — it worked in that direction. But afterwards — oh, God! The undercurrents, the jealousy, the bitterness . . . why do I have to get involved in all that? My mother, perhaps, but why Constance, when she knows . . ." He sighed. "I'm sorry. It's not anything but my own fault. Taking you to Ascot was a mistake, it seems. How strange women are! Would you think . . ." He sighed again.

Charlotte wanted to shout: she was jealous! She was jealous! I saw it. And her corsets so tight she was nearly cut in half, to make herself desirable for you — for you, Milo! To look like a young woman. And she is forty-nine. Nearly *fifty*! And you don't understand, Milo, that Constance was jealous of me (not that she had any reason, Charlotte knew). But Milo didn't understand the half of it. He was more exasperated than upset that Constance was angry with him. Was he starting to grow tired of Constance, without knowing it? Was it as hard to know when you were falling out of love as it was to know when you were falling in? Oh, that he would fall out of love!

Charlotte bit her lip to stop all these stupid thoughts

falling out in speech. Milo would think she was potty. It seemed wonderful to have Milo to herself in the sweet-smelling evening, talking of love, but she could think of no answers. His eyes were far-away, troubled, violet-blue like the lady's sapphire bracelets, the tired cheeks dulled with tomorrow's beard. She wanted to take him in her arms and have him cry his troubles on her breast as she had once on his, but it wasn't the right time for it. So she gathered up his cast boots and clothes and went to light him a candle for his bedroom.

16

In the autumn when hunting started, Constance came home from Scotland, where she accompanied her husband for the grouse shooting, and fell into her winter routine. She came to dinner, but this time, the first time she came, there was no tumbling into Milo's arms before the gaze of housekeeper and butler. Rather, as Charlotte took her cloak, there was a long stare at the two servants. Charlotte was forced to come into the full light when Constance held out her coat, and she had a dark suspicion that Constance remembered her face from Ascot. Mar had resuscitated his wig in order to play butler, for he went hunting now, although he was careful to keep with the grooms and servants and well out of Constance's way. He generally rode one of Milo's young steeplechasers, getting it fit to race. His name had quickly become known for buying and producing young hunters, and usually when Milo's friends called he was one of the party, eating and drinking. Milo had asked Charlotte and Phyllida if they wanted more proper servants to help them, but they declined. It was only for Constance that Mar played butler, and that was partly for his own amusement. "To keep my hand in," he said. "In case I fall on hard days."

Whether Milo was worried that Constance might realize the unorthodoxy of their household Charlotte was unable to discover. She thought he was. It was evident that he was a different person when he was with Constance, far more intense. He did not take their affair lightly, and Constance laid great demands on him, with her tempestuous and scornful nature. For the first time Charlotte, waiting on table, was aware of a row between them, an icy silence falling as she entered, and lasting all the time she handed the dishes. It made her hands tremble. She dropped a spoon, which seemed to crash on the polished table like a tree falling. Constance stared at her angrily, her magnificent eyes glittering with fury. Yet Milo, far from being cowed, was white and distant, like the summit of their lovely Matterhorn, unapproachable. It was he who was impregnable, and Constance the vain climber, trembling with frustration. What were they doing to each other? Charlotte was breathless with agitation and scurried to retreat the moment her job was done. She closed the door behind them with a gasp of relief. Immediately she heard Constance's voice, quiet and vicious, like icicles snapping in the blizzard, on and on.

She went back to the kitchen with the dishes, dropping them with a crash in the sink.

"They're having a row."

The others were agog, Phyllida enraptured.

"How wonderful! At last! Tell us."

"Not before the servants — icy silence. Dagger looks. I think Milo's winning though. She was *fuming* with rage. Milo was sort of — of aloof."

"Oh, what bliss!" Phyllida sparkled like a young girl, her habitual gloom dissolved in smiles of glee. "It's time — oh, it's time. That old woman —"

"He iss not made for old woman," Clara pronounced.

"He's a lovey duck, much too good for 'er," Queenie said. "Time she got 'er comeuppance."

They all worked on the sweet, a complicated confection of meringue and fruit decorated with cream and flowers of angelica and cherries. It was put on a silver tray, awaiting the ring of the dining room bell. They all longed to go in and help Charlotte clear the table and observe the atmosphere. Mar was reading a formbook, with his wig hanging on a chair back. He was not needed for the dining room, only for the closing ceremony when Constance departed and he opened the front door to her waiting carriage. He was amused at the girls' glee.

"You flock of vultures, you. Wait till you're fifty — if you land someone like Milo —"

"She seduced him, at sixteen. That's wicked."

"He must have liked it."

"She rescued him from his mother. But she's as bad. Perhaps he's beginning to see it."

"At last."

Mar thought it was funny. "Rather him than me, crossing swords with that virago."

He was not so amused at Milo's next command.

When Charlotte went in with the sweet, he said, "Order the carriage for Mrs. Mathers, in half an hour."

Mar had to go and change out of butler's gear and into coachman's and rush out to the stable to harness the pair. Roland went to help him with the two-handed job. It was raining softly, and the autumn breeze was blowing wet leaves across the drive. Usually Constance's own carriage came back for her some time after midnight.

Charlotte held out Constance's cloak, and Milo took it and put it round her shoulders. Neither of them spoke. Again Constance stared at Charlotte. There was venom in her look. Then she swung round to the door, which Charlotte had to spring forward to open, Mar being otherwise occupied. Outside Roland stood at the horses' heads. He came round and opened the carriage door for Constance. Somehow he had scrambled himself into some groom's clothes, but his shirttails were showing under the back of his jacket. He closed the door, jumped up onto the box beside Mar, and the carriage departed down the drive.

Milo shut the door and leaned against it, as if exhausted. Charlotte was too intimidated to stop being a servant and waited nervously for orders.

"Shall I clear away?" she ventured. "Do you want anything?" She almost added "sir."

"No," he said. He looked at her and said, "Oh, Charlotte," very quietly, and turned away and went back into the sitting room and shut the door. Charlotte was rooted to the ground. Their unseemly glee in the kitchen was dissolved now into a guilt-wracked pity for the expression on his face. She longed to rush after him and comfort him as he had comforted her when she had

246

cried for Casimir, but she knew she hadn't the authority: he didn't need her silly pity. This was more than the ending of a childish crush. It had at that moment all the drama of major tragedy.

She reported back to the kitchen in a much different frame of mind, but Phyllida's satisfaction could not be hidden. She did not seem to care that Milo was suffering. When Charlotte brought back the unfinished bottles of wine, Phyllida poured them all a glassful and toasted the kitchen: "Here's to Milo's emancipation! Doom and disaster to Constance Mathers!" Clara and Queenie drank, giggling, but Charlotte didn't have the heart and went back to clear up the rest of the dishes. The door of the sitting room remained closed, and the lights were still shining when they all went up to bed.

◆ ◆ ◆

"She is insanely jealous about nothing. She thinks I am having an affair with the girl I took to Ascot, Miss Charlotte Campion."

Milo found it quite amusing in the morning, although how much his attitude was assumed Charlotte could not tell. She could feel her jaw dropping with shock.

"Does she know who I am? That I'm the maid?"

"She didn't say so. But she stared at you, didn't she, in that strange way? Does she recognize you as the same person? I could hardly ask, could I? I could hardly say, 'Don't be so stupid, that was only the parlour-maid.'"

"You could have. Why not?"

"Because I don't think of you like that."

Charlotte refrained from asking him how he did

think of her. They were sitting on a bench at the side of the house, where Roland had said the Elizabethan garden had once been, and which now was a gravel drive leading to the stableblock.

"Don't you see, Milo, if we put the garden back where it was originally, the sitting room doors would open on to it? No one opens them now in the summer because they only open onto the drive. Some stupid person decided they wanted the shortest route to the stables and ploughed over the garden. What sacrilege! The drive can easily go round the other side and link up with the back drive and so to the stables. And I could replant the garden. Look, I'll show you."

He was now planting out a lot of sticks, to reveal his plans to Milo. Milo, ever compliant, said he would consider it. Show him. Roland was showing him. Charlotte had come out with mail on a silver salver, being the housekeeper, and Milo had told her to sit down on the bench and help him decide about the garden. "I'm not much good at gardening. Give me the woman's view." So Charlotte sat with Milo while Roland paced out his new garden.

"Are you going to see her again?" she asked. It seemed an innocuous question under the circumstances.

"She's rather taken up at the moment with Bertie coming to stay — the Prince of Wales. It makes a terrible lot of work and worry. He's coming for a few days' shooting. I don't suppose she'll have time for me until it's over."

"Do you mind?"

He considered for a few moments. Charlotte waited.

"No."

"You've fallen out of love?"

He laughed. "I'm resting, say." Then he added. "I love her when we're hunting. I love the action, I love her courage and her spirit, but I can do without the spite and the recriminations. Like last night. I'm not her puppet any longer. I think I'm growing up, Charlotte. Isn't that nice?" He laughed again.

"Those sticks in the middle mark the sunken pond, with a fountain in the middle," Roland said, coming up to them. "And the birch twigs mark the stone walk. The bamboo canes are the herbaceous borders, and there will be a pleached hedge all round, with archways to the outside. What do you think? Can you see it?"

"I can see the sticks."

"You have to visualize it."

"Visualize it for me, Charlotte."

"Yes. Say yes to Roland. It's exactly what you want."

"Yes, Roland."

"Oh, wonderful!" Roland's face broke into shining smiles, as if he had been given the best present in the world. It was, to him.

"I promise you, on a summer evening, it will be magical, and the sitting room doors will open on to a little terrace, looking down on the water. You will hear the fountain playing and smell all the flowers from inside the room. It will be really romantic. So much better than looking out onto a gravel drive."

"If you say so, Roland. By all means."

"I promise you. I can order the stone?"

"Of course."

Roland went off to gather up his sticks, almost skipping with joy. What a nice boy he was, Charlotte thought. What a pity she didn't love him. He had no time for girls. He always fell asleep.

She picked up the silver salver and got up to depart. But Milo said, "Don't go." As she hesitated he said, "Pretend it's next year and we're sitting in a little garden looking at a fountain playing and smelling the aromatic flowers. Really romantic, Roland said. Sit down."

Charlotte sat. It was a warm, late autumn morning, the sun shining on the wall where they sat, the air very still and slightly misty, a smell of wood smoke from the kitchen garden.

"It will be a mistake, buying this place, if I fall out with Constance," Milo said. "My life is all mistakes."

"Oh no, not at all. Not for us, it's not a mistake. It's lovely. It — you — have been so good to all of us. What would we all have done without you?"

"Probably become splendid, hardworking citizens, doing something that will lead you to fame and fortune. Not cooks and bottlewashers and oddjob men. I don't think I've done you any favours."

"Of course you have."

"Phyllida is wasted — her brain is wasted. Clara should be studying music, according to Kitty; she is very talented. Kitty is going to do something about it, she tells me. Roland, perhaps, is happy. Queenie — fine. Mar will do what he pleases, and you — you, Charlotte, what about you? What are you going to do?"

"Can't I stay here?"

"Yes. I want you to. But not to suit me. To suit yourself."

"It suits me."

250

Sitting with him in what was to be the newborn, romantic Elizabethan garden, Charlotte felt as if its ghosts were already there haunting her. Milo could have been her Elizabethan swain the way he looked at her so gravely, sitting so closely yet not touching her, his voice caressing. She felt herself almost trembling with the suspicion that he might love her. Was it wishful thinking? He was looking at her in what she thought of as a "smoky" way, holding her in conversation for no reason at all. She dare not look up.

"If I were to go away," he said, "would you still want to be housekeeper here?"

She was trapped in a corner. It was unfair. She strived for a clever answer, the sort an Oxford girl would make, tart and witty, but absolutely nothing came to her tongue. All that happened was that she went red and stammered, "I don't know." She got up abruptly. "I have to go shopping. I must go."

"Look at me, Charlotte."

She looked. The blushes were like fire. She found it difficult to meet his eyes, but he demanded it and she stared at him and felt the tears burning behind her eyelids. What was he asking of her? It was unfair, using his native authority to pin her against the wall like a butterfly with a pin through its middle.

"I'm a friend," she said. "Not just a housekeeper. What do you want of me?"

"I'm trying to work it out. Friendship, yes. More perhaps. Certainly not housekeeping. Do you love anyone else, Charlotte, since Casimir? Mar perhaps?"

"No. Nobody."

"Good. Oh, good."

He smiled.

What now, with such prompting, if she were to say to him that she loved him? It was the moment to declare it, but she could not bring herself to speak. It seemed like begging, and terribly unfair to Phyllida, her friend. And besides, she didn't know. She told herself she didn't know, but when she turned her back on him and hurried indoors, she found she was shaking helplessly and quite unable to face anybody in the kitchen. She ran upstairs to her room and flung herself on the bed. Of course she loved him! It wasn't like Casimir because this time it was real, and loving Casimir had always been like living in a dream. And this time she would suffer — oh, how she would suffer! — if he did not mean what she thought he might mean, if he was just playing with her. Now she knew how Phyllida suffered. Now she knew how he had suffered with Constance and, even more certainly, how Constance was wracked with fear that she was going to lose Milo. And she was going to lose him. That was plain. But whether to herself Charlotte had no idea at all.

It took her about half an hour to pull herself together, and when she at last came downstairs Milo had gone out riding with Mar. Phyllida said to her, "You do look queer. Are you all right?"

"I'm as well as you are."

"All right, I only asked."

There was no way of telling Phyllida what was making her feel ill. Phyllida could confide in her, but never could she confide in Phyllida.

❖　❖　❖

A fortnight later, when the Prince of Wales came shooting, it rained.

"Oh, how it rains."

Kitty had come to stay, excited by planning the Elizabethan garden with Roland, but there was little one could do, save make drawings out of the window. It seemed a far cry from sitting by the open doors, smelling the aromatic flowers inside the room. The only water they could hear playing was the rain dripping down the windows.

"Serves Constance right, having Bertie in this weather," Kitty said. They could hear the guns popping away in the woods beyond the kitchen garden. "He'll drive her mad if he has to stay indoors."

Mar had reported that, out hunting, Constance had carved Milo up at a jump and Goodnight Glitters had had to refuse — so violently that Milo had shot over her head into the hedge. Although they were all pleased at the signs of the great love affair coming to an end, both Kitty and Mar were worried.

"She's such a bitch, she won't go without doing him harm," Kitty said frankly.

"Oh, come, what can she do?" Phyllida asked derisively.

Both Mar and Kitty exchanged glances. Kitty said, "In her world, there are ways of harming people that you wouldn't know about."

Phyllida flushed up at the snub, although Kitty had spoken a fact and not meant to put her down. But Charlotte thought that Milo did not care for Constance's social whirl, not as much as he cared for the high snow ridges in Switzerland and the freedom they represented. He had eschewed the world he had been brought up in, and it was only Constance that held him there still. His spirit, Charlotte thought, was elsewhere, and as he grew up Constance was failing to constrain it.

"In fact, I have a feeling —" Kitty stood up abruptly and went to stand at the long window, looking out. "If I were Constance, feeling spiteful —" She shook her head and paused, shrugged. "I can think of a very simple way to harm him. If not harm, deeply embarrass."

They all gaped at her, agog.

"How?"

"He's a Rawnsley. Our mother is a darling friend of Bertie's. What would be more natural, if Bertie is bored, for Constance to suggest they drop in here? They are shooting only half a mile away, and the weather is foul."

They felt the ground rock under their feet.

"The Prince of Wales, to tea!"

They were all in the sitting room. Mar, having been out and gotten soaked, had taken off his boots and socks and hung the socks up on the fender in front of the fire. The baby Lily was attempting her first crawl round the back of the sofa, with Queenie down on her hands and knees encouraging her. Clara had a vast velour curtain spread across the sofa, which she was shortening to fit the landing windows. Phyllida was cleaning some silver at the table, and Charlotte had washed her hair and was trying to comb the knots out of it, covered in a large towel — as domestic a scene as would ever be found in a workman's cottage or student lodging.

Mar looked up and laughed.

254

"Kitty's right. That would be just her style. I wouldn't be surprised if they aren't coming up the drive right now."

The girls all screamed. Queenie went rushing out to the hall to see, Lily started to cry, and Phyllida dropped the cutlery box on the floor.

"Oh no, miss, he isn't. You're joking," Queenie reported back.

But Mar was putting on his socks and boots. "She isn't joking — it could well happen. She must suspect the setup, the times she's been to dinner. And she could well have recognized Charlotte at Ascot. It's only since Ascot that Constance has thrown her tantrums."

"Perhaps she thinks Miss Charlotte's his new lady friend." Queenie laughed.

Charlotte caught the expression on Phyllida's face at Queenie's tactless remark — the expression she had seen too many times, of bitterness and despair.

To cover up she said quickly, "Perhaps we should be prepared, in case Kitty's right. He's only here for three days, after all."

"Yes, we're getting very slack. Where's my wig?" Mar jumped to his feet. "I'm going to get into my butler's gear at once."

Nobody knew if he was joking or not as he left the room.

"I'll dress the part too. It would be wonderful, if it happened, if we were all brilliant," Charlotte said, almost exciting herself by the challenge.

"It would be one in the eye for Constance," Phyllida said. "I'll go and make the thinnest cucumber sandwiches in the world, just in case. Roland sharpened the knives last night, thank goodness."

"And your angel cake, Phyllida — that will charm Bertie. Think how Constance would be enraged, if we gave him a lovely time, and it was all perfection."

Kitty was laughing, seeing how they had all risen to the idea of putting Constance's nose out of joint.

"Oh, but we could do it." Even Clara looked interested for once. She started to gather up the curtain. "I will help Phyllida."

"Of course, if we are ready, it won't happen," Kitty said sadly. "That's the way of the world."

"But for Milo — if you think Constance would be so mean — we would all die to get it right," Charlotte said.

"Of course, it would rebound on Constance — she would have to take the blame if Bertie didn't enjoy himself, as she is his hostess. But she is so wild, she wouldn't care if she offended Bertie, if she could hurt Milo — if that's how it is between them now. Mar seems to think it is. She would be the most vindictive woman in the world if Milo dropped her."

Charlotte felt herself quake at Kitty's words. Remembering the look in those furious eyes, she knew that what Kitty said was true.

When Milo came in for lunch, having been prospecting Roland's new dam down by the lake to see how it was working in the downpour, he was amazed to find everyone at work, polishing and tidying, the kitchen full of cooks cutting and mixing and icing and decorating, and Lily cordoned off in her playpen wearing her best dress.

"Whatever's going on?"

"We thought we were getting slack," Charlotte explained. "In case Bertie calls —"

"He won't call here. What on earth makes you think —?"

"It's an exercise," Charlotte said. "To keep us up to scratch. Kitty says you're to have lunch in the dining room, with her, properly."

Milo laughed. "It's her mad idea — I might have guessed. I suppose I have to change."

"Of course. Look at us."

"My perfect housekeeper. Black becomes you, Charlotte. Has my valet got my dry clothes prepared?"

Kitty had already been in his room and laid out afternoon clothes suitable for a visit from the Prince of Wales.

"Yes, sir," Charlotte said.

She wanted to kiss him, seeing his amusement. He was wet through, his hair slicked down to his skull as he pulled off his hat and shook off his coat. She took his wet clothes.

"The fire is lit in your room, sir."

Milo looked worried. "Don't 'sir' me."

"No, sir."

"Charlotte! This is serious?"

"Yes, sir."

"Kitty is raving mad."

But he went leaping up the stairs and came down ten minutes later in a country tweed suit, waistcoat, high stiff collar and tie. His hair was smarmed down, and he had a gold watch chain dangling from his pocket. Kitty came down at the same time in a different dress with a high lacy neck and a diamond brooch at the throat.

"Shall I serve luncheon now, ma'am?"

"Yes please, Charlotte."

Mar had appeared to everyone's surprise in his wig and white gloves and butler's knee breeches. Between them, he and Charlotte served impeccably. Kitty was very impressed.

"Why, you're brilliant! I'd never have known."

"Thank you, ma'am."

It could become a habit. They all agreed, once they had got into the way of it, it was difficult to stop being obsequious. While she was changing the plates, Charlotte heard Milo say to Kitty, "Constance wouldn't do such a thing. You're being ridiculous to suggest it," and Kitty replied, "You are very sweet, Milo. It's one of the reasons everyone likes you, because you don't believe anything bad about anybody."

"I believed it about the Paynes."

"Oh, such out and out villains — even you couldn't fail to notice evil there. But in ordinary people, it passes you by. Their devious ways, their jealousies, their power games, their petty status-seeking — you just don't see it, do you? Probably because you were languishing in Switzerland when you should have been learning all these things. Evelyn is not very happy there, I learn. He wrote me a miserable letter, poor lad."

"He's well away from trouble, the way it turned out," Milo said. "It might cure his gambling as well as his lungs. I shall visit him when I go again and cheer him up. At Christmas."

"Yes, do that. Poor Evelyn."

When they had finished, Milo and Kitty retired to the sitting room, which Queenie had tidied and polished during lunch, and the servants all stayed in the kitchen. They fetched out the best tea service (never used), washed it ready for use, and polished the best silver tray and the tea urn and anything else that needed polishing. The cucumber sandwiches were all wrapped in greaseproof paper in the cold-room.

"Whose silly idea is this?" Phyllida said at three o'clock, when they were running out of things to do.

"Kitty's."

"At four o'clock, she and Milo are going to have to eat all these sandwiches. Serve her right."

"They're still shooting," Mar observed.

They all listened. The shooting was close, spasmodic.

"Them poor pheasants," said Queenie.

"Perhaps you should keep a look-out, Queenie, just in case," Charlotte decided. "They certainly are close. Go and watch from the landing window. You never know."

The rain was teeming down, harder still, and the lights of their house shone through the grey afternoon. Charlotte thought Bertie would be tempted if Constance were to suggest it. The wood smoke from their chimneys would be hanging in the damp trees, with promise of crumpets and silver teapots. (Phyllida had the crumpets ready.)

Mar took his wig off to scratch his head.

There was a scream from upstairs, and then the rattling of feet flying down the stairs. Queenie burst in.

"Go and look! The front drive. Oh lawks, it's true!"

"It's not necessarily him," Mar said, but he put his wig back on. "I'll go and tell Milo."

They all rushed to the dining room window to look, and Milo and Kitty came hurrying out into the hall.

Two shooting brakes were coming down the drive towards the front door. Charlotte, although prepared, felt her insides quake with horror. It was not letting Milo down that mattered. Even he looked shaken.

"I told you she would," Kitty said to him, angrily. "You didn't believe me."

"No — without warning — what is she thinking of?"

"She'll make the weather the excuse."

Kitty turned swiftly to Charlotte. "Thank God we thought of it! You will be fine, don't worry. You stay here while Mar opens the door. We'll come out of the sitting room when Mar announces them. We mustn't let them see we guessed it. Come on, Milo, back to the fire."

Mar took charge. "Back to the kitchen, all of you. Queenie, if Charlotte wants you, be ready to come and help with the wet coats. Charlotte, stand there. I won't open the door immediately — make it look as if I was in the butler's pantry, where all proper butlers are to be found."

After the others had rushed away he winked at Charlotte. "I still love you, Charlotte. I haven't told you lately. I've a fine leg for a butler, don't you think?" He did a little dance and stuck out his leg in his butler's stockings. "What larks, eh? Cheer up, we'll show 'em."

He gave her a kiss. There was a loud knock on the door. Mar said, "I love you, Charlotte, don't forget."

Charlotte shook herself free, almost spitting at him, and he stepped back and put his white gloves on very carefully and stood pushing them fastidiously down on his fingers. The knock came again.

"Mar!" Charlotte's voice came out like a squeak.

"What shall I do?"

"Go and wait at the bottom of the passage and come up when they're all in the hall. I'll open the door when you're out of sight."

And he stepped forward at last to let them in. His face was utterly expressionless. From the darkness at the end of the passage Charlotte saw Constance standing there, dressed in her shooting tweeds, holding a large umbrella over a bundled-up figure smoking a cigar. Behind them, getting out of the brake, were several shooting gentlemen.

"Tell Milo the Prince of Wales would like to shelter from the rain!" Constance commanded.

"Yes, madam."

Mar stepped back to let them all in and bowed deeply to the Prince of Wales, the man with the cigar.

"Your Royal Highness."

He then backed away and crossed the hall to the sitting room and knocked on the door, as if royalty called every day. Charlotte decided to advance and was in time to take the wet coats that Constance flung at her, aware even then of the intense and angry gaze that came with them. She knew instantly that Constance had expected to find them off guard. When Milo and Kitty came out to greet them in impeccable afternoon dress, welcoming and unworried, Constance was patently seething with disappointment. Milo bowed and Kitty dropped an elegant curtsey, and the Prince of Wales, divested of his outer clothing, was revealed as the familiar figure that Charlotte was used to seeing engraved on mugs and plates and framed on the walls of village halls, a slightly rotund man in his fifties, bald on top and with a moustache and greying beard. She felt herself gaping, instinctively wondering what Elsie would think at the grandeur of it — waiting on the future king! — even aware of his passing appraising glance and his obvious relief at being in a warm house with a civilized welcome.

"I'm happy to let the pheasants be, if there's a warm fire to sit by," he said cheerfully. "We're all chilled to the bone."

They all seemed to know each other; no introduction took place, and they trooped across the hall and into the sitting room, chatting. Mar went in and shut the door behind him, and Charlotte was left to dispose of the vast pile of coats. Queenie came twittering out to help.

"Lor'! Whatever do we do now?"

"Mar will tell us in a minute. Serve tea, I suppose. Which is the Prince's coat? We'd better try and dry it a bit. Heavens, they're all sopping."

"Don't bother with her Ladyship's," Queenie said irreverently. "With luck she'll catch her death of cold."

Mar came out and said Kitty had ordered tea to be served. Everything was going according to plan. Milo had an enormous fire burning in the grate, and they were all standing round burning their bottoms and saying what a splendid little place, eh? How clever of Constance to have such handy neighbours, what good sport, eh? Have a cigar, old chap, mind you don't set on fire, by God! Mar was a splendid mimic, and they went giggling back to the kitchen where the scene was relayed to Phyllida and Clara. Having made such a good start, Charlotte was determined to get the tea right. To her surprise, Clara declined to help and said she must go to her room.

"Miss Kitty say I do it. It iss her orders." Clara looked pale and agitated. "I do as she tell me."

Phyllida shrugged and when she had departed said, "She's so slow anyway, it won't make any difference. Go and get all those sandwiches uncovered, Queenie, and I'll make the tea in the silver urn. Are you going to wheel it in, Mar?"

"I'll take the tea urn and the china. Charlotte can take the crumpets and sandwiches, and Queenie the two cake stands," Mar ordered.

"Kitty said I could pour the tea," Phyllida said. "I don't want to miss what's going on." She was tying on a frilled apron and shoving her hair up into its severe knot. "I'll pour, Charlotte can hand it round, and Queenie can hand the milk and sugar. It's there on the tray, Queenie. Milk or cream. Ask them."

It reminded Charlotte of a vicarage fête, all the bustling preparation, but when they trundled along the passage with the tea trollies, she felt far more nervous than ever she had felt at home.

But the shooting party, nearly all male, were relieved to be warm and fed and not disposed to make too formal an occasion of it, and the atmosphere was relaxed and friendly. The slightly confused service and the one unfortunate "Whoops, sorry!" from Queenie when she splashed the milk on a Harris tweed knee were quite overlooked in the general pleasantries. The Prince was obviously enjoying himself chatting up Kitty, more so, Charlotte supposed, than Milo, who had been appropriated by Constance. Constance was now in sparkling, vicious form, treating Milo like a private possession, at the same time as demanding attention from the admiring male circle around her. Her voice was slightly too loud and her laugh strident. But the cold air had put a wonderful colour in her cheeks, and wet curls corkscrewed across her forehead, escaping from the artful coiffure, with wonderful effect. Even in heavy tweed, her magnificent figure was apparent. Charlotte knew she dwarfed all female competition wherever she went. How could she ever suppose that competition was possible? She noticed the expression on Phyllida's face as she watched her at Milo's side: even those shrewd eyes could not disguise an unwilling admiration.

But Kitty, with her lack of pretension, was charming the Prince without any effort. To Charlotte's surprise, when all the cucumber sandwiches were eaten and the cakes left in crumbs on their stands, Kitty called her over and whispered, "Go and ask Clara to come down."

Curious, Charlotte went up to Clara's room and found her dressed in her long black velvet gown with the rope of pearls round her neck, looking like a prima donna.

"Kitty wants you to go down."

And Clara, without a word, turned and went out of the room ahead of her, sailing along like a galleon with a fair wind, her large shining bun behind sparkling with diamond combs. She did not say a word. Charlotte had to scurry to keep up with her and open the door for her entrance.

"Oh, Clara!" Kitty welcomed her as if she were part of the royal family. She presented her to the Prince, and Clara made a fantastic curtsey right down to the ground. Charlotte felt her eyes coming out on stalks at this extraordinary picture and noticed that Milo was looking bemused, Constance suspicious, and Phyllida as incredulous as she felt herself.

Kitty said to the Prince, "We are very fortunate to have Madame Roskaya staying with us just now. Have you heard her sing? She has the loveliest voice. I sent word to her room about our unexpected guests, and she said she will be delighted to entertain you. If you are agreeable —"

"Of course, delighted."

The Prince lit another cigar, obviously not bothered about the delicacy of the singer's throat and accustomed to such light entertainment at teatime. He was said to take kindly to small amounts of music, although playing cards was his main evening entertainment. Kitty made her way to the piano and arranged some music on the rack, and Clara took her stand beside her, quelling the murmur of conversation with the hauteur of her expression. Charlotte stood marvelling at this unexpected departure, deeply impressed by this unfamiliar Madame Roskaya, who was suddenly unveiled before them. Was Kitty being opportunist or rash? Boring music recitals were commonly given on wet afternoons — there was nothing unusual in that, but Charlotte just prayed Clara wasn't going to make a fool of herself. She was so humourless and stolid! None of them had ever heard her sing, except her soft crooning to Lily to get her to sleep.

Charlotte was standing to attention with her back to the wall beside Phyllida, who was vibrating with similar amazement. Charlotte knew if she looked at her they would get the giggles. Even Mar was exhibiting astonishment; Charlotte could see by the way his eyebrows moved (they were orange again these days, she noticed, making the wig look rather outlandish — she must mention it to him). Milo was standing beside Constance across the room from her, and he sent one quick, amused glance in their direction before composing his features.

Kitty played a short introduction, and Clara opened her mouth.

Having expected anticlimax, embarrassment even, Charlotte was unprepared for the sonorous beauty that suddenly filled the room. Clara's voice was soft and dark as velvet, her control of it utterly professional, and its power and beauty caught them all unawares. Charlotte felt all the hairs rise up on the back of her neck, so unexpected was the impact. Even the Prince put down his cigar and stared.

Clara took on a completely new dimension. Having neglected and even despised the lumpen, introverted girl, Charlotte found herself filled with admiration for the talent she now displayed. The fat-necked, loud-voiced shooting squires were silent, and Milo and Mar were obviously confounded as the voice filled the room with its ravishing sound. It was domestic entertainment on the grandest scale and could not help but impress the Prince of Wales. He was the first to lead the applause as the brief song finished.

"Enchanting! Please let us hear more."

Clara turned anxiously to Kitty, and Kitty whispered, "The Schubert, Clara, the love song."

Whatever was Constance thinking, Charlotte wondered, as the soft, beguiling music filled the silent room? It was clear that everyone was enjoying their emergency shelter intensely — such charming, relaxed hosts, the room full of warmth and light from the enormous fire of logs in the hearth, the brilliant cucumber sandwiches eaten to the last crumb . . . and now the casual introduction of this glorious voice. Charlotte watched Constance, sitting on a small chair by the fire. Milo stood behind her, his hands on the back of her chair. Constance's face was like granite as she sat taking in the failure of her cruel trick — thanks to Kitty's acumen. Only Kitty had realized that Constance had been prepared to offend the Prince of Wales in order to spite Milo. Constance would have taken the blame if the visit had been a total disaster, and offending the Prince of Wales would have meant less to her than the satisfaction of hurting Milo. She was monstrous!

Charlotte lifted her gaze from Constance to Milo and was embarrassed to catch his eye. She felt herself blush as she stared instead into the fire. Clara's voice, very soft, was singing in German, but such was her skill that the meaning of the song was perfectly clear: an outpouring of passion to the absent beloved. As the voice grew stronger and more emotional, Charlotte's gaze was drawn back to Milo's face. She felt the message of the song taking her over, the beauty of the voice quickening her pulse, and again she caught Milo's gaze. This time, she did not look away. She hadn't the will to release her gaze, and Milo made no effort to. It was as if they were locked together, across the room. His face was very grave. The music enmeshed them, as if there were nobody else in the room. Charlotte felt almost faint with the beating of her heart and had to press her hands to the wall behind her to steady herself. She tried to pretend that she was overcome by the warmth of the room — what excuse could she make if she fainted? Milo looked at her.

When the song finished, the spell was broken. There was an impressed silence, which Constance quickly broke by clapping. Everyone took it up and called out their appreciation, but Constance broke up the clamour for an encore with a frosty, "We cannot trespass on our hosts any longer. There will be a search party out for us if we do not arrive home soon."

As they scattered to order the horses, gather the coats, shake out the umbrellas, Charlotte wondered if she had dreamed the whole interlude. When the party left and euphoria broke out amongst the empty teacups, she slipped away to her room and wept on her bed for ten minutes, unable to cope with the confusions in her mind.

Then she felt better, went down pretending she had been to see Lily in her cot, and started on the washing up.

17

The next day Milo and Mar went hunting. The Prince of Wales was scheduled to depart at ten, and the meet was at eleven. Milo and Mar were speculating as to whether Constance would be there.

"I shall be very surprised if she isn't," Mar said grimly.

It was apparent to all that Milo was not anxious to

meet her again so soon. He was in a gloomy mood and unaccustomedly snappy. The meet was nearby, in the village, only ten minutes' ride away. He sat fidgeting in the kitchen while Charlotte ironed his stock — neglected the day before in the fuss and bother over the Prince of Wales. Charlotte thought she must have dreamed the incident during Clara's singing: back now to the clear light of day. The rain had finished, and the morning was frosty and bright. When she had finished and he had tied it and pinned it with a gold pin, she held his coat out for him. He did not say anything.

After he had gone Kitty said, "Poor Milo. Constance won't let him go without a fight. He knows what he's in for."

"She was furious yesterday, because she didn't catch us out. We've you to be grateful for — oh, suppose, if you hadn't primed us —!"

"I know how that sort operates. There are some very ruthless ladies in society, Charlotte, for all their pretty faces."

She took Clara off for some discussions about her future. Apparently Milo had agreed, after last night, that something must be done about Clara. Her talent needed to be aired in London, and Kitty was going to arrange it.

"She will go," Phyllida said. "And good riddance, as far as I'm concerned."

Charlotte was surprised. For all her unrewarding presence, Clara seemed part of the household now, and Charlotte knew she would miss her. She was very good with Lily, and her "hausfrau" qualifications were very useful when it came to the mending, the starching, the ironing, and the sewing. She was better at actually doing housekeeperish things than Charlotte, but slow and lazy, and always needed to be shown what needed doing. She did not naturally work like the rest of them.

"We shall miss her."

"Speak for yourself."

Phyllida was in a very bad mood. Charlotte worried. Phyllida had been standing next to her during Clara's recital, and Charlotte wondered whether — if her imagination hadn't played tricks on her and Milo had really gazed at her during the love song — Phyllida had noticed. Her joy at the apparent undoing of Milo and Constance was short-lived. Edgy herself, Charlotte decided to stop thinking and divert herself — Roland was going to work on the dam and said he would be glad of some help. "The boys" were working in the new glasshouses.

"Why don't you come too?" she asked Phyllida.

"I've the dinner to prepare."

"It doesn't take all day."

But Phyllida did not respond, her lips set in their thin line. When she was old, Charlotte thought, she would be a real harridan.

She put on her boots and her "dirty skirt" and old jacket and went down to the lake. It was high after the rain, the reeds waist-deep. Roland was making what he called the Riverside Walk and was gradually thinning out the wilderness at the far end of the lake where the dam had been built.

"You will be able to walk in a circle, along the side of the lake, past the dam and through the woods — a winding path — which will lead you back to the house via the Elizabethan garden."

He could see it all in his head, exactly as it would one day be. Charlotte saw a dense thicket of overgrown hazel, hawthorn, and sloe with inroads started upon it, no more.

"If I hack it out, you can pull it away and make a heap for burning. Have you got leather gloves? Here, take these."

He gave her his own. His hands were hard as iron and covered in scars. He had grown, Charlotte noticed suddenly — filled out. He had been a lanky youth last year in Zermatt but now would have passed for a mountain guide himself, so muscled and glowing with outdoor health. He struck down the thick bushes as if they were mere reeds. She had a job keeping up with the task of clearing.

Shortly after they started, Milo and Mar rode down the drive on their way to the meet. Charlotte, shielded by the undergrowth, paused to watch. They both rode as if grown to the horse, so easy and relaxed although the horses were excited, and chatting amicably. Constance would be at the meet, in the guise that Milo found the most admirable, displaying not only her beauty but her skill and courage. Charlotte turned and snatched at a large branch. Happy a moment before in Roland's kind and undemanding company, she now felt a surge of resentment and self-disgust, prompted no doubt by jealousy. Today Milo would love Constance, and their estrangement would be over. Milo was as much a dream as Casimir.

And then she remembered that Mar loved her, and laughed. How stupid life was!

While they worked they heard the holloas and whoops of the hunting men and the occasional crying of the hounds not far away. The foxes seemed intent on staying in covert.

Roland, resting his slasher for a moment, said, "They're not getting much of a ride from the sound of it."

"Perhaps they'll come through here."

"We'll open the gate for them and get sixpence for it. What with Bertie and his guns yesterday and this lot today, there's not much peace —"

But shortly they heard the cry of a "gone away" and the thready music of the horn on the far side of the woods. They stopped and listened — a few shouts and the sound of hooves, muffled by the woods. From the direction of the hounds' cries, the fox had crossed the stream below the lake and gone out into the country beyond. After the rain the stream was flowing strongly and Roland said, "If they've any sense, they'll come back this way and cross by the bridge."

"Across your lawn!"

"If Milo leads 'em — it's his lawn, after all." Roland laughed.

There seemed to be a holdup, for there was no sign of any horses in pursuit of the pack.

"They can't get over the stream," Roland decided.

But seconds later they were startled by an excited shout, a scream, and then an outburst of shouting. High above the clamour one voice bellowed, "Milo! Milo!"

"That's Mar," Charlotte said. The tenor of the voice terrified her. "Something dreadful's happened!"

She felt as if her blood had stopped coursing in her veins, so awful was Mar's cry. Roland put a hand on her arm and said, "It sounds bad."

They went forward instinctively, crashing their way through the thick woodland, although dreading what they might find. They could hear hooves now galloping on the home side of the wood, making for the house, the opposite way from the hounds' line, as if going for help. To their left the stream flowed strongly downhill, gathering strength from its damming, and the bank on the side they followed grew higher, up away from the stream. On the far side of the stream was an old manmade bank, to stop it flooding into the fields below, with ancient oaks growing out of it, spreading huge, gnarled roots. If anyone had jumped here, it was fearsome. But in the field below a figure on a horse was coming back towards the stream — a chestnut horse —

"There's Milo!" Charlotte gasped. "Oh, thank God!"

They both slowed, seeing a great milling of people and horses ahead of them where the trees thinned out. Several men were wading in the stream and clambering over the bank while their abandoned horses churned about amongst the trees. Below them in the field a black heap lay in the grass, with steam rising from it.

"That looks like Constance's horse," Charlotte whispered.

Drawn by their morbid curiosity they approached the mêlée. Mar's horse, which Roland recognized, came towards them, and Roland caught it. Mar was down in the stream with some other men, lifting something. Charlotte ran down, sobbing, watching Milo as he galloped up the field and tore to a halt beside the still horse. He flung himself off and ran forward. Charlotte stood on the high bank above the stream, and a man caught her arm and pulled her back.

"Don't cause another accident, silly girl!"

But there was no way she could get down. Milo had jumped this terrible place, a drop of about eight feet with a huge spread, to clear the far bank, and an oak tree overhanging. Constance had failed to make it. Her limp bedraggled figure was being laid out on the grass beside the horse, the face a mask of blood. It was Mar who gently undid the veil and took off her hat. Milo stood staring. His back was to Charlotte; she could not see his face. Goodnight Glitters sniffed the still horse.

The other helpers withdrew, leaving only Milo and Mar with Constance. Some of them ran off to get help — a hurdle to lay her on. They would have to take her out by the field. Roland had already mounted Mar's horse and set off for home to get the carriage harnessed. As the other followers sorted out the horses and started to withdraw, Charlotte was left alone on the high bank, looking down on the tangle of grief below her. Mar had left Constance to Milo, to attend to the horses. Milo knelt by Constance, bending over her, taking her limp hand up to his face. Her hair had come loose and fanned out over the grass, but it was full of blood.

Because she could not get down, Charlotte was stranded on the bank, unable to help. Unable — impossible to even move . . . she felt as if she were turned to stone. She could not look away, yet she did not want to see. Her whole being cried out against it. She could not bear to see Milo kissing the lifeless figure.

Mar straightened up from the dead horse and mounted Goodnight Glitters. He said something to Milo and started to ride towards home along the far side of the stream. Charlotte longed to go to him, but it was impossible. She felt now that she was intruding: Milo was alone with Constance and had no need of her. She crept away from the lip of the bank and turned back into the woods the way they had come. She could not stop crying, yet all her instincts were rejoicing that Constance was felled. Was she dead? She certainly looked it, but there was no way of knowing. Charlotte was not familiar with violent death. But because she was glad she cried the more, for being so wicked.

As she stumbled out by the lake she saw Mar coming across the bridge on Milo's horse. He appeared to be in no hurry. Help for Constance had already been dispatched in the form of the flat farm cart with the two carriage horses. A whole army was running in the opposite direction as Mar came up the drive, and Charlotte went to meet him. He could tell she knew what had happened, and slipped off the horse as she came up to him. He put his arms round her, and she wept uncontrollably with her head buried in his jacket. When she pulled away she was smeared with the mud and blood that covered him.

"Is she dead?"

"I think so." He gave her a little hug. "What a way for it to finish!"

He was as shaken as she was, she realized, and she made a great effort to pull herself together.

"I wouldn't have wished it on her," he said. "But I'm not sorry."

"What happened? Milo jumped it."

"Yes, Milo jumped it, more fool he. She was in a nasty mood and jibed at him when he said it was a bad place. I wasn't close to them but someone told me. She said, apparently, if he didn't jump it she would, and he was very angry and turned Glitters round and jumped it almost from a standstill, right under her nose. Poor little mare, lucky she didn't go the same way as poor Jackdaw. Well, of course, she had to go at it then, and she was in a blazing fury, so they say, and took a bad line and the horse hit the oak tree on landing, and she hit her head on the low branch and was tipped off backwards. Without the oak tree, it wasn't a place that would have stopped either of them ordinarily."

"They are mad," Charlotte said, thinking of the place, shivering.

"You should go on," Mar said. "Get a drop of brandy. You look bad. Go and tell Phyllida the news — she'll love it! I've got to go and find my horse."

"Roland caught it. I think he rode it back."

"Oh good. I'll see to Glitters then and come in. God knows what state Milo will be in when he gets back."

But Milo didn't come back. Not that day nor for several days afterwards.

18

Charlotte was so shaken she had to go to bed. Phyllida said Mar was in a bad way too but went to work it off. If Kitty hadn't been there to organize them, Charlotte thought they would have fallen apart. When Milo didn't come home she was the only one unworried.

"He will be all right, don't fuss. When he can't cope, he goes off on his own."

"How long for?"

"Oh, it could be weeks."

"Where does he go?"

"He never says. Nobody asks. With Milo's moods, there are some things you don't enquire into too closely."

Kitty stayed until the funeral, which she attended as a guest. Charlotte, Phyllida, and Mar went as part of the village turnout, out of grim curiosity and a sense of belonging — for Milo. Charlotte had a crazy vision of Milo turning up and flinging himself on the coffin as it was lowered into the grave but, of course, he didn't. But on the coffin, below her husband's wreath, was a small wreath of evergreen and violets which Kitty had asked to put there, from Milo. It was not refused. Jackdaw was buried where he fell, in a hole dug by Mar and Roland.

Constance was buried in the grounds of Goldstone House in the family graveyard beside the private chapel. The service was held in the parish church, as the private chapel was too small to accommodate the many guests, and afterwards the cortège in all its splendour bore the coffin back to the house. It was a grand ceremony, which kept the village talking for weeks. The representatives from Nettlepot followed on foot as far as their own drive and then turned away and walked home, going in the back way to the kitchen, and gratefully flinging off the black hats and gloves and funereal expressions. It was a cold grey day, entirely appropriate.

"Ah, thank God we are free of her!" Phyllida cried.

But Mar said somberly, "She is the reason we are here. Perhaps we should be grateful to her."

"Never."

"But it's true. Mar's right," Charlotte said.

But later, when Mar and Charlotte were alone, Mar said, "The rift started after she saw you with Milo at Ascot. I sometimes think that she saw something sooner than the rest of us . . . because she was so afraid of it — " He stopped.

"What are you talking about?"

"That you and Milo are falling in love. She suspected it. I wouldn't mention it, save that I am involved too. Loving you."

"Mar!"

Charlotte was dismayed. Mar took everything so lightly; even telling her he loved her was jokily done, and he had never pressed her or become heavy like Mr. Carstairs, but now he had what she recognized as the Mr. Carstairs look. He sat opposite her in a chair by the fireside in the servants' sitting room, his elbows on his knees, his face cupped in his hands, very serious. The others were getting the dinner ready in the kitchen and Kitty was upstairs. The fire between them flickered cheerfully, and the curtains were closed against the dismal wet evening.

"It's true, isn't it?" he persisted. "I saw how he looked at you when Clara was singing."

So it wasn't a figment of her imagination! Charlotte felt a skip of excitement and pleasure in her heart, but took care not to show it in her expression.

She said softly, "Everyone falls in love with Milo, you said it yourself."

"Yes. But who does he fall in love with? Only Constance, to date. And now you. He has very good taste."

"Who says he is in love with me? He hasn't told me."

"The signs are there."

"Oh, Mar." She wanted so badly for it to be true, but she hated to hurt dear Mar.

"Constance knew."

"You are blaming me for her death!"

"For her bad temper, which caused her death. We are all responsible for consequences we can't foresee. You can say Max's foot slipping was the reason we all came here, the reason why Constance acted so rashly. But we can't help these things, any more than we can help who we fall in love with."

"But now that Milo is free of Constance he can love anyone."

"That's true. I hope to God he goes away and finds someone as lovely as you, Charlotte. But why should he, when you are here at hand to come home to?"

"Oh, Mar, stop being ridiculous."

"I'm feeling gloomy. It's the funeral. It's put me in a funereal mood. I'm not good with death. Milo's good at it, being so near himself when he had tuberculosis — that's why he takes such risks, the way he rides, and the way he climbs, because he looks on his life now as a bonus. He told me seven boys out of ten in his ward in Switzerland died. It must alter one's attitude. However, I digress. I love you, Charlotte." He laughed then. "Kiss me."

Charlotte whispered, "I don't love you, Mar. Not like that."

"You can still kiss me."

He stood up and came across to her and held out his arms. She could not repulse him and allowed him to take her into his embrace and kiss her. She was curious, remembering Casimir. What was love? She did not know. She shut her eyes and pretended Mar was Milo.

He lifted up his head.

"You're pretending I'm Milo."

Charlotte laughed. "Dear Mar."

And he said, savagely, "I don't want *dear* Mar!" and held her face in his hands and stared at her. His eyes were golden-green and sparkling with anger. Charlotte was ashamed; but she was angry back.

"I told you, I can't love you to order."

"Oh, God, but I love you, Charlotte!"

And he kissed her again and then flung himself away and crashed out of the room.

"Whatever's the matter with Mar?" Kitty said, coming in a moment afterwards. "I can't believe the funeral upset him that much. It seems to me, dreadful as it is to admit, that it's a matter of good riddance in this house."

"Oh, yes, I think so." Charlotte preferred to discuss this subject than what was the matter with Mar. "What was it like, in the big house?"

"Like most funerals, quite jolly meeting all one's old friends. No one depended on her, after all, and few people loved her. Even her children seemed relatively undismayed. Dear mama was there, being histrionic. I lied to her and told her I was driving home, as I certainly didn't want her coming here."

"Constance's children —?"

"Well, hardly children — they're in their late twenties. Two boys, and the youngest, her daughter, is twenty-five, I believe. She is married to an admiral. A dreadful girl, although beautiful. The nicest person there was

Constance's husband, Willie, a very sweet man who didn't mind what she got into as long as she was happy. He was sad and asked after Milo. He said she would have preferred to go like that, rather than get old and ill, and I suppose that's true. He was very kind about Milo's wreath. I think Milo would have liked that."

"You thought of it . . . where is Milo, do you think?"

"Oh, I think somewhere lonely where nobody knows him. It's not difficult. In his mountains, perhaps, in Scotland, or in Italy. Who knows?"

"He'll come back?"

"Yes, of course. He's happy here. He'll come back."

Kitty got up and started taking the hatpins out of her splendid funeral hat and piling them onto the mantelpiece. "I have to go home tomorrow. My husband is coming back and I have to be there. How are the finances, Charlotte? Shall I leave you some housekeeping money?"

"We've enough until the end of the month. Then we shall run out."

"Fine. If Milo's not back, send word."

"What shall we do?"

Charlotte could not contemplate the house without either Milo or Kitty. Whatever was going to happen, now that the reason for the household no longer existed?

"You just keep the place ready for Milo when he comes back. The same as usual. It's quite simple."

But it wasn't simple, not now, with Mar loving her seriously, and she not knowing whether she was coming or going. Mar said Milo was in love with her, which made her spirits fly so high there was no containing them: she felt sick and dizzy and almost ill, and it was

281

hard to act as if nothing had happened. In reality, nothing had happened. When she told herself this she became deeply depressed.

However, the whole household was lost without its master, and the days passed in restless bickering and inaction. Mar spent all his time in the stables, and even after dinner returned there more often than not because of some equine disorder that needed his attention.

"Are you avoiding us?" Phyllida asked him crossly. "I'll bring your dinner out there if you'd prefer it."

But he did not reply. Why couldn't he love Phyllida, for goodness' sake, Charlotte grieved, so that everyone could be happy? But Phyllida, too, loved Milo.

Kitty returned once, to take Clara to London. She had arranged lodgings for her from where she could study singing with a renowned teacher. "When you are famous, you can pay me back," she said when Clara nobly resisted. Clara departed in a whirl of excitement, jolted for once out of her cowlike calm and sobbing when it came to the goodbyes. For all the appearances to the contrary she had been happy, very happy, with them all at Nettlepot Hall, so she assured them. When she had gone, they missed her more than they expected. The kitchen seemed very empty without her large presence.

"She never said anything much, after all, but she took up a lot of space," Phyllida said, hardly gracious.

"Perhaps she'll become famous, and we shall all go to hear her at Covent Garden."

"Cooks and housekeepers don't go to Covent Garden."

"When we've married our rich husbands."

"Milo, you mean?"

"What, both of us?" But it wasn't a joke, Charlotte could see, only the initial tilt at the difficult situation that would be defused, one way or another, when Milo came back.

He came, of course, without any warning, one evening almost a month after the funeral. He rode into the back yard on a hired horse, chucked the reins at one of the grooms, and came in through the back door, taking the lid off one of Phyllida's bubbling pans and asking, "What's for dinner? I'm famished!"

Phyllida was in the pantry and Charlotte was rifling through the cutlery drawer looking for a sharp knife. Queenie was upstairs putting Lily to bed.

"Milo!"

Charlotte felt as if her lungs had been squeezed of all their breath. Her voice came out in a whisper, and she had to hold onto the table to steady herself. She had dreamed of this moment every day for the past fortnight, and now that it was here she couldn't speak.

Milo looked up, hesitant, and for a moment Charlotte thought he looked as she felt, as if the ground were quaking under his feet, and then immediately she knew it couldn't be.

She said, stupidly, "You're back!"

Phyllida came out of the pantry, carrying a plate of pink blancmange, which she nearly dropped in her shock.

"Milo! Oh, we've missed you!"

And Charlotte saw immediately that she glowed, her grey eyes gleamed with light like sunlight on a winter sea as they devoured Milo's lean figure.

"How thin you are! Where have you been?"

"But you're brown — you've been in the mountains? You've been abroad?" Charlotte pulled herself together.

"I've been in Italy. I've been climbing in the Dolomites. And then I stayed by Lake Como in the sunshine. And went to see Evelyn." He unwound a muffler from round his neck and unbuttoned his mud-spattered jacket. "But I'm glad to be home. My own place. I like this place." He smiled, and Charlotte was touched by how drawn he looked, in spite of the tan, the eyes tired, the hair damp with sweat as he tossed off his hat. "Oh, I'm glad to be home!"

"Does Mar know you're here?"

"I didn't see him. A boy took my horse."

"Oh, we must tell him. He'll be so pleased."

"And my dear Glitters is going strong?"

"Yes. Mar has been hunting her." Charlotte, so eager, wondered the moment she spoke whether it was unwise to mention hunting, but Milo smiled and said, "Good."

Charlotte could not take her eyes off him. She knew that anyone could tell she was in love with him by looking at her. She looked at Phyllida and saw that she too was shining with adoration — the moment so unexpected, so that all their defences were down. And she wanted to laugh at how stupid they were, so feebly revealing their hopeless desires.

By the time Mar and Roland came in the first excitement had been contained. Over dinner it was man's talk, the red wine flowing freely.

"Now the snow is falling, the mountains are magical. And the climbing is quite different — sometimes easier, sometimes harder. We must all go at Christmas and climb together — you must try it. I can't wait until the summer."

He did not mention hunting. Mar looked anxious, but did not broach the subject. He merely said, "It's not easy to leave the horses in the middle of winter."

"Your grooms must be well trained in your ways by now."

Mar shrugged.

"Ten days, Mar. You could spare ten days. I wouldn't stay longer myself. Ben would enjoy it, Charlotte, and even you, Roland — this time of year the garden won't miss you."

"It's very tempting."

"We will go. It's settled. The girls too — you're both tough enough, and it's high time you had a holiday. You can ski — girls are very good at it. It's a great lark. I tried it — you go at an amazing speed, with no effort at all. Downhill, of course. It's not so great climbing up."

Charlotte could not believe the bliss ahead of her — climbing again with Milo. She had no compunction about going. If he invited her, she would go. And if Ben were to be a member of the party . . .

"Oh, what fun! It will be like last year, before Max's accident. All of us, climbing together . . ."

After the men had gone to bed she stayed to clear up the kitchen with Phyllida.

Phyllida said, "It doesn't work like that. If you have a great time and you try and repeat it, it doesn't necessarily happen."

"But we're the same people, the same place, why not?"

"We've changed."

"We're better friends now. It will be better."

"It won't. It's too complicated now."

"How do you mean?"

"You know perfectly well what I mean."

Phyllida spoke with a sudden temper, making Charlotte feel gauche and ashamed. She knew that Phyllida had no reason at all to suspect that Milo was attracted to her; her own excitement and anticipation of the future was fuelled by her optimism that Milo might love her. She could not reply, scolded like a child. They parted and went to their rooms, but Charlotte could not sleep for excitement. Seeing Milo again had started afresh the ridiculous panics, soaring expectancies, and lurches of despair that seemed to characterize the condition of being in love. She turned over and over until all the blankets were on the floor and she had to remake her bed. She wondered if Phyllida was in the same state. But Phyllida had more dignity and resource. Charlotte vowed to be cool and quiet the following day, and full of kindness towards Phyllida.

She woke very early, while it was still dark. A cock was crowing in the stableyard, and the first stirrings of the birds in the ivy came familiarly to her ears. She lay savouring her contentment — that Milo was back — and watching the stars grow pale in the square of her window. It was her turn to do the kitchen fire, but there was no hurry. Mar and Roland went out before it was revived and came back later for breakfast when all was in order. Their routine had fallen into place without difficulty. Milo slept in longer, his privilege.

But her inner excitement prompted her to put her feet out of bed and grope around for her clothes. She did not light her candle, but dressed in the dark, brushed her hair and tied it back roughly with a black ribbon. The old house sighed and creaked all round her as she stole down the passage to the back stairs, and the lingering warmth in the kitchen rose up to meet her as she opened the stairway door. To her surprise the lamps were burning and the fire blazing. Milo stood by the range, watching the kettle that was just starting to murmur on the hob.

Charlotte could not help a squeak of surprise, standing in the doorway. Milo looked up, equally startled.

"Heavens! You're early!"

"I'm sorry." She wasn't sure if he wanted to be alone with his thoughts. "It's my turn for the fires."

"I've saved you a job then." He smiled. "I couldn't sleep. I thought I might as well come down."

Charlotte was too nervous to reply, suddenly wondering what she looked like, hurriedly dressed, her hair not done. As she hesitated he said, "Don't go away. Make a pot of tea, like a proper housekeeper."

Charlotte emptied the teapot dregs outside in the yard. The air was cold and damp, smelling of rotting leaves and sour earth; there was no sign of the sun rising, only a slight lifting of the dark, yet Charlotte felt like singing.

She made the tea, and Milo sat down at the table while she fetched the cups and saucers. He was wearing a camel-hair dressing gown wrapped tightly round his slim frame and his hair, tousled with sleep, fell over his forehead like a child's.

"I shouldn't have run away," he said. "It makes it hard to come back."

"Oh no. I think it was the best thing to do."

"Did you go to the funeral?"

"To the church, yes. Not to the interment at the manor. Kitty went. There was a cortège from the village. It was very fine, and lots and lots of people."

"Willie was always very good to me," he said, as if to himself. "He wanted her to be happy, he said. I didn't repay him."

"Kitty put a wreath on the coffin, from you. There were just the two, his and yours."

It was quiet in the kitchen, the only sound the muttering of the flames in the range. Charlotte was afraid she had said too much as Milo did not reply, but he picked up his teacup to drink.

"It's like losing my *mother*," he said, harshly.

But after finishing the cup of tea he became the old Milo and asked after the running of the house, and Kitty, and whether they missed Clara, and how was Lily? They were laughing over an escapade of Lily's which Charlotte recounted when Phyllida came down. Charlotte had rather lost track of time and jumped up with a flush of guilt. Phyllida gave her a daggers look, nodded a good morning to Milo, and made a great to-do removing the porridge from the oven and stirring it and tasting it and putting it back and crashing the frying pan on the range ready to do bacon and eggs for Mar and Roland. Charlotte felt like a smacked child, and even Milo looked as if he felt in the way.

"I'll go and get dressed."

"I'll fetch up your hot water." Charlotte jumped up, anxious to be seen working.

While she was letting the hot water out of the boiler into the tall tin jug Phyllida said sharply, "That looked very cosy, so early in the morning."

"He came down. I got up to do the fire. It was my turn, remember?" Charlotte spoke coolly, without feeling it.

"Don't get into his bed, when you're up there."

Charlotte did not deign to reply, needled intensely by Phyllida's jealousy. If this was going to be the pattern of behaviour now that Milo was home, the outlook was depressing.

She took the jug up and knocked on the door. When he answered she went in and carried the jug over to the washstand, trying to feel like a proper maid. He was looking for his shaving things, yawning, rattling in the drawers. Charlotte fetched clean towels from the cupboard beside the fireplace and hung them over the towel stand.

"In a minute you'll say, 'Will that be all, sir?,'" Milo said.

Charlotte hesitated, half smiling.

"No."

"Tell me, Charlotte —" Milo looked up from his search. "Did you miss me while I was away?"

"Yes, terribly. We all did."

"I don't care about the others. Did you miss me?"

"Oh yes!"

"Good. Because I missed you too."

Charlotte could not look at him, her breathing hung up in her throat so that she thought she might burst.

"Do you ride, Charlotte?"

"Yes, of course. Not like you — but, yes."

"When you've finished being a housekeeper —

when will that be, this afternoon perhaps? — I thought we could go for a ride. Would you like that?"

"I —" Her voice failed her. Would she like it? Only if it was a quiet horse that would not embarrass her. Her old fawn habit had a hole in the hem. Why did he want her to go for a ride? Was he going to compare her with Constance? She could not control the tumbling thoughts that careered through her brain. *What would Phyllida say when she heard?*

Feebly she heard herself say, "I — I don't know."

"I would like it. A gentle hack. Will you come? Say 'Yes, sir.'"

"Yes, sir."

"Good. At half-past two, after lunch. Mar will give you a quiet horse. One of the greys, perhaps."

What would Mar say when he heard?

Charlotte went downstairs feeling dizzy with shock and excitement. Whatever could he mean? It could surely be nothing but a courting gesture? In the vicarage book of etiquette, nice young men might invite a girl to go for a ride, but only with a groom in accompaniment. Milo had said nothing about taking a groom. Unless Mar was to be invited?

Charlotte was in a dream, stumbling into the kitchen. She did not notice Phyllida's sour looks or hear her snide remarks. She went down to the farm gate to fetch the can of milk left out for them and carried it back without knowing where she was. Roland and Mar and Queenie were sitting round the table, with Milo in his old place at the head, and when she had poured a jugful of milk for the table Phyllida served up the porridge. There was talk of plans, of the Elizabethan garden, the racing of Goodnight Glitters, the rehabilitation of Old Tom as a hunter.

Phyllida said to Charlotte, "I thought we might turn out the pantry this afternoon and scrub all the shelves. We keep putting it off and it really needs doing."

Charlotte looked at her porridge, unable to look at Phyllida. There was a silence into which she had to deliver an answer. She glanced up at Milo, who went on eating as if he had heard nothing.

"I can't. I have to do something else." Her voice was a mumble.

"Such as?" Phyllida asked.

"Something — Milo asked me."

"Oh." Phyllida gave Charlotte a hard and suspicious stare, but enquired no further.

"I asked her to ride out with me," Milo said. "At two-thirty." Charlotte kept her eyes down, tingling with embarrassment. Phyllida made a sort of small exclamation, almost like a snort, and there was a silence, which Charlotte would have described as shocked, but which perhaps was merely a lull in the conversation. But when she lifted her eyes she saw Mar across the table with an expression on his face which made her lower her gaze again instantly. She could not mistake anguish when it faced her and certainly dared not look at Phyllida.

But Roland — dear Roland — said, "Perhaps before you go out, Milo, you could look over my drawing for the garden, because I'd like to get the hedges in this winter if I can, and the sooner the better now that the ground has softened up."

"Of course," Milo said agreeably.

"There are seedlings down by the stream I can use . . ."

Charlotte surfaced as the conversation continued and saw Mar again, back to himself. But Phyllida she could not face. As soon as breakfast was over she went to do some household jobs upstairs and took great care not to go back to the kitchen until the boys came in again for lunch. Her tryst was now accepted, and Mar discussed which horse would be best for her and went to get it ready when he had finished.

Charlotte fled from the table. Phyllida had not spoken a word over lunch, save orders to Queenie, and her face was like stone. I can't help it, Charlotte decided, but her pleasure and excitement were tempered by Phyllida's jealousy. She wondered, had the positions been reversed, whether she would be able to show magnanimity, or whether she too would be torn by bitterness.

At least Mar put on a cheerful face. When she went out to the stable he had the ex-racehorse, Old Tom, waiting with a sidesaddle on his back.

"I can't ride a racehorse!"

"He's no racehorse. He never ever looked like winning — mainly because he's a lady's hack at heart. You'll love him, Charlotte. He's a poor old darling just happy to amble along, quiet as a lamb."

"I hope Milo's not going to compare me with Constance." Milo had not yet appeared. "My habit's a wreck, and I can't ride like her. Oh, do say this horse will behave?"

"Dear Charlotte, I love you too much to have you hurt." Mar's soft Irish voice was so sad that Charlotte was deflected from her silly anxieties.

"Oh, Mar, I'm *sorry.*"

"What, because Milo loves you?"

"He doesn't. Oh — why —?" What a muddle it all was. She wanted to love Milo, but it was hurting her best friends.

"He is courting you. Wait and see."

He helped her to mount and went to fetch Goodnight Glitters. Old Tom felt nice, interested but not too sparky, but before she could take an experimental turn up the drive Milo came out in his riding clothes and hopped up on Glitters with his usual practiced spring. Mar tightened his girth for him and stood back as Glitters skittered across the gravel.

"You've kept her in form," Milo called out, laughing, and then, "Are you fit, Charlotte? Is that nag to your liking?"

"He feels lovely."

As she rode out beside Milo she forgot all the complications that so plagued her and felt excitement and pleasure burning in her cheeks. It was blissful to be alone with Milo, to be his companion, to watch the graceful, gentle way he rode the fractious mare. He was a true horseman, with magic hands, who could get the best out of any horse. Mar said he had bought Glitters for a song, as "unrideable," but now she was the best hunter in the Midlands.

"You missed me, my darling girl, didn't you?" he soothed her, as they rode away between Roland's stakes. Glitters pulled and curvetted, sending the gravel showering. She was underexercised, as no one else would ride her save Mar, all the while Milo had been away. At the bridge, Milo turned away in the opposite direction from where Constance had fallen with Jackdaw, and they went out into the stubble fields.

It was a raw November day, and the afternoon was closing into thick fog. It was luminous, as if the sun would come through, but thick and wet and silent, making a curtain across the distance. They were in a cocoon, isolated from the world, feeling only the horses' warmth as they danced across the golden field, their breath leaving white clouds. Charlotte was in a heightened mood, fixing every stalk of straw, every dewdrop, every sodden leaf in her memory to savour, almost trembling with happiness. Yet it was only a winter ride.

Milo did not talk much or say anything important, but Charlotte felt that he was in accord, not needing to speak any more than she did. She did not think, this time, that it was all in her imagination.

They circled the village and passed the farm where Jester and Old Tom had been hidden. Charlotte felt a pang as they passed the stable door where she had sat with Mar, but it no longer hurt her. The afternoon was dark by the time they got back, and all the lights were on in the stable.

Mar came out when he heard their hooves. He looked disturbed.

"You will be sorry to hear — I couldn't stop her — Phyllida has left."

"Left? Not for good, surely?"

"She said so. She took a suitcase. She wouldn't say where she was going."

"Why?" Milo was astonished. "With no warning?"

"She wouldn't say."

Charlotte knew why, and she guessed Mar did too.

She exchanged a quick glance with him and felt an angry despair ride up over her joy. Her anger was completely selfish, Phyllida's martyrdom taking all the pleasure out of her own happiness. She knew also that she would miss Phyllida's companionship terribly. Phyllida was the only close woman friend she had ever had. She felt like bursting into tears.

"I don't understand it." Milo jumped down from Glitters and started to undo her girth. "Why didn't she say if anything was wrong? Have I offended her? She was happy, I take it, while I wasn't there?"

"She's a temperamental one — it's not your fault," Mar said.

"Of course, she's far too clever to be a household cook. None of this was going to last, it's clear, but I thought she would — well —" He shrugged.

Mar and Charlotte exchanged stricken looks again as Mar helped her dismount. Milo led Glitters away to the water trough, and Mar said, "He's no idea. I nearly went with her, don't tell him that."

"Mar!"

But there was a light in Mar's eye. "Have I told you I love you, Charlotte?"

"I don't remember." She had to smile. Phyllida took life far too seriously; she rarely laughed. But Mar could cover his feelings with jokes. It was hard sometimes to tell how serious he was. Charlotte found her mood swinging, not knowing whether these love complications were fun and exciting, or deeply traumatizing, as Phyllida had found. One's feelings were heightened to such a pitch that plain sense was hard to recognize.

All the same, practical considerations quickly overtook them. There was no dinner, and Charlotte had no idea what was in the pantry. There were three starving men to feed, as well as Queenie and the baby. Phyllida's job had been no sinecure.

"Perhaps she got fed up with it, miss," Queenie said, as they rummaged through the larder. "Just got fed up with it. You know the feeling."

"No. I've never felt like that."

"Nor me neither — not here. But at the other place — well, I can tell you —"

Charlotte thought it odd that neither Milo nor Queenie had the faintest idea.

They fed on half a cold duck, some potatoes baked in the oven, some greens out of the garden, and the remains of an apple pie. Without Phyllida they were all rather subdued. She had certainly been a splendid cook, and Charlotte knew that she would never take her place.

"I can try," she offered. "I would learn as I went along."

"No, it's too much," Milo said. "I'll get Kitty to come over and decide how to arrange things. We shall have to get a cook from the village, I suppose, but —"

They all knew no village woman would accept the way they lived, dish up the dinner, and sit down at table in the kitchen with the boss. She would be too embarrassed. Even Queenie, although she sat down with them, sat apart and never joined in the conversation. She always did the serving and clearing away and removed herself as soon as she had finished while the others sat on, talking and drinking. But now, with both Clara and Phyllida departed, the party atmosphere was missing.

Kitty came as soon as she got Milo's letter. Milo and Mar had gone hunting, and Charlotte was in the kitchen alone, cooking, when the rakish pair of chestnuts flew up the back drive. One of the grooms came out for the horses, and Kitty came in to warm herself at the range.

"Oh, I'm frozen! The wind is bitter. Dear Charlotte, have you turned cook?"

"It's awful. I'm hopeless. Nothing like Phyllida."

Kitty sat down and stuck her feet out towards the fire. She looked marvellous in her caped driving coat and outrageous hat held down with veil and pins. She started undoing this confection carefully, dropping the hatpins on the hearth.

"I can't stay long because my husband is at home. Milo said something about going to Switzerland at Christmas and would I like to come, and this time I thought, yes, I would like to join the party. Is that still the plan?"

"Yes, I think so. It would be marvellous if you came."

Charlotte had decided that without another female member of the party she would be very ill-advised to go. Her grandfather, if he heard of it, would be horrified. Both Mar and Roland were going, and Milo said Ben too, for part of the time, and the thought of missing it had been casting her down. Kitty's declaration cheered her immediately.

"So why did Phyllida go?" Kitty demanded.

Charlotte did not know how to reply.

"I think I know," Kitty said. "It's Milo, isn't it?"

"I think so. He asked me to go riding with him, and I think she couldn't bear it."

297

"Well, it's best. Don't worry. We shall have to hire a proper cook and housekeeper, and you and Mar and Roland will eat in the dining room and use the sitting room as his friends, staying. Milo's original idea was splendid, but it was bound to be temporary. Now Clara's gone, and Phyllida. And your status, Charlotte, is changing, I think. He's never asked you to ride out with him before?"

"No."

"It's good news. Dear Charlotte, I'm full of hopes!" And she jumped up and hugged Charlotte, getting flour all down the front of her bright clothes. "What are you cooking? Shall I help you? We'll have a celebration dinner tonight — what fun!"

"To celebrate Milo's coming home?"

"Milo coming. Constance going. And Phyllida."

"Poor Phyllida."

"She wasn't much fun. I'm not much of a cook either, but I'll do my best. What is there to cook?"

"Queenie went out and got some ribs of beef and there's lots of vegetables —"

"And Yorkshire pudding and horseradish. Good. I'll get changed and we'll start. What are you making?"

"An apple pie. They like apple pie."

"And all those parsnips in the basket — I can make parsnip soup. And I'm good at custard. You must have eggs?"

The atmosphere always changed when Kitty was around. She rushed up to her room and came down in a working dress and apron, ready to start. Queenie was sent to prepare the dining room and light the fire, and Kitty started making the soup. Charlotte fetched the best wine from the wine cellar. When the men came in they were all dispatched upstairs to wash and change for dinner, and Queenie was sent scuttling with the hot water. By the time they were ready, somewhat bemused, the hall was suffused with the smell of roast beef and burning custard. They went into the dining room with the whiskey bottle and stood round the fire scorching their trousers while Queenie came rattling down the hall with the soup in a large tureen on the trolley. Kitty and Charlotte flung off their aprons and ran after her.

"All we need is the Prince of Wales to roll in," Mar exclaimed. "Is this a new regime?"

"Yes. You must learn to toe the line. You're not students any more."

"Come back, Phyllida!" Mar lamented. "All is forgiven."

"I still can't fathom why she went," Milo said. "Without a word, and no message. I would have thought —"

"She went because she was in love with you and couldn't bear it," said Kitty bluntly. "That's why she came in the first place. Why else would a lady of her brain take a job as a cook? Where are your wits, Milo?"

Kitty's tongue was no doubt loosened by the glass of port she had drunk whilst making the gravy, but as it was only Milo himself who did not know the reason for Phyllida's departure, her declaration did not come as a shock. Milo flushed violently and could find no answer. He stood in front of the fire in his evening clothes, the whiskey glass in his hand, and did not move as the others all went to their places. Charlotte looked up and saw the grey-blue eyes, bemused, staring at her. She felt as if she were alone in the room with him, all the chatter behind her with the rattle of the silver tureen lid and Queenie's "Lawks, sorry!" He moved forward and put his arm round her shoulders and gave her a little hug, and then a sketch of a kiss, his mouth brushing the tendrils of hair that curled down in front of her ears.

"Poor Phyllida," he said. "Dear Charlotte."

He pulled out her chair for her, and she sat down next to him, quivering with her bolting emotions. No wonder Phyllida had fled, to preserve her sanity . . . Charlotte could not control her thoughts. And then she looked up across the table and saw Mar's face, like a storm cloud, watching her. She bent her face to the soup, her heart hammering as if she had run in a race. Suppose Mar went too? Her spoon clattered against the soup plate.

But after the shocks the party mood prevailed. The beef was overdone, the apple pie too sour, the custard scorched, the wine too cold, but not a scrap was left. They digressed to the sitting room where Mar and Milo sang songs at the piano with great gusto, until Kitty said they were getting too rude, and then they sat round the fire discussing plans for the winter expedition to Switzerland. Now that Kitty had decided to come, the vague plans Milo had aired were firmly put in place by Kitty, with dates, train times, hotels all to be discussed. The more pressing discussion concerning a cook, housekeeper, and extra maid was eschewed by Milo. "You fix what you think best, Kitty dear. I'm sure it will be correct. And we'll behave however you think fitting."

"I will discuss it with Willie Mathers' housekeeper tomorrow. I'm sure she will know of suitable servants."

Kitty was so assured at running a household. Once she arrived, all problems were sorted out in no time. One scarcely remembered there had been any.

Charlotte went up to bed when Mar and Roland went. Kitty got up too, yawning, but Milo said, "Stay awhile, Kitty. I want to talk to you."

As she shut the door Charlotte saw them sitting together over the fire. They meant a lot to each other; much as Charlotte loved Ben, she knew they had never had the rapport that Milo and Kitty had. Poor Phyllida had nobody. Charlotte ached for the void that Phyllida had left and for the unhappiness that possessed her.

19

To Charlotte's joy, Ben could take a few weeks off for Christmas. They met on the platform at Victoria and embraced wildly.

"We ought to be going home." They both had the same thought and voiced it together.

"We'll go for a few days when we get back," Ben decided.

He was introduced to Kitty and enquired after Phyllida. They tumbled into the train, laughing and joking.

"Phyllida's gone away we know not where. Cooking was getting her down," Kitty said tactfully.

"I hope you're not depending on Charlotte," Ben said.

"No. Her standard is much the same as mine —

we've decided to spare the boys our efforts. We have a proper lady starting when we get home — a Mrs. Armstrong. Not a gorgon — Milo was very strict. She laughs a lot."

With the addition of Ben and Kitty the party was refreshed, and a holiday mood prevailed. Charlotte was relieved to be away, spared the awful chore of cooking, and anxious for a change of scene. She did not know where she stood with Milo, only that she loved him hopelessly. If he turned to someone else, she too would have to go away, like Phyllida, for it would be unbearable. He had made no move to change their relationship, only inviting her to go riding several more times, presumably enjoying her company away from the others. It was only six weeks since Constance had died, and she knew that he was still bound to Constance in many respects, although he never spoke of her or of his feelings. His attitude was inscrutable. She sat opposite him in the train and when during the long ride through France the others dozed, she stayed awake watching him. The dim oil light flickered over his finely drawn features. He was too thin, she thought, and had the look of a consumptive, with the cheekbones prominent because of the spareness of flesh, the nose chiselled and proud with delicately curving nostrils, the lovely mouth tranquil in sleep, not sagging or downturned. He had a very sweet face. It did not boast strength, but she knew he was strong, with his mountain climbing, his long days of hunting, and his authority over people. Watching him, she had a sudden fear that perhaps the consumptive state would return. He never seemed to put on weight and sometimes looked very tired. She had always thought the tired look was because of the strain of the affair with Constance; he had always looked better when Constance was away. And she wondered, with a sinking of despair, how she could possibly take the place of Constance . . . she was deluding herself. It was Mar's jealousy that had prompted him to see love where no love was and fuel her hopes.

She tried to make herself more comfortable, to sleep, as the train rattled its way towards the Alps across the sleeping farmland of France. She was excited about the holiday but knew it marked a change in the pattern of life at Nettlepot, perhaps a breaking up. The future was very uncertain.

They went back to Zermatt, Milo having decided that he liked the place too much to be put off it by Max's death. After all, Max had not been a close friend, only a casual climbing companion. Milo had been going to Zermatt long before he met him.

"Besides, Kitty's not made for roughing it. Kitty likes nice hotels."

He insisted they all stay at the Monte Rosa at his expense. Mar was amused, remembering his hay barn. Charlotte was not anxious to meet Casimir again, but word had it that he was in the Oberland visiting his wife's parents over Christmas, so she was spared the trauma. She shared a room with Kitty, and as they spread out their things and bounced on the beds she realized suddenly how lucky she was — how crazy to make herself miserable with all the things that might or might not happen when she was enjoying this luxurious life, with her best friends, in this wonderful setting. It was scarcely eighteen months since she had been venturing away from home for the first time in her life.

"Kitty, I am so lucky!"

Kitty, putting another log on their fire, looked up and said, "Yes, you are. Indeed you are."

She spoke in such a serious, old-fashioned way that Charlotte was surprised, but then Kitty laughed and said, "Milo knows how to enjoy life. He only likes comfortable hotels, he says, when he has spent a very hard day outside first. Myself, I like them all the time. I don't feel I need to earn them. Milo has a very spartan character."

Zermatt was deep in snow, and in the street one or two horse-drawn sleighs slid past, bells jingling to mark their otherwise silent passage. It was very quiet, unlike during the summer, with very few visitors. In the dusk of the late afternoon the mountains loomed eerily white against the darkening sky. It all looked very different, so still, locked in the snow, the river gurgling softly between frozen banks and the small streams hidden away under great mounds of untouched snow. But Charlotte felt very at home. The head waiter had bowed to her in recognition and had given them the best table.

Milo was not intending to do anything rash.

"Some guideless walks to get our legs working, up to Schwarzsee, or perhaps the Riffelalp, see how it goes . . . if the weather is fine and the conditions right and we can get a guide, we might try the Dom or the Rimpfischorn, sleep in the hut —"

"Oh, not me." Kitty gave a shudder. "Charlotte perhaps, but I'm having my supper down here."

"Just the chaps then. We'll soon find out what conditions are like. How about the Staffelalp tomorrow? That would be a good starter."

They all slept in after the long journey and woke to the strange white light that gleamed from below on the bedroom ceiling. The village was muffled and silent — how strange, with the memories of the summer rabble still fresh . . . Charlotte was enchanted with this world they had to themselves. After a huge breakfast, and loaded with more food in their knapsacks, they set off late up the track to Z'mutt. Charlotte and Kitty wore riding breeches with a skirt over and quite soon abandoned the skirts, feeling that their jackets hung low enough to make them decent. The track was trodden and hard, but even off it the snow was hard enough to walk on without falling through. It crunched and squeaked under their boots, and the air was sharp and glittery, making the eyes water, the breath hang in chill clouds. The pine trees bent under their fretted canopies of snow, occasionally shaking off their burdens as the sun climbed over the shoulders of the mountains. Above them the Matterhorn stood mantled in blinding white, only its highest crags, too steep for the snow to settle on, bared to the milky sky, dominating the valley. From its summit a plume of white vapour streamed out like a pennant, the only cloud in the sky.

"You can be up there, in a great storm of thunder and hail and lightning," Milo said to Charlotte. "Yet only there — all the rest of the mountain is clear and sunny, and when you come down nobody believes you."

"I want to climb it."

"So you shall, when the time is right."

They crossed the gorge of the Z'muttbach, which

was now stifled by snow and ice, and creaked on over the snow. There was a path of sorts but not much used in winter. It passed across the spreading skirts of the great south face of the Matterhorn and on up over a high col to Arolla in the far valley. They were now high and out in the open, and the sun was warm on their backs. They stopped to rest and eat their provisions, vast sandwiches of hard, dark bread with salami and goat's cheese. Kitty wrinkled her nose.

"I'd rather have Phyllida's cucumber sandwiches, as made for the Prince of Wales."

"Where is she? I wish she was with us," Charlotte said involuntarily. "She would love it here, in the snow."

Nobody said anything, and Charlotte realized she had not been tactful. She bent to her man-sized sandwich, and as she did so a sound like an explosion echoed from far up the valley ahead of them. There was a distant rumbling and growling as if the very mountain were complaining, and a haze of what looked like white spray drifted over the horizon.

"Whatever was that?"

"Avalanche," Milo said.

"It sounds like gunfire."

"Even small ones sound dramatic. Imagine being in its path!"

"But snow is soft."

"More than six feet on top of you, you die," Milo said. "And it's not soft. In falling it compacts and finishes up as hard as concrete. And it bowls you down, it knocks you about. Sometimes whole villages go under."

"Not Zermatt, I hope."

"No. Mostly they've learned where it's safe to build. And the forests are a good protection."

"It must be like the mountain eating you, to get caught in an avalanche."

"What a delicious morsel!"

Milo laughed.

None of them felt very energetic, not yet adjusted to the rarer air of the high valley, and as the days were so short — "That's the big disadvantage of winter climbing," Milo remarked — they started back after they had eaten. Yet, so beguiling was the dying day, the shadows lengthening across the crystal snow, the air so still and silent across the valley, that they were loathe to leave it for the prosaic evening below.

When they got down as far as the tree line Mar suggested they make a fire, and the idea was taken up with enthusiasm. They collected a large pile of dead branches, and Mar fanned the flames under a cushion of pine needles and small twigs until the fire caught and was ready to devour the logs. It crackled and hissed, and the sparks spun up into the sky to join the first pale stars. The smell of scorching tweed compelled them to back off as they crowded round, steam rising from their legs — a domestic situation that was completely contradicted when they looked up the valley to the towering face of the Matterhorn, its peak now serene and clear of cloud, the ice sparkling on its sheer crags like diamonds in the firmament. It seemed to fill the sky, austere and remote. To think of men gaining its heights seemed as absurd at that moment as thinking that a man could stand on the moon, so hostile and yet so unfairylike its snowlaced cliffs in the starlight.

Charlotte stood away from the fire, watching, and thought, I shall remember this moment until the day I die. The world seemed a much bigger place than she was accustomed to and its glories prodigious. The beauty of the flames against the icy snow and the warmth of the company made her feel giddy with joy — an adolescent emotion, she supposed, so strong and yet illusory: she had to stand apart, almost trembling. Then Mar closed in and whispered, "I forgot to tell you today — I love you, Charlotte. Have you forgotten? I have to work at it." His eyes were golden points with the flames reflected; they seemed to be laughing, but she could not tell. She saw then by the faces in the firelight that they were all infected with the same fantastic delight in the situation, and nobody wanted to go on their way. The fire stabilized, and a great heap of glowing embers surrounded the burning logs, and they stayed watching it and talking until the sky was quite dark and the stars were bright above the mountains. Down the valley lights came on one by one. Charlotte had a sudden twinge of heartache for Phyllida, missing this.

Of course they stayed too long, and there was still a long way to go, and by the time they came down into Zermatt they were cold and tired and hungry, and the last mile or two seemed like ten. The lights of the hotel were a welcome sight.

◆ ◆ ◆

The next day it snowed. Kitty wasn't going out. She had brought drawings of Milo's Elizabethan garden with her, and when Roland saw them he started discussing it with her.

"Tell me where you're going and I'll catch you up," he said when Milo, Ben, and Mar were ready. He was engrossed in his pet subject, the sheets of drawings spread over the breakfast table.

"You're on holiday," they complained.

Kitty said, "On holiday you do what you want to do most. Roland wants to do this most."

They certainly looked very comfortable, conferring over the table with the big dining room fire roaring in the grate behind them. At the windows a grey veil of snow cut off the outside world.

"I doubt if we'll go far, unless it clears," Milo said. "Just get some exercise."

Charlotte went with them, just to walk through the village. The cold was bitter. From the chalets rich, warm odours of wintering cows drifted from the barn doors, and the manure heaps steamed freshly into the driving snow. Beyond, there was nothing to be seen. Charlotte turned back when the three men made for the path to Winkelmatten, deciding they could walk up through the forest. She could not face passing Casimir's chalet with its humiliating memories, and she knew that they didn't want her to accompany them, although they did not say so.

"If it clears I'll come this way later to meet you."

There was no visibility. They disappeared immediately in the swirling snow, following the path, which was still discernible, and Charlotte went back to the hotel. There, with a fresh coffee pot, she found Kitty and Roland still engrossed in their garden. They made a good pair, she thought, smiling. Perhaps when Kitty's old husband died, Kitty could marry again, and Roland would suit her, even if he was only a gardener.

Fortunately the bad weather did not last long, and they were then treated to two weeks of almost perfect weather. It was more than they had dared hope for. The snow was thick and hard, and walking on it was nearly always easy. After the first week Charlotte found she had acclimatized, and her strength improved dramatically. She had always been active and agile, and she was relieved to find that her natural climbing skill had not deserted her in these different conditions. Where the men went she could go too. Kitty was not so keen but refused to hold Charlotte back, assuring her that she found plenty to amuse herself with down in the village. She had her painting things with her and was absorbed by the very real difficulties in painting the scenery in the ever-changing light.

"Go and play, dears. I have my intellectual pursuits to follow."

"Lazy!" Milo taunted her. "Because you haven't got a horse to do it for you —"

"I hire a sleigh. It's fantastic, driving in the snow."

But Milo was only interested in the heights. Because it was so cold, sleeping high in the mountain huts in order to tackle the peaks was extremely uncomfortable.

"It's not for women," Mar said sternly.

Charlotte did not argue, for she was not stoic enough to want to do it.

"I'll climb as far as the hut with you, then come back."

"You can't come back alone," Mar said. "I will come down with you." He said it in a martyred tone of voice, but his eyes were glinting.

Milo said, quite sharply, "We will have two parties.

310

I will do a day climb with Charlotte, and Mar can lead the two-day climb."

"And then we'll switch, and I will do a day climb with Charlotte, and you can lead the other."

"Why, how popular you are, Charlotte!" Ben said, and laughed.

But there was a strange tension, and Charlotte noticed that neither Milo nor Mar was amused. It was the first time Mar had ever remotely challenged Milo's authority, and the way he spoke was considered, not flippant. Charlotte could never work out how serious Mar was for, although he reminded her at intervals of his love, he did not persist or become boring on the subject. Presumably he knew how hopeless it was while Milo was around, and for his forbearance and dignity Charlotte loved him. But not how she loved Milo.

But Milo, until now, had shown little preference for her company. So what was she to think?

"You are to realize, dearest Charlotte, that I wish to love you. But — how can I explain? — my being is still in thrall to Constance. She is so strong and will not let me go. It takes time to get myself disentangled, like beating my way out of a dense thicket, like swimming up out of deep, dark water towards the light. I must be free of her first before I can make my approach to you. I mention this because I think Mar loves you. The signs are there. Has he told you?"

"Yes."

"And much as I respect Mar, I have no scruples in putting myself first — before Mar . . . that you should love me, not Mar."

Milo said this as they walked next morning up the path to the Riffelalp in bright sunshine. The path was now clear, the visibility brilliant. The peaks towered on every side sparkling with fresh snow; the sky was cloudless and without a breath of wind. Charlotte felt she was walking in paradise with these words in her ears and the peerless landscape all round her. She had to stop to get her breath, feeling the tears filling her eyes at the brightness of the snow — or at the amazing words like crystals hanging in her ears; she could not tell.

The others had hired a couple of guides and departed for the Dom, and Milo had invited Charlotte to accompany him for a day climb. At first she had thought he was doing it out of kindness, foregoing something he would rather have done. But he had dismissed her protests impatiently, and she had been left with mixed feelings — half exasperation that she was burdening Milo with what she thought of as a duty, and half excitement that she had him to herself. And now this — she did not know whether she was laughing or crying.

"I love you," she said. "Mar knows I love you."

Milo did not say anything, steadily climbing the path ahead of her. Charlotte had no breath, both with the climb and her glorious astonishment at Milo's words. When she stopped, putting her hand to her side where the stitch was needling her, he came back to her and put out his hand. They had gloves on, but it made no difference to Charlotte. She felt his commitment in the powerful grasp, like shaking hands on a bargain, and he said, "It will be all right, Charlotte, I promise you. In a little while." Then he added, "Don't love Mar. Please."

He was looking down on her, his head framed by the burdens of snow that lay on the pine branches above him, and she remembered him always like that, the expression of slight anxiety, of compassion, not in any way jokey, and the steadiness of the gaze, very blue as if the sky was lending its brilliance. And the steadiness seemed to flow into her own being through the clasp of their hands so that all the silly, flaring hysterics of schoolgirl passion were calmed into certainty. She knew that he would love her as she loved him.

And after that she climbed steadily, without tiring, like a boy, and Milo had no need to give her his hand.

◆　◆　◆

In the early afternoon they retreated. They turned away from the minor crags they had scaled and started for home down a long snow slope. On one side it fell steeply down to a glacier, but their direction lay on the far side where a path led down into the forest. The day was too short to linger, or to extend. Milo had been tempted to cross the glacier and go down on the other side, but he thought it was too dangerous.

"The crevasses fill with snow and you can't see them. But you can go through, if you're unlucky. I'd miss you, Charlotte, if you disappeared down a crevasse."

"Thank you," she said.

Strangely, she thought of Phyllida. How difficult it would have been if Phyllida had not gone away . . . what had seemed hasty at the time was now revealed as a stroke of wisdom. But, descending, caught in this delicious haze of physical and spiritual contentment,

Charlotte spared her a guilty thought. Phyllida would have loved these winter mountains, the remote peaks swimming palely in the thin, icy atmosphere, and the utter silence that wrapped the valleys, the stilling of the cowbells, the muffling of the waterfalls in cloaks of ice . . . only the scrunch of their boots and their own breathing disturbed the stillness.

There was a steep wall of crags above them at the top of the snow slope, hung with ice. As they made their way down, a stone fell from the top and landed with a soft thud in the snow above them. Milo, in front, stopped and looked up. He stepped back and grasped Charlotte's hand.

As if the falling rock had disturbed its neighbours in some way, a shower of small stones followed, pinging into the snow and disappearing. Then, quite slowly, another large rock seemed to teeter out of the sky, leaving a gap like a missing tooth in a child's mouth. Charlotte heard the whistle of its fall but knew they were not in its path. It crashed into the deep snow with a muffled explosion that echoed all round the surrounding mountain faces, even from the mighty face of the Matterhorn itself. Imperceptibly, the snow on which they were standing started slowly to slide beneath them.

"Milo?" Charlotte was more puzzled than afraid.

But Milo grasped her hands with a grip that hurt.

"Charlotte, will you marry me?" His voice was very urgent, his eyes sharp and excited. "Say you will, promise, before it's too late."

"Yes, of course!"

"Then run! You must fight, Charlotte, don't let it take you! Because I want to marry you."

And taking her hand he started to run across the moving snow, pulling her after him. And Charlotte realized that the whole mountain was moving beneath her feet, the snow unanchored from its grip on the mountain and sliding, faster and faster, towards the glacier far below. As fast as they ran, so faster the snow bore them, and the drifts of soft, loose snow, resting at the top of the slope, unfastened, came sliding and skittering down in innocent-looking clouds. But far from a soft embrace the clouds were heavy as steel and knocked them down, and the sky was blotted out in darkness.

And in the seconds it took to fall, Charlotte's early life flashed through her mind with startling clarity, just as the books always said. One wasn't to guess, until it was actually happening. She saw the buttercups in the field below the vicarage spread yellow and wide in the sunshine, knee-deep to the pinafored children passing. She saw the meadows and woods beyond filmed in the milky blue haze of spring and smelled — yes, smelled — the blossom pungent where it swagged the hedgerow. All in the seconds it took to fall. As the snow overtook her and bowled her body down as if in some joyous mountain game, the buttercups and hawthorn went with her, held tightly before the ultimate darkness, spurring her last not unhappy thought: it has been good, God, it has been good! And her body crashed against Milo's and caught him and they fell together, still holding.

Part Two

20

John Boss, the young reporter, had never travelled out of England before. Nobody did during the war, of course, but he felt at a great disadvantage. The other reporters who were covering the story were all quite elderly. Old hands. They disregarded him. He had been sent because the editor was sorry for him. He had been called up and only had three weeks before he joined the army. The war had been over a year, but conscription would continue — so they said — for years. John was not unhappy about the prospect, but his editor said it was a crying shame to interrupt the career of one so talented — did he mean it or was it a joke? You could never tell with the editor. But the upshot was that John Boss had landed this rather plummy job, which was taking him to Switzerland.

Switzerland, which had remained neutral during the war, was not a particularly popular country. Its blatant preoccupation with self-preservation was not attractive. On the other hand, John thought, if you were Swiss it seemed the obvious course to take: keep your head down, and trust the mountain walls to keep out all invaders. John had never seen mountains such as these, and his eyes were glued to the window as the amazing little train ground its way up to Zermatt. It was April and the snows were melting. The river beside the railway was in full spate, crashing along, and the lower pastures were a vivid green with the fresh uncovered grass. Above, the forests were bursting into growth and higher still, so that the young journalist had to crane his neck to see, the improbable peaks soared in their mantles of snow. He had never seen a hill higher than Kinder Scout and was bedazzled.

The discovery that had galvanised Zermatt out of its winter sleep and provoked the charge of journalists to the village was expected to attract an even greater inrush of gawpers at the weekend. There was a palpable air of expectancy in the throng that was gathered round the station. John Boss realized, if he were to call himself a proper journalist, he would have to try to whittle out one or two characters who had some personal knowledge of the events, rather than rely on the mayor's official story. Perhaps his editor had meant it when he had described him as talented . . . certainly John was eager to make the most of this opportunity. He had the enquiring drive of a terrier and did not look unlike one, with his strong, stocky build and untidy, upstanding hair. This was his chance, and he meant to take it.

The local who seemed to know a lot was an old guide called Casimir something, but when John sought him out he found him already ensconced with seasoned journalists, the schnapps flowing. John could not get near him, nor catch anything of what he was saying amongst the rabble. Most of the journalists were booked into the hotel, the Monte Rosa, but there was no way John's expense account would allow a room here — a drink at the bar was the most he could hope for. So he dumped his bags and elbowed his way forward. With luck he might apprehend Casimir later on his own and get something personal. He could keep an eye on him and watch when he went home. Follow him perhaps.

At the bar he knocked the elbow of a young man and spilt his beer. He apologized profusely and offered to buy him another, but the young man said he didn't want another. He was much the same age as John, about eighteen, perhaps younger, and looked out of place and slightly forlorn. He had ferociously bright orange hair and a pale freckled face with rather arresting violet-blue eyes, and his voice was native English. John fastened on this with relief.

"Are you here because of — of the — "

"Yes, indirectly. But I'm not a journalist."

"Just interested?"

"Well, involved, you might say. A — a sort of relative."

"Blimey!" John could not believe his luck. He had to bite back an excitement that threatened to choke him.

"Of the body, you mean?"

"No. Not exactly. But my grandmother was with him when he fell. She survived. She's on her way out here now. I'm waiting for her."

John fought to maintain his professional front but felt more like passing out from sheer exhilaration. Old

Casimir was nothing compared to the story of this slender, anxious youth whom nobody but himself had noticed.

"They're like vultures, all this lot," the boy said. "It's rather disgusting."

"Yes, but — look, I have to admit, I'm a vulture myself. John Boss, from the *Evening Telegraph.*"

"Oh, Lord," said the boy, looking hunted. And then, his manners taking over — "David Merchant-Fox."

They shook hands.

"Am I the first journalist you've spoken to?"

"Yes. I haven't checked in here — nobody knows my name, so nobody's bothered me. I was already out here, you see — pure coincidence — staying with friends in Grindelwald, so when I read the paper about this body being found in the glacier I hared over here. Because I guessed it was Milo — the story is family history, after all."

"Have you seen it?"

"No."

"But they'd have let you — being a relative — sort of relative."

"Yes. But I'm waiting to go with my grandparents."

John knew he was on the brink of a story so good it made him feel queasy just to think about it. To go with the grandmother to see the body . . . was there a bat in hell's chance that he might be so privileged? Access to the site in the glacier was limited, and journalists were taken in small batches, but most of them were too deskbound or drunk to make it. The body was at the bottom of a crevasse and said to be as perfect as on the day it died, but a lot of the journalists took it as read and honed their prose from the imagination. John, being young and active, knew he could make it to the crevasse if he got the chance.

"When are your grandparents arriving?"

"Tomorrow, I think."

"And this opera woman — the famous one, who everyone's waiting for - Clara Roskaya — I thought she was his lover. She says she was."

"Yes. I read that. Bit of a joke really, because she's making it up. She wasn't even there when it happened, and she was never his lover. Not according to my grandma."

"Was your grandmother his lover?"

"Oh, heavens, no. They were just friends. She always said he was just a friend, no more. She was in love with my grandfather."

"What's she like, your grandmother?"

"My grandmother? Well, old — you know. Nice. Rather handsome, active. The red hair comes from my grandfather, not her. We've all got it."

"All?" John wanted to take notes but was afraid of David being put off. He had been rather scornful of the "vultures," and stood now at the window looking out at the teeming street. He said, "You won't tell anyone who I am, will you? I don't want to be quizzed like that wretched guide — although he seems to be thriving on it, from the look of it. I don't mind just you. Where are you staying, by the way?"

"Nowhere, at the moment."

"No, like me. There's no room anywhere."

"Perhaps we could go and find a bed, before it's dark. You can always find a place if you try hard enough." John had discovered this, being a good journalist (persistent and inquisitive).

"Can you?" David was less optimistic. But he saw a useful ally in this friendly young man.

"And I'm starving. Let's see what we can find."

They went out together. It was true that all the hotels were full, but John had the initiative to wave some Swiss banknotes under the noses of old ladies who lived in some of the cleaner-looking chalets, and quite soon his pushiness resulted in their being offered a room from which a couple of teenage boys were evicted. Nobody offered to change the sheets, but that was a negligible detail. It was under a stout roof, and the night was cold. Bitter. The arrival of the opera star was timed for eight o'clock. As a good journalist John thought he should join the mayor, most of the village, and all the journalists who were thronging the station precincts.

"Why bother?" said David. "I know all about her. I can tell you what you want to know."

"All right." This time John got out his pencil and notebook. He thought he had won David's confidence. The boy had thawed out and was obviously happy to have company.

"She was one of a party who met out here, climbing. But her husband fell off and was killed and Milo Rawnsley — the body in the crevasse — took her back to England and paid for her to study singing. And she became famous. My grandmother told me this."

"But she's going round saying that this Rawnsley chap was her lover. When she arrives, it's to see the body of her lover."

"Wishful thinking," David said. "She's a prima donna, remember — a great show off."

"Yes, she has a reputation, I understand."

"Her voice has faded, but she likes the limelight. This is a great chance to have public hysterics."

"But surely your grandmother — if she was with Rawnsley when he was killed — is worth more limelight. Why wasn't she killed too?"

"Avalanches work in strange ways. He was buried and she was blasted clear. She came to and it was nighttime, and she had no idea where she was and not much recollection of what had happened. She just climbed down until she could see the lights in the valley and got home by herself. Search parties went out for Rawnsley, but he was never found. Until now. Some climbers crossing the glacier saw him at the bottom of the crevasse."

"Why would that be? People have passed by that way for years, I understand."

"The glaciers move all the time. Only very slowly, but new crevasses open up and old ones close over. The body is quite a lot further down from where it fell but by some quirk has never been crushed. It was deep enough under the ice that it never decomposed. But a new crevasse opened up and revealed it."

"It's pretty creepy."

"Yes, him looking just the same as the day he died. He was twenty-four, and nearly fifty years have passed. Really he's seventy-two, but there he still is, looking twenty-four."

John, who was not unimaginative, was awed. "It's lucky your grandmother wasn't in love with him because — seeing him, how he was . . ." God, he'd got to attempt to write this! The mind boggled. How would she feel? Would he get an interview with her? If he played his cards right . . . if he could go with the family when they went to the glacier . . . his mind was racing.

"Is she coming out alone?"

"My grandfather's coming with her. And some of their friends — the ones that knew him. Aunt Phyllida — she's not really an aunt — and Milo's sister Kitty and her husband."

"Quite a party then."

He prayed to God he would manage to accompany them. All these ancients . . . they might need a strong hand across the snows. The story was so fantastic he did not know if his skills would be able to put it across. Pity the old girl hadn't been in love with the corpse. To see the face of one's lover as it had been fifty years ago, now that you were an old crone — that was stunning stuff. He must try to get some of this down while the impact was fresh in his mind: it would go better if the brain was still reeling.

Outside the crowd was gathering to meet the opera diva's train. David had no wish to see her, but John thought he had better get a glimpse and a smell of the atmosphere. He put on his overcoat and went out again to join the crowd.

The great opera singer — great in every sense — descended to a welcome that obviously pleased her, besieged by a huge pack of journalists. She was swept into the big hotel where she held court beneath the bright lights. She was imposing, upright, with a huge chest swagged in black velvet and pearls, jet black hair (although she was nearly seventy-five) combed back into a vast chignon at the back of her head. She had jowls, a nose like a hawk, and flashing black eyes.

She was famous for her once-glorious voice, but her acting in opera had always been hammy, and it was a hammy act she now presented to the assembled throng. Milo had been her lover, the light of her life, Tears coursed down her slightly furry cheeks. He had supported her in her studies and had been the first to recognize her talent. Her first husband had been killed here in these very mountains. Milo had comforted her and taken her home with him.

"Everything I have, I am, I owe to this man," she declared dramatically.

When John went back and reported all this to David, David laughed.

"From what I gather, Milo was a good bloke. He did help her, but that was all. Gran says sending her away to study got her out of the house. They all lived together, you see. I don't mean slept together, but a sort of commune. It must have been quite unusual for the time. Until Milo died, then it was finished."

"What did your grandmother do after the accident?"

"Oh, she got married quite soon after, to my grandfather. He set up as a horse dealer and made a very good living, I believe. He still dabbles in it now, and hunts, and has a few racehorses. He's quite a laugh, my grandfather. I like staying there. My father's their youngest son. They had four children, two girls and two boys. We've all got this terrible hair."

"I don't think it's terrible."

"It's difficult to fade into a crowd."

"Nobody's discovered you yet, save me. That was my luck."

"Spilling my beer. I rather dread tomorrow though."

"What time are your grandparents arriving?"

"Early. They're travelling tonight on the sleeper train."

"Look, I know I'm presuming, but — well — it would be terrific for me if — if you could get me an introduction —"

"You got me a bed," David said, with a grin. "I don't see why not."

"Will you go out to the glacier with them?"

"You bet. I don't want to miss the body."

"Could you take me?"

"I don't see why not. I'd rather you than most of those fat slobs who'll try and get on the bandwagon. Not to mention the town council, the town band, the hoteliers — you can see how it is. Not forgetting the prima donna."

"It'll be a good mule who gets her to the glacier."

"They'll need a crane to get her down. And back again."

They went out for a meal together and got rather drunk, and by the time they got back to their lodgings, John felt he was one of the family.

◆ ◆ ◆

The station was crowded again in the morning when the train that was bearing the friends and relations of Milo Rawnsley was due from Visp. The party had apparently breakfasted at Visp, and they would depart for the glacier as soon as they arrived. They would transfer from one train to another, which would take them up the Riffelalp. From there mules would be waiting to take them to the glacier. There was a vast party of journalists waiting to get onto the Riffelalp train, but David and John elbowed their way to the front where David depended on being recognized. It was a clear bright morning, sunny but very cold and, if David regretted his climbing holiday being interrupted, he did not admit it.

The little train came clacking in on time, and the official welcoming party moved forward as the doors opened. John found he was holding his breath with anticipation, screwed up in case he might get left behind. The crush on their backs increased, and two angry porters tried to hustle everyone back. But David grabbed John's arm, and with a shout of "Dad! Gran! I'm here!" he pushed through the barrier and ran onto the platform. John kept with him, frantic to be his friend.

"David! Darling!"

David was gathered into a warm embrace by a lady who was far from being the ancient crone John had envisaged: a strikingly handsome and athletic-looking, if elderly, woman with beautiful eyes and thick curling grey hair cut rather short. Her husband was the source of the fiery hair, John could see, although his was much greyed as well. Rather amazing eyes, golden-green like a tiger's, flicked over John's hesitant figure.

"Who's this young chap? One of your climbing friends?"

"This is John. I met him here. He got me a room —
you know, it's dreadfully crowded. Let me introduce
him —"

John, without his notepad, honed his brain to take
in and not forget every name he was offered, every first
impression. It was the most important assignment of
his life and could make or break his career — a scoop,
if he got it right. Those journalists behind the barrier
would be giving their right arms to be in his place now.

"My grandmother, Mrs. Merchant-Fox, and my
grandfather . . . my father . . . my Aunt Phyllida, Mrs.
Carstairs; my aunt Kitty, Mrs. Palmer; and her husband, Mr. Roland Palmer."

To John they were just names, but he took care to
get them correctly memorized to the right faces. David
could tell him who they were when he got a chance.
David's father stood out by reason of the red hair and
also by the fact that he was in the uniform of an army
major. He, by force of habit, organized the party, greeting the formal deputation from the town worthies and
deciding the plan of campaign.

"We have breakfasted — I think we are ready to go
straight ahead. Our luggage can be taken to the hotel
for us, I trust? None of us will rest until we have seen
the body, that's plain. So full speed ahead, and we can
talk to the journalist chappies when we come down.
Does that suit your arrangements, sir?"

"Oh, most certainly. Everything is ready for you up
the mountain."

"Fine. Off we go then."

And John was swept along as one of the party, hardly daring to believe his luck. Behind the barriers the
journalists jostled and fought to get their places and

were eventually let in like sheep from a corral to fill the train. A large proportion were left behind. There but for the grace of God, John thought. He shrunk down in his corner, not wanting to stare, but needing to take in every nuance of feeling, of dread, of bewilderment amongst the party he was with.

And it was quite plain that, even after fifty years, this was no casual identification party. One would have been very thick not to sense the painful atmosphere that permeated the small carriage as the rack-and-pinion train ground its way up through the forests of the Riffelalp. On either side the journalists chattered loudly and laughed, but here there was silence.

John was able to stare because they were all plainly deep in disturbing thoughts, unaware of the stranger in their midst. David's grandmother was pale and she shivered several times, although her woollens and tweeds were thick enough. She was the one who had survived the avalanche, John remembered, and got herself down the mountain alone. She looked strong, with her fine jawline and the brilliant eyes that were fixed on the view of the Matterhorn that filled the valley above Zermatt. The higher they rattled up the icy slopes the larger and more imperiously the Matterhorn lowered through the window, and the more glittering grew the smoky eyes with unshed tears. But she had only been a friend, John remembered. For mere friends, these women were intensely moved. The ugly one, Aunt Phyllida, was white and stony, as if carved out of granite, her lips quivering occasionally. She looked hard as nails, like an old-style hospital matron, yet her thin lips were out of control. The other woman, Kitty — the sister? — was the most composed, a small neat woman with expensive clothes and a very sweet face. Her husband's name seemed familiar — Roland Palmer, but John couldn't remember why. He was famous for something. Gardens sprang to John's mind, but he did not see how anyone could be famous for gardens. His brain was racing like an overheated engine. He pulled out a notebook and jotted down the names, a sentence or two, but the Major was watching him, and he put it away, trying to seem nonchalant. The Major was not affected with grief, it was plain. He was of another generation and not concerned.

The train struggled higher and higher up the glittering snow slopes and came to a halt at a small platform. Here a deputation of guides and mules were waiting. The sun was very warm and the snow was soft and wet. The amazing face of the Matterhorn shimmered across the glacier, peerless in this morning light with its single pennant of cloud floating like a halo across the resplendent brow. There must be all sorts of good stories out here, John thought, of endeavour, suffering, and near-death. Perhaps when he had finished his army stint he might try for a travelling job, a roving reporter. It would be hard to go back to weddings and summer fêtes after this.

The ladies eschewed the mules.

"We're not that old," said Mrs. Palmer firmly. "It's downhill, we can manage. On the way back, perhaps."

One of the guides came forward. It was the old boy Casimir, John noted, very wizened and bent. He had once been a handsome man, but a hard life had caught up with him by the look of him. He shook hands with them all. But when he came to the grandmother — John gathered that her name was Charlotte — he

332

stopped in front of her, clasped her hand, and kissed it. And, astonishingly, Charlotte lifted her face and kissed him on the lips.

"Dear Casimir," she whispered. And then, "Have you seen him?"

"Yes."

"Is he all right?" Her voice wavered.

"You will be pleased. He is very peaceful."

"All these people — they mustn't — spoil — desecrate —"

"We have guarded him day and night; don't be afraid."

"These awful journalists —" She waved her hand towards the mob disgorging from the train. John flinched. "You mustn't let —"

"No. We are going alone. They stay here. If they go later, they will be strictly controlled."

She looked relieved. And Casimir took her arm, and they went down the shining track towards the glacier in front, together.

"He climbed with us, the old chap, when we first came here," Charlotte's husband said to his son. "That's Casimir. He was a splendid young man then." Then he smiled. "Weren't we all?"

They all went down quite a good path that looked as if it crossed the glacier ahead of them. The old women walked ahead, strongly. They were an impressive bunch, John thought, Aunts Phyllida and Kitty in their strong brogues and pre-war Harris tweeds cut in thirties style with sensible pleats and belted jackets. How on earth had they climbed up here in Victorian long skirts and corsets? They must have been tough. And perhaps — even in those days — they were girls

333

that rebelled, that went against the grain and did things well-brought-up girls wouldn't do. John's thought processes were sparkling out like a fountain in all directions.

Getting down to the glacier was steep, and the path down it, away from the main track, was difficult, over tumbled blocks of ice. But a path had been chopped away for them and a fixed rope hammered into pitons to hold on to. Casimir and Charlotte went first, and then John pushed himself in to help the old man, Merchant-Fox, as his son the Major was hampered by a gammy leg, and it was all he could do to manage himself. Below them was a gaping crevasse with ladders laid across it and ropes fastened to iron stakes to make a fence in front of it.

Casimir stopped before it, and they all came to a halt.

"Oh, God."

The man John was helping suddenly started to shake. John put his arm tightly under his own. "Are you all right, sir?"

"Oh God, poor Charlotte," he said.

Some young men who had been guarding the crevasse were helping Casimir and Charlotte down over the lip, where apparently ropes and ladders had been installed. They disappeared from view. The others waited, frozen in different attitudes on the rough ground.

It seemed an age before Charlotte climbed back into view. Her face was as white as the snow and, if she hadn't looked old before, she looked old now, John thought. He was stunned by the image of the old lady of seventy meeting again her young lover of twenty-four, for whom time had stood still. He didn't believe a word of David's "They were just friends." No one looked like Charlotte did for a mere friend. She came back to her husband, and he put his arms around her and held her tightly, murmuring into her ear. She was shaken to the core. John moved away and helped with the job of lowering the others of the party down into the crevasse. He could not see the body from where he worked. Below him, two guides helped him onto a ledge from where the body could be viewed, and one by one they stood there and returned. They were all deeply shaken. At last only he and David had not gone down, and the Major who had declined the invitation. He was shepherding the return up the fixed ropes, which was difficult with the party in its demoralized state.

David dithered. "I don't know if I want to see it."

"I do! Come on! You'll regret it bitterly if you don't."

John sat down and took the fixed rope in his hands. The two guides below looked up enquiringly, obviously wanting a break from the frozen depths. The sides of the crevasse were of shimmering blue ice, incredibly beautiful, the depths of deep violet, cold as the tomb they actually were. On a solid bridge between the walls, about ten feet down, the body of the young man lay on its back in a quite natural sleeping position, the arms flung out, the face upturned. It was a peaceful and very beautiful face. The eyes were wide open, gazing up towards the sliver of sky, which showed the glorious light of an April morning. They were still as blue as the morning, yet empty as the sky above the clouds. The man was seventy years old, John remembered. Yet his hair was a rich brown, carelessly long, and naturally curling. His clothes were the climbing clothes of the 1890s, the close-woven cloth of the breeches and coat torn in places, the old-fashioned cravat of navy-blue spotted silk loosely tied, with a gold pin holding it, embossed with a little fox's mask with tiny diamond eyes. John, hypnotized, stayed staring so long that David called down, "Are you still there?"

"Oh, my God, it's unbelievable!"

He climbed back up, enthralled by the beauty of the find. For it was beautiful, the tranquillity and the walls of azure ice containing like a pearl the shell of what had been a vital life, quenched in the full flow of its energy and enjoyment. Not — like those old men and ladies — withering irrevocably through the decades, slower and slower. But no, snuffed out in the fullness of its flame. It was splendid, John thought. He was drunk with the emotions that he had both experienced and witnessed. And crazily exultant at the privilege of seeing it. When David had come up, the guides closed the site, apparently shrugging off the journalists' clamour: "They would never get down, the fat twerps. And if they did they would never get up again." John guessed that the ones who had enough to spend on bribes might see the body, and it would cost them dearly.

"What will you do with it, when all this is over?" he asked one of the men.

"We will fill in the crevasse, or take him down to the church. It is for the relations to decide. Bodies turn up all the time; you would be surprised."

"Not so long after as this, though?"

"No. This is very rare." He shrugged, laughed. "Good for trade," he said.

They scrambled up the ice slopes to catch up with their party. Halfway up David was sick. "It's really gruesome," he said.

But John thought it was stunning.

◆   ◆   ◆

In the evening, David invited John to join the private supper party in the hotel.

"They're giving us a private room, away from the hordes. The opera singer is coming. One more won't make any difference. We'll be treated like royalty. You'll enjoy it."

"Are you sure?"

"Yes, you count as my friend now. They asked you. They don't mind your being a journalist."

John, having been writing nonstop since he had arrived back from the glacier, knew he was a journalist all right. His head was reeling with the pressure that had sent the words spinning over the pages. By the time he had telegraphed it out, he felt ready to pass out. But the invitation was not to be declined. The party had spoken to the journalists during the afternoon, and those journalists were probably in their rooms composing their copy now. But John was three hours ahead of them, and his story was already in London. He was still on a high from his amazing day.

"It's been fantastic meeting you. I can't thank you enough for all this."

"Oh, no. You were a great help up there. Better than me. My dad said so. He said bring your friend."

"That's great."

He hadn't any decent clothes, only what he stood up in, but when he went to the hotel nobody seemed to mind. Everyone was hanging around now to meet the opera singer again, but they didn't know she was already sitting down in the private dining room to which he was admitted. His luck knew no bounds.

"Why, John, good fellow." The Major came to greet him.

They were all just about to sit down to the table. The Major was arranging them, and John found himself next to the ugly Aunt Phyllida on one side and David on the other. The lovely old Charlotte sat opposite him, now composed, although still looking very strained. Her husband, who seemed to be addressed as Mar, was worried about her but did not fuss. The prima donna was at the head of the table where she obviously felt she belonged, with the Major on her right and the man called Roland Palmer on her left.

"Poor Roland," Phyllida whispered across to Charlotte, "he always gets the short straw." Her eyes shone maliciously.

"It's because he's so nice," Charlotte said.

Certainly old Roland had a very benign expression, rather sleepy, as if his thought processes were slow and steady, not mercurial like a journalist's. Gardening did seem to fit. John decided to chance his luck.

"Is Mr. Palmer famous for something?" he asked Phyllida. "His name is very familiar."

"He designs gardens. At least, he did before the war. I suppose he can go back to it now."

Phyllida was a bit formidable with her face like a rat trap, but John had learned that a journalist got nowhere by being awed. He asked her, "Were you in the climbing party when Mr. Rawnsley was killed?"

338

"No," she snapped.

At that moment from something Charlotte said to Kitty, Kitty and Phyllida changed places, Kitty coming to sit next to John. She said to him, "Charlotte doesn't see Phyllida very often. They don't want to shout across the table at each other. Charlotte and I see plenty of each other."

"Do you live near?" What luck! Unlike Phyllida, Kitty was a little old dear to talk to.

"Yes. I live in Milo's old house. Roland was Milo's friend and rebuilt the garden there, and after my first husband died I married him and went to live there. It was my house, you see, after Milo died. And Charlotte married Mar, and they went to live in my old house, which isn't very far away."

"And was Phyllida — Mrs. Carstairs — one of the party too?"

"She lived in Milo's house with the others — yes. But she left. She met Charlotte's brother Ben, and he arranged for her to live at his old home and help nurse their old grandfather who was dying. Charlotte has always had a guilty conscience about this, because she always said it was her job and she should have done it. Of course she did go, at the end. And it worked out very well, for Phyllida married the curate there, and they went to work in the East End, and that suited Phyllida really — a hard life doing something very worthwhile. She's a very tough lady. And underneath, deep down — you might not believe this — there lies a heart of gold."

Kitty giggled like a girl.

"She's very clever, not like me. I'm just a gardener."

She was like a little wren, John thought, very bright and quick. Or like a robin on a garden spade. He could see that she had the same finely drawn features as her brother in the crevasse.

And then she said, "It was wonderful to see Milo like that, don't you think? It's a miracle. Unbelievable, after all these years. If he were here now he would be like us, grey and worn-out. And there he is today, as beautiful as he always was, untouched, unspoilt . . . it's strange because he once said we should all meet here when we were seventy and see what had happened to us all. And we have."

Of them all, Kitty seemed to be the least affected by the day's experience. Even if, as old friends, they were meeting all together after a long period of time, they were not laughing and reminiscing. The table was subdued, and some members lapsed into long, withdrawn silences as if contemplating the day's shocks. They were tired, after all, and old. John still found it hard to suppress the overwhelming joy he felt at his luck in gatecrashing this extraordinary gathering and had to restrain his urge to chatter and laugh. He noticed that Clara the opera singer was proving rather a pain at the top of the table, but the imperturbable old Roland and the sharp Major were managing rather well. She was being rather emotional about how much she owed to dear Milo — her career, her life — and her hammy acting was much in evidence.

In a pause in Clara's outpouring, Charlotte suddenly looked up and said to her, "How long are you staying? Will you be here for the funeral?"

"When is ze funeral?"

"We haven't discussed it yet. It's something we

have to do. We've been told we can have the body brought down and buried here in Zermatt, or else they can fill in the crevasse and leave it there. It's for us to say."

The Major said, "They are slightly worried about leaving it where it is as they think, with the glacier on the move, the body could well be revealed again. And people are very humid — the authorities think the place might be disturbed. It is relatively easy to reach — not, as in most of these cases — very high up or in a remote valley. Strictly speaking, Aunt Kitty is the next of kin and should make the decision."

Kitty said, "Charlotte can decide."

Nobody questioned this — what John thought — rather odd statement.

Charlotte said, "I would like him to remain there. The mountains were where he always wanted to be. But I think the danger of it not being a permanent grave is too great, and he should be brought down to the church."

There was a silence while everyone considered. Nobody contradicted her opinion.

Mar said softly, "He will be in good company in the churchyard. It's full of climbers."

"It will finish it decently," said the Major. "A Christian burial in the English church."

John had noticed that there was an English church in Zermatt, presumably because so many English people had always gone there. Rather strange, he thought — or did so many of them need a funeral?

"Yes, I think that will be best," Kitty said. And added, "For us too, as well as Milo."

"Yes." There was general agreement.

341

Then Charlotte turned to Clara again and said, "Because if you can stay, Clara, I thought you could sing at the funeral. Just one song."

Clara preened herself happily. "My dear, of course."

"The Schubert you sang that day for the Prince of Wales. And Kitty played for you. Do you remember?"

"Of course I remember. Should I ever forget?"

There was a long silence. John sensed wavelengths buzzing that he could not connect to but recognized that the matter was very delicate. Mar, at the end of the table, looked stricken.

Then the Major cleared his throat and said, "I think that would be very nice. We will try and arrange for the body to be brought down tomorrow and then the funeral the next day perhaps. None of us wants to stay here longer than is necessary, especially as it appears we will get very little privacy."

"We could go for a walk tomorrow and Casimir can guide us," Phyllida said suddenly. "Like old times."

"We'll go down the valley on the train and walk from there," Charlotte said, "and the press will be too interested in what is happening up on the glacier to bother us."

"We'll have the day all to ourselves!"

The mood improved rapidly after that, and talk became general, about their children and their grandchildren. They all seemed to have plenty of both. John drank too much (a journalist's habit), and when it came time to leave he went alone, for David had been offered a spare bed in his father's room. He went out into the bar, which was still swarming, and had yet another drink, but he wasn't drunk enough to divulge his wonderful secrets. Tomorrow he would stay and watch the disinterment along with the mob, and with luck he might get a place in the chapel — but if not, his luck was already abundant, far more than he deserved. He did not think he would ever get a break as good as this one.

He went out into the night. It was freezing and the stars were brilliant. There were very few people about, but coming back to the hotel, having taken a turn outside after the supper, were Charlotte and her old husband. They were arm in arm, well wrapped up. John stood to one side, and they came past without recognizing him.

As they passed John heard the old boy say, "When Clara sings that song again, this time it won't be Milo telling you with his eyes that he loves you. It will be me. Still. After all this time."

And Charlotte laughed. She sounded like a girl.

John wished he wasn't so tired, his brain too addled to pick up the nuances of this fag-end of conversation. He must get to bed.

The hum of the evening excitement in the big hotel faded as he lurched away down the street towards his lodging. Above him, steel-bright in the moonlight, the great spire of the Matterhorn seemed to swim towards him, haloed in stars. John felt himself diminished, extinguished almost, watching the clouds moving over the snow-fretted pinnacle. This had been a splendid story, yet he sensed that his newspaper words had only scratched the surface of what had happened. He would know no more. It was locked in the hearts of those amazing old people who had once, like him, had the whole world before them and their mountains still to climb.